THE APOCALYPSE CODEX

Ace Books by Charles Stross

THE
APOCALYPSE CODEX

CHARLES STROSS

ACE BOOKS, NEW YORK

THE BERKLEY PUBLISHING GROUP
Published by the Penguin Group
Penguin Group (USA) Inc.
375 Hudson Street, New York, New York 10014, USA

Penguin Group (Canada), 90 Eglinton Avenue East, Suite 700, Toronto, Ontario M4P 2Y3, Canada
(a division of Pearson Penguin Canada Inc.) • Penguin Books Ltd., 80 Strand, London WC2R 0RL,
England • Penguin Group Ireland, 25 St. Stephen's Green, Dublin 2, Ireland (a division of Penguin
Books Ltd.) • Penguin Group (Australia), 250 Camberwell Road, Camberwell, Victoria 3124, Australia
(a division of Pearson Australia Group Pty. Ltd.) • Penguin Books India Pvt. Ltd., 11 Community
Centre, Panchsheel Park, New Delhi—110 017, India • Penguin Group (NZ), 67 Apollo Drive,
Rosedale, Auckland 0632, New Zealand (a division of Pearson New Zealand Ltd.) • Penguin Books
(South Africa) (Pty.) Ltd., 24 Sturdee Avenue, Rosebank, Johannesburg 2196, South Africa

Penguin Books Ltd., Registered Offices: 80 Strand, London WC2R 0RL, England

This is an original publication of The Berkley Publishing Group.

This is a work of fiction. Names, characters, places, and incidents either are the product of the author's
imagination or are used fictitiously, and any resemblance to actual persons, living or dead, business
establishments, events, or locales is entirely coincidental. The publisher does not have any control over
and does not assume any responsibility for author or third-party websites or their content.

ISBN 978-1-937007-46-1

PRINTED IN THE UNITED STATES OF AMERICA

FOR TERESA NIELSEN HAYDEN

ACKNOWLEDGMENTS

As usual, I'd like to thank my regular test readers for their sterling work in kicking the tires. In addition, I'd like to thank my agent Caitlin Blasdell and her assistant, Hannah Bowman; TNH (the best editor I never had); and Marty Halpern (who has gone above and beyond the call of duty for any copy editor in his work on the Laundry Files).

In a hierarchy every employee tends to rise to his level of incompetence.

—Dr. Laurence J. Peter, The Peter Principle

Prologue

OFFICE JOB

THINGS ARE GETTING BETTER: IT'S BEEN TEN MONTHS, AND I only wake up screaming about once a week now. The physiotherapy is working and my right arm has regained eighty percent of its strength. The surviving members of the Wandsworth Cell of the Brotherhood of the Black Pharaoh have been arrested and detained indefinitely at Her Majesty's Pleasure, in accordance with the secret supplementary regulations in Appendix Six of the Terrorism Act (2003); and every day, in every way, my life is getting better and better.

(The happy pills help, too.)

Please ignore the nervous tic; it's an unavoidable side effect of my profession. The name's Howard, Bob Howard: I'm a hacker turned demonologist, and I work for the Laundry, the secret agency tasked with protecting Her Majesty's Realm from the scum of the multiverse. The nightmares, scars, and post-traumatic flashbacks are the fault of the bad guys, some of whom *also* work (or rather, worked) for the Laundry—which fact is currently causing a shit-storm of epic proportions to rage through the corridors of government.

Ten months ago, while seconded to the BLOODY BARON committee, I stumbled across evidence of a leak inside the Laundry. That sort of thing is supposedly impossible (our oath of office supposedly binds us to service on peril of our soul) but, nevertheless, Angleton—whose assistant I am, and who is not entirely human—set a trap for the mole, with yours truly as the tethered goat.

Things got a little out of hand, and before the dust settled the Black Brotherhood attempted to raise and bind an ancient evil called the Eater of Souls, using a ritual that required a human body for it to possess. (Guess who they had in mind for the starring role?) Luckily for me they hadn't quite worked out that the Eater of Souls already *is* incarnate in a body—Angleton's—but before the Seventh Cavalry arrived I discovered the hard way that Nietzsche was right: if you stare into the Abyss for too long *it* stares into *you*, and likely finds you crunchy with ketchup and a little relish on the side. Bad dreams ensued all around, and it left me with a disquieting new talent that I've been doing my best to avoid thinking about too hard.

Well, they arrested Iris and her surviving minions and sent them to a camp in the Lake District where it rains sideways five days out of four, all technologies invented after 1933 are forbidden, and if you walk too far beyond the perimeter fence you find yourself walking back towards it. I imagine that's where they live to this day, when they're not answering questions in a room where the patterned carpet makes your eyes burn if you stare at it for too long, and your tongue writhes like a tapeworm in your mouth if you try to stay silent.

As for me, I got to go home four months ago. I finished writing up my confidential report, and the nightmares have mostly stopped: I only dream about the fence of living corpses around the step pyramid on the dead plateau a couple of times a week now, and the hole in my right arm has mostly healed. So I'm all right, at least on paper.

A month ago, I went back to work. I'm on light duty for the time being, but I'm sure that'll change once management decides to feed me back into the meat grinder.

BEFORE I CONTINUE. I'VE GOT A CONFESSION TO MAKE.

A couple of years ago, Angleton told me to start writing my memoirs. Which should have struck me as really fishy—why on earth should a junior civil servant in an occult intelligence agency be required to *write a memoir*? (Especially as ninety percent of the stuff therein is classified up to the eyeballs and protected by wards that will make steam boil out of your ears if you try to read it without the right security clearance.) But I'm older and more cynical these days, and I understand the logic behind it.

The deadliest threat to any covert organization is the loss of institutional knowledge that comes with the death or retirement of key personnel. The long-term survival prospects for those of us who practice the profession of applied computational demonology are not good. Let me put it another way: I've got a *really generous* pension waiting for me, if I live long enough to claim it. As we drift helplessly into the grim meat-hook future of CASE NIGHTMARE GREEN, the final crisis when "the stars come right," the walls between the worlds dissolve, and the monsters come out to play, we're going to need more sorcerers than can be trained by conventional methods; we're going to have to drop a lot of our existing security practices, allow the stovepipes between departments to melt, lower the firewalls, and get these sorcerers up to speed and mixing new metaphors as fast as possible. These memoirs are therefore intended to feed into an institutional knowledge base that, by and by, will help my successors (including new operations management personnel) to survive by allowing them to avoid my non-fatal blunders—blunders I only lived through because I made them in a kinder, more forgiving age.

(Also, there is this: writing down nightmares is a *really good way* to exorcise your demons.)

However, as I record this account of the events surrounding the Apocalypse Codex, I'm going to have to take some liberties. For starters, even if *I'm* dead when you read this, other people affected by the events in this document may still be alive—and what you learn from it may hurt them. So I'm going to have to redact some sections. Also, I'm in line management these days, and although I debriefed all the surviving participants and read all the reports, I didn't personally witness *all* the action. In fact, I spent much of my time following the trail of broken bodies, explosions, and general mayhem that BASH-

FUL INCENDIARY left in her wake—and praying that I wouldn't be too late.

(Praying? Well, yes—metaphorically speaking. As you doubtless know if you're reading this memoir, there is One True Religion; but I wouldn't want you to get the idea that I was a follower of N'Yar lath-Hotep, or The Sleeper, or any of their nightmarish ilk. My prayers are secular, humanist, and probably futile. It's one of my character flaws; I was a *lot* happier when I was an atheist.)

Anyway, I'm going to use a simple convention in this memoir. If it happened to me, I'll describe it in the first person, from my own point of view. If it happened to someone else, I'll describe it in the third person, from the outside. And if there's something you really, *really* need to understand if you're to avoid having your brain eaten by gibbering monsters from beyond spacetime, I'll take time out to harangue you directly.

Finally, if it happened to one of us but it has the potential to be damaging if disclosed, you'll have to come back with a higher security clearance in order to check out the version with the spicy bits.

And so, to business.

A MONTH LATER.

Dear diary . . .

No, scratch that. *Two* months ago I went back to work.

The first month was light duty, pottering around the office, catching up on a backlog of training courses and paperwork, filling in time.

And of course I let myself be suckered into a false sense of security, into thinking that everything was, in fact, getting better and better. Despite the nightmares and the security protocols and the ever-present awareness of the fast-approaching end of reality as we know it—I began to relax.

Big mistake, Bob.

A lot of things can happen in a month. In the context of the *last* month, I have . . . well, I'm not dead, even though I've acquired my first gray hairs. I'm not insane, or back in hospital, under arrest, or even slightly maimed. All things considered, that's a minor miracle.

A little light duty, filling in time. Ho bloody ho. "We want you to keep an eye on some departmental assets that are going walkabout," Angleton said, as if we were talking about paper clips or rubber bands. So of course I didn't think to ask what kind of assets he had in mind. Silly me.

The last month's asset-watching has been something of an eye-opener. I've got a whole new bundle of guilt, not to mention a bunch of secrets to see me through the sleepless nights. *Assets, going walkabout.* That's a euphemism, you know, as the actress said to the bishop. Sort of like the French prime minister describing an H-bomb test as "a device which is exploding."

So here without further ado is my recollection of the events classified under APOCALYPSE CODEX.

1.

BLOODSTONE CAPER

A CLEAR SPRING NIGHT OVER BAVARIA, CLOUDLESS AND CHILLY.
The setting moon is a waning crescent, the shadows lengthening to
the southeast. A distant propeller drone splits the sky above the foothills of the Bavarian Alps as a late-flying Cessna 208 works its way
slowly northeast towards Munich. The single-engine utility plane is
nearly six kilometers up as it cruises over the forested slopes of the
west Allgäu.

It's cold and noisy in the unpressurized cabin, which is unfurnished
and bare but for anchor points and tie-downs: this is nobody's idea of
business class. Nevertheless, three passengers, all with oxygen masks,
crouch on the floor. One of them wears overalls, a safety harness, and
a headset plugged into the crew circuit. He waits by the cargo door,
listening for a word from the cockpit. The other two passengers wear
helmets and parachute packs in the same color scheme as their midnight camo overalls.

At a terse instruction from the cockpit, the jump-master leans forward and tugs the door open. As he does so, the taller and heavier of
the midnight skydivers leans his helmet close to his companion's ear
and speaks. "Are you sure this is entirely safe, Duchess?"

"Come on, Johnny! A midnight HALO drop over mountainous terrain, then a rooftop landing on a madman's folly guarded by unholy nightmares?" Her laugh is a rich, musical chuckle. "What can *possibly* go wrong?"

"It's not *that*." Her companion raises a hand, adjusts the fit of the night vision goggles that half-obscure the front of his helmet, lending him the face of a giant cubist insect. "I mean, it's the payload. We're getting a bit too damn close to the deadline, if you'll pardon my French."

"Oh, really." She looks out the door, at the screaming midnight gale and the invisible forest below, as one hand moves to touch the bulge at her left hip. "Yes, we are very late. Blame the ash cloud from Grímsvötn: we should have been able to do this last week. But if you think I am going to abort now, and risk landing at Franz Josef Strauss Airport with that thing still in my pocket—"

The jump-master interrupts: "Sixty seconds."

"I thought you'd say that," Johnny says gloomily.

"Relax. Everything will be fine once it's back in its wards. Just try not to get hung up on the battlements."

"Thirty seconds."

Johnny gives the jump-master a thumbs up and stands, holding the rail beside the open side-door. His companion rolls to her knees and tugs the strap connecting her harness to a kit bag the size of a large carry-on, then stands up behind him. Pausing, she turns to the jump-master and hands him an envelope. "For yourself and Darren," she says, meaning the pilot. "With my undying love, Oscar."

"It has been a rare pleasure, Ms. Hazard." The jump-master raises his hand. "Five seconds! Three. Two. One. *Go*—"

And then he's alone with the night and magic.

PERSEPHONE IS FALLING INTO DARKNESS.

Kilometers below her, the tree-shrouded slopes of the alpine foothills are growing rapidly closer. The wind is a constant roaring drag at her arms and legs as she stops her spin, then scans the grainy green disk of her night vision goggles around until she can see a light green St Andrew's cross perhaps a hundred meters below her, and Johnny, free-falling towards the target. He begins to crab sideways, and she checks her altimeter and the compact GPS receiver on her wrist. Off course by a couple of hundred meters: Johnny has noticed and is correcting. She makes sure to keep her distance to one side. Despite her nonchalant act, she's keyed up and apprehensive: she'd think twice before trying to pull a caper like this with anyone else.

Nearly a minute later she's just two thousand meters above ground level. The target is in view over the ridge line as her altimeter begins to beep. She brings her right hand in and pulls the handle. There's the usual moment of screaming tension, then the whoosh and lung-emptying jolt as the chute opens—cleanly, no messing, *excellent.* The falling stone has hatched into a drifting feather, gently circling towards the ground. She reaches up and grips the rigging handles, spots Johnny's chute. She's fallen past him and he's now fifty meters above her and off to the left. That's either too damn close, or not close enough—depending on how the landing goes. She spots a hand wave. He's aware of her position. *Good.*

One thousand meters up. The target is visible, sitting proudly atop a rugged hill overlooking the Alpsee and Schwansee lakes. Schloss Neuschwanstein was the last and greatest architectural folly of Mad King Ludwig of Bavaria, model for a million Disney fantasies. Today it is one of the most popular tourist attractions in Germany, with a newly opened gallery of baroque art in the lower stories below the king's staterooms.

From the perspective of a nighttime parachute drop, the roofline is a nightmare—steeply pitched gables surrounded by pointed conical towers, like an enormous meat tenderizer poised to slam into flesh and bones.

Persephone focuses on the roofline, picks out the craggy pitch of the Palas with its gables and chimneys and turrets, and steers towards it.

Sane people do not go skydiving at night. They especially don't go skydiving at night over mountainous terrain, then try to land on the steeply angled tiles of a castle roof, with a twenty meter drop to a cobblestoned courtyard off to one side . . .

. . . But nobody has ever accused Persephone Hazard of being sane.

She flares and lifts her knees to clear the spine of the roof, spills air and drops towards the tiles, slides jolting sideways towards the cornice below—and is yanked to a stop by the cable attaching her harness to the peak of the roof by a specially shaped grapple. There is nothing random about the grapple: she and Johnny went to great pains to study the roof earlier, taking photographs and measurements from the Marienbrücke hillside. The grapple is locked to the roof, held in place by her weight. The chute, in contrast, drapes loosely around her. Persephone rolls, putting her back to the roof, and gathers in the chute with both arms. Thirty meters away on the other side of the roof, Johnny is doing much the same. She can see movement at the other end of the Palas, fabric sliding across tiles. *Good.* She relaxes infinitesimally. So far, the plan is on track.

Five minutes pass.

Persephone has rolled up her parachute, knotting it in its own cords, and secured it to the strap of the kit bag dangling below her. Now she begins to pay out one end of the loop of rope that runs through the eye of the grapple, lowering herself towards the edge of the roof. The nearest of the high skylights, surmounted by its own steep gable, is below her and only three meters to her left. Removing an anchor from her sling and reaching out sideways, she levers between slates, feeling for a roof timber to drive the anchor into. Working in darkness takes time: fifteen minutes pass as she crabs sideways in silence, driving anchors every meter and carefully moving her attachment away from the roofline grapple. Finally she is in position, ready to lower herself alongside the gothic arch of the window. And so she descends.

The window is leaded, with a cast-iron frame. There are no security contacts on the glass or its surround; who would break into a castle from the rooftop? Persephone peers inside, sees no telltale shimmer of infrared LEDs. The castle security is tightly focused on the lower windows and outer approaches, and the display cabinets and paintings.

Up here there's nothing to worry about but the fire alarm. And the watchers.

A minute later, she lowers her kit bag and then herself to the parquet floor of the Hall of the Singers.

A shadow moves swiftly in the end gallery: "What kept you?"

"Bad positioning. Help me with this." She kneels and begins to unpack components from the bag while Johnny assembles them. He's still tightening bolts as Persephone removes her helmet, unfastens her harness, then unzips her coveralls. Beneath them she wears leggings and a black leotard; her dark hair is knotted in a tight chignon. She has a dancer's physique—but a dancer would not be wearing the equipment webbing and pouches, or the mummified monkey's hand strung on a leather cord around her neck. She puts her climbing harness back on over the leotard, dons the night vision goggles, then pulls a shoulder bag from the sack and stuffs her discarded overalls and helmet inside it.

"Okay, I think I'm ready, Duchess."

Persephone checks her watch, a Seiko chronometer, synchronized to a broadcast time signal. "We are running late—ninety-six minutes to the conjunction."

"Shit. Well, I suppose I'd better get moving, then."

Johnny pulls out a pair of bent wires from his pocket and walks to the end wall. Whistling tunelessly he paces backwards, holding them before him; then, having found his distance, he switches direction and moves towards the middle of the floor. "Let's see . . . just about here, I think."

Persephone, who is watching from the gallery, narrows her eyes. "Fifty centimeters closer to the window."

"If you say so, Duchess." Johnny squats and begins to work at the parquet tiles. They form a beautifully polished herringbone pattern in rich mahogany, glued to the floorboards below with hot bitumen. With less than two hours to do the job, there's no time for subtlety: Johnny systematically vandalizes them with the aid of a battery-powered jigsaw. First, he uses a cord to draw a circle a meter in diameter around his measurement point. Next, he carefully cuts a groove in the flooring.

Persephone, meanwhile, rolls the metal framework close to him. Then she pulls out a compact caulking gun, inserts a cylinder, and begins to draw a much larger circle on the floor around them. The oozing paste is silvery in the diffuse moonlight, gravid with metallic particles. She periodically pauses to draw arcane symbols around the outer perimeter. Once the circle is closed she retreats inside and then removes a ruggedized tablet computer from one of her pockets. It sports an expansion port, and this she attaches to the circle by a short cable.

"We're locked in," she announces calmly as Johnny pauses to empty the saw's dust bag again. The inner circle is two-thirds cut through.

"This will take another five minutes." He reaches into a pocket, pulls out a compact power screwdriver and a couple of attachment points, and screws them into the cut-out circle. Without looking up he threads a wire through the hook-and-eye attachments and fastens it to the metal frame. Then he picks up the saw and cuts out the rest of the circle. Another minute with a pry bar and then the hand-crank on the portable crane, and the disk of flooring is dangling on a wire.

"Allow me." Persephone leans forward and shines a penlight into the dark recesses below the floorboards. Thick timber joists as strong as a ship's yardarm run from side to side of the dusty under-floor space, half a meter apart; it stinks of mouse droppings and ancient history. About forty centimeters below the floor there is another surface—the ceiling of the Arbeitszimmer, the royal study.

She winces slightly at the thought of what she's about to do to the gloriously paneled and painted interior of the royal suite. Mad King Ludwig bankrupted Bavaria building this castle; he spent over six million marks on it—close to half a billion euros in twenty-first-century currency. But there's a job to be done, and the price of failure is even higher.

She reaches into the pouch on her left hip with one gloved hand and pulls forth a velvet bag. Opening it, she teases out a chain of bright-polished white gold, each link of which is encrusted with glistening emeralds. She lowers the bag by its chain over the dust-strewn roof below. It stirs slowly, dangling away from the vertical. "The amulet points to the warded containment," she says quietly. "We are out of position—at least two meters, perhaps three. Pass me the hand drill."

"Are you sure? It's no bother to raise another lid—"

"It may not bother *you*, Johnny, but I don't like desecrating a work of art. Pass me the hand drill and hook me up."

"It's your funeral." Johnny passes her the drill, then ropes her harness to the crane. Persephone takes a deep breath, then worms her way underneath the floor boards.

THEY HAVE BEEN ON, IN, AND UNDER THE HALL OF THE SINGERS in the Palas of the Neuschwanstein castle for nearly an hour at this point. There are no burglar alarms on this upper story.

That does not mean, however, that there are no guards.

PERSEPHONE HAZARD IS AT PEACE AMONG THE DUST BUNNIES of the under-floor spaces, mentally and physically in the zone as she worms her way towards the ceiling directly above the amulet's indicated spot. Every fifty centimeters she stops and uses the drill to tap a hole in the floorboards above her, then screws another anchor into the woodwork, and walks one of her load-bearing cables forward. It's slow, laborious work, and the palace is not cold—with the central heating running, so too is the sweat.

The amulet is dangling straight down now, and Persephone has begun to orient herself, rolling over to face the floor below, when the hair on the back of her neck begins to tingle. She reaches her left hand up to grasp the monkey's fist at the base of her throat. A thrill of terror washes through her for a moment before she forces herself to stillness. Whatever is happening overhead, she can't crawl backwards fast enough to be out of the hole in time to help Johnny deal with it. But there are other options. She rolls onto her back, raises the hand drill, swaps out the bit for a thirteen-centimeter-hole saw, and applies it to the boards above her.

Meanwhile, Johnny—Jonathan McTavish, accomplice and loyal lieutenant and sometime *adjutant* in the *2ème Régiment Étranger de Parachutistes*—has become aware that he is no longer alone in the ballroom.

No door has opened, nor window slid ajar. No human lungs breathe the still, nighttime air with him. Nevertheless, he is not alone. He knows this by a prickling in the tattoo on the biceps of his left arm, by the warming of the warding amulet on the chain around his neck, by the goose bumps in the small of his back, by the strange blood running in his veins. And he knows it by the faint luminous glow coming from the warding circle that Persephone inscribed around him before embarking on her dive beneath the floorboards.

Johnny slowly scans the room, looking for traces. His nostrils flare. This is not strictly a visual talent, nor does he expect his night vision gear to spot the heat trace of a living body in the gloom. He and the Duchess are here tonight to lay something to rest; there are beings that will not appreciate this work. Entities that will go unfed if the amulet is restored to its rightful place in the display cabinet of King Ludwig's study, replacing the artful forgery that a long-dead cat burglar replaced it with decades ago. Things that do not appreciate the way the amulet's power is blocked while it is confined in this place.

Johnny has what used to be called Witchfinder's Eyes by the old women in the highland village where he was born. And there are some kinds of trouble he can see in the dark with his eyes closed. The gothic architecture and baroque decorations in the Hall of the Singers cannot disguise one aspect of the design of the room—that it is essentially a box chock-full of right angles.

The Schloss is a museum and a tourist attraction by day, a small and significant part of Bavaria's cultural heritage owned and maintained at arm's reach by the agencies of the state government. But it wasn't built here, in the foothills of the Bavarian Alps, solely for the picturesque view. Ludwig Friedrich Wilhelm II was not known as the Mad King by reason of mere psychiatric diagnosis alone, nor was the coup and subsequent assassination that ended his reign a matter of mere realpolitik. The Schloss was not built to be a temple to the Moon King's Wagne-

rian fantasies. Tonight, on the eve of a certain recurring celestial alignment, the temple's night watch are padding through the passages and
stairs of the castle on black velvet paws, their eyeless muzzles questing
for the stink of fear.

There is movement at the end of the room.

Johnny raises his hands round the back of his neck: he draws a pair
of strange knives from their sheaths, their twin blades carved from flat
slivers of some black glassy material.

Claws click on the parquet floor as a doglike darkness stalks into
the hall.

There is no panic, but Johnny wets his lips. These things have no
ears or eyes, but rely on other senses to find their prey. "Duchess," he
says quietly, "we've picked up a hound."

The dog-thing fades in and out of view as it walks towards the warding circle. Shards of leg and head and torso ripple and stretch, rotating
and distorting around an invisible reference point as it moves. When in
motion it is an occult blur, but when it pauses its entire body is visible:
a nightmare-black dog-shape, a gaunt eyeless hunter that doesn't seem
to be all there.

The ward is doing its work, for by its movements the hound appears
baffled and uncertain. Nevertheless, Johnny tracks it tensely, throwing
knife raised and ready. The knives snarl silently, eager to drink souls.
They carry words of banishment, hopefully enough to send the hound
back from whence it came . . . but perhaps not. One thing is sure: the
instant one of the knives crosses the perimeter of the ward, the ward's
protection will vanish. At this range, if he misses his target, the hound
will be on top of him within two seconds. And while Johnny wouldn't
blink at facing off against a timber wolf, these things are different.
Even a momentary skin-to-skin contact with its rippling integument
means death. He's only going to get one shot at it.

The hound casts its blind muzzle from side to side, then pauses a
couple of meters short of the ward, right in front of Johnny. It lowers
its head towards the floor, and freezes, muzzle pointing straight down.

He throws once, in a blur.

There's a blue flash as the knife splits the warding circle; simultaneously, a loud thudding noise comes from the vicinity of the hound. The dagger strikes the hound directly, splashing ribbons of green light from its flank. But it isn't the hungry knife that causes the hound to thrash wildly and keel over, huge jaws snapping at its own belly. There's another door-slamming sound. "Clear!" he calls, pitching his voice low as he steps over the shorted-out warding circle and approaches the hound, which is lying still now, limbs twitching tetanically. "It's not quite gone yet," he adds, as he sets the point of the other knife to the side of the hound's throat and pushes.

There's a moment of resistance, then he topples forwards, reaches out to catch himself with one hand against the floor. Of the hound there is no sign, save the knife and the splinters around the firing hole Persephone had drilled beneath it. "It is now," he adds.

THE REST OF THE OPERATION GOES EXACTLY ACCORDING TO plan.

Using the amulet as a guide, Persephone drills a thirteen-centimeter hole in the ceiling of the Arbeitszimmer. She fastens the amulet to a fishing line and lowers it through the hole. Peering through a compact fiber-optic probe, she lowers her payload towards a display cabinet in the shape of a grotesque miniature oak chapel that squats beneath a mural depicting scenes from the legend of the Holy Grail. There is a glass screen and velvet ropes to keep visitors from getting too close, and there are under-carpet pressure sensors and infrared body heat detectors—hence the ceiling approach. The amulet descends towards the front of the cabinet, tugging like a magnet beside an automobile. Then there's a sudden yank on the cord, a crunch of fine woodwork, and a shattering of glass. The amulet slams into the center of the display, where its identical twin rests on a velvet pad; the replica is sent flying as the wards inlaid in the floorboards under the parquet around the cabinet flash lightning-bright.

Persephone tenses; but there is no shrill of bells. Pressure plates are seldom tuned to hair-trigger sensitivity, lest the security guards are called out every time a mouse scurries across the floor at midnight.

Nor do body heat detectors work on pieces of extravagant jewelry, whether or not they are imbued with grotesque and unpleasant powers by their former owner. She permits herself a sigh of relief. Then she turns her attention to retrieving the replica of the Moon King's amulet from the bottom of the cabinet: a fiddly fishing job, but one familiar to any child who has wasted their pocket money on an amusement arcade grab-machine—and far more rewarding. It's just like old times, really.

Finishing, she coils up the fishing line, weights it down on top of the ceiling boards with her hand drill, and retreats back to the Hall of the Singers—making sure to take the spent cartridge cases from her silenced pistol with her.

"Done here," she says as Johnny pulls her out of the hole in the floor. "Just the one hound?"

"The next time I see 'em hunting in a pack will be the first." He checks his chronometer. "Thirty-two minutes to alignment. Is it in place?"

Persephone glances at him, scrutinizing his face: he's as stoical and imperturbable as ever. "Ever walked past a big electromagnet with a ring of keys? It knows where it belongs. The wards still work after all these years. Nothing to worry about." She smiles, buzzing with exultation. The amulet is back in place, another chink in this world's defenses repaired just in time. The replica installed in place of the stolen original by an uninformed but highly proficient jewel thief is safe in her bag, earmarked for delivery to its final resting place. The incursion will be exposed tomorrow, recognized for what it is by security guards boggling at the ingenuity of the cat burglars who came so close to stealing the Mad King's crown jewels the night before.

"Let's go!"

Persephone gathers her climbing ropes and stalks towards the windows, ready to abseil to the forest below in preparation for the long midnight walk to the rented safe house in Füssen. Tomorrow they will dispose of their equipment and meet with an agent who will take the not-invaluable forgery (itself containing over a hundred carats of blue diamonds and black fire opals, supplied to the jewel thief by a very special collector to whom the original was vastly more interesting than any collection of unenchanted gems) and make it disappear. Then they will depart by light plane, and it's back to the cover of the everyday whirl of the celebrity culture vulture circuit for her, and the adventure tour business for Johnny.

As she pauses on the window ledge to check her harness, Persephone feels more alive than she has in *ages*.

2.

SKILLS MATRIX

MS. MACDOUGAL SQUINTS AT ME DISAPPROVINGLY OVER THE top of her Gucci spectacles: "This year you're going to take at least three weeks of Professional Development training, Mr. Howard. No ifs, no buts. With great power comes great authority, and if you want to stay on track for SSO 5(L) you will need to acquire an intimate and sympathetic understanding of the way people work outside the narrow scope of your department."

I will say this for Emma MacDougal: she may be a fire-breathing HR dragon, but she doesn't short us on training opportunities. "What should I be looking at?" I ask her.

"The Fast Stream track: leadership and people management skills," she says without batting an eyelid. I nearly choke on my coffee. (It's a sign of how far I've come lately that when I'm summoned to the departmental HR manager's office I rate the comfy chair and the complimentary refreshments.) "This is foundation work for your PSG and Grade Seven/SCS induction." Which is HR-speak for promotion: *Professional Skills for Government* and *Senior Civil Service*. "Your divisional heads have endorsed you for SCS, and I gather you've shown up on the radar Upstairs"—she means Mahogany Row—"so they'll be taking a look at you in due course to decide whether you're suitable for further promotion. So it's my job to see you get the grounding you need in essential operational delivery and stakeholder management. You're going to have to go back to school—Sunningdale Park."

I grin uncertainly at her buzz-words. Where I come from, stakeholder management is all about making sure you've got your vampire where you want it. "Isn't Sunningdale Park for *regular* Civil Service?"

"Yes. So what?"

"But"—*we don't exist* is on the tip of my tongue—"this is *the Laundry*." Which really *doesn't* exist, as far as most of the civil service is concerned; we're so superblack that the COBRA Committee has never heard of us. (In actual fact we're a subdivision of SOE, an organization that was officially disbanded in 1945.) Our senior management, Mahogany Row, are so superblack that most of *us* don't ever see them; as far as I can tell, you hit a certain level in the Laundry and you vanish into such total obscurity that you might as well not be in the same organization. "Isn't Sunningdale Park big on teamwork and horizontal networking across departmental boundaries? Who am I supposed to tell them I work for?"

"Oh, all our fast track candidates are assigned a plausible cover story with backup documentation." Emma stares at me thoughtfully. "I think . . . Yes, wait a minute." She turns to her very expensive tablet PC and rattles off a memo. "You're going to be a network security manager from, ah, the Highways Agency. Securing our nation's vital arteries of commerce against the scum of the internet, road tax dodgers and drunk drivers, and so on." A carnivorous smile plays across her lips as she continues: "You're being promoted because they need someone who understands these machines"—her fingers linger on the keyboard—"to supervise the GPS and number-plate recognition side of the National Road-Pricing Scheme."

"But I'll be about as popular as herpes!" I protest. The NRPS is the nanny state poster-child project of the decade—monitoring vehicle number plate movements and billing the owners for road usage, automatically fining them if they move between two monitoring sites faster than the national speed limit permits. It's hugely overambitious, hated by everyone from Jeremy Clarkson to the Ambulance Service, supposedly due to be self-funded out of revenue raised from fines, and destined to overrun its budget faster than you can say "public-private prolapse."

"Exactly; nobody's going to want to get too close to you." Her wicked grin erupts. "Isn't that what you were worried about a moment ago?"

"But—but—" I surrender. "Okay." I've got to admit, it's the perfect cover. "But what about the networking and schmoozing side of things?"

"Your second-level story is that you're looking for an exit strategy from the Highways Agency; they'll talk to you out of pity." She shrugs. "You don't need me to draw you a diagram, Mr. Howard. I'll set up the training account and book you in as soon as possible; the rest is up to you."

THAT EVENING I BREAK THE BAD NEWS TO MO. "THEY'RE SEND-ing me to management school."

"That'll be an eye-opener, I'm sure." She peers at me over her rimless spectacles, then picks up the open bottle: "More wine?"

"Yes please. They're trying to turn me into one of *them*." I shudder slightly at the memory of managers past. Bridget and Harriet, banes of my life, who lost a game of king-of-the-castle to Angleton. Andy, who is a nice guy with a bad habit of dropping me in it occasionally. Iris, the best line manager I ever had, who turned out to have hidden depths of a most peculiar and unpleasant kind. I generally have terrible luck with managers—except for Angleton, who isn't a manager exactly (he just scares the crap out of everyone who tries to use him as a chess piece). Sitting uneasily somewhere outside the regular org chart, off to one side, doing special projects for Mahogany Row, he hardly counts.

"You're wrong," Mo says crisply, and pours a goodly dollop of pinot noir into my glass. "If they tried to turn you into another pointy-haired clone they'd destroy your utility to the organization—and beating swords into plowshares is not in the game plan. They're gearing up to fight a shooting war." She tops up her own glass. "Here's to your imminent officer's commission, love."

"They'll make me wear a tie!" I protest.

"No they won't." She pauses to reconsider. "Well, if they're sending you on regular civil service training courses at the National School of Government you probably ought to dress the part, but there's no need to go over the top." She looks at me appraisingly, and there's something very *professional* about her gaze. Like me, my wife works for the Laundry; unlike me, she keeps one foot in the outside world, holding down a part-time lectureship in Philosophy of Mathematics at King's College. (Maintaining that much contact with everyday life is central to keeping Agent CANDID sane—I've seen what the other half of her job does to her, and it's heartbreaking.) "You're going there as a student so you can probably get away with business casual, especially at your grade and given a technical specialty as a background."

"Huh." I finally raise my glass and take a sip of wine. "But I'm going to be stuck there for a whole week. Stranded in deepest Ruralshire without you. There's on-site accommodation, run by some god-awful outsourcing partnership; there probably isn't even a pub within a fifteen kilometer radius."

"Nonsense. It's suburbia; you can get into town of an evening, there's a bus service, and there are bars and restaurants on campus."

The kitchen timer goes off right then, yammering until she walks over and silences it, then opens the oven door. That's my cue to stand up and start hauling out plates and serving spoons. Dinner is a for-two curry set from Tesco, and we've been married long enough to have worked out the division of labor thing: you know the drill.

(It's funny how, despite the yawning abyss that has opened up beneath the foundations of reality, we cling desperately to the everyday rituals of domestic life. Denial isn't just a river in Egypt . . .)

Mo tugs at the frayed edges of my management-phobia over the wreckage of a passable saag gosht and a stack of parathas. "Sending you on a course on leadership and people skills sounds like a really good idea to me," she says. Tearing off a piece of the bread and wrapping it around a lump of lamb and spinach: "They're not saddling you with stuff like public administration, procurement policy, or PRINCE2. That's significant, Bob: you're getting a very *odd* take on management from this one." She chews thoughtfully. "Leadership and people skills. Next thing you know they'll be whisking you off to the Joint Services Command and Staff College."

"I am *so* not cut out for that."

"Oh. Really?" She raises an eyebrow.

"Marching around in uniform, spit and polish and exercise and healthy outdoor living, that kind of thing." I'm making excuses. We've both worked as civilian auxiliaries with the police and military on occasion. I chase a chunk of spinach around my plate with a fork, not meeting her eyes. "I don't get it. This particular training schedule, I mean. There's a lot of work I should be doing, and there are courses at the Village"—Dunwich, our very own not-on-the-map training and R&R facility—"that I could be auditing. Stuff that really *will* improve my survival prospects when the tentacles hit the pentacle."

Mo sighs and puts down her spoon. "Bob. Look at me. What's coming next?"

"What's—dessert?" I try to parse the precise nuanced meaning of her frown. "The big picture? DEEP SIX rising? Um, the Sleeper in the Pyramid's alarm clock going off? The Red Skull Cult taking the sightseeing elevator up the Burj Khalifa with a black goat and a SCSI cable—oh, you mean CASE NIGHTMARE GREEN?" She nods: kindly encouragement for the cognitively challenged. "The end of the world as we know it? Lovecraft's singularity, when the monsters from beyond spacetime bleed through the walls of the universe, everyone simultaneously acquires the power of a god and the sanity of an eight-week-old kitten, and the Dead Minds finally awaken?" She nods vigorously: clearly I'm on the right track. "Oh, *that*. We fight until we go down. Fighting. Then we fight some more."

I look at my plate, at the smeary streaks of drying curry and the mortal remains of a dead sheep's slaughtered, butchered, and cooked haunch. "Hopefully we don't end up as someone else's dinner." For a moment I feel a stab of remorse for the lamb: born into an infinite, hostile universe and destined from birth to be nothing more than fodder for uncaring alien intelligences vaster by far than it can comprehend. " 'Scuse me, I'm having a Heather Mills moment here."

Mo makes my plate disappear into the dishwasher. That's what my Agent CANDID does for the Laundry: she makes messes vanish. (And sometimes I have to hold her in the night until the terror passes.) "What you missed, love, is that it's not enough for you to be good at your job. When the shit hits the fan your job's going to get a lot bigger, so big that it takes more people to do the work. And you've got to show those other people how to do it; and you've got to be good at leading and motivating them. That's why they want you to go on this course. It's about getting you ready to lead from the front. Next thing you know Mahogany Row will be taking a look to see if you've got what it takes to be an executive."

I stare at my wineglass for a moment. That latter bit is so wildly out there that it'd be laughable, if the big picture wasn't so dire. What do executives do, anyway? It's not as if there's ever anyone in the posh offices when I'm called upstairs to deliver an eyes-only report. It's like they've transmigrated to another dimension, or moved outside the organization entirely. Maybe they're squatting in the House of Lords. But she's right about the job getting bigger and the need for rad management skillz, that's the hell of it. "I suppose so," I admit.

"So. When do you start?" she asks.

I blink. "I thought I told you? It's next Monday!"

"Oh, for—" Mo picks up the wine bottle. "*That's* a bit sudden." She drains it into our glasses, then adds it to the recycling bucket. "*All* next week?"

"Yes, I'm supposed to check in on Sunday evening. So we've got tomorrow and Saturday."

"Bugger." She looks at me hungrily. "Well I suppose we shall just have to make up for time apart in advance, won't we?"

My pulse speeds up. "If you want . . ."

* * *

BY MONDAY AFTERNOON THE TORTURE HAS NOT ONLY BEGUN, it is well underway.

"Hello, and welcome to this afternoon's workshop breakout session exploring leadership and ownership of challenging projects. I'm Dr. Tring and I'm part of the department of public administration at Nottingham Trent Business School. We like to keep these breakout sessions small so we can all get to know one another, and they're deliberately structured as safe space: you all work for different agencies and we've made sure there's no overlap in your roles or responsibilities. We're on Chatham House rules here—anything that's said here is non-attributable and any names or other, ah, incriminating evidence gets left behind when we leave. Are we all clear with that?"

I nod like a parcel-shelf puppy. Around me the three other students in this session are doing likewise. We're sitting knee-to-knee in a tight circle in the middle of a whitewashed seminar room. The powder-blue conference seats were clearly not designed by anyone familiar with human anatomy: we're fifteen minutes in and my bum is already numb. Dr. Tring is about my age and wears a suit that makes him look more like a department store sales clerk than an academic. As far as my fellow students go, I'm one of the two dangerous rebels who turned up in office casual; the rest are so desperately sober that if you could bottle them you could put the Betty Ford Clinic out of business.

This morning we started with a power breakfast and a PowerPoint-assisted presentation on the goals and deliverables of this week's course. Then we broke for an hour-long meet-and-greet get-to-know-you team building session, followed by a two-hour pep talk on the importance of common core values and respect for diversity among next-generation leadership. Then lunch (with more awkward small talk over the wilted-lettuce-infested sandwiches), and now *this*.

"I'd like to start by asking you all to introduce yourselves by name and department, then give us a brief sketch of what you do there. Not in great detail: a minute or two is enough. If you'd like to begin, Ms. . . . ?"

Ms. . . . gives a quick giggle, rapidly suppressed. "I'm Debbie Williams, Department for International Development." Blonde and on the plump side, she's one of the suits, subtype: black with shoulder pads, very formal, the kind you see folks wearing when they want to convince their boss that they're serious about earning that promotion. (Or when they work for a particularly stuffy law firm.) "I'm in the strategy unit for Governance in Challenging Environments. We work with the Foreign and Commonwealth Office to develop robust accounting standards for promoting better budgetary administration for NGOs working in questionable—"

I zone out. Her mouth is moving and emitting sounds, but my mind's a thousand kilometers away, deep in a flashback. I'm in the middle of a platoon of SAS territorials, all of us in full-body pressure suits with oxygen tanks on our backs, boots crunching across the frozen air of a nightmare plain beneath a moon carved in the likeness of Hitler's face as we march towards a dark castle . . . I pinch myself and try to force my attention back to the here and now, where Debbie Somebody is burbling enthusiastically about recovery of depreciated assets and retention of stakeholder engagement to ensure the delivery of best value to local allies—

"Thank you, that's very good, Debbie!" Dr. Tring has the baton again. "Next, if you'd like to fill us in on your background, Mr.—"

"Bevan, Andrew Bevan." Andrew has a Midlands accent, positively Mancunian, and although he's another suit-wearer, his is brown tweed. "Hi, everyone, I'm with the Department for Culture, Media, and Sport, and I'm really excited to be part of the Olympic Delivery Authority's Post-Event Assets Realization Team! As you know, the Olympics went swimmingly and were a big hit for Britain, but even though the games are over the administrative issues raised by hosting the Olympics are still with us—"

And I'm gone again (*four thousand holes in Blackburn, Lancashire*), held prisoner in a stateroom aboard a luxury yacht—a thinly disguised ex-Soviet guided missile destroyer—with a silver-plated keel and a crew of jump-suited, mirrorshade-wearing minions, cruising the Caribbean under the orders of a madman who is trying to raise a dead horror from the Abyss (*and though the holes were rather small, they had to count them all*)—

I pull myself back to the present just as Mr. Bevan explains the urgent necessity of documenting best practices for monetizing tangible assets including but not limited to new-build Crown estate properties in order to write down the balance sheet deficit left by the games.

"Thank you, Mr. Bevan, for that fascinating peek inside the invaluable work of the DCMS. Ah, and now you, Mr., ah, Howard, is it?"

I blink back to the here and now, open my mouth, and freeze.

What I was *about* to say was something like this: "Hi, I'm Bob Howard. I'm a computational demonologist and senior field agent working for an organization you don't know exists. My job involves a wide range of tasks, including: writing specifications for structured cabling runs in departmental offices; diving through holes in spacetime that lead to dead worlds and fighting off the things with too many tentacles and mouths that I find there; liaising with procurement officers to draft the functional requirements for our new classified document processing architecture; exorcising haunted jet fighters; ensuring departmental compliance with service backup policy; engaging in gunfights with the inbred cannibal worshippers of undead alien gods; and sitting in committee meetings."

All of which is entirely true, and utterly, impossibly inadmissible: if I actually said it smoke would come out of my ears and my hair would catch fire long before I died, thanks to the oath of office I have sworn and the geas under which Crown authority is vested in me.

"Mr. Howard?" I snap into focus. Dr. Tring is peering at me, an expression of faint concern on his face.

"Sorry, must be something I ate." *Quick, pull yourself together, Bob!* "The name's Howard, Bob Howard. I work in IT security for, uh, the Highways Agency, in Leeds. My job involves a wide range of tasks, including: writing specifications for structured cabling runs in departmental offices; liaising with procurement officers to draft the functional requirements for our new automatic numberplate recognition-based road pricing scheme's penalty ticket management system; ensuring departmental compliance with service backup policy; and sitting in committee meetings."

I blink. They're all staring at me as if I've grown a second head, or coughed to being a senior field agent in a highly classified security organization.

"That's the system for handing out automatic fines to people who exceed the speed limit between cameras anywhere on the road network, isn't it?" Debbie from DFID chirps, bright and menacing.

"Um, yes?" Living as we do in central London, inside the Congestion Charge Zone, Mo and I don't own a car.

"My mum got one of them," observes Andrew from the Olympics. "She was driving my dad to the A&E unit, he swore blind 'e'd just got indigestion, but 'e'd already 'ad one heart attack—" The dropped aitches are coming out; the mob of angry peasants with the pitchforks and torches will be along in a moment.

"*I* think they're stupid, too," I say, perhaps a trifle too desperately; Dr. Tring is focusing on me with the expressionless gaze of a zombie assassin—*don't* think *about those things, you're in public.* "But it's part of the integrated transport safety policy." I hunch my back and roll my eyes as disarmingly as any semi-professional Igor to the Transport Secretary's Frankenstein, but they're not buying it. "Speed kills," I squeak. From the way they stare at me, you'd think I'd confessed to eating babies.

"That's *enough*," says Dr. Tring, finally condescending to drag the seminar back on course. "Ah, Ms. Steele, if you don't mind telling us a little about your specialty, which would be managing an audit team for HMRC . . . ?"

And Ms. Steele—thin-faced and serious as sudden death—launches straight into a series of adventures in carousel duty evasion and international reverse double-taxation law, during which I retreat into vindictive fantasies about setting my classmates' cars on fire.

FOUR HOURS OF SOUL-DESTROYINGLY BANAL TEDIUM——VAPID nostrums about leadership values, stupid role-playing games involving pretending to be circus performers organizing a fantasy big top night, sly digs from the Ministry of Sport—pass me by in a blur. I go upstairs to my bedroom, force myself to shower and unkink my clenched jaw muscles, then dress again, and go downstairs.

They've set up a buffet in one of the meeting rooms. It's piled high with tuna mayo sandwiches, cold chicken drumsticks, and greasy mini-samosas, evidently in a misplaced attempt to encourage us to mingle and network after working hours. Halfway across the campus there's a bar, although the beer's fizzy piss and the spirits are overpriced. I check the clock: it's only six thirty. If I do the mingling thing they'll start badgering me about their aunts' speeding tickets, but the prospect of drinking on my own does not appeal.

I make the best of a bad deal and strike out across the campus to the nearest bar, where I order a pint of lemonade to calm my nerves and contemplate the menu without much enthusiasm. The ghastly truth is beginning to sink in when one of my fellow victims walks in and approaches the bar. At least I *think* he's a victim; he might be staff. Three-piece suit, mid-fifties, distinguished gray hair and a salt-and-pepper mustache. Something about his bearing is familiar, then I realize where I've seen it before—ten to one he's ex-military. As he taps the brass bell-push he catches me watching him and nods. "Ah, Mr. Howard."

I stare at him. "That's me. Who are you?" It's rude, I know, but I'm not in a terribly good mood right now.

"I heard one of you young people would be here, and thought I ought to meet you." The barman, who looks younger than most of the single malts behind the bar, sticks his head up. "Ah, that'll be a Talisker, the sixteen-year-old, and"—he looks at me—"what's your poison, Mr. Howard?"

"I'll try the Glengoyne ten," I say automatically.

"Bill it to my tab," says my nameless benefactor. "No ice!" he adds, with an expression of mild horror as the barman reaches for the bucket. "That will be all." The barman, to my surprise, makes himself scarce, leaving two tumblers of amber water-of-life atop the bar. "Make yourself comfortable," he says, gesturing at a couple of armchairs beside the empty fireplace. He makes it sound like an order.

I sit down. He sits down opposite me. "You still haven't introduced yourself," I say.

"Indeed." He smiles faintly.

"Indeed." There's nothing I can say to that without being rude, and we in the Laundry have an old saying: Do not in haste be rude to whoever's buying the drinks. So I raise my tumbler, take a good sniff (just to make sure it isn't poison), and examine him over the rim.

"You surprised Dr. Tring, you know. Most of the students here are aiming to network and make connections; you might want to pick a slightly less objectionable cover story next time."

Cover story. I give him the hairy eyeball. "For the third time. Who's asking?"

He reaches into his jacket pocket with his right hand and withdraws a familiar-looking card. Which he then holds in front of me while I read the name on it and feel a prickling in the balls of my thumbs (and a vibration in the ward that hangs on a chain around my neck) that tells me it's the real thing.

"All right, Mr. Lockhart." I take a sip of his whisky and allow myself to relax—but only a little. "I'll take your helpful advice under consideration, although in my defense, I have to say, the story wasn't my idea. But what—if I may ask—are *you* doing here?"

"I'd have thought it was obvious; I'm enjoying an after-work drink and networking with a useful contact in the Highways Agency." Gerald Lockhart, who at SSO8(L) is a stratospheric four grades above me—that's four grades up in the same organization—replies without any noticeable inflection.

"Uh huh." I think for a moment. "We couldn't possibly be running an ongoing effort here to identify suitable candidates for recruitment from within other branches of the civil service—or to implant geases in up-and-coming players fast-tracked for promotion that will enable us to work more effectively with them in future. Could we?"

"Certainly *not*, Mr. Howard, and I'd thank you to stop speculating along such lines. You're not cleared for them."

Oops. "Okay, I'll stop." But I can't avoid a little jab: "But you're obviously cleared for *me*, aren't you?"

Lockhart fixes me with a reptilian stare: "James warned me about your sense of humor, young man. I think he indulges you too much."

Young man? I'm in my early thirties. On the other hand, I can take a hint that I'm in over my head: when your sparring partner turns out to be on a first-name basis with Angleton, it's time to back off.

I put my glass down, even though it's not empty. "Look, I don't need this. You obviously want to talk to me about something. But I've had a bad day, I'm not terribly happy to be here, and I'm not handling this very well. So I'd appreciate it if you'd just say your piece, all right?"

I can see his jaw working, behind the salt-and-pepper topiary on his upper lip. "If that's the way you want it." He takes a sip of his single malt. "I expect you've noticed that there are a lot of high-flyers here. Civil servants who are being groomed for upper management roles, where in ten years time they'll deal with members of the government and represent their departments in public. You should be making notes, Mr. Howard, because although you won't be dealing with the general public, you'll certainly be representing us in front of *these* people. You're going to need those people-handling skills. If we all live long enough for you to acquire them. Ha, ha."

"Ha"—I try not to look unsuitably unamused—"ha. So?"

"James is assigning you to my department for a little project—nothing you can't handle, I assure you. I'll see you in my office next Monday morning at eleven o'clock sharp. In the meantime, you have some background reading to catch up on." He slides a dog-eared paperback towards me across the table before I can respond. "Good night, Mr. Howard." He rises, and before I can open my mouth and insert any additional limbs he vanishes.

I pick up the book and turn it over in my hands. *Spy-Catcher*, it says, by Peter Wright. *A* New York Times *bestseller.* I stare at it. *Background reading?* Wasn't he a rogue Security Service officer from the seventies or something? *How bizarre.* I pick up my whisky glass, and open the book.

Oh well, at least I've got something to pass the evenings with now . . .

3.

BIG TENT

A BLOCK OF SIX GEORGIAN TOWN HOUSES CLUSTER DISCREETLY together on one of the leafy avenues behind Sloane Square in London, south of Victoria and west of Westminster.

In the house at the west end of the row there lives a witch.

A man stands waiting on her doorstep. He wears a pin-striped suit of conservative cut and his hair is graying in late middle age; he might be a senior partner in a law firm, or an accountant paying a house call to a rich, elderly client to discuss their affairs. But appearances are deceptive. He is in fact SSO8(L) Gerald Lockhart, and he is visiting on business.

There are many types of self-identified witches. The common or garden variety is generally harmless—women of a certain age who wear purple disgracefully, have two or more cats, run a new age shop, recycle fanatically, and sometimes believe in fairies at the bottom of the garden.

The witch who lives in this particular house doesn't wear purple, can't be bothered with pets, prefers wholesale to retail (but quit both trades some years ago), pays a cleaning firm to take care of the recycling, knows several demons personally, and is not even remotely harmless.

Gerald Lockhart puts his finger on the doorbell and, with an expression of grim determination not obviously warranted by such a trivial action, pushes it.

Somewhere behind the glossy black door, a bell jangles. Lockhart relaxes his finger on the button after a second, then glances up at the discreet black golf ball of the camera above the door. A few seconds later he hears footsteps approaching. Then the door opens.

"Good afternoon." The man who opens the door is in his late twenties, with shaven head and a slacker goatee; however, he wears a suit so funereal in cut that he could be taken for an undertaker, if undertakers wore black open-necked shirts with their weeds. "Ah, Mr. Lockhart? I believe Ms. Hazard is expecting you. If you'd care to follow me, sir? I'm sure she'll only be a minute."

Lockhart follows the butler across a tiled hallway and through a side door that leads into a parlor at the front of the house. There are side tables, armchairs, and a sofa, the latter items recently re-upholstered but clearly dating to an earlier century. The butler leaves him; as he turns to go, Gerald notes with interest the earring, the tattoos on the back of his neck, and the cut of his jacket, tailored to draw attention away from his broad, heavily muscled shoulders. Ms. Hazard does not employ household staff solely as an affectation of personal wealth. Lockhart makes a mental note to have the fellow's background checked. It's always useful to have a little extra leverage.

Somewhat closer to three minutes later, the parlor door opens. "Good afternoon," Lockhart says, rising reflexively. "And thank you for making time to see me at such short notice."

"It is a pleasure, as always." Persephone beams as she steps closer. Her diction is very slightly stilted, with the echo of an Italian accent lending it a musical trill: her elocution tutor is clearly first-rate. "How are you, Gerald? And how are the children?"

The witch wears an understated gray wool dress with black tights and kitten heels; with her hair pulled tightly back and minimal makeup, she exudes a gamine charm. She moves fluidly, as if only loosely bound by gravity. Lockhart thinks she carries herself like a dancer; but he notices the hardened skin on the backs of her hands—deftly obscured by a smudge of concealer across her knuckles—and the loose sleeves that conceal her shoulders and upper arms. *The Nutcracker* ballet, for Karate and Krav Maga, perhaps.

"Polly is fine," Lockhart says gravely. "Darren is recovering from a bug he brought back from play group, and we're watching in case Nicky comes down with it too—"

They make small talk for a few minutes as Persephone listens, nodding. To an ill-informed observer she could be a thirty-year-old ballet dancer who has married a man with serious money, a man of the very highest rank—seats in the country and the House of Lords, on a first-name basis with minor royalty, reserved place at Eton for the firstborn male issue, that sort of thing. And Lockhart might simply be a family friend, a senior civil servant of the old school, filling her in on the gossip.

Of course, appearances are deceptive: their official relationship is that of a controller and the intelligence officer they direct. But they keep up appearances in semi-private, to ingrain the habit, lest their paths should meet in public.

After a while, Lockhart runs out of pleasantries to spin around his family life. "But enough of that," he signals. "I'm wasting your time."

"Oh, hardly." She half-smiles, then reaches for a device resembling a TV remote control. "All right, we can talk now. Within the usual limits." A thin mosquito-whine from the windows behind her hints at the presence of transducers in the frames, designed to defeat laser mikes or other snooping devices.

"Good." Lockhart pulls a notepad and pen from his jacket pocket. "Did you have anything to add to the agenda . . . ?"

"Not at this time." She pauses. "Okay. The LUDWIG NIGHT outcome—that's positive, as per my report, although it was closer than I'm happy about. I take it the asset has been returned to inventory?"

"Yes." Lockhart nods. "The valuation committee have been asked to report on it but I don't think there's going to be any problem authorizing full payment of all your expenses. A job well done, after all."

"Good." She watches while Lockhart flips the page.

"Next item. There's a candidate from within the organization—"

"*Within* the organization?" She leans forward, suddenly attentive.

"Yes," says Lockhart. "He's been tapped for advancement on the basis of his track record in general operations, but he really needs a spin around the block and an evaluation by . . . well, someone like yourself. I gather Mahogany Row want to know if he's got the *right* stuff. So he's been assigned to me, and I was thinking, if you don't object, of assigning him to you as liaison on the next suitable excursion?"

"You want me to test-drive your new assistant?"

"Yes, more or less. I don't think you'll find him a spare wheel, I hasten to add, although first appearances can be deceptive: he's a poor fit within the regular civil service framework, too prone to picking his own targets and going after them unilaterally—but he gets results. So the promotion board thought it might be worth trying him out on a more, ah, independent command, as it were."

"Really? Well, hmm. If you could send me his HR file, that would help me make my mind up. But we can always use a bit of free-thinking in this line of work. If you want to saddle me with a field liaison officer, it'd be best if you pick one who doesn't expect me to file reports every sixty minutes."

"Noted." Lockhart pauses to jot down her request. "I'll have it seen to later today." He folds his notepad and slides it away.

"Are we done, then?" she asks.

"Mostly. There's another job I'd like to talk to you about, but not here. It's urgent, I'm afraid."

"Really?" She looks at him sharply. "Do you have a tight schedule?"

"Yes; it's a rush job and we need to get the ball rolling by close of business today. Most hush-hush."

"I see. Well, depending on how long it takes . . . I've been summoned for jury service next month, did I say? Terrible nuisance. Perhaps we should continue in the studio?"

"Of course." Lockhart follows her out into the hall. "And I shouldn't worry about the jury duty; these things have a habit of falling through cracks. Unlike other types of public service I could mention."

Persephone walks back into the house, past the broad staircase and the dining room and kitchen, into a narrower, stone-flagged passage obviously designed for servants' use. She opens a narrow wooden door: there is a spiral staircase, ascending into brightness.

At ground level the house appears to be the residence of a society lady: afternoon tea at Fortnum & Mason's, dinner parties for Ruperts and Jocastas, season tickets to Glyndebourne. But as he climbs the staircase the illusion falls away. And as ever, Lockhart can't quite shake the feeling that he's entering the wicked witch's tower.

They ascend a long way—almost fifty steps, clearly passing through the first and second floors of the house. There are no exits below the top, but daylight bulbs behind tall frosted glass panes like arrow-slit windows provide illumination.

Lockhart has seen external photographs of the house, and the floor plans on file with the council planning department, and he knows there's no spiral staircase from the former pantry to the attic according to the official deeds. Nor would a casual intruder even be able to see the entrance to the stairwell. Persephone Hazard is not the kind to skimp on security.

The staircase ends at another door. Persephone waits for him at the top, looking as cool and collected as ever; Lockhart is breathing more heavily than he likes to admit. "Come on in," she says, and turns the handle. "You haven't been up here recently, have you? I've made some changes."

The space on the top floor is open plan, and huge. It appears that the attic spaces of the entire row of town houses have been combined into one enormous room, rafters boarded over with a sprung floor, roof beams replaced in situ with steel girders to provide an unobstructed space fifty meters long and ten meters deep. There's a clear space at one end big enough for a dance floor or a dojo; the rest is broken up by movable partitions. "Welcome to my workshop. It's why I finished buying up the entire row of houses—just so I could build this," Persephone explains, a note of quiet pride in her voice. "I rent out the other units, so I can vet my neighbors for security."

Lockhart swallows. "Very impressive," he says. Previously he's only seen the interior of the town house she lives in. She doesn't invite social callers up here, as a rule, and he can see why.

There is a metal ring in the middle of the eight meter by eight meter square of open flooring at the far end of the room. Cables connect it to a pair of nineteen-inch racks that would not be out of place in a server room. Tool cabinets and other equipment, including a pair of backup generators, are positioned around it.

She walks towards him until they are standing nose to nose. "So, Gerry. What *really* brought you here today?"

"I like to get out of the office from time to time." He nods at the huge summoning grid at the far side of the room. "Is that in proper working order? The new job really *does* require containment rather than just a sweep for bugs."

Persephone stares at him for a moment, then turns and walks towards the grid. Lockhart hurries to catch up with her—she's a tall woman, and she moves fast. "This is a class six grid," she explains over her shoulder. "Kimpel-Ziff deflectors and four different safety interlocks. The control module"—she points at the first equipment rack, which is full of shiny server blades—"is three-way redundant and has two separate power supplies, two UPSs, and two different generators. Just in case. It also has a secondary containment grid around the outside, *just in case*. Which is to say that it is as secure as anything your organization could provide. So the answer to your question is yes, it's in proper working order." She stares at Lockhart, nostrils flaring. "Will that do?"

"Yes." He nods. "If you don't mind firing it up? This briefing will take some time."

SUMMONING GRIDS——PENTACLES WITH ATTITUDE——HAVE A number of uses. Unsurprisingly, summoning spirits from the vasty deeps of Hilbert space is one of them. They can also be used, by the foolhardy or terminally reckless, to open gateways to other spaces (most of which are utterly inhospitable to humanlike life). Finally, they can be used to create a firewall, like a science fictional force-field only buggier and prone to hacking attacks by extra-dimensional script kiddies with pseudopods. Which is why nobody with any sense uses them casually.

The ward that Persephone programs into the management console of her grid isn't aimed at summoning squamous horrors or opening a doorway to hell: it's just there to provide thirty minutes of uninterrupted high-quality privacy, protected utterly from bugs, listeners, and remote viewing exploits. It takes her a minute to set the script up and hit return on the keyboard; then she steps into the middle of the grid and beckons Lockhart forward.

They stand in silence at the center of the silver schematic diagram, ignoring each other, watching opposite ends of the room. Then, suddenly, the room isn't there anymore. Neither is the ceiling. The only light is the LED lantern that Persephone places carefully on the floor at the center of the disk they are standing on, an eight-meter circle of reality in the middle of a universe of absolute night.

"We can talk now," she says tonelessly. "Twenty-nine minutes until the field decays. Sorry about the lack of soft furnishings."

"That's all right." Lockhart's shoulders slump. "I'd like to apologize for springing this on you. I had no choice."

"*Not* clever. You could have blown everything, turning up on my doorstep like that! I'm being watched; they'll be watching you too now, you know."

"Yes. I know."

She stares at him. By lantern-light the bags under his eyes are dark, his cheeks gaunt. "You'd better explain."

"A situation has come up. You're the best asset match for it, precisely because of the arm's length arrangement. Dealing with this situation is probably more important than preserving your cover—"

"Really? There are at least two foreign intelligence services and three crime syndicates looking for me under a variety of former identities. You're not at risk of being shot by the Oaxaca Cartel if—"

"Nevertheless."

"This had better be good."

"It's a unique situation. We believe a situation has arisen that the organization itself, as a branch of the civil service, is incapable of dealing with at an institutional level: our hands are tied. Your Mr. McTavish may have some insights to contribute."

"Now wait a minute!" Persephone struggles visibly for self-control. "Are you accusing Johnny of malfeasance, or—"

"No, absolutely not. But you are familiar with his upbringing, yes?"

"What, his father's church?"

"Yes, that."

"You're kidding. Tell me you're kidding?"

"No." Lockhart takes a deep breath. "They're out there, Ms. Hazard. As you well know. And unfortunately something has come up that—well, I suspect he may have some valuable insights to contribute. However, we, as an organization, aren't allowed to investigate."

"That's idiotic!"

"Is it? It's in the very nature of this particular threat. Eldritch horrors from beyond spacetime? Not a problem, that's our job. Al-Qaida terrorists trying to blow up the London Eye? Again, not a problem: that's the Met's Counter-Terrorism Branch and/or the Security Service. Foreign intelligence services playing footsie? Again, that's SIS or us, depending. But these are all external threats."

"So it's an *internal* threat?"

"I sincerely hope not." Lockhart shakes his head. "But there's a line all of the security services are required not to cross: the cabinet, the actual executive arm of government, is off-limits to us. That rule is there for a very good reason . . . but enough of that. Tell me." Lockhart leans close: "When was the last time you went to church?"

JOHNNY MCTAVISH IS IN BED WHEN HIS PHONE RINGS. UNCHAR-acteristically, he is asleep, but one eye opens immediately. It's Persephone's ringtone, which means business. Johnny blinks, trying to orient himself. The bed in question is half-familiar, the furniture around it less so. Then the phone trills again. His view is obstructed by a shapely back, spray of honey-blonde hair across the pillow, curve of buttocks resting against his upper thighs—*oh, it's Amanda*—she mumbles something sleepily and thrusts her buttocks against him as he elbows his torso upright and reaches past her to the bedside unit.

"'Lo," he says to the phone.

"Afternoon, Johnny." The Duchess sounds amused. "Got company?"

She knows he has a special ringtone for her; the laconic greeting gave him away. "Of course." Amanda is still half-asleep. Hardly surprising—they didn't get to bed until 6 a.m. The poor thing must be worn-out. He feels himself begin to stiffen against her ass-crack.

"Do you have any plans for this evening?" asks Persephone.

Johnny yawns deliberately to force carbon dioxide out of his bloodstream, levering himself to a higher state of awareness. "Nothing definite," he says. "Got something in mind?" His three days and nights with Amanda are drawing to an end: in another few hours her banker hubby will be back home from the Arabian Gulf, and it'll be time for Johnny to disappear.

"Yes, there's a little evening event I want to attend, and I think you should come along. How about Zero and I swing round to pick you up from home at seven? Smart casual will do."

"All right." He swallows her name; Amanda is showing enough signs of awareness that tact is the better part of valor. "Seven sharp. Bye." He puts the phone down.

"Who was that?" Amanda murmurs, catching his arm as it crosses her chest.

"Work," he says.

"Work." She sounds doubtful, but guides his hand down until his fingers lightly stroke one of her nipples. "Your boss expects you to work evenings?"

"Oh yes." He feels her aureoles pucker beneath his fingertips. She sighs and leans against him. First-class booty, the best that oil money can buy. He strokes her flank regretfully, already half-certain that this will be the last time. "My boss is evil," he whispers in her ear. "And I'm going to have to go to work soon."

"But not just yet." She tenses as his hand slides between her legs. "Please?"

"Not just yet," he agrees.

THERE IS A GARAGE ATTACHED TO PERSEPHONE'S HOUSE, occupying most of what was once a garden. It's a very large garage, by Central London standards. Right now it's semi-occupied by two vehicles—a diesel Land Rover and a squat, brutally powerful Bentley coupe. The third resident, a Rolls-Royce Phantom, is cautiously nosing its way out into the street. The chauffeur and occasional butler, Oakley shades and hipster goatee packaged in a black suit, is clearly trying too hard to look like a gangster in a Tarantino movie.

In the back, Persephone has the windows dimmed to near-opacity as she skim-reads reports on her smartphone. Head down, intent and focussed, she pays no obvious attention to the sway and surge of the car, but grips the device tightly in one gloved hand, zipping through a series of pages pre-digested and highlighted for her convenience by a very private research bureau. It's not that Persephone can't use a web browser herself; but some of the material in this briefing would be hard to come by without a lot of tedious legwork and access to some expensive databases, and time is the one thing money can't buy.

It's a February evening in London: cold but not yet chilly, dank and dark beneath clouds that promise rain but never quite deliver. The chauffeur drives smoothly, but behind the gold-tinted reflective surfaces of his shades his eyes are constantly flickering, evaluating threats, looking for trouble. A few months ago, a banker had his Aston-Martin hijacked at knife point while waiting for traffic lights not far from here. It would be most unfortunate if thieves were to target this particular vehicle: explaining their injuries to the police might delay Ms. Hazard.

"Zero."

He glances in the mirror at her voice. "Yes, boss?"

"Tune to Premier Gospel, please."

Zero blinks slowly, then switches on the sound system and brings up the radio control panel. "What do you want that rubbish for?"

"I couldn't possibly say." She sounds coolly amused. "Mood music, maybe."

Zero's knuckles tighten on the steering wheel for a moment, then he goes back to scanning for hijackers, tails, suicidal cyclists, and other threats.

It takes them half an hour to drive out to the North Circular, then a further twenty minute detour into the wilds of London suburbia— estates of 1930s semis with privet hedges and fences out front. Finally they come to a pub with a mock-Tudor half timbered frontage and a sign declaring it to be *The Legionnaire's Rest*. Zero pulls into the abbreviated car park and stops. Behind him, Persephone is finishing a phone call. Moments later the back door opens and a man climbs in.

"I thought you said *smart casual*, Duchess," complains Johnny. His accent switches seamlessly to cod-cockney: "Wotcher, Zero old cock."

"Same to you, motherfucker," the chauffeur says cheerfully. "Strap in so I can go."

"Smart casual for *you*," says Persephone. She's wearing a Chanel suit and a hat. Gucci handbag, designer heels. "You're going in the main audience. I've got a VIP backstage pass. Going to see the Man."

"What's the gig?"

"Revival meeting. Have *you* found Jesus yet?"

"Isn't he down the back of the sofa?" Johnny stares at her for a moment, his face set in a grimace of distaste. "Revival meeting. Have you gone freaking insane?" He looks at the back of Zero's head, then asks plaintively: "Is it something in the water?"

"Button it up, we're on a job."

"Oh." He shakes his head. "You had me for a moment there. What kind of job?" He notices the music, barely audible over the road noise. "Is the Church of England hiring us to take out the Pope? Or are the Scientologists—"

"Neither." She passes him the phone. "Start reading."

Johnny takes the phone and begins to skim. Then he stops abruptly and stares out the window, his expression haunted. "Tell me this isn't what I think it is."

Persephone is silent for a few seconds. Then: "Gerry Lockhart thought you might have some special insights."

Johnny pauses, doing a slow double take. "Gerry wants *my* insight? Since when?"

"Since you grew up in a very wee highland kirk that practices the baptism of the sea and other, odder traditions." She looks at him. "He figures you're quite the expert on what's going on here."

"Does he now," Johnny breathes.

Persephone nods. "We're to sit at the back—or at the front, in my case—and sing along with the music. And we need to make notes. Your job is to apply your highly experienced eyeball to their particular brand of religion. What are we looking at, what do they believe, what species of animal are we dealing with? *I'm* going to be in the front row." She unfastens the top button of her blouse, raises a button-sized leather bag on a fine silver chain from around her neck. "I'm warded." She lets it drop between her breasts, refastens the button, then rummages in her bag and pulls out a small cross and pins it to her lapel. She passes another cross lapel pin to Johnny. "Here, use this. Camouflage."

Johnny is wearing chinos, a polo shirt, and a fleece. After some fumbling, he pins the alien symbol to the fleece. "I'm allergic to churches," he says glumly. "As you should well know."

"Yes. But are you warded?" Persephone persists.

Johnny sighs. "Does the Pope shit in the woods?" He doesn't bother to show her the wrist band.

"Good."

"You think we're going to run into trouble?"

"Not on this occasion."

"Are you *sure*?" He pushes. "*Really* sure?"

Persephone sighs. "Johnny."

"Duchess."

"We are going to a church service. Evangelical big tent outreach, singing and clapping, that kind of thing. No more and no less. Doubtless your dear departed dad would disapprove, but ours is not to question why, etcetera. Take notes, do not draw attention to yourself, we can discuss the where and the why of it afterwards." She pauses.

"We've got a lunch date with Gerry and a junior co-worker tomorrow. That's when you get to hear what the caper's all about, *capisce?* For now, just finish reading that report and take notes."

Johnny glances back at the phone. "There's nothing here that a hundred other churches aren't doing. They're millenarian dispensationalist Pentecostalists and they're trying to spread the happy-clappy around. Film at eleven." He sounds as if he's trying to reassure himself, and failing.

"Let's hope that's all it is." She takes a deep breath. "Either way, we're here to find out."

THE GOLDEN PROMISE MINISTRIES ARE NOT UNAMBITIOUS: they've booked the O2 Arena for a week now, and another week in a month's time.

It takes Zero the best part of an hour to drive into Greenwich. He drops Johnny just around the corner from the O2 complex, then drives on to find a spot in the VIP car park. Traffic is heavy—the arena is able to hold more than 20,000 spectators, and a lot of them are coming by car for this one. It's not just a church service—it's an evening out for all the family, with a gospel choir, a band, and a star-studded cast led by Pastor Raymond Schiller of the Golden Promise Ministries.

The arena itself is huge—a domed performance space the size of a medium-scale sports stadium. Tiered blocks of seats tower above the central stage, lit by distant spotlights far overhead; the atmosphere among the audience is as deafeningly expectant as at any rock concert or football match. Johnny, who walks in among the regular punters, finds himself a roost halfway up one of the rear stands, with a bottle of Pepsi and a cheeseburger. He settles back in his seat and scans the crowd below him. Somewhere near the front of the stage there's a roped-off VIP area, accessed via a red-carpeted subway. The Duchess is down there now, chatting and laughing with the others on the restricted guest list: company directors with sick wives and children, wealthy widows, the children of the idle rich come in search of some additional meaning for their lives. Potential deep-pocket donors for Christ.

Back here in the bleachers it's another matter. It's an everyman (and everywoman) cross-section of London, emphasis on the cross. Family groups with children, some couples without, fewer men and women on their own, and larger groups—church trips, youth groups, some that Johnny can't identify or can't credit. (*A hen night?* he jots discreetly in his notepad.) There are a lot of non-white faces: religion is a minority pursuit in England these days. They come from all walks of life: builder, trader, website-maker. They're here for the music, the pizzazz, the excitement, the joy, and the sense of common purpose. It's like a reflection of his misplaced childhood, cut off behind the broken mirror of his adult cynicism.

Johnny watches with studied detachment as the show begins. People are still arriving, filtering in in knots and clumps and talking in quiet, excited tones as the warm-up man starts on stage, a younger preacher from Golden Promise Ministries' Mission to Miami: "Welcome, Welcome! Open your hearts to the golden promise of a love that will make everything right—"

He's an inspiring speaker, and he promises joy on a plate, heaven on a stick. There is a prayer. Everybody joins in. There is a chant. It's impossible not to stand and clap in time with twenty thousand other sweaty, excited pairs of hands, as Johnny rediscovers: they've got the script letter-perfect. Then the warm-up man segues into an introduction for the first act, a squeaky-clean rock band who are impossibly young and skinny behind the electric guitars they grip as tightly as their faith. There follows half an hour of power ballads where the punch line is Jesus.

Johnny gives up on the notepad, and settles down to wait. An old professional, he gives no outward sign of his irritation. *Three more hours of this shit,* he thinks disgustedly. Amanda's banker was stuck overnight in Zurich; he won't be home for hours yet. What price an immortal soul, when booty beckons? He makes a private guess with himself, and wins a fiver when the band give way to Warm-Up Man in his shiny electric-blue suit, who invites the audience to pray with him and starts the workup towards the main act. Johnny's boredom is just beginning to strengthen towards anomie when Raymond Schiller strides on stage, arms spread in benediction, a larger-than-life figure.

Johnny forgets everything else and focuses on the stage with the total nerveless calm of a sniper.

The Duchess was absolutely right to bring him here. He realizes, to his dismay, that Lockhart was also right to finger him for this caper: you can take the boy out of the church, but you can't take the church out of the boy. And like the devil (in whom Johnny does not believe), the boy will know his own.

4.

EXTERNAL ASSETS

THAT MONDAY MORNING I MAKE A POINT OF SETTING MY ALARM
fifteen minutes early, bolting my bowl of muesli, and skidding out the
house fast enough to leave trainer burns in the hall carpet. I'm pulling
my coat on while Mo is still half-asleep at the cafetière, working on her
second mug of the morning. "What's the big hurry?" she asks blearily.

"Departmental politics," I tell her. "I've been told I'm being temporarily reassigned and I want to get the skinny from Him Downstairs,
just in case."

"Him Downstairs? At nine a.m.?" She shudders. "Rather you than
me. Give him my regards."

"I will." And with that I'm out the door and double-timing it up to
the end of the street and the hidden cycle path which runs along the
bed of the former Necropolitan Line that transported corpses to London's largest graveyard in the late nineteenth century. It's a useful shortcut, affording those who know how to use it a one-kilometer journey
between points that are five kilometers apart on the map. I'd normally
get the tube—the ley lines are best used sparingly: human traffic is not
all that they carry—but I want to beard the lion in his den before I get
sent up to groom the tiger.

Fifteen minutes later I surface in a back alley off a side street a block from the New Annex. I look both ways for feral taxi drivers, cross the road briskly, and insert my passkey in the drab metal panel beside a door at one end of an empty department store frontage.

Welcome to my work.

My department of the Laundry is based in the New Annex for the time being. Dansey House, our headquarters building, is currently a muddy hole in the ground as a public-private partnership scheme rebuilds it. Despite the current round of cuts, our core budget is pretty much inviolate. I heard a rumor that our unseen masters in Mahogany Row found it quite difficult to get the message across to the treasury under the current bunch of clowns, but once fully briefed not even a cabinet of sadomasochistic monetarists would dare downsize the department charged with protecting their arses from CASE NIGHTMARE GREEN. Unfortunately neither Mahogany Row nor the Audit Department can do anything to make Bob the Builder complete a major new inner-city property development on time. And so we're nearly two years into a twelve-month relocation, and it's beginning to feel painfully permanent.

I'm early. The night watchmen have retreated to their crypts in the subbasement, but most of the department are still on their way in to work. I trudge to my office—I have an office all of my own these days, with a door and everything—collect my coffee mug, shuffle to the coffee station, fill it with brown smelly stuff, then head down the back stairs and along a dusty windowless passageway towards an unmarked green door.

I pause for a moment before I knock, and a hollow voice booms from within: "Enter, boy!"

I enter.

Angleton is sitting behind his desk, a huge gunmetal-gray contraption surmounted by something that looks like a microfiche reader as hallucinated by Hieronymus Bosch. (Or perhaps, going by the fat cables that snake under its hood, H. R. Giger.) Tall, pallid, with skin like parchment drawn tight across the bones beneath, he's the spitting image of every public school master who held the upper fifth in an iron grip of disciplined terror on TV in the 1960s. Which is appropriate, because for some years in what passed for his youth he was indeed a public school master. Only now he's my boss, and even though I'm well into my third decade he still calls me *boy*.

"Hi, boss." I pull out the creaky wooden guest chair and sit down.

It's a funny thing, but ever since the clusterfuck last summer I've lost some of my fear of Angleton. I don't mean to say that I don't treat him with respect—I give him exactly the same degree of respect I'd give a live hand grenade with a missing safety pin. It's just that now that I know exactly what he is, I've got something concrete to be terrified of.

Eater of Souls.

"Make yourself at home, Bob, why don't you." His glare is watery, a pro forma reprimand delivered with sarcasm but no real sting. "To what do I owe the honor of your presence?"

"Interesting training course at Sunningdale Park." I bounce up and down on the rusty mainspring of the chair. It must be the coffee, or something. "I ran into an interesting fellow. Name of Gerry Lockhart." I grin. "He gave me a book." Bounce, *squeak*, bounce, *squeak*.

I'm bluffing, of course. They kept me so damn busy I didn't have time to read more than the first couple of chapters—but I checked the Wikipedia entry, just in case.

"Do stop that, there's a good boy." The wrinkles around his eyes deepen into a scowl. "What precisely was the book, may I ask?"

"Oh, some potboiler about a wild man who used to work for the Dustbin, back in the day." *MI5.* "Reds under the bed, that kind of thing."

I wait for a few seconds. Angleton continues to stare at me, his expression icy. Finally, he thaws—but only by a degree or two.

"Peter Wright." The way he pronounces the name I'm pretty sure he intends it to rhyme with *Wrong*. "A dangerous crank."

"Oh, really? I suppose you knew him?" Never mind that Wright retired in 1976; Angleton's been with the Laundry for a very long time indeed. "What exactly did Wright do wrong?" *What lesson am I meant to draw from this book?* in other words. (See, I'm not above cheating at homework.)

Angleton closes his eyes, then leans back in his chair. "Crazies and loose cannons," he mutters. Then he opens his eyes again. "Bob. The cold war ended in 1991. How old were you?"

Huh? "I was fourteen. I saw it on telly; I remember being scared of a nuclear war when I was a toddler. Afraid of my ma being burned to a crisp if Maggie or Reagan were serious about the 'bombing in fifteen minutes' thing."

"I see." I see Angleton contemplating the situation from a very different perspective, trying to work out how to explain something to someone so impossibly young that the Vietnam War was ancient history before he was born and men haven't walked on the moon in his lifetime. "That was indeed one aspect of the confrontation. But only in the later stages. Earlier on, things were, if anything, crazier. And today we are required to work within the constraints established to keep the bad crazy, as you youngsters would call it, from breaking out again."

"The bad crazy?"

"In the early 1960s—you've heard of Philby, Burgess, and Maclean?"

Toothpaste or spy? "Yes." At least, I've heard of them since I read Lockhart's book.

"Then, in light of recent events you will appreciate just how . . . crazy . . . MI5 went in the aftermath of their exposure as Soviet moles. Yes?"

I shudder. "Yes." Eight months ago our own mole problem broke surface. I rub my right upper arm with my left hand. It aches savagely for a moment, then subsides. Moles are voracious underground predators; they're poisonous and they'll eat anything. Some of the latest crop even tried to eat *me*.

"There were excesses," Angleton says blandly. "Then they went too far. Wright was on the FLUENCY committee, investigating possible Soviet moles that had been missed. They began seeing spies everywhere, especially after someone upstairs who shall remain nameless gave them access to GREY CADAVER remote viewing intel. Trade union leaders, senior civil servants, television comedians, politicians, cabinet ministers. It went right to the top. They forced out a junior health minister who was suspected of spying for Czech intelligence. Then they branched out into the broader media. They bugged the FBI team who were bugging The Beatles. Some say that Mary Whitehouse got her start as one of their junior inquisitors. By 1968 they'd commissioned a study on installing a pyre in the former Star Chamber in Whitehall so they could burn witches—using North Sea gas, of course. It was a terribly *British* witch hunt. Their paranoia knew no bounds—they wrangled the BBC into canceling the fifth series of *Monty Python* because they thought the canned laugh tracks might contain coded messages to KGB sleeper agents.

"Finally, they began to investigate the prime minister, Harold Wilson. Wilson, Wright was convinced, was a KGB agent." I'm nodding along like a metronome at this point. "There was a group, a cabal if you like, of MI5 officers. About thirty of them. They actually planned a coup d'état in 1972. They were going to stick Lord Louis Mountbatten in charge of a provisional military government, herd all the suspected spies into Wembley Stadium, and shoot them. They were even going to replace the House of Commons with Daleks."

I roll my eyes. I can tell when Angleton is yanking my chain: "Even the tea lady?"

"Yes, Bob. Even the tea lady." Angleton looks at me gravely. "*When* will you learn to read your briefing documents?"

"When they don't land on my head disguised as a pulp bestseller when I'm in the middle of an intensive training course." I sit up. "So, the 1960s and early 1970s: deeply paranoid, or merely full of obsessive-compulsive witch hunters? How does this affect us *now*?"

Angleton leans across his desk and makes a steeple of his fingers: "The point, boy, is that ever since that time of unbound paranoia the one unbreakable law of the British secret services has been: *Thou shalt not snoop on Number Ten.* Because we are not in the business of generating policy—it's not a task for which agencies like ours are suited, and in those countries where spooks set policy, it always ends in tears. We vet politicians on the way up—that's an entirely different matter—but by the time they're moving into Number Ten they should already be above suspicion; if they aren't, we haven't been doing our job properly. And that's very important because *we are ultimately answerable to them.* Our loyalty is to the Crown; the Prime Minister, as leader of the government, is the person in whose office that authority is vested. He or she issues our marching orders. So we obey Rule One at all times. Are you with me so far?"

"Um. I guess so. All very sensible, I suppose. Except . . ." I frown. "What has this got to do with me?"

"Well, boy . . ." Angleton fixes me with a bright, elfin smile—and I am abruptly *terrified*. "What do you think happens when an investigation in progress runs into the Prime Ministerial exclusion zone?"

TWO HOURS LATER AND TWO FLOORS UP IN ANOTHER WING OF the New Annex I knock on another door. It's a wider and much more imposing door, with a brass nameplate screwed firmly to the wood: LOCKHART, G. And there's a red security lamp and a speaker beside it.

The speaker buzzes. "Enter." It's like a visit to the dentist. I go inside, unsure of the ailment I'm here to have diagnosed—just gripped by an unpleasant certainty that it's going to hurt.

Gerry Lockhart rates a big corner office with a window, decent carpet, and *oil paintings*. I have no bloody idea where those come from—presumably Facilities have a sharing arrangement with the Government Art Collection—but it's a new one on me; aside from the always-empty offices on Mahogany Row, nobody in this organization rates any kind of eyeball candy unless it's a Health and Safety or Security poster. When the door opens he's sitting, poring over some papers on his desk; he hastily flips a black velvet cloth over the documents, slips off his half-moon reading glasses, then stands and extends a hand.

Gosh. He's offering to *shake hands*. For a moment I hesitate and almost glance over my shoulder to see who's behind me: then we shake.

"I trust you had a good weekend, Mr. Howard? Recovered from last week's dog and pony show?"

I roll my eyes. "It was very educational." I am officially educated: it says so right there on my personnel record. I'm not sure I *learned* anything, but that wasn't exactly the object of the exercise. "It's good to be back at work."

He gestures at one of the visitor chairs—opposite his desk, not off to one side, I note. "Have a seat." I sit down; it's better than standing. "I suppose you're probably wondering what this is about. And if you've got any sense, you're wondering why it involves *you.* Aren't you?"

His manner is precise, fussy with an edge of ex-military discipline to it. But thanks to last Monday evening's encounter I knew what to expect, so I ironed my trousers and wore a clean and un-scuffed pair of trainers. I see the ghost of a frown of disapproval at my lack of a tie, but he's almost making a point of not mentioning it. Which is interesting in its own right. "Yes, I'm curious. I've never been assigned to Externalities before. Or worked with your people." I draw the line at asking *What exactly is it that you do?* Sometimes people can be a bit touchy about that sort of thing.

"Your reluctance to sound ignorant does you credit, but there really is no reason to dissemble, Mr. Howard." Lockhart's cheek twitches, nudging the hindquarters of the hairy caterpillar that is sleeping on his upper lip. "There's no reason for you to have heard of Externalities, and every reason why you shouldn't; need to know and all that." He clears his throat. "You've been to see Angleton, of course. What did he tell you about me?"

That's easy: "He didn't."

"Good." Lockhart's sudden smile is feral. "And what does that tell you? Feel free to speculate."

"Oh?" *Now* I glance round, just in case a couple of blue suits from Operational Oversight have sneaked in behind me. "Well . . . Externalities is a really suggestive name for a small subdepartment, isn't it? Utterly ambiguous—meaningless, really. There's a box on the org chart under Facilities, and a couple of dotted lines leading to Ways and Means and Human Resources, and that's *it.* Small staff, boringly mundane subdivision of the paperclip police. Nobody would ever look twice at it, except . . ."

"Yes?"

I take a deep breath. "You're borrowing *Angleton's* assistant. I think that says it all, doesn't it?"

"Don't get above yourself, Mr. Howard." His smug expression be-
lies his tone. "Just so that you know where you stand, everything I am
about to tell you about this particular asset is classified BASHFUL
INCENDIARY. Dr. Angleton is on the approved list, and—now—so
are you. Your line manager (that would be Mr. Hinchliffe this month,
would it not?) is not so cleared. Neither are your barber, your wife, or
your pet cat, and I'd appreciate your cooperation in not spreading the
magic circle. Under pain of your oath of office."

I nod, jerkily. This is some heavy shit he's drawing down. The oath
of office here in the Laundry is rather draconian: forfeiting your eternal
soul is only the beginning. "Uh. You asked for me for a reason. Can I
ask why?"

"Hmm. I did *not* ask for you. You were *recommended*, and after due
discussion it was agreed that you were eminently qualified for, and in
need of the management experience that you can gain in, this posting."

Management experience? I feel an oh-shit moment coming on.
"Um. Question mark?"

"Here in Externalities, we monitor organizational assets that are
largely outside the usual lines of control—beyond regular management." Lockhart smiles blandly.

"Paperclips? Attached to interdepartmental memos?" That's improb-
able enough on the face of it. Most intelligence agencies are fanatical
about locking down the hardware, banning phones and USB sticks and
iPods from the premises. The Laundry takes a different approach, and
focuses on securing the people, not the property—although sometimes
this leads to, shall we say, *misunderstandings* in our dealings with other
agencies.

"Paperclips, other assets." Lockhart waves dismissively. "People on
external assignment, for example. We provide support for senior executives on request. And it goes both ways. We also keep track of external contractors."

"External *what*?" I stumble into disbelieving silence. External
contractors? I've never heard of such a thing. Not here, not in an
agency that promiscuously hires anyone and everyone who stumbles
across the truth—makes them a job offer they can't refuse, inducts

them under the authority of an appallingly strong geas, and keeps them busy chasing paper until it's time to retire. "But we don't employ external contractors! Do we?"

"No, we don't. Not as such." His expression is so arch you could hang a suspension bridge from it. "Tell me, Mr. Howard, have you eaten recently?"

"No—"

"Then you'll have no objection to accompanying me to lunch at a restaurant, will you? The organization's paying."

I boggle. "Isn't that against accounting regs or something?"

"Not when I'm briefing a pair of contractors, Mr. Howard. Your job is to sit tight, ears wide, and *listen*. When we get back here afterwards there will be an exam. If you pass, *then* I shall explain what I want you to do for the next couple of weeks."

"And if I don't pass?"

"Then you go back to Dr. Angleton with a recommendation for some more training courses. And I shall have to do the job myself." His cheek twitches at the prospect. I am beginning to get a handle on the code. That is an *unhappy* twitch: the caterpillar has indigestion. "However, that would not be an ideal outcome, because the job in question appears to be well-matched to your strengths."

Damn him, he's clearly been taking lessons from Angleton on best practice for baiting the Bob-hook. "Okay, I'll bite. Lunch with a contractor, then an exam. Where do I start?"

"Right here." And Lockhart folds back his black cloth, picks up a slim dossier headlined BASHFUL INCENDIARY, and watches vigilantly while I read it.

AFTER AN HOUR'S READING, MY HEAD IS SPINNING. MIDWAY through the dossier, Lockhart—evidently satisfied by my absorption—tiptoes out of the office for a quick fag or something. I hear the door lock click behind him. Luckily I don't need a toilet break. The file is quite slim, but the contents—or rather, their implications—are explosive.

Here's the rub. The Laundry runs on three inviolate rules:

1) We make a point of recruiting—conscripting, really—everyone who learns the truth. That's how I ended up here. We have a place for everyone (and make sure everyone knows their place).

2) It is a corollary of the preceding rule that we never employ external contractors. There are no independents.

3) Finally, and most importantly, the security services—of which we are one—do not snoop on Number Ten.

But *all* of these rules come with a sanity clause.

Take the first rule. It's how everyone I know (Angleton excepted) came to work for the Laundry. We stumbled across something ghastly that we couldn't handle, and before it could apply the Tabasco sauce and find us crunchy but good with fries the Laundry came and rescued us, then made us a job offer we weren't allowed to refuse.

In my case, I nearly landscaped Wolverhampton with an unfortunate experimental rendering algorithm. (For my sins, they stuck me in IT Support for three years; on the flip side, I didn't die.)

The B-team players we hire so we can keep an eye on them and protect them from the consequences of their own actions. The A-team players end up doing the protecting—both for the second-raters and for the Crown—defending the realm against things with too many tentacles and eye-stalks.

As for the second rule: if we employ everyone in the field, so to speak, then it follows that there are no external contractors. Anyway, external contractors would be a security risk. So even if there *were* external contractors, we couldn't put them on the payroll without them taking the oath of allegiance, going the whole nine yards, etcetera. At which point, they wouldn't be external.

As for the third rule . . . I'm guessing that's where I come in. But I'm getting a bit ahead of myself at this point.

HALF AN HOUR LATER LOCKHART COMES BACK AND REMOVES the dossier from my nerveless fingers: "Are you coming?"

"Uh? Lunch? Sure." I struggle to my feet. "I'll just get my coat."

He picks up the dossier, adds it to another that he's carrying—I spot the subject JOHNNY PRINCE on the cover before I force myself to stop—and turns to stash them in his large and exceedingly secure-looking office safe. I make myself scarce.

We meet downstairs, just outside the empty department store window. Lockhart flags down a passing taxi. We ride in silence: fifteen or twenty minutes to Wardour Street, in the heart of London's Chinatown. Pocketing a receipt, Lockhart leads me through the crowd of shoppers to a surprisingly familiar destination, if only because it's infamous: the Wong Kei. "We're meeting *here*?" I ask.

"Where better?" Lockhart says ironically as he leads me inside. It's lunchtime and deafeningly loud inside the landmark restaurant. I'm expecting us to end up queuing, but no: as if by magic Lockhart flags down a waiter, mutters something, and we're whisked through a *Staff Only* door, into a cramped lift that squeals and grinds its way up to the third floor, then along a narrow passageway to a private dining room. He pauses before we enter. "The budget will only stretch so far." But my reading of his mustache is getting better, and right now it spells: *caterpillar is hungry for Cantonese*.

The room is cramped, illuminated by flickering fluorescent tubes and a tiny window outside which throbs a bank of kitchen extractor fans. But the table is already laid out with chairs for four and a pot of jasmine tea on the lazy Susan. "Remember what I said," Lockhart warns me, "keep your ears open and your mouth shut. Within reason. Understood?"

I nod, and mime a zipper. I'd normally put up more of a fight, but after reading the BASHFUL INCENDIARY file I find myself curiously uninterested in making a target of myself: she might turn me into a toad or something.

A minute later—I've just filled both our cups with steaming hot tea—the door opens again. Lockhart stands, and I follow suit. "Good afternoon, Ms. Hazard." The caterpillar is delighted. "Ah, and the estimable Mr. McTavish! How are you today?"

Handshakes and smiles all round. I take stock, then succumb to a brisk flashback: a disturbing sense that I've met these people before.

McTavish is easy to pigeonhole, hence doubly dangerous: in jeans and a hooded top he looks like a brickie, except I know what the side-long flat stare and the ridges on the sides of his hands mean. He reminds me of Scary Spice, one of Alan Barnes's little helpers—specialty: ferreting down rabbitholes full of blood-drenched cultists and undead horrors. The resemblance isn't perfect, but I've met NCOs in special forces before and he's got that smell. Although there is a slight *something else* about him as well: he punches above the weight.

She, however—

"Charmed to meet you," she says, and smiles, impish and vampish simultaneously. "I have heard so much about you, Mr. Howard! May I call you Bob?"

"I'm Bob to my friends," I drone on autopilot as my brain freezes in the headlights. Stunning beauty in a minidress over black leggings, studiously casual yet somehow managing to send a bolt of electricity straight down my spine and drop my IQ by about fifty points on the spot . . . *Yes, I've seen her like before.* "That's a nice glamour. Class two?"

Her smile freezes for an instant. "Class three, actually." Then she lets it slip slightly and the starry soft-focus dissolves, and I'm merely shaking hands with a strikingly pretty dark-haired woman of indeterminate years—anything between twenty-five and forty—with Mediterranean looks and a dance instructor's build, rather than a sorceress with a brain-burning beauty field set to Hollywood stun. "You have much experience of such things?"

"My wife doesn't bother." Is that a palpable hit? "But I've met them before, yes."

Lockhart keeps a stony face throughout, but at this latter bit of banter he begins to show signs of irritation with me. "Bob, if you'd care to sit down, perhaps we could order some food?"

We sit down. I pointedly pay no attention to McTavish pointedly taking no slight at my pointed rejection of his mistress's pointed—and unsubtle—attempt to beguile me. I'm somewhat disappointed. Do they think we're amateurs or something?

"That was a very interesting service you sent us to last night," Hazard tells Lockhart. She's working on the English understatement thing, but her hands, expressive and mobile, give it away: she's spinning exclamation marks in semaphore. "Absolutely fascinating."

"Yes it was, wasn't it?" Lockhart deadpans. He glances at McTavish. "You took a different angle, I assume?"

McTavish nods. "Penthouse and pavement." His expression is oddly stony.

"Good—" Lockhart stops as the door opens. It's one of the Wong Kei's crack assault waiters, pad in hand. They're famously rude; it's all part of the service.

"You ready to order?" he barks.

"Certainly." Lockhart is clearly a regular here. "I'll start with the hot and sour soup . . ."

Two or three minutes later:

"Where was I?" Lockhart asks.

"You were grilling us about last night, as I recall," says McTavish. Hazard nods, eyes narrowing.

Lockhart glances at me briefly. It's barely a flicker, but enough to warn me: *The game's afoot.*

"Did you notice anything unusual about the, ah, performers?"

"What? Apart from the way they programmed the event to build the audience's emotional investment in the key payload, then love-bombed them from fifty thousand feet with the warm floaty joy of Jesus?" Hazard props her chin on the back of her hand and pouts, sulky rather than sultry. "You should send Bob. He doesn't like glamours. Do you, Bob?"

"Hey, it's not you—it's just that the last time someone put one on me I ended up buying an iPhone!" My protest falls on deaf ears.

"It's not the glamour that interests me," Lockhart says deliberately, "but the person it's attached to."

"You're asking about Raymond Schiller, of the Golden Promise Ministries," McTavish says lazily. "More like the Golden Fleece Ministries if you ask me, Duchess."

"Mm, that tends to go with the territory." Hazard is noncommittal.

"You didn't see the average take in the collecting buckets at the back. Lot of people going short on luxuries this month, if you ask me."

"The O2 Arena doesn't rent for peanuts."

"Unless it's a charity loss-leader and they make up their margin on the food and entertainment franchises." McTavish is a lot sharper than he looks. "Or someone with a glamour as good as Ray Schiller gets to the management committee."

"Does he, ah, preach the prosperity gospel?" asks Lockhart.

"After a fashion." McTavish's lips are lemon-bitingly narrowed. "There are doctrinal shout-outs, dog-whistles the unchurched aren't expected to notice. The prosperity gospel is in there, of course—it's a Midwestern mega-church, after all. That's what their appeal is all about. But there's other stuff, too. It put me in mind of the church of my fathers, and not in a good way."

"You didn't say that last night." Hazard sits up. The door opens as a pair of waiters appear, bearing trays laden with soup and starters. She continues after they leave, addressing Lockhart: "It was a very non-specific love-bombing, but it was a very public evening. I thought it was a recruiting drive for foot soldiers rather than a second-level indoctrination aimed at officers. Very skillful, though."

"I'd use a different word for it," McTavish says darkly.

"Yes?" Lockhart focusses on him.

"You'll have read my file." McTavish winks and picks up a prawn toast. "Let's not disrespect the food, eh?"

As I dive into my chicken and sweetcorn soup I'm trying to place Hazard's accent. It's not remotely American, but not British, either; there's a hint of something central European, but it's been thoroughly scrubbed—all but erased—by very expensive speech training.

"Ray is an interesting character," Lockhart explains over the starters. "We don't know much about him. US citizen, of course; he came out of Texas, but his background is rather vaguer than we're happy about. There's a worrying lack of detail, especially about what he did before he found Jesus in his mid-twenties and joined the Golden Promise Ministries, back when it was a converted shack in the Colorado mountains."

"Aye, well." McTavish is busy with his ribs—I can't tell whether he's genuinely hungry or using them as a smoke screen—but Hazard is suddenly abruptly intent on Lockhart, her gray eyes as tightly focused as a battleship's range-finder. "You think . . ."

Lockhart clears his throat. "Please don't say what you're about to say. I'm implying nothing, Persephone. There's no evidence and there are no witnesses—none we've been able to locate. I may be barking up the wrong tree. Nevertheless, we are *concerned*."

"I am not sure I see why," she says slowly. "As long as he simply takes the marks for their marks, what's the problem?"

Johnny McTavish has gone very still and very distant, gaze fixed and unblinking in a sniper's thousand-yard stare. A cold chill runs up and down my spine. I'm the only person at this table who hasn't been fully briefed on whatever is being spoken of here, and I feel horribly exposed, because I've read enough of the BASHFUL INCENDIARY dossier to know what Persephone is capable of, and Johnny is her lieutenant—and I suspect the subject of the other dossier, the JOHNNY PRINCE one I saw on Lockhart's desk—which means he shouldn't be underestimated either.

"Did you stay for the laying on of hands?" Lockhart asks after a moment.

"Yes." Her eyes narrow. "And the speaking in tongues, and the reeling and writhing. Thank you very much."

Johnny is pointedly silent and dour.

"Did they say anything interesting?" Lockhart leans forward.

"Hard to tell." She frowns. "Glossolalia is always hard to follow, even with my—assets. The music and chanting and clapping and cheering from the back, they make it really hard to hear. But if I had to guess, I think—I might be wrong—it was all coming through in High Enochian. And one lady in particular—she was facing in my direction as the Holy Spirit took her—she was calling, *He is coming, he is coming*, over and over. And it was definitely in that tongue."

Johnny looks up and nods. "The faith of my fathers, for sure," he says quietly. "I could feel the siren song in my blood."

"Well that tears it." Lockhart looks at me sourly.

"What?" I say, surprised.

"Gerry, would you mind explaining, preferably in words of one syllable, just why this particular hedge-wizard occultist turned preacher-man is suddenly a person of interest to Her Majesty's Government?" Hazard stares at Lockhart, openly challenging.

Johnny looks uncomfortable. "Duchess—"

Lockhart shakes his head. "That's the wrong question."

"What's the right one, then?"

"The right question," he pauses for a final mouthful of soup, "is why Her Majesty's Government has suddenly become of interest to Raymond Schiller. And in particular, why our prime minister is hosting a prayer breakfast for the pastor the day after tomorrow." He puts his spoon down and fixes Hazard with a chilly stare. "There are aspects of Pastor Schiller's mission that were not on display at the arena. Call it the uncut, X-rated version of yesterday's PG performance. As you can imagine, we find his faith disturbing."

McTavish fixes me with a lazy smile. "Are *you* a man of faith, Mr. Howard?"

"In a manner of speaking." I use my napkin to wipe my lips while I work out how much I can say without Lockhart putting me on latrine duty afterwards. "I'm fully aware of the One True Religion. I know where I stand with respect to it." I stare right back at him. "And I know what to do with worshipers when I find them."

His smile widens. "We must get together and compare notes some time."

Hazard cuts across us: "If you gentlemen have quite finished? I believe we still have a main course to eat." She smiles indulgently. "You can continue plotting deicide later. I, for one, am looking forward to the Hoisin duck . . ."

Jesus, that woman's got a strong stomach, I think as the waiters come to clear away our starters and Lockhart looks at me and gives a stiff, very quick nod.

Little do I suspect what's in store for dessert.

5.

BASHFUL INCENDIARY

I KEEP MY GOB SHUT UNTIL WE GET BACK TO LOCKHART'S OF-fice. He shuts the door and flips the security lamp switch—to warn passers-by not to enter—then turns to me. "Sit down, Mr. Howard. I must congratulate you on not giving away the *entire* kitchen sink, along with the silver teaspoons . . ."

I sit on the edge of the hard visitor's chair. I will confess to a slight degree of tension. *There will be an exam*: no shit, Sherlock. The real question is, who is examining whom?

"Do Operational Oversight know about this?" I ask bluntly.

Lockhart's response is characteristically terse. "They aren't cleared to supervise Externalities. We answer directly to Mahogany Row. The Auditors keep an eye on us, in case you were wondering about ac-countability."

Great. Just when I thought things couldn't get any dicier, it turns out we're going behind the backs of the folks normally charged with keeping us on the straight and narrow, because the Big Bad them-selves are giving us the hairy eyeball. "So, let me see if I've got things right . . . You've got wind of a televangelist who is in too tight with the Prime Minister. He's got, at a minimum, some rudimentary talent; at worst, he may be a cultist. The PM is completely and utterly off-limits, so we're going to set up a surveillance op that bypasses Operational Oversight *specifically* so we can violate our organization's equivalent of the prime directive. Right?"

"Not exactly." The caterpillar is unamused. "We are going to obey the letter of the law, Mr. Howard, and don't you forget—"

"I'm so glad to hear that—" I begin before I realize he's got more to say: "I'm sorry?"

"What did I tell you about using your ears?" I bite my tongue and give him the nod he's waiting for. "When you're not filling the external assets' ears with your own opinions . . . anyway. As I was saying, we are bound to obey the law. The Laundry does not snoop on the PM or his associates. Caesar's wife and all that. Nor does the Laundry employ external contractors."

Then what was lunch about? I manage not to ask; instead I nod, trying to fake a thoughtful expression.

"It is possible that from time to time outside interlopers who, I emphasize, do *not* work for the Laundry, and who feature nowhere in our org chart, might take an interest in people associated with Number Ten. Wild cards, loose cannons." Lockhart aims for the arch expression of a Sir Humphrey Appleby: on his round face it looks as authentic as a six pound note. "In which case we would of course be required to investigate *them*: strictly to ensure that the PM's security was not violated, you understand."

"Outside interlopers like BASHFUL INCENDIARY and her pet thug?" I stare at him in ill-concealed disbelief.

"You appear to be slightly perturbed." Lockhart walks behind his desk and sits, stiffly. "Would you care to explain why, Mr. Howard?"

You gave me the dossier—I flap my mouth: noises come out. *Get a grip, Bob.* "Where shall I start?"

"At the beginning." Lockhart laces his fingers together. "Tell me about BASHFUL INCENDIARY, then explain why you are uneasy."

"Huh. Okay, then. We have a woman with no history before the age of eight. She first appears on the scene in Bosnia during the war, already aged eight, via a refugee camp. Doesn't speak and is believed to be mute. After four months in the camp a couple of teenage thugs try to rape her. The UN peacekeepers notice the aftermath of the incident but write it off as a freak accident; by the time someone asks what sucked the soul out of two gangbangers, she isn't there anymore. To this day, it's an open question—precocious talent or a protective agency? There are isolated reports over the next two years. Living with a family of Roma in Albania, caught begging in Trieste, shoplifting in Milan. She slips through the net every time. Then, a year later, the trail firms up. She is formally adopted by Alberto and Marianne di Fonseca, whose lawyers convince the magistrate that despite the lack of paperwork it's in the kid's best interest for her to have a stable, loving, and fairly well-off family."

I take a deep breath. "The di Fonsecas are persons of interest: a professor of theoretical mathematics and a former fortune teller with a reputation as a witch. He's titled—duke of a historic statelet that hasn't existed since the eighteenth century. There's old money and influence there, not to mention his membership in a politically influential but very secretive masonic lodge—"

Lockhart makes a cutting gesture: "Fast-forward, if you please."

"Okay. Our ten-year-old girl is enrolled in an expensive *Liceo Scientifico* where her academic performance goes from subpar in the first year to meteoritic in the second and subsequent. By fifteen she was taking her, ah, diploma di scuola superiore—ready to enter university four years early. Wednesday Addams, the Italian remix: a quiet, reserved pupil, doesn't make many friends, spends holidays at home with her adoptive parents. Pay no attention to the word among the local lads about town that she's a, a succubus; probably she's just very good at creeping out teenage boys who hit on her.

"She's staying with the di Fonsecas in their holiday villa—but not at home on the evening of July 19, 2002, when they are murdered. The murderers are gunmen reported variously to be members of the Palermo Mafia, the Brigado Rosso, or the Red Skull Cult, depending on who you ask. The girl, aged sixteen, is the sole survivor. Her claim to have been out on the town at the time is accepted by the local magistrates. She inherits roughly two million euros and the contents of the di Fonsecas' library, changes her legal name, and moves out."

I draw a deep breath. "Fast-forward two years—I'll back up in a minute—and two badly decomposed bodies are dredged from a lake in Tuscany. DNA evidence places them at the scene of the massacre. The remains show signs of paranormal intervention." That's Laundry-speak for *they were chewed on by extradimensional horrors.*

"Inconclusive." Lockhart frowns. "What next?"

How to summarize . . . ? Oh, that's *easy.* "She embarks on a five-year reign of terror. Instead of going to university, from September 2002 through to November 2007 BASHFUL INCENDIARY ran the most successful private occult intelligence service in history. The Hazard Network. An eighteen-year-old genius with a private income, the looks of a model, and a knack for identifying and hiring raw talent. She is, as it turns out, a very talented ritual practitioner"—one who risks their own cerebral cortex by working magic, raw, by force of will—"with a speciality in sex magic and, if that isn't sickening enough, she's a damn fine paralogician and a skilled programmer." Ritual magic is rare enough; combining it with a talent for our kind of business is distinctly unusual.

"Let's see: White Hat work. We know the Sultan of Brunei hired the Hazard Agency to track down a deep-cover Al-Qaida cell attempting to infiltrate the army intelligence service and the Sultan's own personal bodyguard. A Swiss bank retained her services as a Tiger Team to test security on their new deposit facility—verdict: it needed serious improvements. That sort of thing.

"As for her Black Hat work, there's nothing anyone can prove well enough to stand up in court—but a certain stench of brimstone attaches." I begin checking off crimes and outrages on my fingers. "Suspected removal of occult artifacts and jewelry from sunken Roman merchant vessels in the Adriatic. Suspected involvement in smuggling of Egyptian antiquities. Suspected theft of previously stolen old masters from a rich collector's hoard in Vienna, subsequent resale and blackmail—sexual as well as handling stolen goods—of their previous custodian. And an investment portfolio that bottomed out at 1.2 million euros in 2002 and peaked at just over *one hundred million*"—I do the Doctor Evil little-pinkie gesture at this point—"before the bottom fell out of the market in 2008."

Lockhart nods. "Since that time?"

"In 2008 she retires to London. Waits six months, then dumps the thick end of twenty million pounds of her personal wealth into the property market—right after the initial crash—and another hundred thousand pounds in political donations that make her very difficult to dislodge. By this time she's only got five or ten million left in the bank—she's paid off her team—but she plays her hand expertly. She's an EU citizen thanks to the di Fonsecas, a twenty-four-year-old millionairess who invites herself to the right parties and makes friends with the right Bright Young Things. Any crimes she *did* commit are swept under the rug, and she's kept her nose clean for the past seven years. In fact, she's done a terrifyingly professional job of turning herself into a pillar of the establishment. There's absolutely *nothing* on her record after 2008 except for the financial and social work. To all intents and purposes it looks as if she dropped out of the whole occult world completely."

"Yes, that's always the way it works." Lockhart nods.

"So why isn't she *one of us*?" I ask bluntly. "She'd be a major asset . . ."

"You have no need to know." The caterpillar stretches in a thin line: curls over and plays dead. "That decision was taken above your pay grade—or mine. However"—Lockhart places a hand on top of the BASHFUL INCENDIARY file—"you will doubtless have realized by now that if she *was* in here she would be required to work under the same constraints as you or I, which would severely reduce her value to us. And I am led to believe that, within certain parameters, her loyalty is absolute."

I can't help myself. "What's that supposed to mean?"

Lockhart's cheek twitches. "For one thing, it means that she really *does not like* the Culto del Teschio Rosso and their playmates. And for another thing, if you ask her why she moved here, she will tell you that she conducted a rigorous survey of European occult defense agencies and concluded that we have the best chance of surviving CASE NIGHTMARE GREEN. In her opinion." His tone is dry enough to curdle milk. "It would be unwise to confuse a finely tuned survival instinct with loyalty to the Crown, Mr. Howard, but it counts for *something*."

"So we're her lifeboat and you trust her to bail if you hand her a bucket?"

"Something like that. Or so I have been led to believe by Mahogany Row. And what's good enough for them is, ipso facto, good enough for us."

"Jesus." I shake my head. (So this is coming down from the very top of the organization: the stratospheric, secretive executive country that mere mortal scum like me don't get to see even from a distance unless we're very unlucky.) "So, let me see if I've got this straight. Ray Schiller of the Golden Promise Ministries is doing breakfast with the PM, and you're a little upset because he's disturbingly convincing and gives off bad vibes. We can't snoop on the PM ourselves, so you point this loose cannon at the pastor—" I stop. "Oh no you don't."

"Don't what?" Lockhart's face is as unreadable as a professional poker player's.

I'm on my feet and leaning over his desk; I don't remember standing, and I am so damn angry that I'm shaking: "You're setting me up! You're going to spin it as a rogue operation with no oversight and if anything goes wrong—"

"Calm down, Mr. Howard!"

I'm not sure quite what it is about his tone, but his words are like a bucket of cold water in my face.

"You are *not* being framed. Quite the opposite. Your role in this operation is to monitor and report on BASHFUL INCENDIARY's officially unauthorized and unsanctioned activities; nothing more and nothing less. You will have . . . noticed . . . that *at no point* did I instruct BASHFUL INCENDIARY to act on our behalf. In fact I have no

authority over her. What Ms. Hazard chooses to do next is entirely up
to her. It is not impossible that she will decide to occupy herself with
the Grand National and the Chelsea Flower Show instead. Or to emi-
grate to Brazil, or paint herself orange and join a Buddhist nunnery.
The point is, she is *not under our control*. Not under yours or mine.
You don't have command authority; your job is to keep an eye on the
external asset, not to direct it."

"But"—I begin to slow down: the implications are sinking in—
"with what she knows, what if she's a threat?"

Lockhart looks at me grimly. "I think that is very unlikely, Mr.
Howard, otherwise I would not have mentioned our little problem to
her. However, in the hypothetical case that the loose cannon were to
explode in our faces, your job would be to deal with the consequences
as you see fit. *If* you happen to be one of the survivors."

"I"—*squeak*—"survivors?" It wouldn't be the first time an operation has blown up under me with fatal consequences, but I *really* hate
the way this is shaping up, with Hazard carrying the detonator and
me trailing along with bucket and spade. But Lockhart evidently mis-
understands the nature of my reservations.

"This is not a game, Mr. Howard. Your new pay grade comes with
strings attached; I am not referring to the management training. Further advancement as an officer within this service will put you in situations where you will be responsible for whether other people live or
die—this is inevitable as we move closer to CASE NIGHTMARE
GREEN. Worse: it is likely that you will encounter situations where
you must choose who to save and who to cast adrift, answerable only
to your oath of service and your conscience. I understand from your
personnel file that you have been placed in situations where you have
been required to use lethal force in self-defense. *This is not the same.*"
He fixes me with a gimlet stare. "There is a huge difference between
returning fire in personal self-defense and ordering an artillery strike
on an inhabited civilian settlement suspected of harboring enemy
forces. Do you understand?"

I sit down. My mouth is dry. Lockhart's gaze is directed through me, almost as if he's talking to a younger version of himself. *Military background,* I think. It's his personal metaphor. Nightmare, whatever. Then I have a flashback of my own, to a buried temple: writhing bodies, hungry revenants in the surrounding darkness, a sacrifice of souls. "I'm afraid I do," I say slowly. "Too bloody well."

"Good." His shoulders relax like an over-wound spring. "I trust that you were not suffering from the misconception that your promotion was directed towards a routine management role."

"This doesn't sound very routine to me." As a joke, it falls flatter than a Brick Lane chapati.

The caterpillar twitches. "Ninety-eight percent of management work in this organization is routine. The other two percent is a tightrope walk over an erupting volcano without a safety net. Congratulations: here's your balance pole."

I lick my lips. "So what exactly am I managing?"

"Trouble." Lockhart glances at his wristwatch. "Hmm. Well, I must be going—I have a meeting at four. I suggest you take the rest of the day off. Go home, check your go-bag, that kind of thing." He looks at me again. "Make sure to wear a suit tomorrow."

"What?" The phrase *wear a suit* does not fill me with joy.

"Be here tomorrow morning, nine thirty sharp. We'll start by collecting your new passport. They'll need to photograph you. Then we have a field trip."

"New passport?"

"In all probability this operation will require you to travel outside the country." Lockhart picks up the BASHFUL INCENDIARY file and bends over his office safe, putting his back between me and the keypad. "In which case you will need a passport with a diplomatic visa. In my experience, when pretending to be a diplomat working for the Foreign Office it usually helps to look the part." He glances over his shoulder at me. "Well? What is it?"

I put my brain back in gear. "Where am I going?"

"Probably the United States, because that is where Schiller's Golden Promise Ministries is headquartered—but in any event, wherever Ms. Hazard leads you. Remember: economy class on flights of less than six hours duration. Oh, and don't forget to write." He flicks his fingers at me. "Shoo."

I shoo.

I AM IN THE BEDROOM PACKING MY GO-BAG WHEN MO GETS home.

There is a clattering from the front hall, then more noises from the kitchen—cupboard doors, the fridge, a dirty coffee mug rattling in the sink. Finally a loudly pitched question mark: "Bob?"

"Up here." *Five pairs of socks, six, or hit M&S for a new one-week pre-pack?* I hear footsteps on the stairs.

"Who died?" she asks from the doorway.

"No one," I say, straightening up. She's seen the suit.

Actually, I own *two* suits these days. The other one is a black-tie job for formal bashes like the Institute of Chartered Demonologists' annual ball. *This* one is my Reservoir Dogs Special. It does duty for all occasions that require a suit—court appearances, weddings, graduation ceremonies, funerals, and those situations when work absolutely requires something other than a tee shirt and jeans. It's the kind of suit that is worn at arm's length by a suit refusnik; the kind of suit that trails a screaming neon disclaimer overhead, saying: *the occupant of this garment is clearly alive only because he wouldn't be seen dead in one of these things*; the kind of suit whose afterlife is destined to be spent surrounded by mothballs in a charity shop window display. I did not buy it willingly: when it became half past obvious that I needed one, Mo dragged me round the shops for seven solid hours until I finally surrendered.

"They're sending you somewhere," she says. "Diplomatic cover?"

"Er—"

Laundry employees are not supposed—in fact, not allowed—to discuss their work with civilians. But Mo is not a civilian. And (I don't think Lockhart knows this) she and I have a special waiver to our binding geas to allow us to vent on one another's shoulder. But this business with Raymond Schiller and BASHFUL INCENDIARY is a cut above the ordinary, and I'm not even sure she knows about Externalities and Lockhart's little sideline.

While I'm vacillating over how much I can tell my wife, she works it all out for herself and nods, briskly: "Well, if they're running you under FO cover they'll want you to look like a junior FO staffer, and that won't do. Let me see what you've got so far, then we can work out a shopping list to fill in the gaps."

"A shopping—"

"Oh Bob." She looks amused. "What do you think they pay me *for*?"

"Personal shopper?" It's a bad joke; of course I know what they pay her for. Mo owns several suits, because part-time university lecturers are expected to look the part—and when she isn't teaching, or researching, she's traveling on business with one of the aforementioned diplomatic visas.

"Good guess." She bends over the case. "Any idea how long you'll be gone for? Or where?"

"You missed an 'if' out of those questions." I shrug. "I may not be going anywhere at all. Or I may be going several places, in a hurry."

"Oh, one of *those* jobs." She frowns. "Okay, you pack for five days and work the hotel room service on expenses for priority cleaning if you overrun. Underwear, shirts, huh . . . is this your only tie?"

"Apart from the bow that goes with the dinner jacket, yes." It's a black silk tie with Wile E. Coyote's head embroidered on it in raised relief, black-on-black. I've had it for two years; I was forced to buy it for my uncle's funeral after the last neck-strangulator was disemboweled by the washing machine. (How was *I* to know they're dry clean only?) I was wondering how long it would take her to notice.

"Jesus, Bob." She shakes her head. "Okay, I'm taking you to work tomorrow. By tube, via the shops in Liverpool Street station. And I'm buying."

"Why?" I will confess to sounding a tad querulous at this point.

"So you don't end up with a diplomatic mug shot that makes you look like a hung-over hipster, that's why." She glares at me. "It's *work*."

I deflate. "No, it's management bullshit," I say weakly.

"Tell me about it." For a moment her expression is bleak beyond anything her years entitle her to. And she's five years older than me.

I take a chance. "There's a department called—"

My tongue sticks to the roof of my mouth and a taste of acrid brimstone fills my nostrils. So, being me, I try again.

"I'm working for—" There's an immediate electric prickling in my eyes and a crawling on my scalp. *Nope, oath of office ain't having it.*

"Looks like our usual waiver doesn't apply to this job." The ward of office agrees and refrains from frying my ass for explaining this to her.

Her eyes narrow thoughtfully. "You'll forgive me for saying so, but that's some serious shit you're in." I nod enthusiastically, which seems to be allowed. "Coming right on top of that course on, what was it, leadership skills . . ." She walks around the bed and prods disconsolately at the graveyard of trainers. "You'll be needing a good pair of running shoes, then. And something that doesn't call you out as anything other than your normal boring embassy desk pilot. Assuming you're doing what I think you're doing." She pauses. "Have you been to see Harry yet?"

"That was on my to-do list for tomorrow," I admit. Harry is our armorer. "But if I have to tool up, everything will already have gone to shit."

"In which case you will need to be carrying, in order to evacuate and report." She pauses. "Scratch Harry; if you're going overseas, guns are a liability. I think you want to have a word with Pinky tomorrow. He's been working with a new application of SCORPION STARE, and you might be an ideal candidate for beta tester."

I HNOCK ON LOCHHART'S OFFICE DOOR AT NINE THIRTY SHARP the next morning, wearing a sober suit and a new tie—one of three that Mo insisted on buying for me in Noose Hutch International on the way to work (which meant she got to vet them for cartoon wildlife first). It's uncomfortable but I'm not panicking yet—I've got a compact

Leatherman tool in my pocket, which means I can always stab it to death if it wakes up and tries to throttle me.

"Ah, Mr. Howard." Lockhart's stare is judgmental. "Come on, we're running late." He sweeps out of the office and I tag along in his wake.

Normally, when I apply for a passport I get some pictures taken in a photo booth, fill out a form, then go round to a post office and pay them to check the paperwork and send it off to the Identity and Passport Service. A couple weeks later a fat envelope flops through the letterbox. This is a bit different, and involves visiting an office about which we shall say as little as possible, because the Dustbin are not our friends (except when they're arranging official cover documentation for our people, including shiny new passports with genuine diplomatic visas accredited by the US Embassy in Grosvenor Square without the need for an actual visit and interview).

After the photo-and-fingerprints session at Spook Central, Lockhart leads me outside the MI5 headquarters building and hails a taxi. Twenty traumatic minutes later we arrive at the sucking vortex of existential despair and chaos that is Euston, whereupon Lockhart hands me a rail ticket and leads me through the barriers. "Where are we going?" I ask. He ignores me, but pauses to buy a copy of the *Daily Telegraph*. The ticket, I note, is first class—something I thought was a strict no-no under our current hair-shirt expenditure controls.

Half an hour later, he folds his newspaper, stands up, and leads me off the train onto a platform in Milton Keynes Central. I shiver and look around, counting cameras. "Where are we going?" I ask again.

"To an obscure industrial park on the outskirts of town," he replies as he strides out of the front of the station, head swiveling in search of taxis like a vigilant blackbird after a juicy earthworm. We pause beside a row of pantone-colored concrete seagulls. "A place called Hanslope Park. Home to an organization called HMGCC."

"Her Majesty's GNU C Compiler?" I blink stupidly at the daylight.

"No, Her Majesty's Government Communications Centre. Very much *not* open source, Mr. Howard."

"Oh." Something about the address rings a bell from years ago, but I'm not certain yet. I stare at the seagulls. My skin crawls; I have bad memories of Milton Keynes, but they mostly center on the concrete cows and a compromised research station that may or may not have been located close to Hanslope Park. A sign beside the station entrance tells me that the local schools are having a seagull parade, with a charity draw and a prize for the best avian paint job. "So we're making the rounds?"

"It generally attracts less attention than an external request." A taxi pulls up between a puce seabird with bright red eyes and a startled expression and another gull wearing authentic 1940s Luftwaffe insignia. We climb in.

HMGCC is one of those boringly standardized cookie-cutter government installations that look like a blighted industrial estate: crappy seventies brutalist office architecture and prefabricated concrete warehouses with an open car park behind razor-wire-topped fences and signs saying BEWARE OF THE DOG. For all I know it *could* be right next door to the unit where I had my happy-fun encounter with Mark McLuhan; these places are so anonymous they could be anything. A bonded whisky warehouse, a bank cash center, or a factory where they build nuclear warheads. Further back, behind the buildings and out of sight of the road, there will be satellite dishes and exposed runs of cabling and pipes between buildings, and stuff of interest to spies and trainspotters—but first you have to get inside.

Lockhart stops our taxi driver at the front gate, pays, and we walk up to an impressive set of wire gates that are overlooked from three directions by white masts bending under the weight of CCTV cameras and antennae. My skin is just about ready to crawl off my neck and sprint screaming up the street—I know what those cameras are for!—but Lockhart pulls out his warrant card and advances on the gate guard. "Gerald Lockhart and Robert Howard to see Dr. Traviss. We're expected."

Half an hour and the electronic equivalent of a body cavity search later—I swear they're using me as a guinea pig for the scanners for next decade's airport security theater—we arrive in a small, dingy office with high, frosted-glass windows and too much furniture. It's clearly one of the graveyards where the MOD filing cabinets go to die. There's a too-small meeting table, and three occupied seats. The occupants stand as Lockhart shakes hands. "Bob, this is Dr. Traviss." A tall, gloomy-looking fellow in a suit and horn-rimmed glasses, Traviss seems only marginally aware of his surroundings. "This is Alan Fraser"—a government-issue scientific officer, subtype: short, hairy, and explosive, probably screeches all over the home counties on a monstrously over-powered motorbike every weekend to reassure himself that he still has a life—"and this is Warrant Officer O'Hara"—a blue-suiter, middle-aged, clearly along for the ride with orders to shoot the boffins if they try to think too hard. "Dr. Traviss, Bob is the individual you were briefed on yesterday." *Oh, really?* I think. "He's going overseas. Bob, these fellows are going to equip you for inventory tracking."

I stifle the urge to roll my eyes. "You aren't planning on using destiny entanglement on me, are you? Because last time—"

Lockhart cuts across me: "Nothing of the kind," he snaps. "Destiny entanglement *leaks*. It's a security violation waiting to happen."

Warrant Officer O'Hara pulls a file folder out from under his blotter and extracts a fearsome-looking document. "Read this and initial each page please, Mr. Howard." His avuncular smile draws some of the sting from his words, but it's quite clear that I'm not going to hear another word from these folks until I sign.

I read the first paragraph, clock that it's the standard Official Secrets Act boilerplate with added Laundry special sauce that we use to bind people to silence under threat of a fate worse than prosecution, skim-read the rest to make sure there are no surprise whoopee cushions buried in it, and sign in blood, using the sterile lancet and pen that O'Hara provides for that purpose. The unusually heavy paper itches under my fingertips, a dry prickling sensation that reminds me of dead insects. O'Hara removes the form and slides it back into the folder as I apply a cotton wool pad to my hand.

"Now we can proceed," says Traviss. He walks over to one of the filing cabinets and unlocks it, withdraws a zip-lock bag containing something that looks like a small photo album—the old dead-tree variety—and sits back down in front of me. He pulls the booklet out. "Mr. Howard. Have you ever seen one of these before?"

I squint at it. "A photo album. Yes?"

"Exactly." Traviss looks glumly satisfied. "Nine pounds from WHSmith's." He carefully folds the first page open. "And this is a pre-paid phone card."

I nod, fascinated.

He flips to the next page. "This is a temporary tattoo." Just like a million other tramp stamps sold on rolls of transfer paper in tat shops for kids who're too chicken to let a weekend biker scribble on their skin with a needle gun. "And, oh look, another. Inventory tags, Mr. Howard."

"Right."

"The phone card goes in your wallet. There's nothing special about it except that any call you make using this number will go through a switch that is monitored around the clock, so everything you say will be overheard." He nods at Lockhart. "I believe Mr. Lockhart has a list of codewords for you to memorize."

"Isn't that a little crude?" I probe.

Traviss pulls a face. "There is a man behind the curtain but you should pay no attention to him, Mr. Howard. We've put a lot of effort into ensuring that if you ever use this phone card, nobody will pay it any particular attention. In fact, we encourage you to use it a lot—if you're overseas, you can use it to call your wife." I suppress a twitch. Clearly he doesn't know that Mo is also a Laundry employee. "Would you rather engage in some cloak-and-dagger antics involving ad-hoc wifi networks running at set times in Starbucks, and laptops with hardware encryption dongles? So that when the black hats come to arrest you they find all your incriminating equipment and beat your password out of you with rubber hoses?"

I swallow. "I'm not used to that particular threat," I admit.

"I suppose not." Traviss looks satisfied.

"What about the tattoos?" I ask.

"Ah. Let's see." He flips rapidly through them: a goth's trophy pentacle, a cherub's kebab-skewer of love hearts, a hieroglyphic squiggle of ankhs and eye of Horus, even a couple of crosses. "Put these on your, ah, inventory items. They're waterproof and will last until they rub off—typically three to six days, but possibly longer if the inventory items refrain from bathing or cover them with an occlusive dressing. The image itself is non-signifying—the ink contains suspended nanoparticles impregnated with—" O'Hara clears his throat. "Right." Traviss pauses for a few seconds. "This is the master controller." He flops to the back of the book and shows me a kitsch clockface tat. "Apply this and you can communicate with the satellite tattoos."

"Um. How?" I ask.

"Contagion and blood magic," says Fraser, with relish. He grins fiendishly. "Use a needle to prick yourself through the tat and you'll be able to drop in on your subject. Or just use pain, in emergency pinch skin—but that can damage the tattoo. You can talk by subvocalizing or thinking the words—you can communicate silently."

I blink. It sounds almost too good to be true. "What are the drawbacks?" I ask.

"Well, there's some sensory leakage; while you're connected, you can feel their emotional state to some extent, see through their eyes. And physical pain—that transfers much too easily. You really don't want to call one of your satellites right after they've been shot in the stomach. The second real risk is that the opposition will find the tattoo and deduce what it is and what it's for before one of you can remove it. Oh, and you really don't want to activate it while you're in proximity to an unshielded trophic resonator—soul-suckers, or demons, or anything that can get a lock on your nervous system—they're attracted to such channels, and a ward won't save you."

I shiver. Suddenly it's not looking that convenient after all.

"It's a tool," O'Hara explains slowly, as if to a particularly stupid schoolboy, "to allow you to silently and untraceably talk one-on-one with field operatives, or snoop on their activities. In enemy territory, under the nose of the bad guys. It is not a magic wand. There are countermeasures, and if you are not careful and run into them it can betray you as thoroughly as being caught with a shortwave radio and a code book. But not to civilians." By which he means the likes of the FBI and police.

I take a deep breath. "Got it. Is there an FAQ?"

"I'll email it to you." Traviss's words are directed to Lockhart. "You can share it with Mr. Howard, I'm sure."

I do not like this. I do not like the way Lockhart takes the slim flip-book and pages through it, frowning thoughtfully—the caterpillar is disturbed—or the way these cowboys are tag-teaming us. "Is that all?" I ask sharply.

"Is that all?" Traviss sounds appalled.

"Yes, Bob, *that is all*." Lockhart stares at me with watery, dyspeptic eyes. "I think we'll be going now," he says, sliding the book back into its bag. "Thank you, gentlemen." He stands, and we file out.

LOCKHART DOESN'T SAY ANYTHING UNTIL WE GET BACK TO THE New Annex; he takes the admonitions about careless chatter so seriously that while we're out and about he's as conversational as a badger that's been dead for three days. Once back in his office he opens up—in my direction, unfortunately.

"You will not discuss our operational parameters in the presence of members of external organizations ever again," he says coldly. "Do I make myself clear?"

"Uh?"

He walks around me where I stand, more or less rooted to his office carpet. "You mentioned *destiny entanglement*, Mr. Howard. How do you know that Dr. Traviss and his companions were cleared to know about that technology?"

I blink rapidly. "My geas didn't—"

"No, it *didn't*, Mr. Howard. But you should not rely on your oath of office as an infallible guide to the perimeter of our security cordon. It relies on your own cognizance of threats to determine what level of security to apply. You of all people should understand that there are individuals who your geas would passively allow you to talk to who are nevertheless enemies—moles, enemies within who have official clearance. It may be that Dr. Traviss and Mr. Fraser and Warrant

Officer O'Hara are familiar with destiny entanglement tools like the one you used in conjunction with agent RANDOM a few years ago. Very probably they are, because the inventory tracking tags rely on a very watered-down version of the same technology—one that does not risk your mind fusing with that of your target if it isn't forcibly disconnected after a handful of days. The problem is that they now know that *you too* are familiar with such tools."

Enlightenment dawns, somewhat too late. "Oh. Shit."

"That is the correct word, Mr. Howard. Most likely it is an insignificant slip—but if, for example, Mr. Fraser turns out to be a mole in the employ of the Thirteenth Directorate, you have just delivered valuable information about your own capabilities to an unfriendly organization. Security is not just an externally directed process, it must be an *internal* one. Do you understand me?"

I nod jerkily. "Good." He makes a cutting gesture with one hand and suddenly my feet can move again. "You're a smart lad. If you have any concerns, you can bring them to me whenever you like. I will not mock you for asking stupid questions; we all have to start somewhere. But I would appreciate your keeping them private."

"Um," I say again.

"Yes?"

"If I'm going overseas, do I have any defensive issues?"

"Are you expecting to be physically attacked?" He raises an eyebrow.

I pause for a few seconds. "I am not *expecting* anything," I say slowly. "But I try to be prepared for all circumstances. I really don't like being held at gunpoint. And it's happened before."

For a few long seconds Lockhart stares at me. Then he nods approvingly. "Use your discretion," he finally tells me. "No firearms; remember you will be traveling under diplomatic cover." I wonder why he's so certain about that, but now is probably not the time to poke him. "I've got a meeting in ten minutes. Go. I'll send you the FAQ on the tracking tags when I receive it."

I can take a hint; I go.

* * *

I HATE FIGHTING. I'M NOT PARTICULARLY GOOD AT IT. COMpared to some of my acquaintances. Hell, I'm not even as good at it as my wife. If you have to fight, it means things are already badly out of control. So I generally try to avoid physical confrontations; my preferred defensive tactic is to run away. However, I can handle a Glock 17 and a Hand of Glory, and I'm certified for certain classes of occult self-defense. Mo said something about a device that Pinky and the Brain are testing over in Facilities . . . so after grabbing a quick lunch in the canteen I bail out of the office and head across town to what they used to jokingly call Q Division.

Unlike HMGCC, which is not part of the Laundry, Field Support Engineering *is*, and my warrant card is enough to get me inside. Whereupon I make my way through a drab corridor floored in carpet tiles that look to be a decade past their replace-by date, to an office door with a frosted-glass window and a *No Entry* sign. A pair of concrete seagulls to either side serve as gate guardians—these ones are unpainted, and unpleasantly lifelike—and there's a bumper sticker instead of a name plate. *Q: What are we going to do tonight, Brains? A: The same thing we do every night, Pinky: Try to take over the world!*

I enter, and close the door behind me. Pinky—not his real name—is hunched over his computer's screen, messing around with a digitizer pen. After a moment he blinks and looks up at me. "Bob?" He grins enormously and comes bounding out from behind the desk. "Bob!"

"Long time no—"

"Bob! You really must see this! It's brilliant!" He zips across the room and begins sifting through a mountain of what looks at first sight like junk (but probably isn't). "You're going to love this," he promises, turning round and offering me a slim box. After a second I recognize it.

"It's a camera, right?" Digital, subtype: compact. I take it.

Of an instant, Pinky's expression is all concern. "Hold on a minute! Don't switch it on yet."

I turn it over in my hands. "Huh." There's a legend on the front: Fuji FinePix Real 3D. Suddenly I remember the seagull gate guardians and my blood turns to ice. "Jesus, Pinky. Tell me this isn't what I think it is?"

"I don't know, Bob." He cocks his head on one side. "What *do* you think it is?"

I lick my suddenly dry lips. "What happens if I turn it on?"

He shrugs. "It switches on."

"And what happens if, say, I took a photograph of you?"

He shrugs again. "It takes a rather crappy 3D photograph. Why?"

"Where's the special sauce?" I ask tensely.

"On this." He produces an SD memory card with a flourish. "It's just a 3D camera until you reflash it with this special firmware."

"And then . . ." I lick my lips again. "Don't tell me. It's SCORPION STARE in a box that looks like a consumer digital camera. Right?"

"Yup." And Pinky, the idiot, looks indecently pleased with himself. "Mo said you might be needing a personal defense weapon and, well, you've used a basilisk gun before? Only bigger, bulkier, and much crappier."

You *could* put it that way.

Most of the magic we work with here in the Laundry is about using computational transforms to send messages that induce certain entities from outside our universe to sit up and pay attention. But sometimes there's cruder stuff.

We've known for years that sometime soon we'll be living through a crisis period; magic gets easier to perform the more people are around to perform it. It's a computational, cognitive process and humans are cognitive machines . . . so are computers. We've got a population bubble, and a computing bubble, and they coincide. For the next few decades conditions are right for rupture and invasion by entities from outside our universe.

Some folks (ritual magicians) actually do the symbol-manipulation thing in their heads, risking death by Krantzberg syndrome and worse. It's not an approach to defending the realm that scales, because you can't take a random reasonably bright teenager and reliably turn them into a sorcerer. But you *can* turn some of them into computer scientists—and a whole lot more into IT support drones who can use a canned toolkit to perform a limited range of occult manipulations.

One of the weapons Her Majesty's Government is developing to deal with the threat is the SCORPION STARE network. Two or more observing viewpoints—cameras—feeding the right kind of hardware/software network can, shall we say, impose their own viewpoint on whatever they're looking at. In the case of SCORPION STARE, about ten percent of the carbon nuclei in the target are randomly transformed into silicon nuclei as if by magic. Messy pyrotechnics ensue: gamma radiation, short-lived muons, some really pretty high-energy chemistry, and *lots* of heat. We worked out how to do it by reverse-engineering basilisks and medusae—animals and unfortunate people suffering from a peculiar, and very rare, brain tumor. Now we've got defensive camera-emplacements on every high street, networked and ready to be controlled centrally when the balloon goes up. Street cleaning by CCTV-controlled flame thrower.

"What are its capabilities?" I ask Pinky, holding up the camera.

"Right now, it's running the camera firmware," he says. "Slide the lens cover down to switch it on. Point, shoot, it's a camera." I slide the lens cover down. As expected, the display back lights up. There's a honking great gunsight frame superimposed over it. I turn it off hastily. "Load the basilisk firmware and you'll see a gunsight. Point and shoot and instead of taking a snap, it sends a bang."

"You've been practicing on the seagulls," I accuse. "In Milton Keynes."

"They're vermin, Bob. They've been driven inland by over-fishing and now they're spreading disease, attacking waste collections, keeping people awake in the small hours, and carrying away stray cats and small dogs. Next thing you know they'll be cloning credit cards and planning bank robberies."

"Yes, but . . ." I see no point in arguing; it's not as if I *like* seagulls.

"It's got an effective range of about a hundred meters, and enough juice to fire eighty times on a single battery charge," Pinky adds. "It looks innocuous, which is more than you can say for a Glock; you can carry it on an airliner or through a security checkpoint, right?"

I sigh. "I *hate* these things." Being shot at with them is a good enough reason, in my books.

"So use it wisely!" Pinky beams brightly. "Mo said you'd be calling, so I took the precaution of booking it out to you as a beta tester. Sign here . . ."

He's learned from Brains's mistake last year: he's got the correct release forms in triplicate, *and* a memorandum of approval from the head of FSE, *and* a fearsome-looking end-user agreement that commands and compels me to ensure that the said device shall be returned to FSE, whether intact or in pieces, and all usage documented—this isn't going to be a repeat of the JesusPhone fiasco.

"Okay." I read the small print carefully and sign, repeatedly, in blood before he hands me the rest of the kit—charger, sync cables, spare SD card full of dodgy firmware, and a neck strap. By the time I leave his office, my suit pockets are bulging. But at least if any bad guys try to shoot me I can snap right back.

Interlude

ABSOLUTION

BREAKFAST AT NUMBER TEN.

Normally the Prime Minister and his family dine in the apartment upstairs, in the relative privacy of their home rather than the imposing wood-paneled rooms of state below. But today is different. The PM has invited four of his senior ministers, a handful of senior advisors, and a party of industry leaders to a breakfast meeting in the State Dining Room at 10 Downing Street, his official residence. It's not a press-the-flesh session—all the invitees have met the PM before—so much as it is a promotional session for one of the PM's pet hobby horses, the Caring Society initiative.

The Prime Minister is young, pinkly scrubbed and shaved, and privileged: a self-congratulatory scion of the upper social ranks of the Conservative party. He's bright as a button and sharp as a razor, with a mesmeric oratorical ability that served him brilliantly in his political pre-history as a barrister. He's an impressive performer—made it to the top of his party less than a decade after entering Parliament. And in no small part it's because he's clearly a man with a mission: to restore personal integrity, honesty, and humility to government (and to get government out of people's private lives and pocket books along the way).

"Good morning," says the PM, beaming and bobbing slightly as he shakes hands with the chief executive of a private academy trust with eight schools to his name: "Morning, Barry"—to the Home Secretary, an old war horse with pronounced progressive views about the value of rehabilitation over imprisonment (if only because it's cheaper)— "have you met Raymond before? Barry Jennings, the reverend Raymond Schiller."

"Can't say I have." The Home Secretary's tone is avuncular, friendly. "Pleased to meet you." He turns sideways, accepts the offered handshake, and stares into Schiller's eyes: *So this is the god-botherer Jeremy keeps banging on about? Doesn't look like much.* It's always best to keep a weather eye on the PM's joie du jour, however, lest one be caught out off-message by the carnivorous press. As Barry sizes up the preacherman, Jeremy—the Prime Minister—keeps on with the grasp'n'greet routine. An aide behind him keeps the hand sanitizer ready.

Schiller smiles and stares right back at the Home Secretary. "I've heard a lot about you, Mr. Jennings," he says, his voice deep and rich. "I gather we have a mutual interest in saving souls."

Barry's eyes crease slightly; then he smiles, slightly less warmly. Religious zeal is not a career asset in British politics; quite the opposite, in fact, and (like about half the members of the current cabinet) Barry's church attendance is limited to weddings and funerals and affairs of state. "I'm sure you do," he agrees, amiably enough. "But my job is more concerned with the here-and-now, I'm afraid. I can't speak for the hereafter."

"That's perfectly all right," Schiller agrees, baring his expensively whitened teeth. "The one generally goes before the other in my experience."

Other breakfast guests are arriving: the chairman of the largest merchant bank still based in London, a columnist for News International's leading broadsheet newspaper, the founder of a successful budget airline. Schiller turns his attention to them, working the influx discreetly and professionally. The Home Secretary pays brief attention. He always finds it informative to watch a high-level operator from a related profession at work, but something about Schiller irritates: a hangnail of the mind.

It's not as if he particularly wants to be here—there are never enough hours in the day when you're running the Home Office—but it's the PM's idea, and Barry has to admit that he's got a point. Jeremy's got this bee in his bonnet about enlisting community support for rehabilitation of minor offenders—nothing new there; the twist is that he's trolling for corporate support. He wants the private sector to pay for uniforms so they can *take pride in their work* while they're busy picking up the dog turds and used condoms: "building structure for empty lives" is what the PM calls it. *Workfare for chavs* according to the papers. It's easy to mock, but Jeremy has the same messianic zeal as his last-but-two predecessor, the Vicar. And Barry needs to back him up visibly on this one (as well as discreetly riding herd), lest he and his faction look weak in front of the 1922 Committee and the restless natives encourage one of the Back Bench Neanderthals to mount a leadership challenge. Which would be bad for the party, bad for the country, and very bad indeed for the Home Secretary. So: breakfast for thirty with businessmen and sky pilot. Barry takes a deep breath, and collects himself; then turns to glad-hand the newspaper columnist.

Eventually everyone's seated and greeted, the coffee is poured, the buffet is opened, and then—stomachs filled—the PM's chief of staff rises and introduces the first guest speaker. Who is, predictably, the visiting American preacher. Barry sits back with his coffee and fakes up an expression of polite interest as Schiller gets fired up.

"Good morning, my friends." Schiller beams. There is the usual pro forma boilerplate burble, thanking Jeremy and his staff for delivering unto him a captive audience. Barry can time it to the fractional second. Then Schiller gets the bit between his teeth and everything is somehow *different*. "I'm sure we're all happy to be here, and grateful for the great spread and our host's hospitality—and the company. But I think we ought to spare a thought for the unfortunates who aren't here today, and who never will be: the homeless and the abused, the poor and the sick—and the young men and women with empty lives who every day face an uncaring society that looks away . . ."

Barry finds himself drifting off on a wave of—not boredom, exactly, which is odd, because boredom is what he would have expected— but euphoria. *How strange,* he thinks dazedly. Schiller, once he hits his groove, isn't as annoying and preachy as he'd expected. Schiller's got a vision, a vision of charity and joy that he wants to share with everybody. "Good works are central to faith," he explains: "My creator wants me to do good, and rewards those who do good. And the best reward is another hard job. The job, my friends, is central, and our job here today is to work out how we're going to raise tens of thousands of young people out of deprivation and debasement and lend new purpose to their shattered lives."

Barry submerges again, diving in the torrent of words. Which he finds mildly astonishing because, as a sixty-year-old cynic (risen to the second-highest ministerial tier, but too old to raise his aim to the PM's office itself) with no little experience in rhetoric himself, he has long considered himself immune to such blandishments. But they feel so *good.* Schiller is painting a picture of redemption, of a joyous coming-together in pursuit of the commonweal that reminds him momentarily of why he went into politics in the first place: the conviction that he can make a difference, change things for the better.

When Schiller finishes, he claps with the rest—then shakes his head, dazed. Schiller is obviously *right* about something. What is it? The Caring Society initiative? Or could it be something deeper? Barry finds it hard to think, because now the airline founder is standing up, striking a pose, outlining his plans to bootstrap a network of community-centric work exchanges to match up the needy with the jobs they so obviously desire—there's no time to think about Schiller's inspirational words, and by the time Mr. McGready is wrapping up his pitch the actual neon-limned words themselves have faded into rosy memories.

On the way out, he makes a point of clasping Pastor Schiller's hand once more. "We'll have to talk again some time," he says effusively.

Schiller smiles. "I'm sure we will."

* * *

A CAR IS WAITING OUTSIDE NUMBER TEN TO WHISK RAYMOND Schiller away. It's a stretched BMW limo with mirror-tinted windows. Roseanne, his current number one handmaiden, is waiting in the jump seat with his briefcase. A blonde and high-cheeked twenty-something, dressed in a trim gray skirt-suit with only modest makeup, she could easily pass for a lawyer or a political aide. Schiller approves silently, letting his gaze rest on her. There is a flash of futile lust, but nothing more, for which he is duly grateful. The lust often tries to overwhelm his will right after he has worked a blessing, testifying before the Unsaved. She waits until the driver starts the engine before she opens the case. "How did it go, Father?"

"It went well, Daughter." The formalities of their relationship reaffirmed, he sinks back in the leather and closes his eyes. His stomach is full: not gluttonously so, but enough to make him torpid and lazy. Two sins in one. "Hmm. Make a note: I need to focus on Barry Jennings. His heart is open."

"Barry Jenning?—Or with an 's'?"

"He's their Home Secretary. Like the Attorney General, only more powerful. One of the top five posts in the administration. He's ripe for a weekend retreat. Phase one, of course."

"Yes, Father." Roseanne has some kind of high-tech digital pen; she can scribble notes and add them to his BlackBerry without re-typing anything.

The car sways heavily on its suspension as it noses past the barriers at the end of Downing Street and turns into Parliament Street. They're heading towards Victoria Embankment, and then out east in the direction of Docklands, less than fifteen kilometers away, but three-quarters of an hour through the heavy Central London traffic.

"Another note. John McGready. We need to invite him, too."

"The airline executive?"

"Yes." He hears Roseanne flip pages on her notebook. "A letter to the prime minister. Begins. Insert appropriate salutation. I'd like to thank you once again for inviting me to breakfast today. I found it deeply humbling and moving to discover a kindred spirit in you; truly the Lord moves in mysterious ways, and it is our duty to perform wonders on his behalf. I look forward to contributing to your Caring Society program, and if there is anything I can do on your behalf I would be delighted to help. Insert appropriate conclusion. Send."

"Got it." Roseanne clears her throat tentatively. "Father, Lindsay sent an update on yesterday's correspondence while you were inside . . . ?"

Ray opens his eyes and looks at her directly, showing no outward sign of the turmoil in his soul. Gluttony, sloth, lust: it's a good thing he's Saved. Even so, some prayer is indicated. And mortification. These excursions into the carnal world of the fallen are increasingly wearing, but also increasingly hard to avoid as the mission proceeds. "Tell me the news," he says evenly.

"Yes, Father." Roseanne glances down at the tablet computer in the briefcase. "Item: Operation *Castitas*. There has been a suspected security breach, level two, in the research and development conclave. One of the external contractors—a researcher in an essential post—has apparently been talking to his sister by phone. We don't have a log of what's been said but he has made an increasing number of long calls to her from within the campus. Security first verified that there was no change in her family circumstances—no babies, no deaths, no obvious explanation—then escalated. Fowler wants to know how to proceed."

Ray suppresses a sigh. "How replaceable is the contractor?"

Roseanne glances down again. "He's part of the core team working on the ventral tegmental area and the amygdala, Father. A parasitologist specializing in neurochemistry." Her lips tighten in disapproval.

"In other words, not." Ray thinks for a moment. "All right. Tell Fowler to focus on the sister. Double-check for options, just in case—if we can save her, that will be sufficient. Otherwise, our Father will know His own."

"Yes, Father." Roseanne makes a note. "Next, the arrangements with the New Life Church for next weekend's mass outreach service need attention. Brother Mark is having problems negotiating with the

PD for crowd management services, and we're seeing some push-back from the Church board of overseers—a couple of them are not yet Saved and, reading between the lines, Gilbert managed to offend them during the negotiations. He hadn't been briefed on the progress of our outreach mission to them."

Ray sniffs. "All right. Remind me to call him personally"—he glances at his wristwatch—"after six p.m., British time. I'll need a printout of the report." He pauses. "Anything else?"

"A final note, Father. You asked me to remind you—"

"About the presence in the audience at the arena on Sunday, yes." He thinks for a moment. "I'm *certain* it was another of the elect: I'd recognize the scent anywhere. But there were too many people." He frowns, frustrated. "Remind me again tomorrow. I shall make enquiries once we are home. If there is already a church cell in London, that would save us much trouble." He breathes out. "Is there anything more?"

Roseanne shakes her head. "That's all from Lindsay." The head of Ray's office staff. "You're set, Father."

Ray unwinds somewhat. Doubtless there will be more tiresome administrivia for him to render judgment over when they get to the airport—his staff defer to him as before the throne of Solomon—but for now he can relax. Everything is running along just fine, and in about half an hour he'll be boarding a Falcon 7X bound for Baltimore. While he doesn't own the executive jet himself, the Ministries hold a controlling interest in the fractional aircraft ownership group: enough to guarantee him a plane of his own whenever he needs one—and, more importantly, guarantee that it is kitted out to his very exacting requirements.

He focuses on Roseanne, who is squaring away the travel kit in the bag. She is, he thinks, wholly delectable; a younger and wilder Ray would have jumped her bones as soon as look at her. Those days are long behind him, thanks to God and Mission, but she still inspires a ghost of possessive lust in his shriveled heart, if not his loins. *Young and zealous*. His pulse speeds. She closes the briefcase and looks at him evenly. "Yes, Father?"

"I require mortification, Daughter."

"Ah. Of course." She bites her lower lip. "Right now? We're less than half an hour from the airport."

"Now." It's inevitable. He can't tear his eyes away from her. If he has to wait, it could be too late for both of them.

Her chest rises. "I hear the call, Father."

The seat belt clicks. His neck is abruptly damp with sweat. Blood speeding, he watches as she kicks off her heels and slides down to the floor of the limo before him to kneel in stockinged feet. She kneels as he begins to recite: "In the name of the Father, and the Son, and the Holy Spirit—"

His handmaiden leans towards him, pure and terrible: clean and untouched, a virgin, just the way he requires. *Have to marry her off soon,* he thinks with mild regret. Slim fingers that have never seen nail gloss reach out and gently unzip his fly. *Let her do her duty.* He continues to pray, quietly awaiting her deliverance. The younger Ray would have risen for her, exulted as she went down on his manhood—or worse, he might have spoiled her, yanked up her skirt and thrust himself into her—*unclean. I'm better now. So much better.*

She slides her hands between his legs, privy to his shameful secret, forgiving and obedient as she touches the place where his manhood used to be and performs the service he requires.

"—mortify me, for I have sinned."

The pain is monstrous, but absolves all guilt.

All guilt.

6.

JET LAG

FORTY KILOMETERS AWAY, DANGEROUS MEN ARE STALKING A woman.

It's a sunny day in Surrey, out beyond the M25 motorway, and the horizon-spanning urban sprawl has given way to ribbon development and scattered commuter dormitory towns separated by farms and green belt land and isolated strips of woodland. Many of these are privately owned; and the owner of one particular eighty-hectare chunk of ancient forest is in the habit of renting it out to murderers by the hour.

The woman is clearly aware that she's being pursued. Equally clearly, she isn't prepared for this. She's dressed for the office, not for a hike in the wild woods, and it's a hot day. She's slung her black suit jacket through her handbag's straps and is walking barefoot through the undergrowth, smart shoes clutched in one hand. Breathing deeply, she backs up close to a three-hundred-year-old oak encrusted with ivy and lichen. Her eyes flicker from side to side, mistrusting. They searched her bag and took her phone—otherwise she could get a GPS fix and call for help. She's unarmed; she has no idea how many men are pursuing her, but doubts there are fewer than two. And they *will* be armed.

On the other hand, she knows there's a perimeter wall. On the other side of it, there's a main road—if she can get over it, she can flag down a ride. Or she can backtrack along it to the gatehouse, assuming her pursuers aren't waiting for her there. If. *If.* She glances up at the sky, but the foliage is so thick she can't spot the sun. She's running out of options, and as she realizes this her heart beats faster.

Less than a hundred meters away, her closest pursuer crouches on top of a muddy bluff and inspects the ground at his feet. Unlike his target, he's dressed for the occasion in woodland camo and para boots. He wears a webbing vest and a helmet with headset, and carries a chunky machine pistol. Right now he's examining a couple of telltale smears in the mud. Not boots. Not animal paw-prints, either; the only large animals he's likely to meet in this over-tame forest are deer, and possibly the odd fox or badger. He taps his mike. "Found a trail," he says. "Recent. Looks to be barefoot." *She came up here for a look-around, slipped and fell,* he considers. Or did she? There's no crushed patch of shrubbery nearby. He peers over the edge of the bluff, looks down three meters. *If she'd gone over, I'd have heard.* Probably.

Hunting around, he spots a clump of nettles. The ground around them—someone or something has given them a wide berth and, in doing so, they've left traces: bent stems, broken twigs. He grimaces. *Clueless.* It's not what he'd expect of a smart fugitive. But nevertheless, it's a trail. He follows it, scanning for more signs of passage. *Careless,* he thinks.

It's nearly the last thing he thinks. The trail winds close to the edge of the bluff again, then through a disturbed tangle of ferns and nettles between beech trees. As he steps close to it, something catches his eye and he drops into a crouch. It's almost invisible when he's standing, but from beneath . . . "Nasty," he whispers. Stretching between the trees, about one and a half meters up, is a nearly invisible nylon wire, smeared with mud and vegetable sap. He taps his mike again. "Rabbit showing its teeth." He tightens his grip on his gun and swings round. Which is why the woman's field-expedient blackjack—doubled-over nylon hose filled with pebbles from the bed of the stream that feeds the ferns—catches him on the side of the helmet rather than on the back of his neck.

They close and grapple and two seconds later it's all over.

"How do you score that?" Johnny is lying with his back against one of the beech trees, the paintball gun beside him.

"The usual handicaps apply: I make it one all." Persephone rolls over on her back. "You shot me, I cracked your skull."

"That tripwire was *most* unpleasant, Duchess." Johnny sits up and rubs his untouched throat. "Where did you conceal it?"

"Up top." She sits up. "Hair extensions are one option; I can loop it through the roots in a continuous run. Takes ages to untangle, though. This time I just tucked it into the lining of my bag—metal detectors don't see it, and if you do it properly even a trained X-ray tech will assume it's just a seam."

"Right. And the cosh—"

"Any sufficiently advanced lingerie is indistinguishable from a lethal weapon." She smiles enigmatically, then holds up one of her shoes. "Heels, too." Then she sits up. "Okay, back to base then we'll run it again. This time"—she reaches out and taps him on the shoulder with the shoe—"*tag*, you're *it*. Let Zero know, will you?"

It's a game they play about once a month: escape, evasion, and ambush. The object of the exercise is training—not merely for the pursued to avoid capture but to turn the tables on their pursuer, trapping or killing them. Often they run it in the wild, as on this rented paintball range—which they have to themselves for the day—and sometimes they play it on deserted industrial estates, at night. Sometimes they drag in other players to beef up the pursuit side, and sometimes they play it one-on-one. The only constant is that the game only ends when one of them is down.

They're standing up and Johnny is calling Zero to tell him round two is on when his phone rings. He answers it. "It's for you." He passes it across.

"Yes?" She listens intently for a minute, nodding silently. "All right, I'll do it. Thanks." She hangs up, glances at Johnny. "Playtime is cancelled. Tell Zero to bring the car round; we have a date."

"Uh-huh. Where?"

She starts walking, back the way they've come. "That was Lockhart.

Schiller's on his way to the airport and his pilot's just filed a flight plan for Denver. As his Mission has a compound outside Colorado Springs, that's probably where he's going. Also, Lockhart's got me a gilt-edged ticket. They run a weekend spiritual retreat for interested outsiders from time to time—with a remarkable track record of generating born-again believers. In fact, the conversion ratio is one of the things that got his attention."

"So you're going to go in and sniff around?" Johnny's expression makes his reservations glaringly obvious.

"Of course. What could possibly go wrong?" She gives him a sardonic look. "Better hurry; I want to see if we can make the four p.m. shuttle to JFK."

I'M AT HOME THAT EVENING, ENJOYING A LONG HOT BATH, WHEN my phone rings.

It's been a trying day. From the whole suit-wearing thing to the offsite visit to HMGCC, Pinky and the amazing pyroclastic pigeon-zapper, and then the usual tiresome bullshit in the COBWEB MAZE working group, which is trying to nail down the extent of the damage caused by the BLOODY BARON committee being infiltrated by—no, let's not dive in the acronym soup just yet. I go home early out of sheer brain-dead exhaustion, hit the Tesco Express for a ciabatta, microwave curry, and a bottle of wine, and just as soon as I get into the steaming hot bath in hope of unwinding, I hear my phone begin to call from the kitchen table downstairs.

(Do *you* take your phone to the bathroom? I reckon it's one of the fundamental dividing lines of modern civilization—like whether you hang the bog roll so that it dangles in or out, or whether you eat your boiled eggs big-endian or little-endian. Anyway, I'm an old fart now—I'm over thirty—and I feel the need to actually put the bloody thing down for a few minutes a day. Even though it *is* a JesusPhone, and all JesusPhone users eventually wind up crouched in a dank, lightless cave, fondling it and crooning *"preciousss . . ."*)

So there is a loud *slosh* from behind me, and a baby tsunami rolls across the bathroom floor as I leg it for the stairs, swearing and hoping I left the kitchen window blinds down. Naturally I stumble on the third step and take the rest of the stairs with three bounces of the left buttock, rebound from the passage wall, and topple into the kitchen, reaching the phone on the table just as it goes silent. And then the front door opens.

"Bob? What *are* you doing?"

It's Mo, back from the office earlier than I'd expected, clutching a couple of shopping bags. Unfortunately she's not alone: trailing behind her is Sandy—a civilian teacher, friend of hers from way back—also clutching the shopping. I make a dive for the tea towel and manage to slip on a floor tile and go arse over tit—or maybe the tit is busy making an arse of himself: by this point I'm thoroughly confused.

"I was having a bath," I explain when I stop swearing and the pain in my head, where I whacked it on a cupboard on the way down, subsides enough to permit business as usual to resume. "Then the phone rang." The penny drops with a loud clang. "We're meant to be doing dinner, aren't we?" With Pete and Sandy, old friends of Mo's who go way back. Pete's a witch doctor—sorry, a priest of some sort—and Sandy is a high school religious education teacher with a sideline in pottery. Nice enough folks as long as you keep the conversation away from work.

"I'll just be in the living room," Sandy says helpfully, and disappears, leaving her smile hanging in the air like the Cheshire cat. (I'd say "smirk" but I have it on good authority that women do not "smirk." At least, that's Mo's story, and she's sticking to it.)

I manage to catch my balance just in time to help Mo deposit the shopping bags on the table. "Let's have a look at that," she says, then inspects the back of my head for a few seconds. "Hmm, everything seems to be intact, but you're sprouting a lovely egg." She kisses it, making me wince at the sudden pain. "Why don't you go upstairs and finish that bath, then join us when you're human?"

"My thoughts exactly," I agree fervently, then retreat towards the stairs, dignity in tatters.

Half an hour later I make my way downstairs, drier, cleaner, and fully clothed. Mo and Sandy are bickering good-naturedly over the makings of an M&S meal, so I make myself useful and lay the table. Partway through, the doorbell rings; I answer the door, carving knife in hand (you can never be too careful) and find Pete on the doorstep, clutching a couple of bottles of wine. "Come in," I say, and drag him through to the kitchen. For the next couple of hours Mo and I have the opportunity to lose ourselves in the clichéd middle-class role-play of hosting an informal dinner party—just as long as we remember our employment cover stories: Mo teaches history of music at Birkbeck (about a quarter true) and I'm a civil servant working in IT support (also about a quarter true these days).

The first course is leek and potato soup a la Marks and Spencer, accompanied by a rather acceptable New Zealand sauvignon blanc while the filet of trout is steaming in its own juices in the oven and Sandy unburdens herself of some workaday frustrations. Teaching is changing again, or something of that ilk—which in turn means more work for teachers, juggling lesson plans and learning new jargon. "Policy-making in RE tends to be very hands-off," she explains; "it's political poison, so they usually leave it alone." Religious education in schools may be the law of the land, but aside from de-programming successive generations through boredom it's turned into as much of a political third rail as public transport policy: whatever you do will be wrong for someone.

"Take class Ten B. I've got three Hindus, four Muslims, six Catholics, one Jew, two random pagans, and a Jedi. That's going by what their parents tell us, on top of the default Church of England types who wouldn't know a chasuble if one bit them on the pulpit. There are another three militant evangelicals and a Seventh Day Adventist who've been withdrawn, lest I pollute their precious ears with knowledge of rival faiths, and a couple of out-of-the-closet atheists who sit in the back row and take the piss. Now there's this"—she's waving her hands in counter-rotating circles—"*spiritual centeredness* program coming from the top down, and a whole new four-year curriculum for comparative religious education along with coursework, and *my* performance is evaluated on the basis of the averaged continuous assessment scores of said Jedi, pagans, and atheists . . ."

(Her hair's turning gray and she's only in her late-thirties.)

"Huh. What kind of evangelicals withdraw their kids from RE?" I ask.

Mo looks at me pityingly, but Sandy is allergic to ignorance, bless her: "Oh, you'd be surprised. Churches often behave more cultishly the smaller they get, trying to hold on to their children by making it hard to leave—and one of the easiest barriers you can put in someone's way is to convince them that everyone else is some kind of satanic monster, doomed to hell and all too keen to take you with them. Comparative RE is pure poison to that kind of mind."

"There are two types of people in this world," Pete volunteers helpfully, "those who think there are only two types of people in the world, and everybody else." He sips his wine thoughtfully. "But the first kind don't put it that way. They usually think in terms of the saved and the damned, with themselves sitting pretty in the lifeboat." He manages to simultaneously look pained and resigned. "Sometimes they find their way out of the maze. But not very often."

"Huh. Speaking of which, I've been getting an earful at the office lately," I say. Mo glances at me sharply as I continue. "One of my colleagues keeps banging on about some televangelist or other who's been running a mission. You'd think he farts rainbows the way Jim talks about him. The, uh, Golden Promise Ministries? Do you know anything about them?" Mo's eyes narrow to a flinty stare, but she holds her peace. Pete nods thoughtfully.

"Golden Promise? The big tent revival meetings in Docklands?" I nod. "Pastor thingummy, um, Schiller—he's one of the bigger American Midwestern TV Charlies"—he glances at Sandy apologetically—"but there's something not quite *right* about him. Did I tell you about Dorothy"—Sandy nods—"one of my parishioners? Special needs, learning disability. And no, we've got two or three Dorothys, I'm not telling you which one it is. Anyway, she went along and found it very disturbing. Well, not at first, but he's actively recruiting. And trying to get people to go along to a series of church meetings his people are running in South London. They're clearly Presbyterians who are hot on fundamentals theology, but there's a bit more to it than that. Stuff that smells a bit cultish, frankly. They've got the usual unhealthy obsession with homosexuality and so on; but what upset Dorothy was that they were trying to fix her up with a *husband*. Trying to get her to join a Christian dating ring. Which might be fine if they'd bothered to *ask*, but Dorothy has—let's just say she has *issues*. They were quite pushy, and really freaked the poor girl out."

Mo nods slowly. Looking at me, she asks Pete out of one corner of her mouth, "Are they by any chance a quiverfull ministry?"

Pete's lips thin. "Yes."

The word "quiverfull" sets my alarm bells ringing, and clearly upsets Mo. It goes back to Psalm 127, which refers to having many children as having a *full quiver*. They're arrows for the Lord, and a number of evangelical churches have adopted the theory that you can never have too much ammunition. The Brotherhood of the Black Pharaoh has a history of using such churches as cover for their cells. They have other uses for children, as recruits and—let's not go there over dinner.

"You disapprove?" I ask.

Pete sniffs. "I'm in the business of providing spiritual and pastoral care for my parishioners," he points out. "Pressuring a confused and vulnerable young woman into an arranged marriage in order to turn her into a baby factory is *not* how you look after her spiritual needs—" He stops, revealing a momentary flash of anger. "Sorry. Not your problem." He pauses. "I probably said too much there," he adds.

"It will go no further," Mo assures him.

"Absolutely."

Sandy, who has been holding her breath without me being consciously aware of it, exhales loudly enough that I nearly jump. I notice that her wineglass is empty. I pick up the bottle. "Can I offer you a refill?" I ask, a little white lie because now I think about it she didn't ask for one in the first place—

"No thanks." Her cheeks dimple. "I'm avoiding alcohol for the next few months."

Mo catches the dropped penny first: "Congratulations! How long—"

"It's been nearly ten weeks. We're not out of the first trimester yet, I wasn't going to announce it for a little longer."

Opposite me, Pete's expression has switched from muted disapproval to the smug anticipation of fatherhood-to-be.

"Congratulations to the two of you," I say slowly. "Well, good luck with that." I lower the wine bottle and pick up my glass. "Here's to sleepless nights ahead, huh?"

Mo raises her glass, too, keeping her expression under rigid control. But I can see right through it; right to the core of delight for their joy, and suppressed envy for Sandy's condition, and above all else, horror at the fate they've unwittingly condemned themselves to.

LATE THAT NIGHT, AS WE LIE IN BED, I FEEL MO'S SHOULDERS shake. I slide an arm around her, try to provide comfort. She's crying, silently and piteously to break a man's heart; and the worst part is that I can't do anything about the cause of her grief.

We're not going to have children.

For months now, and for decades to come, we've been living on borrowed time. I can feel it in the prickling in my fingers and toes, in the strange shapes and warped dead languages of my dreams. We're living through the end times, but not in any Biblical sense—the religions of the book have got their eschatology laughably wrong.

Outside the edge of our conscious perceptions, the walls between the worlds are thinning. Things that listen to thoughts and attend are gathering, shadows and fragments of cognition and computation. The Laundry has a code name for this phenomenon: CASE NIGHTMARE GREEN. Magic is a branch of applied mathematics: solve theorems, invoke actions, actions occur. Program computers to do ditto, actions occur faster and more reliably. So far so good, this is what I do for a living. But consciousness is *also* a computational process. Human minds are conscious, there are *too damn many* of us in too small a volume of space on this planet right now, and we're damaging the computational ultrastructure of reality. Too much of our kind of magic going on makes magic easier to perform—for a while, until space itself rips open and the nightmares come out to play.

But that's not why we aren't going to start a family. Abstract principles aren't sufficient. No, it's a lot simpler: we know the sort of thing that's likely to happen during CASE NIGHTMARE GREEN, and we're not selfish enough—or evil enough—to condemn a child of ours to die that way.

There's going to be an epidemic of dementia—not mad cow disease, new variant CJD, but something our house doctors call Krantzberg syndrome: if a sorcerer unintentionally thinks the wrong thoughts, performs magic by mind, the listeners and feeders and actors they invoke from the quantum foam take tiny bites out of their brains. Dream the wrong dreams, and you can wake up with a palsy or an aneurysm.

There will be amazement and miracles, too. Magic wands stuffed with silicon chips that work wonders. Twisted biological creations that obey our directives. Ordinary people discovering they have the power to summon demons and angels and warp reality to their will. Somnolent sentient species rising from the deeps to take an interest in the suddenly interesting land-dwelling aboriginals. Alien emissaries, and powers beyond our comprehension like the Sleeper in the Pyramid—

—Monstrous conquerors no bullet or atom bomb can kill—

—And their willing servants.

No, this isn't a sensible decade to start a family. Especially not for the likes of Mo and me, insiders and experts with a ringside seat at the circus of horrors.

WEDNESDAY MORNING DAWNS, GRAY AND MOIST. I YAWN, ROLL out of bed, and stumble downstairs to the kitchen to switch on the kettle. I glance at the clock: it's a quarter to seven. I shiver, the skin on the soles of my feet sticking to the cold linoleum. We talked, for a bit, when the tears dried, then I slept fitfully. No dreams of the plateau and the pyramid, which is a small blessing. But today is a workday, and I've got at least one meeting booked in the office. I reach for my phone, which is still sitting on the kitchen table where I left it last night—

There's a notification. A call. I blink, bleary-eyed. Six forty-two last night, from *oh fuck* it's Lockhart. There is voicemail. I listen to it. "See me first thing tomorrow morning. Bring your bag. Be prepared to travel." *Click*. He doesn't sound happy: probably expected the good little minion to be in the office until whenever he felt like going home. I yawn, then get the coffee started.

Half an hour later Mo and I are sitting opposite each other across the table. Toast, marmalade, a cafetière full of French roast. Mo is showing signs of sleeplessness, yawning. "I had a bad dream," she remarks over the coffee.

"Bad enough to remember?"

"Very." She shivers. "I was alone in the house. Upstairs, in the attic." The roof space is big enough that we've been planning to add a dormer window and turn it into a spare room one of these years. "There was— this is going to sound cheesy, but it was just a dream—a window. Under the window, there was a cradle, and a woman in a chair sitting next to it with her back to me. I couldn't see very clearly, and her face was in shadow, or she was wearing a veil, or there was something between us. She had a bow, and she was playing—lullabies. Except I couldn't hear them. To the crib. Although I couldn't see anything in it."

"Um." There's no way to say this tactfully, so I don't. "Are you sure it was empty? Because if so, that's classic projection—"

"No." She shakes her head. "I know what you're thinking." She looks troubled. "The thing is, in my dream I knew the melody. It was familiar from somewhere. Only I don't. It's not a tune I've ever heard. And I'm not sure the crib was empty. But it was *definitely* my instrument."

And now it's my turn to look troubled, because nobody in their right mind would play lullabies to a baby on Mo's violin. It's an Erich Zahn original, with a body as white as the bone it's carved from, re-fitted with electric pick-ups and retuned to make ears and eyeballs bleed. It has other properties, too.

"Have a bagel," I suggest, buying myself some time to chew on the problem. "It sounds like projection, but if you think it's something else . . . well." A thought strikes me. "The violin?"

"Huh." Mo glances at the corner of the room. She brought the violin downstairs. It's still in its case. Come to think of it, the only time she leaves it in another room is when she's having a bath or a shower. "Think it's jealous?"

She shivers. "Don't *say* that."

"My new boss phoned," I say to change the subject. "Told me to bring my go-bag. I might be late for dinner."

"Oh." She stands up and walks around the table. "So soon?"

"Can't be sure. Hope not." I stand up and we embrace, awkwardly because of the coffee mug glued to the palm of my right hand (it's a shape-shifting leech that feeds on fatigue poisons in my blood; it'll fall off when I'm fully awake).

"Take care. Remember to write. Or call, if you can keep track of the time zones."

"I shall." I remember something. "Pinky had a little toy waiting for me. Not the kind of toy that's supposed to go walkabout, I think. Your doing?"

"What toy—oh, *that*. I don't think so. But last week Angleton made a point of asking me the kind of hypothetical question that's not so hypothetical: I reminded him about that time in Amsterdam." The hole in a hotel corridor's wall, blowing air into vacuum in a dead-cold world beneath the blue-shifted pinprick stars of a dying cosmos. Pinky's little toy is the direct lineal descendant of the machine they issued me for self-defense back then. "Promise me you're going to make sure you don't get into a situation where you need it. Please, Bob?"

I shudder. "I promise. You know what I think of violence."

"And you'll draw a new ward. And a HOG. Two HOGs. And you'll brush your teeth every night. Okay?"

I kiss her. "Sure."

And, oddly, when I go in to work later that morning my first stop is the armory, just to draw a new and unused protective ward and a pair of mummified pigeons' feet in leather bags. I draw the line at toothpaste, though.

"AH. MR. HOWARD. COME IN. YOU'RE LATE." LOCKHART IS CHAR-acteristically curt, but despite the routine chewing-out—I am getting a feeling that this is his usual way of relating to his staff, in which case it's bloody juvenile and I wish he'd get over it—he seems somewhat pleased with himself.

I shut the door. "Has something come up?"

"You could say that." The smugness is threatening to burst out. "Yesterday BASHFUL INCENDIARY's invitation to attend a session of the Omega Course came through. It's a weekend residential session held at the Golden Promise Ministries headquarters, just north of Colorado Springs, and it starts this Friday. We've been trying to get someone inside there for weeks. She's already on her way there by way of New York, along with Mr. McTavish. So you'd better get moving, eh?"

"Wait a minute. The tattoos—"

"You'll just have to play catch-up with her in Colorado, Mr. Howard."

"Okay. What then? What's the plan? What's she doing, do we know?"

"I couldn't possibly say." Lockhart's eyes narrow. "BASHFUL INCENDIARY is not one of your, or my, or our department's employees, so *in principle* she could be doing *anything*. As it is, she's clearly engaged in surveillance activities directed against a protégé of the PM. We are therefore sending you to Denver to keep an eye on her and find out what's going on. We devoutly hope that she will find it amusing to confide in you from time to time, Mr. Howard. That is all you or I *know*, to be sure. Do I make myself understood?"

"I think so." I pause. "Isn't this a little bit open-ended . . . ?"

"Clever boy. Yes, it is." He nods sharply. Then he picks up a black nylon travel document wallet from his desk and hands it over, along with a form. "Sign this."

"Sign what—" It's a receipt. "Just a sec, you know I need to check the contents."

"Take your time."

I open the wallet. It contains a passport and a bunch of boarding passes. Return from London to Denver, business class, fully flexible— my eyebrows are clawing at the ceiling even before I see the next item.

"You'll need to sign that, too," Lockhart adds.

"But, bu-but—" I don't usually stutter, honest, but it's the first time I've seen one of these things in the wild: Aren't they supposed to come on a velvet cushion escorted by a couple of snooty liveried footmen and an armed guard? "This is a gold Visa card. A *Coutts* gold Visa card."

"For expenses." Lockhart sounds perfectly matter-of-fact.

"But, but . . ." Coutts is a small, obscure, remarkably stuffy financial institution in London. It used to be private but these days it's the posh subsidiary of one of the mega-banks. Owner of banking license 002—001 belongs to the Bank of England—they won't even give you a cheque account unless you maintain a minimum balance of a quarter of a million. *The Queen* banks with Coutts. (Although apparently they had second thoughts about her son: maybe he lowers the tone, or something.) They've become a little more accessible since the RBS takeover—I gather they'll give accounts to rock stars and presidents these days—but even so. "What will the Auditors say?" I finish weakly.

"Nothing, as long as you keep proper records."

"But, but . . . *what*?"

"Mr. Howard. Robert." Lockhart lowers his voice and speaks slowly and clearly, as if to an idiot child: "You are pursuing an investigation on behalf of *External Assets*. It's an open-ended assignment. Let us be very clear, I am handing you a sufficiency of rope with which to hang yourself, should you choose to do so—but we have no way of anticipating what you may run up against. So we're equipping you accordingly."

He taps the rectangle of plastic. "This card draws against an account held by the Ministry of Defense—supposedly for entertaining visiting Saudi royalty or equally dubious people. You can pay for your incidentals and subsistence, within reason: hotel bills and car hire and so forth. Just keep receipts. This particular card comes with a call center in London, manned around the clock by a concierge service that will arrange just about any personal service you desire at the drop of a hat—as long as it's legal. You can hire an executive jet or pay for an emergency liver transplant. You can draw ten thousand pounds in cash per day. It's the most powerful weapon in your inventory, notwithstanding the silly little toy camera your friends in Facilities have loaned you, or the dead pigeons' feet in your toilet bag."

He clears his throat. "I gather you've met the Auditors. Just remember that this isn't your own money and you won't have anything to worry about."

"I thought you said that we're outside Operational Oversight?"

His gaze is icy. "We are," he says. "But the Auditors make random inspections. And we can always make an exception if you really fuck up."

"Urp." I flip the card over and scrawl on the signature strip. Then I sign the receipt. "Okay." I open the passport. It's for me, okay, but it's shiny and new, with the enhanced security biometrics, and there's an extra page bonded into it—a diplomatic visa good for the United States, accrediting me as a junior cultural attaché at the British embassy in DC. "We still have cultural attachés?"

"We still have pulse-dialing electromechanical Strowger telephone exchanges in the basement"—Lockhart startles me by suddenly rattling off the correct but decades-obsolete terminology—"just in case we experience a need for such equipment. And you are now discovering just *why* we also have cultural attachés in the embassy in DC."

"Ri-ight." I glance at the first boarding pass. "Hey, this leaves Heathrow in less than three hours!"

"So you'd better get moving, Mr. Howard. The tag for your reports is GOD GAME BLACK. Don't forget to write!"

THE NEXT FOURTEEN HOURS HAVE THEIR HIGHS AND LOWS.

The highs: taking a cab to Paddington, breezing through the barriers onto the Heathrow Express, arriving at the airport nineteen minutes later, and zipping through all the usual inconveniences and impediments of air travel as if they barely exist. Priority check-in, special security screening arrangements with no queue, then forty minutes to catch my breath in a slightly run-down business lounge (with free wine and beer! If only I wasn't on business) and then priority boarding.

There are *no queues*—at least nothing worthy of the name—and my ticket comes with a reclining chair and the kind of meal service that convinces me British Airways are engaged in a sinister conspiracy to prepare their frequent fliers' livers for sale to a pâté factory.

The lows: arriving at JFK to change flights, entering the diplomatic queue in the vast, echoing cowshed that is the immigration hall, and waiting as the uniformed immigration officer stares at my passport, types at his computer, then stares some more until I get that familiar old-time sinking feeling.

"Is there a problem?" I ask, pitching my voice for curious-casual.

He glances up and looks at me. "Please look into the camera, sir." There's an eyeball on a stalk—that's new since I last visited the USA—and I mug for it. "Fingerprints." That's new, too. Come to think of it, I haven't been over here for a decade and my last visit didn't end well. "Hmm. You're traveling on an embassy visa, sir. Can I ask the purpose of your visit?"

I've been briefed on what to say. "I am here on official business of Her Majesty's Government." I try not to look apologetic. "I am an accredited member of a diplomatic mission—accredited by your own State Department—and I am not required to discuss my business."

I don't see him press the magic button, but there's some discreet movement behind him: another Customs and Border Patrol officer—this one a guard—is drifting over, and an office door at the other side of the barn is opening, someone coming out. "If you wouldn't mind waiting a minute, sir, my manager will take this from here." Another officer has sidled across the entrance to the tollbooth-like tunnel I'm occupying, effectively blocking my retreat.

"May I have my passport back?" I ask.

"Not yet."

Palms damp and pulse racing, I try to look bored. It takes an endless minute for the woman in the suit to get here from the office. The immigration goons are courteous but distant—and they're armed, and a law unto themselves. Also, some kind of shit has *definitely* hit the fan because they're absolutely *not* supposed to stop someone traveling on a diplomatic visa. At least (I remind myself) I shaved halfway through the flight, and look reasonably presentable—credit Lockhart for making me wear a suit—but—

"Mr. Howard?" The CBP manager is a woman, about my age, east Asian. "Would you mind coming with me?"

"Is there a problem?" I ask.

She looks at me, assessing and evaluating. "Hopefully not, but you must appreciate we need to ensure that only people entitled to use the diplomatic channel do so"—she takes my passport from Goon #1—"so if you'd come this way, please?"

I don't have any alternatives unless I want to escalate drastically, and they haven't actually done anything that amounts to good cause yet. I fall in behind her, and try not to pay attention to Goon #3, who is trailing us at a distance, his belt clanking under the weight of handcuffs, pepper spray, and a sidearm.

The office is spartan, bare-walled and furnished with a desk, two chairs, a computer, and a telephone. The CBP manager waves me to the seat opposite the desk, then sits down and starts mousing around on her computer. I pointedly don't glance at the door—I'm pretty sure Goon #3 is standing outside. Presently she looks up. "Mr. Howard, I believe that these documents are genuine, and I recognize your diplomatic immunity. However, you're identified by our records as being a covert asset. I must warn you that failing to register as an agent of a foreign government is a felony, and potential grounds for denying you entry to the United States. Do you have anything to say?"

Her body language clearly adds: *Aside from oh shit?* She looks smug. It's clearly not every day that Little Ms. Smarty-Pants here catches a spook.

"I'm not in your Big Book of Registered Spies? Is that the problem?"

She looks down her nose at me. "One of them."

"Well." I roll my eyes. "That's a nice Catch-22 you've got there, isn't it? *Real* shiny, that Catch-22."

(I blame the Russians for spoiling everything. Time was when a spy could just breeze through US immigration and be about their business—but the CBP have been pissed ever since the FBI caught a battalion of barely competent FSB agents who waltzed in behind a brass band and set up shop in Manhattan. And this is, of course, a representative of the NYC local chapter of the Cantankerous Bastards Patrol that I'm dealing with, not the State Department.)

"Let me see: I think in the next five minutes you're going to"—I notice her neck muscles and shoulders tensing—"call DC and talk to State. Who will in turn talk to an officer from one of your government's black agencies which do not exist, and then State will tell you what you need to know, which is that they've heard of me and you are to let me go. *Or* we can do this the hard way. You can refuse me entry, provoke a diplomatic incident, and then an agency which does not exist will arrange for your superiors to tear you a new asshole." I lean back, cross my arms, and try to look confident. "Your call."

It's only about twenty-five percent bluff. I *am* on the books: the Black Chamber know who I am, and if I've come up on the CBP radar there'll be a contact number in the office directory. What happens to her if she's stupid or insane enough to phone and attract the Black Chamber's attention is anybody's guess—eaten by Nazgûl, spirited away to a detention center at the bottom of Chesapeake Bay, compelled to listen to Rick Wakeman until her brain melts—but I don't really care. The Black Chamber will ensure that I cease to be a person of interest to the CBP. The only question that interests me is whether the phrase "of interest to the CBP" belongs at the end of that sentence.

(*Aha,* I can hear you asking, *but what about the UK-USA intelligence treaty? Why didn't Lockhart just call the Black Chamber and ask them to keep an eye on our turbulent priest?* Well, there are several reasons. Firstly, our turbulent preacher is American; it's even possible he's one of theirs. Secondly, we're really not supposed to give foreign agencies blackmail-grade information about the Prime Minister. And finally: they're the *Black Chamber.* They're not so much our sister agency as our psycho ex-girlfriend turned bunny-boiler.)

In the event, Ms. Smarty-Pants glares at me and calls my non-existent bluff. "Okay, that's your choice." Then she reaches out and picks up the phone and dials.

I am jet-lagged, tired, and—I will admit—a bit scared. I wait, wondering if it wouldn't be better to simply let them declare me PNG and stick me on the next plane home. But it's too late for that: someone answers the phone. "Sir, I've just taken custody of a traveler on the DSR watch list . . . yes, I'll hold . . . hello? Yes, I have a traveler on the DSR watch list, he's flagged as a POI to AGATE STAR . . . thank you, sir, yes, his name is Howard, Robert Oscar Foxtrot Howard, record number 908 . . ."

She stops talking and listens for a couple of minutes, nodding from time to time. Her eyebrows furrow slightly. Then whoever's at the other end of the line hangs up on her. She stares at the handset for a few seconds, almost angrily, then puts it down. "That makes *no* sense," she mutters, as if she's forgotten I'm there. Then she glares at me. "What are you doing here?"

"You've got my passport," I say helpfully.

"I—" She blinks rapidly, then looks at the offending document, sitting on the desk. "Oh." She looks unhappy about something: probably me. She pulls open a desk drawer, withdraws a stamp, and whacks away at a blank page in the passport. "Get out."

"Am I free to enter?" I ask.

"Yes! You're free to enter." She's angry—and clearly frightened.

Interesting; things have definitely changed since I was last here. "Aren't you required to register me as an agent of a foreign power?"

Her pupils dilate. "No! Just go! You weren't here, I'm not here, this never happened, nobody stopped you, go away!" She stands up and yanks the door open. "Nick! Escort Mr. Howard to baggage claim and see he gets through Customs without any delays! He has a flight to catch!"

Nick—Goon #3—looks puzzled. "Isn't he under arrest?"

"No! His papers are all in order. Just get him out of here!"

Her concern is contagious. Nick looks at me and gestures. "This way, sir."

And so I enter the United States with a Border Patrol escort—desperate to see me on my way as fast as is humanly possible.

What strange times we live in . . .

7.

COMMUNION

PERSEPHONE HAZARD AND JOHNNY MCTAVISH ENTERED THE
United States on Wednesday, twenty-four hours ahead of me. Their reception was somewhat different. Flying into JFK on the pin-stripe express from London City Airport, they bypassed the Immigration queue
entirely: they had their passports stamped by an obsequious immigration officer during the refueling stop at Shannon, along with a dozen
bankers and discreetly ultra-rich fellow-travelers.

At the arrivals terminal, they checked their bags onto a flight bound
for Denver, paused long enough to shower and freshen up after the trans-
atlantic leg of their journey, then headed to the gate for their five-hour
onward connection.

Uneventful. Boring. Tedious. All good adjectives to apply to long-
haul travel; much better than *exciting*, *unexpected*, and *abrupt*. With
Johnny sacked out in the window seat to her right, Persephone leaned
back in her chair and plowed determinedly through the bundle of documents she'd compiled before the trip. *Homework.* Everything her staff
had been able to find about the Golden Promise Ministries. Everything
about other organizations that members of GPM's board of trustees
held seats on. The whole intricate interlocking machinery of religious

lobbying and fund-raising that wheeled around the person of Raymond Schiller.

Schiller was not an isolated phenomenon, Persephone noted. He had connections. Connections with John Rhodes III, a scion of Washingtonian blue-bloods and a pillar of The Fellowship—Abraham Vereide's C Street prayer breakfast and power broker mission to the Gentile Kings. Rhodes had a visiting fellowship at the Institute for American Values, and sat on the board on the National Organization for Marriage. One of NOM's board members, Chuck Parker—CEO of a Christian textbook publisher—also sat on GPM's board. GPM was a sponsor of NOM, and Schiller had run pledge drives on his TV show, urging his flock to "stand tall and defend marriage." Parker was a shareholder in Stone Industries, an arms manufacturer, and—

Persephone blinked. *Uneventful. Boring. Sleepy.* That was the problem with trying to cram while leaning back in a recliner with a tumbler of Wild Turkey at forty thousand feet: it was too easy to doze off. Johnny found this stuff interesting (his upbringing had, if nothing else, exposed him to some of the wilder reaches of fundamentalist Christianity) but she was making heavy weather of it, finding their feuds and arguments as arcane and recondite as Trotskyite ontogeny or cultist schismatics. *Pay attention now.* This stuff was—would be— important. Golden Promise Ministries, the Fellowship, National Organization for Marriage, True Path Publishing, Stone Industries Small Arms, Pillar of Fire International, the Purity Path Pledge League— they were all merging into a whirling tattered spiderweb of Christian Dominionist pressure groups and fund-raising organizations. Deeper connections to shadowy ultra-conservative billionaire sponsors were hinted at but coyly elided—nobody wanted to speak truth to the power to launch a million libel lawsuits.

Johnny honked, a sluggish bass. Persephone reached out and poked his shoulder.

"Yes? Duchess."

"You were snoring."

"Was I? Oh bugger." He stabbed at the power button on his seat, then waited until it tilted up to Persephone's level. "Something come up?"

"In a manner of speaking." She closed the folder. Quietly, she added: "I make a sky marshal two rows ahead, over to the left, aisle seat. Deadheading pilot to his right. Four businessmen, a retired couple, one woman and child. Am I missing anyone?"

By way of reply, Johnny stood up clumsily and stepped across her legs, then walked aft towards the toilets. A couple of minutes later he returned. "I match your count. We're green."

Over the years, Persephone and Johnny had frequently needed to discuss confidential matters in public, so they'd long since worked out a protocol to improvised security. A first-class airliner cabin was pretty good—lots of background white noise, little opportunity for adversaries to plant bugging devices (especially after they'd arranged last-minute seat changes with the cabin crew), an easy environment to monitor for eavesdroppers. By color-coding it green Johnny was agreeing that it was—conditionally—safe to talk.

Persephone relaxed infinitesimally. "Do we know any forensic accountants on this side of the pond?"

"Accountants?" Johnny frowned. "We're going to *Denver*. If you wanted to pick up an accountant, couldn't we have stopped on Wall Street?"

"I didn't know we'd need one until . . ." She gestured irritably at the folder. "It's a real mess. As bad as mafia money laundering, all barter and back-scratching."

"You're assuming this is about cash, Duchess."

"It usually is." She looked pensive. "Except when it's about power."

"What about religion?"

"Religion *is* power, to these people. And power is religion, of course. If you're a humble believer set on doing your deity's will, then what are you doing spending the take on Lamborghinis and single malt? The real believers are running soup kitchens and emptying bedpans, trying to do good while the televangelists preaching the prosperity gospel are doing it to keep up the payments on the McMansion and the Roller."

She spoke with quiet vehemence, fingers whitening on the spine of the folder. "Power and money. It's about all of those things, otherwise why is Schiller trying to gain access to the highest levels of government? He's a fraud and a dabbler, and Mr. Lockhart shall have his evidence."

Johnny thought for a while. Then he shook his head slowly. "You're wrong this time, Duchess. Snark or Boojum. What if he *is* a true believer, have you thought about that?"

"A true believer in *what*? The prosperity gospel? New Republican Jesus who rewards his faithful flock for their faith with the ability to make money fast? That's self-serving cant, and you know it. Wish-fulfillment as religion." A twitch of the cheek: Persephone unamused. "Don't get me started on the gap between the Vatican and their flock."

"I know the church I grew up in." McTavish is silent for a few seconds. "I could smell it on him. He's one of the unconditionally elect, Duchess, and it's *quite probable* that he holds to the old rites."

"If it's a shell, what's going on under cover of the church?"

"Well." Johnny shuffles uncomfortably. "*You* know about the five points of Calvinism, yes? Total depravity, unconditional election, limited atonement, irresistible grace, and the perseverance of the saints. Up in the western isles they take it all too damn seriously. That, and the, uh, cousins under the sea. They hold that they're unconditionally elect; and that the bloodline of the elect are going to usher in the new age and summon Jesus back to earth—but only when he's good and ready, you understand. Pay no attention to the gill slits and fins, they're signs of grace. It's come to a pretty pass when the bastard spawn of the Deep Ones turn into Presbyterian fundamentalists, hasn't it? But anyway, that's what we could be looking at, worst case."

"So you think they're a cover for a cell of cultists who are planning on raising something?"

"If you pray to Jesus on the cosmic party line and something at the other end picks up the receiver, because you happen to have an affinity for the uncanny and your prayers attract attention, what are you going to assume?" Johnny shuffles again. "But they're not cultists in the regular sense, Duchess. Quite possibly they're just your regular prosperity gospel preaching televangelists. There's a certain point beyond which any sufficiently extreme Calvinist sect becomes semiotically indistinguishable from the Brotherhood of the Black Pharaoh. But even though their eschatology is insane, it doesn't necessarily follow that they're trying to summon up the elder gods."

"In which case we're back to money again." She smiles triumphantly.

"Some of these Pentecostalists, Duchess, they're not all con men. From 3 John: 'I pray that you may prosper in all things and be in health, just as your soul prospers.' Suppose rather than passing the plate in church, they get a radio show and pass the plate and half a million listeners donate. Isn't that going to convince a preacher that it's all true? Wealth comes to the faithful, that's the message they're going to take. An' I never yet met a con man who wasn't the better at the job for believing his own spiel."

"That's not . . . untrue. But money corrupts. Almost invariably, powers that arise around money are corrupted by it. He might have started out as a true believer, but money has a way of taking over. A church is a business, after all, and those employees or executives who are good at raising money are promoted by their fellows."

Johnny shrugged, helpless in the face of her conviction. "I still reckon you shouldn't discount belief, Duchess. They may be after the money as well, but they're motivated primarily by faith. I *know* Schiller's kind: I was born and raised to be one of the elect."

"But you broke out," she observed. "And that was a couple of decades ago, and you don't know Schiller personally. He's an American cousin, not one of your relatives."

"All true."

"So. We've got a situation to investigate. Is Schiller fronting a cult or merely making money? That's worth knowing, but what we really want to find out is why he's putting so much effort into getting in deep in the UK. Recruiting hands and doing breakfast with VIPs."

"So you've got a plan?"

"Not much of one." Persephone's lips wrinkled. "The provisional plan is that there is no plan. First we scope the site and designate accessible dead-letter drops. Then I go in, I do the course, and I come out. You'll be sitting on the outside monitoring the message drops—I won't make contact directly unless I want to abort. Gerry's little helper will make contact with you while I'm inside; if I learn anything, pass it on to him. I think it'd be useful to customize a penetration toolkit for the job, and have two escape routes planned in case things go *really* off the rails. But I'm not expecting any trouble. It's a residential retreat and bible study course aimed at recruiting new blood, not a Gulag or an army base."

"What kind of penetration toolkit do you want? You planning on worming their computers?"

"Yes. You can research the religious angle if you want, but I think we'll have difficulty getting access and working out what they're trying to do if Schiller really *is* running an inner circle. We're under time pressure here, so I'm aiming for the low-hanging fruit: if it's about money or power there'll be an audit trail. So I'm thinking in terms of installing a back door, and after the course is over and I'm out of the zone we will use it to take a look inside Schiller's email inbox."

"Hmm." Johnny thought for a moment. "I think there's an updated release of the Zeus toolkit I can use to knock something suitable up with. We'll need to buy a new zero-day exploit, but that's affordable. What's your level one cover story if they catch you?"

"I keep my email on a memory stick. There'll be an infected message in my inbox, so when I plug it into one of their computers it'll auto-run. If I'm caught, I'm just an ignorant, technically illiterate socialite with an infected email set-up—the security trail can lead back to a spear phishing attack on my bank account. Victim not perp, in other words."

"That sounds very good. So . . . you go in, read your email, finish the course, leave, then we have a party with his email. Hmm. Exit strategies?"

"I want you to buy three cars and locate two safe houses downtown. If I need to run I'll signal you, then drive out, swap plates and wheels, pick up new ID, and keep driving. I'll charge up the NetJets account to cover seats on standby and we can prepare an evac plan via the nearest airports—but that's conspicuous. Much better to just drop off the map and turn up in Utah or New Mexico twenty-four hours later. Then revert to regular ID and fly commercial."

"Okay, three cars, two pads. One escape car, plus a remount and a decoy? We'll be sourcing proper motors, for appearances sake?"

"Perfect: you read my mind."

"Okay. So let's make that a hot four-by-four with off-road capability for the escape car, then two boring mom taxis with tuned-up engines. Why not a bike?"

"Too conspicuous. Also, hard to ride one in heels and a skirt. I'm a well-dressed society matron in this scenario, don't forget."

"Noted. You're going to do this unarmed?"

"*Johnny*—" She smiled. "I'm a foreign VIP guest; they'd smell a rat if I went with concealed carry."

"Okay, field-expedient gear only. May I say that I don't like this, Duchess? Whether or not you trust Gerry, you don't know what these cults can be like—you've never been in one. You're going to be totally exposed if anything goes wrong—"

"Nothing's going to go wrong." Her self-assurance was complete. "I'm a VIP guest on a study retreat week, not an armed intruder, and you'll just be a lonely foreign tourist taking in some church services. The deadliest thing I'll be carrying will be a corrupted email box on a memory stick. Unless they turn out to be a front for the Red Skull Cult or the Malaysian Presidential Guard, it should be a walk in the park."

"That's what I'm afraid of," Johnny said gloomily.

"So we'll just have to liven things up in round two." Persephone grinned, impishly: "Once we know for sure who we're dealing with."

HOTELSPACE IS A PARTICULAR SUBSPECIES OF HYPERSPACE that links the service corridors and bland, beige-carpeted halls of chain hotels. I've always had an uneasy feeling that if I open the wrong *Staff Only* door and turn a corner, I could find myself stepping out of the vending machine room on the seventh floor of a Hilton in Munich or a Sheraton in Osaka. At about 8 p.m. local time—or three in the morning back home—I find myself padding along one of the aforementioned dim, soundproofed corridors in the center of Denver, this time on the thirtieth floor, towing a suitcase behind me and clutching my room keycard in my other hand. (All arranged by the concierge service on my magic credit card, of course.)

Along the way I have a minor flash of déjà vu, echoing a check-in in Darmstadt many years ago that segued into a near-disastrous encounter in the hotel bar. My collisions with the Black Chamber over the years have not been happy; luckily the odds of me running into certain past acquaintances are low. Nevertheless, I'm as awake as I can be with my hindbrain telling my eyelids it's half past sleepy time.

Approaching my room's door, I haul out my phone and poke tiredly at it. OFCUT works like a charm. There's no sign of tampering anywhere up or down the corridor, and the lock's clean: no wards, no geases, no nasty little hidden surprises. Relieved, I stick my card in the lock, shove the door open, and tow my bag after me. Welcome to slumberland.

What can I say about the generic American hotel room? External Assets punch well above the usual Laundry expenses budget: I've got a decent king-sized room rather than the usual broom closet. The bed is the size of a small aircraft carrier, piled invitingly high with pillows, and pulses in my travel-stressed vision like some kind of carnivorous cotton plant. There's a desk, a clinically tiled bathroom, a TV set, an ethernet jack—

Ethernet.

Even before the door has swung shut behind me I'm into my travel bag to haul out the small and rather naff Dell that Facilities issued me with. The contents of the hard disk are carefully designed to look as if the laptop belongs to a mid-ranking idiot with a heavy Plants v. Zombies habit, and there is nothing remotely confidential about the machine. Laptops are an inherent security risk—they're too easy to steal—so the classified stuff all sits on a thumb drive. It has a fingerprint reader, the contents are encrypted, and if someone who *isn't me* tries to use my severed thumb to log in, then may dead alien gods have mercy on their soul (because the guardians of the Laundry email system won't).

I dash off a quick "arrived alive" message to Lockhart's publicly visible email address, then catch myself yawning. A quick glance at the bedside alarm radio tells me it's only half past eight. *Shit.* If I succumb to sleep before 10 o'clock I'll be up with the birds, which is not exactly my kind of lark—I should really go downstairs and get some food and hang out in the bar. Except both food and alcohol, in my current condition, will make me sleepy. If I want to stay awake, I need company. It's way too late to phone Mo, but—

Aha.

My IronKey is loaded with an address book. I send a quick email to Johnny McTavish, attaching my US phone number and hotel room: *Are you on site yet? Need to meet stat.* It's the tattoos: I should have passed them over before they left—but he and BASHFUL INCENDIARY lit out for the Golden Promise Ministries' bible study and brainwashing B&B too soon. But there's still a chance he can get one to her before she checks in, if I get them to him immediately.

Clearly McTavish is on the ball, because I'm listening to the coffee maker gurgling and choking into a mug five minutes later when my phone rings.

"McTavish here." He sounds alert.

"Howard."

"I'm in Denver."

"You are? Me, too. We need to meet up as soon as possible."

"Huh." A pause. "Meet me at the corner of Colfax and Fourteenth. Half an hour?"

"I'll do my best." Luckily I have Google Maps on the JesusPhone . . .

"Over and out."

He cuts the call. I guess I'm not the only one around here who finds jet lag eats away at the social veneer.

Colfax turns out to be the main east-west drag in town—the nearest thing to a high street in central Denver, all wall-to-wall shops and daytime diners. My hotel in the central business district is only about half a kilometer away, and while the weather's a bit chilly by my standards it's moving out of the depths of winter—the sidewalks are scraped bare of snow, and there's only the odd grimy mound in the gutters to remind me that I'm in the middle of a continental deep-freeze. So I pull the overcoat out of my suitcase, drag my shoes and jacket back on, stuff the book of tats and Pinky's funky little camera in my jacket pockets, and head downstairs to pound pavement.

We're on a plateau halfway up a mountain range, and I can feel it on my chest before I've gone three blocks. It's dusk: the cloud base overhead is low, and a lazy wind cuts through the streets, working its way through my coat. I'm wishing for a hat by the time I pass Thirteenth and start looking for Johnny. There aren't many people out, and traffic is light: either the center of Denver on a spring evening with a smell of snow in the air isn't the best place to hang out, or I'm missing a big ball game.

"Wotcher, Bob." I nearly jump out of my skin; for someone who's most of two meters tall and built like a brick shithouse Johnny is surprisingly hard to notice.

"Yo," I manage, glancing round quickly. I see no sign of anyone tailing us, and relax slightly. "There's something I need to fill you in on. Got ten minutes for a coffee?"

"This way," he says, and disappears into the murk between street lights. I do my best to follow him.

He leads me to a small indie coffee shop that, for a miracle, is both open and hasn't turned itself into a restaurant in time for dinner. We find a booth with padded vinyl seats and a good view of the doorway and slide in. I unzip my coat and rub my hands together. I'm cold; I didn't realize it until we got indoors. A waitress ambles over while I'm still shivering. "What'll it be?"

"Mug of Joe," grunts Johnny.

"Mocha venti with an extra shot for me, no cream," I add.

"Anything else?"

I shake my head and she wanders off. Johnny looks suspicious. "Since when do you speak Starbucks?"

I shrug. "It's not as if I can help it; they've got our office surrounded, and they don't like it if you try to order in English."

We wait in silence until our coffees arrive and the waitress departs again. Then Johnny asks, "What's the problem?"

"A little something for the weekend." I pull out the tat book. "You guys left before I could hand these over." I slide it towards him.

"Not our fault, the travel agent was *most* insistent . . ." Johnny opens the book. "Hmm." He squints at the contents. "That's neat. Are these what I think they are?"

I sip my coffee. "I don't know. What *do* you think they are?"

Johnny slides one of a pair of matching stabbed love-hearts out of its transparent sleeve. "Sympathy and contagion. If I wear one of these and you wear the other, we get a private walkie-talkie channel, right?" His gaze flickers back to me. "Whose bright idea was it?"

I shrug. "Don't ask *me*, Lockhart just thought they might come in useful. Dead-letter drops are *so* twentieth century, don't you think?"

"Huh." Johnny is looking thoughtful. "Yes, I should think the Duchess will be most interested in these. Thank you kindly." He raises his mug and takes what is clearly a throat-burning swig of coffee. "Well, I'd better be going."

"Wait!" I stop. "Firstly," I take the book and leaf through it, removing the control tattoos, "I need to keep these. Secondly—what are you guys planning?"

"We're going to get Mr. Lockhart exactly what he wants," Johnny says blandly. "Tomorrow, the Duchess is driving down to the Ministries' compound to start the Omega Course. It runs three days, Friday through Sunday, and she'll be there the whole while. Don't expect to hear from us—I'm moving on as well. I'll get in touch afterwards. In emergency"—he flips to a control tat—"I'll page you. Okay?"

Great. So just when Lockhart expects me to report back, all I can say is, *They've dropped off the map.* "And if I need to get in touch with you?"

He taps the book with a thick, stubby finger: "Use the force." Then he finishes off his coffee and vanishes, leaving me to pick up the bill.

YR. HMBL. CRSPNDNT. DOES NOT HAVE EYES IN THE BACK OF his head. Also, he's pretty shit at the whole spy tradecraft shtick.

Which is why what I'm about to relate came to me at third hand, some time after the event.

PERSEPHONE WATCHED THE DOORWAY OF THE COFFEE HOUSE from the far side of the road until she was sure the Laundry bureaucrat wasn't following Johnny. Then she slid the Flex into gear and circled the block slowly, keeping a weather eye open for any sign of company. Half a block past the coffee house she pulled over and popped the passenger door. Johnny clambered aboard, a stray snowflake preceding him. "Drive."

Persephone headed south, sticking to the speed limit. Traffic was light; she hung a left, then a right, checking her mirrors each time. "We're clear."

"Good." Johnny slumped slightly in his seat. "Save us from innocents, Duchess, they've stuck us with a bloody *amateur*."

"You think?" Persephone's lips peeled back from her teeth in a humorless grin.

"Bubblegum sympathy tats and a trench coat. What *is* the world coming to?"

"Never attribute to incompetence that which can be adequately explained by jet lag, my dear. So, these tats. What do you think?"

"I think you'd be mad to wear one," said Johnny. "They're too big, and these fundie nutjobs got some whacky ideas about real tattoos—mark of Cain, stuff in Leviticus, that kind of thing—and if they strip-search you—"

"They won't."

"Or if they lift Mr. Chinless-Wonder and find *his* tat—"

"They won't." Persephone spoke with complete assurance. "You underestimate Mr. Howard, his rap sheet's nearly as questionable as yours. People underestimate him: that's his game. Probably why it's taken Mahogany Row so long to notice him, at a guess. If we'd met him, back in our Network days . . . Well. I'm going to, let's see, burn myself on a steam iron? Blistered heel from running? Yes, that should explain the gel plaster. I'll keep the tattoo covered. You don't need to be so twitchy."

"But—"

Persephone turned to stare at him. "We *are* trying to get word out to Lockhart, aren't we? It's their preferred channel—and it's a lot harder to eavesdrop on than a phone call or a dead drop."

He looked away first, helpless before her confidence. "I got a bad feeling about this whole deal, Duchess. *Very* bad."

Coming up on the intersection with North Speer that would carry them out to the interstate, Persephone floored the accelerator. Gas gurgled into the huge V8 as the big mom-wagon accelerated. "Your opinion is noted. So doesn't reducing our risk of exposure help?"

Johnny shivered, a surprisingly delicate gesture for one so outwardly stolid. "Yeah, but I've still got a feeling there is something *wrong* with the picture. We're missing a piece. Something enormous."

"Very likely." Her fingers whitened on the steering wheel. "But it's our job to find out, isn't it? That's what we do."

MEANWHILE, SIXTY KILOMETERS AWAY . . .

Off US85, about seven kilometers north of the Air Force Academy in the vicinity of Palmer Lake, there's a road leading due west into Pike National Forest. It looks like a dirt track, winding around the wooded hillsides, but once it's out of sight of the township there's a fence, and a gate bearing the sign of the cross, and then single-track blacktop hugging the hillside above the Lower Reservoir until it reaches another discreet fence, and turns into a proper road, with driveways leading off either side to landscaped car parks and low buildings. One building is surmounted by a trio of large satellite dishes; another cluster is backed by a complex of specialized gas supplies and air conditioning units that would do justice to a small hospital. There's a mansion, a motel, a 7-Eleven, and a surprisingly small church.

Welcome to the Golden Promise Ministries compound.

Whenever the gates down near Palmer Lake open to admit a vehicle, eyes up in the security center track them on closed-circuit TV screens, check their registration plates online on license databases. Golden Promise Ministries has its own fire service, ambulance, and police force. Golden Promise Ministries has its own kindergartens and schools. It's the hub of an entire town, in miniature: a gated community with its own rules and regulations.

And the prophet is coming to town.

A black stretched Lincoln with mirror-tinted windows is rumbling up the blacktop path, preceded and trailed by a pair of black Explorers, also with mirrored windows. A police department cruiser leads the way, lights flashing in lazy salute. It's been a long day's journey, chasing the terminator around the spinning globe, but Raymond Schiller is finally coming home.

It's late in the evening when the Lincoln draws up outside his combination office and residence, a neoclassical-styled mansion fronted by a horseshoe-shaped drive at the end of the road; but his people are there, waiting for him. Here are his secretarial and administrative staff hoping for an audience at this late hour, a Judgment of Solomon in some cases. Next to them are a gaggle of trimly uniformed nursemaids and teachers from the crèche and kindergarten, vital handmaids to the progress of Project Quiver; a small group of visiting cadets from the Air Force Academy, doubtless here for one of the workshops the junior outreach ministry run in his absence; and a double-handful of other onlookers, well-wishers and members of the flock come to welcome him home.

Raymond musters up a broad smile as he climbs out of the limo and stretches his travel-stiffened muscles. He raises his hands: "What a welcome! Thank you, my friends. Let us pray together. Oh Lord, we thank thee for this safe homecoming . . ."

It's what they're here for, and he appreciates their thoughtful welcome, although a bath and his bed would be more welcome at this point. Benediction complete, he strides towards the front door. As he does so Alex Lockey slides into place at his side, a slim attaché case clamped under his elbow; to his other side, Doctor Jensen waits impatiently. "Can it wait?" Schiller asks quietly.

"No, sir." Alex matches stride as the door opens; Jensen echoes him. They move in convoy towards Schiller's office, leading a comet-trail of followers: his handmaiden Roseanne, Sheriff's Deputy Stewart, one of the senior teachers. "We've had a heads-up from the FBI in Denver . . ."

"And I need a moment of your time, too," Jensen says snippily. "Clinics don't run on air and promises, you know. We're getting an earful from a busybody at the Joint Commission over our accreditation and they're threatening to send an audit team."

"Intolerable." Schiller keeps his voice low. "Unless they are fellow travelers."

"Well yes." Jensen's gaze flickers to Brooks: "That would be Alex's department, but in the meantime what do I tell them? They're threatening to revoke our certification."

Schiller suppresses the urge to utter a profanity. "Can these items wait for two hours? I need to compose myself for the midnight communion; these are temporal matters, are they not? I'll see you both after the service."

Alex takes a deep breath, then nods. "Sir. It can't wait. It's critical."

"How critical?" Schiller focusses on his security coordinator.

"Our sources in the FBI passed on a warning while you were en route: apparently during your time in London you were being monitored by a deep black intel organization, and now MI5—the British counter-intelligence agency—are asking questions on behalf of another department. The FBI don't know who, which is worrying in itself. And then they got a tip-off from the DHS, that at least one British intelligence agent was tracked through JFK, en route to Denver."

"Didn't they arrest him? Forget that, son, that wasn't a question." Schiller thinks for a moment. "You're saying they're on to us?"

Alex nods. "It looks likely." Time to give Schiller a nudge: "Almost certain, sir."

"But the hour cometh, and now is," Schiller mutters under his breath. "Well, it's earlier than I wanted, but I see no reason to delay; we'll just have to bring everything forward as fast as we can. Schedule a meeting of the inner circle for tomorrow morning. Operation Multitude will simply have to go into effect as soon as possible." He turns to Pastor Dawes: "I assume you have blessed the hosts?"

"They're in Stephen's keeping. Tonight's communicants are being prepared."

"Good." Schiller unwinds slightly. "Doctor Jensen, I assume the certification matter will not actually impact your existing patients? It will merely hold up the admission of new cases?"

Jensen nods reluctantly. "Yes, but the audit—"

"Need not concern us; by the time they get around to sending someone, we shall have completed phase one of Operation Multitude and nothing short of the Antichrist in the White House ordering a nuclear strike on Colorado will be able to stop us." Then he turns back to Alex. "As for your British agent—if you find him—" He smiled thinly. "I am innocent of the blood of this person: see ye to it.'"

AN HOUR AND A HALF LATER, IN THE CHAPEL ATTACHED TO the back of the residence, Raymond Schiller conducts a service of midnight communion.

It's a small chapel, and windowless, as befits its unusual purpose; the congregation is equally small, and not entirely willing. Schiller is slightly late, red-eyed and tired, but his vestments are nevertheless immaculate. Pastors Dawes and Holt conduct the service, leading the confession. Ray enters from the rear of the chapel, climbing the steps to take his place behind the altar, just in time for the climax: "The Lord Jesus Christ is faithful and just to forgive us our sins and to cleanse us of all unrighteousness; therefore you are forgiven!"

He scans the upturned faces before him, the ecstatic joy of the Saved, the apprehension and fear of the new members attending their first communion. "You are cleansed of all unrighteousness, and you are worthy to participate in this holy meal!" A wave of fear so clear and cold he can feel it in his marrow sweeps through the twelve unshriven, kneeling in the two front rows between their guards. He smiles, beatific with the knowledge of their coming salvation. Then he leads off: "The Lord be with you!"

The congregants—those who are Saved—answer: "And also with you." The others, the Unsaved, have a harder task of making their voices heard, for they are gagged: Who needs to hear the cries of the damned? They will be Saved soon enough, willing or no. "Christ has died. Christ has risen. Christ is coming again!"

And finally it is time. Schiller licks his lips, shaking with emotion. "As Paul said to the Corinthians, I say to you: Christ our Passover is sacrificed for us. Let us keep the feast!" He gestures at the front row. "Let our new brethren be brought forward to join us . . ."

At the other side of the altar, Brother Stephen lifts back the silver-trimmed white linen cover from the incubator that holds the supply of hosts for tonight's ritual. The cymothoans are torpid, legs rippling along their pale flanks. Schiller accepts a pair of silver tongs from Pastor Holt and reaches for one of the divine isopods as two deputies frogmarch the first of the unshriven up to the altar. A healthy young male hipster, now handcuffed, gagged, and robed as befits a first-time communicant, his eyes bulge with terror. Schiller feels for him, a keen stab of compassion and empathy: the poor fellow seems to think he is about to be murdered! Which is anything but the truth. Raymond leans forward and makes the sign of the cross. "May the Body and Blood of our Lord Jesus Christ keep you unto eternal life," he says, and, as Pastor Dawes pushes the fellow's head back and unhooks the ball gag, he shoves the host into its new home.

The man convulses silently, choking in the grip of involuntary communion as the host goes to work, eager to save his soul. He's unconscious already as the deputies carry him back to his pew. Then the next communicant is kneeling before Schiller, a young African-American woman with dreadlocks and scared-deer eyes.

Raymond reaches out with his tongs for the next slowly writhing host and thanks the Lord from the depths of his heart, for giving him these souls to save and the means whereby to do His holy work.

8.

OMEGA COURSE

I'M STRANDED IN LIMBO, OTHERWISE KNOWN AS DOWNTOWN Denver.

After the handoff to Johnny I wander around for half an hour, glancing in closed storefront windows until I get too cold, too tired, or both. I go back to my room, run a long bath, order a slab of pizza on room service, and force myself to watch an episode of an inane sitcom just to remind myself how far from home I've come . . . until my eyelids start to drift shut at semi-random intervals. Jet lag will get you in the end, and by 10 o'clock my hindbrain is screaming at me for sleep. So I give in and go to bed.

Which is stupid of me, because I don't actually *need* to discover that downtown Denver doesn't look any prettier at five o'clock on a damp Friday morning than at ten at night on a Thursday. On the other hand, it's nearly noon back home so I don't have to suffer in solitary boredom. I fire up the laptop and check into my non-work Gmail and Facebook accounts to say "hi" to Mo and various relatives and friends; then I log out, shove my IronKey in the slot, and fire up the encrypted connection to the gateway machine outside the Laundry's firewall.

I am greeted as usual by a happy fun burning goat-horned skull in a pentacle followed by a prompt to enter my password. Which is the first thing that bubbles up into my subconscious (because I am destiny entangled with my own warrant card, which does double duty as an authentication token), and lets me into a webmail service that, despite all the to-ing and fro-ing and blood-curdling threats, isn't cleared for any messages above PROTECT—"may cause mild embarrassment if published in *The Sun*; curdles milk and causes stillbirth in sheep: significant risk of accounting errors." (And when I say *isn't cleared*, I mean that any attempt to type certain codewords for restricted or confidential topics will cause smoke to rise from the keyboard. Laundry IT have a very literal-minded approach to designing firewalls . . .)

There is a memo from HR about the correct format for minor expense claims. I read it and, with mild dismay, discover that I've cocked up the hotel reservation. Hopefully it's fixable; if not, they'll try and debit £2895.50p from my next month's payroll run, which would be bad. I swallow a mouthful of weak coffee and make a note, then move on.

There are several more irritating memos from HR. (Time off in lieu for medical issues does not cover jet lag; conversion of foreign currency expenses to sterling needs competitive tendering from at least three competing *bureaux de change* for amounts exceeding 50 pence and staff are reminded that currency triangulation arbitrage is strictly illegal; requirements for time sheets *do* cover jet lag, but only from west to east because the 1970s payroll system doesn't understand negative time differentials . . .)

Then I come to an email from Angleton asking why I missed the CENSORED CENSORED weekly committee meeting yesterday. I do a double take, then realize that (a) it's COBWEB MAZE, and (b) Angleton himself did not write the message—it was automatically generated by our in-house calendar system, which doesn't understand time zones terribly well either (the design brief focussed on converting cultist Great Cycle sacrificial festivals into Gregorian dates rather than pandering to jet-setting executives).

And finally there is a short, enigmatic message from Lockhart:

Your arrival was noticed. You should avoid direct contact with sub-
jects. You must avoid any contact, repeat any contact, with local
FBI, USAF, and police personnel. Infection more severe than initially
suspected.

I gulp down the rest of my coffee and re-read it, just to make sure
I'm not wrong and I really *am* in the shit up to my nostrils.

In the Laundry, we use certain words with extreme caution. "Should"
means what it says—it's strongly worded advice, but it's discretionary.
"Must" is another matter entirely: it's an *order*.

If Lockhart is ordering me to avoid the FBI and the cops and saying
"infection more severe than initially suspected" then, reading between
the lines, those agencies must be presumed hostile. I note with interest that he *didn't* order me not to consort with the Nazgûl—sorry, the
Black Chamber. Not that there's much chance of me going to them
without lots of kicking and screaming and splintering of fingernails
along the way, but it tells me that the warning about the FBI and the
blue-suiters is based on specific intelligence.

Which means they've been penetrated and compromised. By a
church?

RIGHT NOW, MY JOB IS TO HURRY UP AND WAIT. WATCH. MON-
itor, and report back to Lockhart; all those things will come in due
course. So after I've been up for a while I go down to the hotel restaurant for breakfast, after which I head out for a morning constitutional—
and, I will admit, to nose around and familiarize myself with the area
on foot.

I am not, at this time, tailed by police cars, monitored by serious-
faced G-men in trench coats, or hovered over by black helicopters.

After an hour or two in an indie bookstore and coffee shop, I head
back to my hotel room. It's neat, sterile, the bed made, and the coffee station resupplied. As I touch the doorknob the ward I left there
tells me the only person who has been inside is a Columbian maid
called Maria, who is either a tooled-up occult operative from the Black

Chamber with a terrifyingly effective line in countermeasure invocations, or exactly what she thinks she is. I go inside, lock the door, sit down in the swivel chair at the desk, and open the book of tats.

It's time to go to work.

My last experience with destiny-entanglement protocols was not, shall we say, a happy one. Anything that involves telepathic bonds with other parties is pretty damned dangerous. If you've got a skull full of classified files, the other party you're forcibly entangled with turns out to be a BLUE HADES/human hybrid succubus working for the Black Chamber, and you've got a week to get disentangled before your neural states start to merge, you might develop a slight aversion to the procedure.

Luckily, this time it's different. The tats don't result in a direct merging of minds; but if I close my mind and try to daydream, I find I'm daydreaming myself into someone else's skull. Try and visualize something else—pink elephants, say—and after a moment I find myself drifting back into the headspace of a dangerous woman trying to play the part of a wealthy ingénue on a religious retreat . . .

PERSEPHONE LOOKED AROUND THE CONFERENCE SUITE LOBBY with politely veiled curiosity. Calling it a conference center was a bit of an exaggeration; a timber-fronted motel with an attached car park and a picturesque chapel nestling against a pine-tree-infested hillside, it clearly catered more often to weddings than to business events. On the other hand, the combination of a secluded lodge with an event center and chapel was clearly a good match for Golden Promise Ministries, with the added bonus feature of execrable mobile phone signal—her BlackBerry had been showing one bar ever since she arrived, and no data.

She'd driven up that morning, checked into the lodge with a matched set of Mandarina Duck luggage, and engaged the concierge with a barrage of bubble-headed questions about the facilities. For his part, the concierge humored her: no complaints there. Once in her room she'd taken time to install her extensive wardrobe in the closet, then retired to the bathroom for the best part of an hour. Finally, she sneaked downstairs for lunch—a tuna salad—and across to the event center where the course was due to kick off at three o'clock with an afternoon reception.

Palmer Lake, Persephone was displeased to learn, lay outside the Golden Promise Ministries' compound. Her target was at the far end of a private road, beyond a gateway just around the corner of the hill from Pinecrest. In between interrogating the concierge about nearby beauticians and whether the fitness center had an elliptical trainer, she'd pumped him for details: GPM ran these courses regularly, and usually gave participants a guided tour of their ministry on the final day. *Not good,* she told herself. If they were going to keep her exposure down to a supervised tour, how was she going to plant her spyware? More importantly: What were they trying to keep out of sight?

The timbered hall was furnished for a talk—a podium at the front and rows of chairs facing it—but there was a buffet spread at the back, with coffee urns and trays piled high with cookies, cake slices, and sushi rolls, as for a corporate motivational junket.

Aiming to stay in character (a London high-society divorcee or widow, hunting for meaning in an over-privileged, sterile existence), Persephone drifted towards the coffee urn. It was already the focus of some attention by a handful of over-groomed men in office casual and a corresponding gaggle of women who, from their costumes, were desperate not to fade into the invisibility of middle age. As she took in faces, a woman of a very different sort—young and perky, blonde, clipboard-armed and badge-wearing—stepped in front of her. "Can I help you?"

"I do hope so." Persephone injected a faint quaver of uncertainty into her voice. "This *is* the Omega Course reception, isn't it . . . ?"

"Sure! My name's Julie, and I'd just like to take a few details if I may, ma'am? If you wouldn't mind telling me your name?"

"Persephone Hazard. Um, this *is*—"

"Don't you worry, Mrs. Hazard, you're in the right place." Julie patted her arm, clearly intending reassurance, then scored through a line on her clipboard. Persephone took note, careful not to snoop

visibly: from the size of the list they were expecting fewer than thirty
people. "From London, I see? Wow, you've come a long way today!"

"I flew in yesterday," Persephone confided. "There are no direct
flights via British Airways so I caught the afternoon shuttle from—"

Two sentences and Julie began to nod like a metronome; it was
amazing how fast most people zoned out if you babbled at them, in
Persephone's experience. (It was all true, easily verifiable—drown 'em
in data and they won't suspect you're holding out.)

"Thank you, that's wonderful," Julie gushed as soon as Persephone
gave her a crevice to lever her way back into the conversation-turned-
monologue. "Now I absolutely have to go and take other names? But
make yourself right at home! Help yourself to the spread and Ray will
be right along in a few minutes to introduce everything. Meanwhile,
why don't you circulate?"

Persephone nodded and thanked Julie fulsomely, then went about
putting her advice into practice. If bonding was the name of the game,
then over the next twenty minutes she scored: a property developer
called Barry, a local TV anchor called Sylvia, a state senator, and a
newly minted partner in a corporate law firm—*work that smile!*—half
the men were divorced or newly upgraded to wife 2.0, so it wasn't
entirely a gold-digger's paradise, but they were all united by a common
factor: the need for something else in their life.

Persephone was discreetly pumping Senator Martinez about his
stance on right-to-work legislation when she felt a sudden change
in the atmosphere in the room. Allan Martinez wasn't looking at her
anymore: his gaze tracked over her shoulder, and she turned, following his eyes round towards the doorway. Which was open, to admit
Raymond Schiller, beaming, and a couple of assistants—a bald man in
smoked glasses and a gray suit, and a homely-faced, middle-aged woman
in a blue dress.

"Hello, everyone!" Schiller called, raising his arms. His suit was im-
maculately cut, his white shirt worn with a power tie, a small silver
cross pinned to his lapel. "Welcome to the Golden Promise! I'm glad
you all could make it here today. I mean to make it worth your while.
I think this could be the most important meeting of your lives—and by

the time we're through, I'm hoping you'll find your way to agreeing with me."

He clasped his hands together—not in benediction, but in a gesture of defensive self-deprecation. "I want to wish you all a very warm welcome. Some of you may be wondering, 'Hey, what have I gotten myself into?'" A ripple of nervous laughter spread around the room. "Well, don't worry. We're not here to pressure you; you can leave any time you want. This might just not be the right time for you. That's okay; you can leave whenever you like, and come back whenever you like. Nobody's going to stop you. It's a free country."

Once started, Schiller kept going for nearly a quarter of an hour, tickling his audience, playing on their nervous curiosity with self-deprecating humor, bringing himself down several pegs until he presented himself as seeing eye-to-eye with them: no longer a mega-famous preacher on a pedestal, but a down-home fellow the men in the audience could see themselves sharing a beer with. Persephone nodded along, happily in her element, taking mental notes. There were tricks here, flickers of eye contact, hand gestures designed to manipulate the onlookers' perceptions. His focus wandered the room, meeting eyes and engaging like a jolt of lightning recognition from the base of the spine. When he spoke to the women his spin was slightly different, less overtly masculine, stressing the mystical; when he spoke to the men his manner became more laconic, less emotionally loaded.

He's brilliant, she realized, with a flash of admiration normally reserved for a deadly freak of nature like a black widow spider or a sleeping tiger. He hadn't even gotten started on the subject of the course—the Omega, humanity's destiny, the answer to the greatest question, as the promotional pamphlet put it—and he was already establishing himself in his audience's minds as a trusted guide, an old and reliable friend, leader, and helpmate.

Ray was good: it went beyond being an inspirational speaker. He had a grip on his audience's attention span and interests, not just their ears. The talk was more like an afternoon chat show than a sermon. Stomachs full of cake and coffee, heads full of questions, and the audience were nodding along with him enthusiastically rather than nodding off to sleep. Schiller was going to supply the answers—but not until after dinner.

Persephone leaned back and waited for her opportunity, a vacant smile fixed to her face.

I BLINK AND OPEN MY EYES. "OW." I MUMBLE VACANTLY. THE tat on the inside of my left wrist aches and shimmers before my eyes, my bladder's full, my neck's stiff and sore, and while I've been sitting in this bloody chair the sky has begun to darken in the west. I shake myself and stand up, wobbly from being in one position for too long. *Slide time*—I must have been experiencing the show in real time with Persephone.

I'm acutely aware of her self-image, her body feel mapped onto my own—I feel odd, squat and narrow-hipped and dumpy. It's quite strange; I thank my lucky rabbit's foot that she's not having a period. I waddle to the bathroom and empty my bladder, worrying. Am I going to have to do this the whole time? Sixteen hours a day in a chair (hell no, I ought to be in bed) kibitzing on someone else's sensorium? How about—

Huh. I completely forgot about Johnny. Should I call him up, too? But not like that; I just need to talk to him, make sure everything's running to plan. Traviss said I could use the tats to talk. I try to remember the protocol; unlike the straight over-the-shoulder monitoring function, it requires a drop of blood and a minor invocation.

There is this to be said in favor of posh hotel rooms: they come with handy stuff like an adjustable shaving mirror in the bathroom, a sewing kit (for needles), and most of the stuff you need in order to whomp up a field-expedient summoning grid (class one, minor). I take my time, puttering around for half an hour as I round up the ingredients, jot down a recipe, take the time to step through it in search of fatal errors, jot down a second—this time, non-fatal—version, then execute.

It's a good thing I took my time and I'm sitting down because for a moment I *can't see*. I know my eyeballs are still where they belong—they haven't fallen out or anything—but I'm not registering what they're looking at. Then, with a really uncomfortable mental crunching of gears, I land back in my own head. Except I'm hearing things. Like: ***Wotcher fuck d'you think you're doing, fuck-head?***

It's Johnny. And he's not terribly happy.

Testing, testing, one, two, three, Peter Pepper picked a—

Fuck off, son. You trying to cause an accident? Coz I'm on the highway, overtaking . . .

Whoops. ***Sorry.***

There is a pregnant pause. ***Fuckin' A.*** A longer pause, synonymous with a sigh. ***Okay, say your piece and get out of my head.***

Update from head office: they say to avoid all contact with law enforcement, especially the FBI.

No need to teach your grandmother to suck eggs. His disgust is palpable. ***Got any other good advice for yer maiden aunt?***

I rack my brain and apply some spare rusty pilliwinks to my thought processes. ***I've been kibitzing on your boss's session. Trouble is, there's just the one of me and no shift relief. So I'm going to have to rely on you to alert me if anything goes wrong. Hence the chat.***

Kibitzing— I have the most peculiar feeling that he's rolling his eyes. ***Jesus, son, that's not clever. The Duchess has a short way with snoops when she finds them: if yer skull's still intact that's only 'coz she were distracted. Knock before entering, wipe yer feet on the mat, and wash yer hands on the cat, do I have to draw you a diagram?*** Another pause. ***Anyways. You're calling 'coz you want me to drop everything and page you if Schiller takes a crap. Right?***

That draws me up sharp, and I do a double take followed by a brisk self-test. ***No.***

There is good management and bad management: good management is like air—you don't know it's there until it's gone away. Looking at the back of my head, I have a feeling I'm not being a good manager right now. So I take a deep breath and try to explain myself: ***I'm hanging out alone, in an information vacuum, and it's doing my head in, so I'm acting out. Right now I have no idea what you two are planning or what you expect me to do if things go adrift and you two have to cut and run. Or if there's any support you need.***

There's a long silence. ***Like that, huh?*** He sounds thoughtful. ***Okay, Howard. It's like this: you don't know where I am because I don't *want* you to know where I am. And we haven't asked you for any support yet. And if we have to run, you'll know about it. Like *this*.*** I scream and clutch my upper right arm. Bastard feels like he's twisting it between his hands—not hard, but he got the scar that Jonquil left in it last year. ***If you get that, it means you want to leave town *now*, do not pass Go, do not collect two hundred kilos of China White, because everything has gone to fuck. Got that?***

Jesus, I mutter verbally. ***I get the message. But use the other arm, please.***

Any particular reason?

No. I *might* just be a bit snippy right now. My eyes are certainly watering. ***Just do it. In case I'm pointing a gun at someone.***

You and guns don't mix, unless I mistake my man. The bastard sounds amused.

He's not as right as he thinks he is, but I pass. ***Next. I gather the course is outside the GPM compound, so your boss is looking for a way to get in and plant her bug. Which is fine, if she can do it—but I don't want her to take any unnecessary risks. Put it this way, I don't think it's worth her life. If she can't get in, we'll figure out what to do later. But I want *you* to get that message across, because I've got a feeling if I tell her directly she'll take it as a challenge. Am I right?***

Silence. Followed by more silence. Finally he says, ***You're not wrong.*** For a moment my vision fuzzes again, almost as if he's decided to drop the mental firewall. But no: ***I don't reckon she'll take that from me, either. But she's not stupid, son. Sit back, stay out of our hair, and I'll feed you updates when it's safe.***

Okay.

****Okay,**** he says, and there's an empty moment that feels like I've just been punched in the head, minus the pain—then I'm staring at a cracked mirror and clutching my right bicep, which is aching like a pulled molar.

This management gig isn't as easy as it looks at first sight, is it?

I ORDER UP DINNER ON ROOM SERVICE. WATCH A SHITTY COM-edy on the in-room TV channel, then hit up the minibar for a half bottle of wine. Drinking on my own is a bad idea but I manage to keep to just the one serving, and anyway, going out and looking to get drunk in company is an even worse prospect under the circumstances. I am not merely stranded in hotelspace, I am adrift in hoteltime in my very own personal air-conditioned TARDIS. Eventually I drift off to sleep, at first to dream of burning goats checking my time sheet for accounting errors, and then—

Oh shit, is my first reflexive thought as I wake up inside a dream: *I've been here before, and I didn't like it the first time.*

I'm in a dream, and in this dream I am awake, and I am immobilized, and I am very, *very* thirsty for something other than water.

Above me the sky is dark from horizon to horizon, dark but not black: a gossamer streamer of varicolored dust clouds splashes across the night like a Thuggee strangler's silk scarf. The starscape itself is crammed with the red and dying stellar wreckage of a prematurely aged galactic core. Below the horizon I can sense the dying sun, bulbous and red, choking on the corpses of its planetary children. But not this world. The moons—plural—have set, but the dim radiance of the nebula overhead casts long shadows across the parched plateau and the Watchers and the Pyramid.

The Pyramid.

I'm one of the Watchers—or rather, I'm a passive, helpless passenger inside the skull of one of the dead, mummified Watchers who the Bloody White Baron impaled in a huge circle on the dying plain nearly a century ago, to form a ring of human sacrificial guards around the Pyramid. The Baron, himself a figure out of nightmares and a necromancer of no small talent, had nightmares of his own about the thing that sleeps in the Pyramid: the Opener of the Ways, some call it. The sleepers are quantum observers, eyeless and dead but still alive, condemned to collapse the wave function of the thing in the mile-high tomb so that it is forever *asleep*—

(Because if the Watch on the Pyramid fails the Black Bird of Hangar 12B will fly its one-way mission, the last forlorn hope of the British strategic nuclear deterrent, and then all hell will literally break loose.)

—Why am I here?

I am, it occurs to me, having a lucid dream. Which is an utterly horrible experience when you wake up inside an impaled, mummified corpse propped up on a stainless steel spike in front of a geometric shape that makes your imaginary insides curdle with terror. I'd pinch myself if I could move the withered, blackened claws I have instead of hands. The peripheral nerves of this body have shriveled and decayed along with its flesh, but I can still feel the other Watchers to either side of me. Indignant and hungry and incoherent with rage and grief and the shattering of life's dream, they recognize the presence of a not-dead soul and lust to eat my identity, to pour my waters into the drained pool of their deaths—

I strain at my imprisoning flesh, but it won't move. Dead, of course; silly me! I may have learned a thing or two about death when the Cult of the Black Pharaoh were busily trying to feed me to the Eater of Souls, but that doesn't mean I can reboot the cellular machinery from scratch once the algorithms of life have run their course and halted for good. And while there may be some kind of animation trigger that'll make the mummy dance, I don't have it.

Something brought me to wakefulness here. What? Or who?

I shiver involuntarily. There's a low rumble, resonating through the tiny bones of my inner ears. Moments later I feel, as much as see, the corpses on the spikes to either side of me vibrate in sympathy. A dusty ripple spreads out across the plain in front of the Pyramid, rising on a blast of shocked air. The vibration intensifies, the ground rocking, setting my jawbone clattering uselessly against my skull. Somewhere a phone is ringing off the hook.

Earthquake?

The phone is ringing as the earthquake intensifies. It's *my* phone, I realize, and I reach for it, and the dream disintegrates around me on the darkling plain as I roll sideways and swipe, my arm spasming across the bedside table until I grasp the phone and hug it like a drowning man with a lifebelt.

It's still ringing. I clutch it to my ear and hiss, "*Yessss . . . ?*"

An unfamiliar female voice says, "Hello? Can I speak to Mr. Howard, please?"

"Speaking." My blurry eyes slowly focus on the bedside alarm clock.

"I'm conducting a survey on behalf of Scamworth and Robb Double Glazing; would you be interested in doing a short questionnaire? Our salespeople are in your area and I wonder if you'd—"

"It's four thirty in the morning." Everything comes into very sharp focus. "And I very much doubt you're in my area, unless you are flying a helicopter over downtown Denver. Where did you get this number?"

"Oh, I'm terribly sorry Mr. Howard—"

"*Where did you get this number?*" I repeat, a horrible focal point of *hunger* crunching itself tighter and tighter inside my head. "Tell me!"

"You're . . . in our database . . ." Her voice begins to slur.

"You will remove this number from your database." My voice is deathly and controlled. "Then you will tell your supervisor that if any of your people ever call this number, men in unfamiliar uniforms will drag them away in manacles and they will never be seen again. Do I make myself understood?"

"Wha . . . ! There's no need to be rude!" She sounds indignant. Obviously she doesn't get the message.

A silvery spike of pure rage flashes through my head: "*Listen! Obey! Submit! I bind you in the name of—*"

I bite the back of my tongue with my molars, hard enough to draw blood. High Enochian is harsh on the vocal chords; more importantly, *what the* fuck *am I thinking?* I switched to a metalanguage of compulsion because I was about to tell a double-glazing call center sales drone to go and—*oh Jesus, no*. That's the sort of thing the Black Assizes nail you for.

I hang up, hastily, with a shudder. Then I swallow something warm. Blood. I've bitten my tongue and it's bleeding.

It's four thirty in the morning. I roll out of bed, stumble to the bathroom, and welcome in the new day by throwing up in the toilet. After which I can't get back to sleep.

I SLEEPWALK THROUGH SATURDAY MORNING IN A STATE OF borderline shock, unable to trust myself. The world outside is still there, just the same as before, but somehow it feels different, more distant. Tenuous and breakable. I go downstairs and hit the hotel swimming pool, but after a couple of dozen lengths I'm gasping for breath. Denver air is thin and unsatisfying. So I wander out, find a coffee shop to hang out in with a pretzel and a mocha and something that claims to be a newspaper.

Towards late morning I go back to my room. It's been made up, as before. Good. I make myself comfortable on the bed then cold-bloodedly drop myself back into Persephone's head.

There have been changes.

Persephone is standing in the open courtyard outside the timber-framed conference hall. Consternation: so are the other students. There's a trestle outside, and the door handles are taped shut. "I'm sorry," one of Schiller's assistants from the night before is saying, "we can't use the conference hall today, there's been a leak. We're waiting for the bus right now, so we can continue off-site in one of the Ministries' buildings. And the reverend has been delayed—he's in a meeting this morning, some kind of business that couldn't wait."

"Are we going to run late?" asks one of the men from the previous night—Persephone's memory prompts, *Jason*, an accountant from Colorado Springs—thick-set, red-faced, hypertensive. "Because if so, I've got a—"

"It's coming now," interrupts the woman. (*Christina*, according to Persephone. Slightly heavy, ruddy-faced, wears a cross that's just slightly too large for her neck.) Persephone turns. There is indeed a smallish shuttle bus, outfitted with leather-upholstered seats.

"He's worried about being late," Darryl the real estate agent confides in Persephone's ear. "You ask me, he should worry more about being *late* before he's got himself square with Jesus."

"Are you square with Jesus?" Persephone asks with a bright and elegant smile.

"I surely am." Darryl is smugly self-satisfied about his salvation status. His eyes wander around Persephone's person, unconsciously undressing her—she briefly fantasizes about rabbit-punching him—then settle on her wrist. "That's a pretty bracelet." He focuses on the engraved silver band as the bus draws up, its doors opening to take the course participants up to the Golden Promise compound. "What's it say?" She raises it, turns her wrist. "Huh. W. W. L. J. D.—does that mean 'What Would Lord Jesus Do'?"

"Something like that." Her smile widens. *Thank you, Johnny,* she thinks, and I glimpse in the front of her mind what the bracelet *really* stands for and choke, which is when she notices me.

For a moment I'm somewhere very very dark and very very bright, like a bug on a microscope slide the size of a galaxy, pinned down by laser-bright spotlights beneath the inspection of a vast, unfriendly intelligence.

Mr. Howard. Get out of my head and *stay* out.

She is *not* pleased, but I get to live—this time.

Uh . . . okay, I manage.

With an effort of will I begin to disentangle myself from her senses. But I'm not fast enough, and she is obviously not happy, because suddenly she *shoves*, chucking me out of her mind so hard that I lose consciousness.

WHICH IS WHY I DON'T HAVE A RINGSIDE SEAT IN PERSEPH- one's and Johnny's heads when everything goes right to hell.

9.

SPEAKING IN TONGUES

"IT'S IMPORTANT TO UNDERSTAND GOD'S PLAN," SCHILLER says, clasping his hands behind his back, chin lowered to his chest, braced against the force of his own wisdom.

"First, we must follow His instructions. Go forth, be fruitful and multiply and fill the Earth with souls obedient to His will. Live good lives, obey His rules, be faithful members of His flock, and when the end comes we'll be safe forever in heaven. That much is clear. But. *But.*"

He's pacing back and forth across the stage now. "That isn't enough." He stops in the middle of the stage, turns and faces his audience. His expressive face, lit from below, is suddenly shadowed and ominous. "There are one and a half billion Muslims on this Earth. A billion and a half Chinese communists, a billion Indian Hindu elephant-worshippers. One point two billion Catholics, misled by the Vatican. And I'm afraid they're all going to go to hell if we don't manage to save them in time. This is a tragedy; the great, besetting tragedy of our age is that at least ninety-five percent of currently living humanity is going to burn in hell. To make matters worse, this is the most populous century ever—there are more than seven billion of us! We know the truth, and the necessary steps to salvation are simple: accept Jesus into your hearts—you're all

Saved, there's room for you in the lifeboat, but why aren't we saving *them*?"

Ray is clearly anguished, Persephone realizes; he believes this stuff with all his soul and all his guts. He believes in the viral metaphor of a bronze-age rabble-rouser from the Levant, as interpreted by his syncretist followers scattered throughout the Roman Empire. He believes in heaven and hell as real, literally existing destinations you can book an airline ticket to. He believes salvation is a deterministic, card-punching exercise in holding faith in the right god; believes that there's a coming End of Time in which his godhead will return to Earth, reading minds and separating the sheep from the goats. No need to ask *why* his God might prescribe eternal torture for the unbelievers, no need to engage with the problem of free will—Schiller's eschatology is either brutally truncated or sublimely simple, depending on viewpoint. One thing it isn't is nuanced.

Persephone rubs her bracelet uneasily. (*WWLJD indeed.*) True believers unnerve her, for she has seen the Red Skull in their observances, witnessed the rites of the Cult of the Black Pharaoh, and she knows the abhorrent truth: the things humanity call gods are either lies or worse, alien and abhuman intelligences that promise something not unlike hell but without any heavenly insurance policy. The pre-existing destination for humanity is death. But Schiller doesn't see it from that angle; in his own way he is an idealist and an optimist.

"Everyone who isn't square with Jesus is destined to go to hell. That means about seven billion souls at this moment. Golden Promise Ministries was established in 1896 by Pastor William Gantz to honor a promise he made when he first realized the magnitude of the crisis, and I am personally sworn to follow him, unto death if necessary. Our mission is simple: *We're not going to let it happen.* We're going to save every human soul it's possible to save before our Lord returns. And his return is imminent, within our lives: closer, it could be next year, next month, even next week. So we've got to work *fast*."

Schiller pauses for a moment to take a sip of water from the glass on his lectern. Persephone glances around the room. Her fellow Omega Course attendees are rapt in the grip of his glamour, mesmerized by his bullshit. She shivers. He's a powerful speaker. Despite her occult knowledge—for Persephone is fully cognizant of the dismal message of the One True Religion—she'd be in his grip too, were it not for the cross-shaped ward she wears.

"Our Lord Jesus Christ is going to return sometime within our lifetimes. The signs are there before us, the turmoil and decadence and chaos of these last days. The corruption of Western civilization. We've formed a team to pray for guidance—the forward observer study group, we call them—and the signs are clear to read: Jesus is coming. Well, short of actively trying to *delay* him"—Schiller chuckles drily—"we can't do anything about the timing; 'For as the lightning cometh from the east and flashes to the west, so also will the coming of the Son of Man be.' But we can do our best to sort out the tribes of man first.

"We need bodies to wage the war for Christ. We can increase our numbers by adoption—you may have noticed the crèches and kindergarten facilities here—and we can raise large families and guide our children to the path of righteousness. If you're not raising a large family, even if you're infertile, then you're not doing all you can for Jesus.

"And we can work on other strategies. Our missions leverage the latest marketing and narrowband consumer targeting protocols to make best use of the internet to reach—"

Persephone discreetly stands and sidles towards the doorway.

She's taken a seat at one end of the back row, just to make this move possible. And she's consumed two cups of coffee in the past hour. "I need the restroom," she quietly tells Julie, or maybe she's a Christina or a Roseanne—the mousy-haired young woman in a gray maxi-dress who stands by the door.

"Sure thing, ma'am." The handmaiden opens the door and they duck outside. Behind them, Schiller is rattling on about Web 2.0 communications strategies for evangelical outreach. "If you'd like to follow me?"

Persephone slides into place behind her escort, eyes wide open and scanning the passageways to either side as she is escorted down a corridor and round a bend to a discreetly camouflaged restroom, where her escort leaves her and hurries back to the conference room.

(Which means the clock is ticking.)

Persephone waits out her guide and guard's departure, then steps out into the hall. Her badge is flipped round, the big red V (for visitor, presumably) hidden as she paces rapidly in the opposite direction from the lecture hall. *Three minutes,* she thinks. She adjusts the bracelet again: *What Would Leeroy Jenkins Do?* It's Johnny's little joke, dating back to an experiment with World of Warcraft as a global conferencing system for the Network. The intel team that raids together stays together.

This part of the conference center is set up around three lecture theaters and a hall, plus support offices. And it's a Saturday. It doesn't take Persephone long to find an unoccupied receptionist's station, complete with a PC. She does a quick risk assessment. Pros: it gets the job done, and today's a Saturday, which minimizes the chance of discovery. Cons: her pre-canned excuse won't work. The pros win. She touches the mouse, thumbs the screen to life, sticks her USB stick in a free socket at the back, then yanks and re-inserts the power cable. The PC's BIOS isn't password protected, and it's the work of a minute to start it rebooting off her memory stick.

While she waits for the PC to come up, she heads back toward the toilet (temporary excuse: *I got lost on my way back*); but she has to return to the reception station for long enough to log in, fire up the copy of Outlook on the PC's hard disk, and open her contaminated mailbox.

(Mission accomplished.)

The skin on the back of Persephone's neck is crawling as she shuts the PC down again. Everything seems to take impossibly long, the animation in Windows moving with nightmare slowness. But finally the job is done. She pulls the USB stick, walks back to the toilet cubicle, and flushes it just as there is a tentative knock on the door.

"Ma'am? Are you all right?"

"Never better," Persephone says fervently. "Well, aside from breakfast. I'm sorry, I'm just freshening up in here. I'll be with you in a minute."

"Take your time."

When Persephone comes out, the mousy woman is waiting. She isn't showing obvious signs of anxiety, but the mere fact of her presence is sufficient to put Persephone on alert. *They don't want to lose track of me.* She smiles. "Have I missed anything important?" she asks.

"Oh no." Her escort shakes her head very seriously. "I'm certain Father will take time to help you." She turns, then pauses, looking over her shoulder. "Follow me, please."

There's something oddly affectless about the woman, and it gives Persephone the creeps. But she tags along behind her. After a few seconds Persephone realizes something else: the slight heaviness in her guide's hips, something about her body fat distribution, her shape in profile. She's pregnant: not hugely so, but certainly well into the second trimester. *Odd,* Persephone thinks, but she remains silent and unquestioning until they come to an elevator. "Hey. This isn't the way back to the hall, is it?"

"No." Her guide pushes the call button. "Father led everyone to the chapel after you left, so he sent me to show you the way there. He decided to invite everyone to attend holy communion. Wouldn't you like that?"

Persephone blinks as the doors open. *What would a true believer say . . . ?* "I suppose so. I mean, absolutely!"

The doors slide closed behind her and the elevator begins to descend. "You sound a bit conflicted," her guide says guilelessly. "That tells me you *need* the host in your heart. It'll make everything better."

"I guess so." The elevator stops and the doors open. The guide leads Persephone out into a wide corridor, windowless but lined with illuminated niches holding spotlit stained-glass panels. At the end, the wide double doors gape open. "This way." They reach the doors and step through. "See, everyone is waiting for you!"

Persephone sees everything, taking in the timeless scene in front of her with horrified eyes: the waiting flock, the guards holding an unwilling inductee before the altar, the pastors and the silver bowl full of things that to her warded eyes are not what they seem to everyone else—

Persephone turns at bay, ready to fight her way to freedom.

*　　*　　*

IT'S LATE.

I shudder and awaken on my hotel room bed.

As I turn my head fireworks explode in my skull, accompanied by a wave of unbelievable pressure. I have a headache, my tongue feels as if something died on it, and I ache all over. In fact, my body has an eerie not-quite-me-here feeling that I've had only a couple of times before, most notably in a dank room under Brookwood Cemetery—a really disturbing sensation, and not one I care for. I figure the headache is the after effect of being given the oneiromantic heave-ho by an angry sorceress; but I can't account for the not-me feeling. Outside my thirtieth-floor window the sky is slate-gray and angry-looking. (Luckily it's turned cold outside, and the temperature's too low for tornadoes. That's one of the local attractions I really don't mind missing.) I check the clock and realize with a start that I've been asleep for about eight hours.

The bathroom is calling. I stumble through and splash water on my face. One thing leads to another, and ten minutes later (by way of the toilet and a brisk application of my shaver) I'm feeling a little more human, if still somewhat grumpy from the slowly subsiding headache.

I stare at my red-eyed face in the bathroom mirror. *What am I doing here?* I feel like an eight-year-old who's been handed a laser pointer and a bag of catnip and told to go amuse the kittens behind the chain-link fence labelled *Siberian Tiger Enclosure*; my so-called External Assets are off the reservation and halfway to the horizon while I sit here with my thumb up my ass, nursing a dream hangover, with nothing to do but fill out expense accounts while Rome burns.

Pull yourself together, I tell myself.

Once you start managing other people, you can't control every aspect of how they do their jobs or keep yourself informed on everything that's going on. I'm supposed to be taking on a managerial role, for very small values of management (Look at me! I've got two contractors working for me! Whoop-de-do!) and I should bloody well stop trying to act like an over-stressed prima donna and start doing my job.

Beginning with sending Lockhart a brief sitrep, an expenses update, and a revised estimate on when I expect to have something concrete to report—

There's a knock at the door.

I'm not expecting anyone, the room's made up, and it's evening: all this passes through my head before I'm even off the bed.

I'm halfway to the vestibule, the narrow corridor running past the bathroom to the doorway, when I hear a rattle, then the thud of the door coming up against the security chain. For a moment I think I'm hallucinating: in the back of my head I'm hearing the crunching, munching sound of brain cells dying in the skulls on the other side of the portal, their waiting bodies occupied and animated by something blind and segmented and possessed of a vast, unthinking faith.

Possessed. Not human anymore. These aren't the feeders in the night; I'd recognize those guys anywhere. These are something else. *They seek and they save—*

(Where am I getting this from?)

"Who's there?" I ask aloud.

"Hotel security. Open up."

There's something wrong with his voice, as if he's speaking around a mouthful of chopped liver. I mutter a macro in High Enochian, a pre-canned invocation that will open up my inner ear and let me listen again, eavesdropping on what's left of his mind with a corner of my own consciousness that was only fully awakened last summer, and this is what I get:

A vast and wistful inner peace has stilled the fragmentary thoughts of the once-frightened human vessel. He knows he's Saved, for he has eaten the blood and the body of Christ—and the host trans-substantiated into something that has in turn eaten his mind. He isn't alone, he has a companion in arms. They are barely separate individuals anymore, for their hosts bind them together and control them. They're united not merely by a common mission but a shared hunger for salvation. They want to help me. They're *dying* to help me. And they've been sent here to help me find a friend in Jesus.

I left my phone and my warrant card beside the laptop on the table, didn't I? *I'm going to have to do this myself,* I realize queasily.

"Open *up*," says the seeker, its voice breaking into a very inhuman rasp.

I crunch down on them hard and fast, and I feel their savior-damped fears and needs stab at the edges of my mind like shell splinters as I engulf their shattered minds swiftly, a squid reaping a pair of unwary crabs from the seabed.

There is a heavy double-thud from the corridor. My stomach lurches. I feel queasy: bloated and simultaneously light-headed as I unhook the security chain and open the door.

Two men lie on the beige hotel carpet, looking for all the world as if they've just decided to take a nap. White shirts, black suits, black ties, like they came to audition for a role in *Reservoir Dogs: The Musical.* Focussing on the discreet cross lapel pins I see no motion: they aren't breathing. *My bad.* I grab the nearest arm and pull; his jacket spills open, revealing a leather holster nestled in his armpit. I pull harder. Corpses are heavy, but I keep dragging until he's well inside the doorway, then force myself to go back for the other one. I feel numb, like my emotions are wrapped in cotton wool. It's not as if I murdered them—they barely had enough soul left to keep their bodies breathing and responsive—but I still feel responsible. Most of what was left of their minds was given over to experiencing a weird ecstatic rush of surrender, a feeling of being *saved.* I don't think it's any kind of salvation that Pete the Vicar would recognize, though.

I get the door shut and chained and I'm just about to fire up the corporate intranet and look up the regulations for dealing with the metabolically challenged when the jaws of the nearest stiff begin to open. His cheeks distend and something begins to pulse in his throat—almost as if he's getting ready to vomit. Except he's dead. (Actually he's been soul-dead for weeks, if not months, but that didn't stop him walking around.) Now it looks as if the death of the body isn't any kind of obstacle to indigestion. I watch, repelled, as something forces its way out through the corpse's lips: a pale white head, eyeless, with whiskery antennae, followed by a segmented body with tiny little legs. *It* isn't dead, and I can feel its tiny little mind searching—an atom of desperate awareness, eternally hungry, seeking a soul to save—

I rush to the desk and grab the shitty Dell laptop, moving so fast I'm not consciously aware of my actions until afterwards. Then I look at the splattered mess I've created, and the bodies, and an abrupt wave of nausea seizes me. I make it to the toilet ahead of the dry heaves, then realize with a sense of near-panic that there are *two* parasites and I only had the one computer, and now it's all broken and covered in blood and bits of the giant isopod from hell. (Fucking netbooks; you can't even use one to beat an alien brain parasite to death without it breaking.)

Luckily there's a trash can in the bathroom. I carry it back into the hotel room, where the second savior is just pulling its whip-tail free of its deceased victim's jaws. It leads me a merry chase around the desk for a minute or two, but I have the tongs from the hotel ice bucket, and it does not; eventually I get it in the can, and weight the lid down with one of the missionary's pistols.

I sit down, breathing heavily. This is not good. Above and beyond the whole self-defense thing—and I'm going to sleep badly over that, even though they were soul-dead to begin with—it opens a giant can of worms. Someone sent these things to . . . well, given what was on their tiny minds I'm fairly sure they weren't just going to try and sell me a subscription to *The Watchtower*. But what worries me is *who* sent them. It appears Golden Promise Ministries have been alerted to my presence.

Which in turn leads me to wonder: What if my tigers have run into a big game hunter?

IT'S LATE AFTERNOON. THE SKY IS THE COLOR OF STONE AND occasional fat snowflakes drift below the street lights, glistening as they melt before they reach the sidewalk.

Johnny has spent the day patrolling the exit routes he has carefully laid out for Persephone. Tomorrow, if all goes well, he'll see about dropping in on one of Schiller's church's public services; but first it's his job to ensure that Persephone's needs are covered.

Each of the rented apartments is kitted out with the necessities for either a short or a long stay: fast food, sterile prepaid mobile phones, a couple of off-the-shelf outfits—weekend-casual and office drag—and medical kits. But that's not enough. He's also keeping an eye on the safe houses, checking for surveillance, nosy neighbors, environmental hazards like crack houses and off-duty cops. And he's checking out each house in turn, driving from one to the next and watching from down the street. Lamplighting, the spooks call it; attending a single safe house is usually rated a full-time job, but Johnny's got three lamps to tend, in different cities. He's driven maybe two hundred miles today, back and forth between Denver and Colorado Springs and Pinecrest, and he's almost sufficiently fucked off with the job to phone that geeky bureaucrat guy and set him to work. (Howard wants to help? *Let* him.)

He's driving back towards the safe house in Washington Park when he realizes that he's being tailed.

It's not a new sensation for Johnny, but it's always unwelcome. A crawling on the back of the neck, awareness that there are at least one set of headlights behind him that are keeping their distance—he experiments, taking an exit fast and a right turn on a red light, and the lights follow.

Johnny's lips peel back silently in something like a smile. This boring legwork is his least favorite part of the job (though he'd rather die than admit as much to the Duchess while she's depending on him). He's more than ready for a rumble, though he's professional enough not to seek one out while he's on a job, but if someone *asks* him for one—*Got you, my son,* he thinks at the lights in his mirror, and looks for a suitable location.

He passes an alleyway between two shuttered brick-and-steel shops in a block that shows little sign of night life. Half a mile later Johnny circles and turns back towards it, slowing. He indicates in plenty of time, then noses into the alley and kills his lights. His vehicle is a stick-shift pickup with a big block engine, selected specifically for its ability to carry out maneuvers like the one he's about to pull; and he's already disabled the airbags and the reversing light. Johnny believes in living dangerously.

There are lights in his mirror, approaching. Still rolling forward, Johnny slams the truck into reverse, guns the engine, and smokes the clutch. The truck lurches to a standstill and rolls backwards without stalling. It's got enough torque to haul a ten-ton trailer; the clutch is probably glowing cherry-red. There's a crunch, more felt than heard, and he lets his headrest absorb the impact. Then he's out of the cab and into the alley before the engine stops.

He finds the driver of the crunched car beating back the airbag and struggling with his door, swearing. Johnny tuts admiringly as he scans the passenger seats and the alleyway for spectators; the pickup's trailer hitch has done a real number on the radiator of the tail car—a Neon, now bleeding out between a pair of overflowing dumpsters. He yanks on the door handle with his left hand, holding his weapon where the driver can see it. "Hands on top of the wheel," he says, taking care to speak clearly and loudly. "Where I can see 'em."

The driver freezes, an expression of profound disgust on his rabbit-like face. "Jesus, Johnny," he whines, "whatcha have to do *that* for?"

Johnny squints at the driver. "Patrick?" Sixty-something, with white receding hair and a salt-and-pepper beard, he's a dead ringer for a certain former associate of the Network. Johnny takes a step back—ensuring his knife is out of range of a quick grab—glances up and down the alleyway, then turns back to the driver. "Small world, mate." An old and unwelcome memory prompts him: "Show us yer tongue."

"Yer wot?" Patrick looks genuinely perplexed.

"Like this." Johnny sticks his tongue out at Patrick, rolls it. "Do it. *Now.*"

"Sure." Patrick looks disgusted, but does as he's told; his tongue is clearly normal. "What's that about, for the love of God?"

Johnny sighs. "Why were you following me?"

"I just saw you drive past and recognized—"

"No, Pat. I don't have time. Listen, I'm doing you a favor just letting you talk. But I don't have forever. Tell me the truth, okay? Who are you working for?"

Patrick's fingers tighten on the steering wheel. For a moment, under the shadows cast by the street lights, he looks a century older than his age. "The Nazgûl."

Johnny wears a couple of small wards in a leather bag on a cord round his neck, tucked under his check shirt. One of them should— just over ninety-four percent of the time, to within two standard deviations—prick him when someone is lying to him with malice in mind. It is quiescent in the face of Patrick's quiet despair. "Well, mate, this is yer lucky day." Johnny lowers his knife.

Patrick's eyes widen. "I don't understand. What's with waving that thing at me if you're not—"

"Case of mistaken identity: we're not the only players in town." Johnny scans the alley again. "Tell you what: let's you and me go some- where an' catch up on the news over a cup of tea. It'll be just like old times again. You on, mate?" Patrick is, in truth, not exactly the rumble Johnny was looking for. His pulse slows, adrenaline rush receding.

"What about me car? That's me wife's wheels you fucking minced." The airbag is deflating slowly; Patrick slowly eases out of the driver's seat, wincing. "Jesus Mary, my fucking *knee* . . ."

"Wipe the steering wheel and leave it. You've got triple-A? You can call it in as stolen later. Do me right and I'll front you the dosh for repairs."

Patrick raises his hands in a gesture of surrender. "Okay, Sarge, you win." That was Johnny's tag in the Network: it brings back a rush of memories, not all of them welcome. "You're not angry with me?"

Johnny shakes his head. "Climb in the cab. Front seat." He walks round the pickup, opens the driver's door. "The Nazgûl. You freelanc- ing? Expensing?"

Patrick climbs up into the high cab slowly, wincing. "They're paying Moira's medical bills."

"How is she?" Johnny asks, checking his mirrors and turning over the engine. He's never met Patrick's other half, but it's the right ques- tion to ask when you're building trust prior to a debrief.

"Cancer." Patrick's voice is flat. "'Ad it for three years. You know 'ow it is over here."

"Jesus, Pat." The truck jolts forward with a screech of fiberglass and metal. Johnny sees Patrick wince, checks the rearview to ensure the Neon's bumper isn't still fouling the tow hook. "Why didn't you go home?"

"She's got family on this side of the pond." Patrick closes his eyes. "Like I said, the Black Chamber offers a generous medical insurance package. Even for stringers."

Johnny reaches out sideways without taking his eye off the alley and takes Patrick's left wrist. It's bony, the skin loose as a chicken carcass; he rotates it, glances sidelong at the symbol tattooed there. It's quiescent right now. He lets go. "Jesus, Patrick," he says softly. "How long?"

"Two years. It was that, or bankruptcy and no high-quality chemo for Moira."

Johnny does not want to hear this, so he leans forward, scanning, as he guides the big truck down the narrow alleyway. Putting a human face on the oppo is never welcome: it feels like staring into a bathroom mirror and seeing a skull. Learning that an old workmate has taken the Dark Mark—signed on as a freelance stringer for the Black Chamber's mind-riders to spy through—is harsh; that he's done it for the love of a good woman is all the worse, like a moral bullet to the kneecap.

At the end of the alleyway there's a car park and a row of dumpsters. Johnny slides the pickup round and out towards the street exit on the far side. Pulling out into the traffic he asks, "What do the Nazgûl want with me, Pat?"

There's a pause. Then, "Mister McTavish. What are you doing in Denver?"

The voice is Patrick's, but it speaks with a Midwestern twang quite unlike his Northern Irish tenor. The other ward around Johnny's neck is suddenly choking and hot, gripping tight; there's a pale violet light in the cab, coming from the vicinity of Patrick's wrist.

"Cut that out: I'm not your bitch." Johnny's hands clench the wheel, but his mind is abruptly calm. He's got his rumble; the potential for collateral damage is simply an unwelcome addition.

"You are on our soil. Under normal circumstances that makes you my bitch."

"You want to talk to me, get a fucking cellphone." Johnny pauses. "What precisely do you mean, *normal* circumstances?"

A laugh forces itself out of Patrick's larynx, followed by a wheezing series of coughs. "You will tell us who sent you here."

"Nobody sent me." Johnny slows, seeking a parking space. He's acutely aware of the sleeping, hungry knives holstered inside his jacket, a million miles from the hand that grips the gear stick.

"You are here with your mistress, Persephone Hazard, who is inside the Omega Ministries' compound." The creature that animates Patrick's body speaks assertively. "This we know. Eight hours after your arrival, an agent of the British Special Operations Executive also arrived in Denver. You were observed together."

Johnny pulls over, kills the engine, and switches off the lights. He turns to face Patrick's body. "Why are you telling me this?" He demands. As he turns, he palms a small item from beneath the steering column. "Who are you?"

"We are Control." The amber glare of the street lamps casts deep shadows across Patrick's face, but not so deep that Johnny can't see the faint fluorescent trails writhing in the empty gaze. "The unblinking, red-rimmed eye, as Peter Jackson frames it. We see everything we look for. Usually."

Johnny waits. The pressure on his ward is oppressive: he can feel it around him, as dark and implacable as the waters of the Challenger Deep, a chilly, soul-crushing dread.

"But we cannot see your mistress. And now that we know where to look, we cannot see inside the Omega Ministries' domain."

"You're having trouble seeing—" Johnny stops. (*The Black Chamber* is having trouble with remote viewing? Is there some grit in the unblinking panopticon gaze? Or a detached retina?) "What do you want?"

"We want. Co-operation. Yours, mostly. Freely given."

Johnny chuckles nastily: "Fuck off." His grip tightens on the item he palmed. Control has got Patrick. It's a dilemma. Usually he wouldn't think twice about doing the necessary, but there's no telling what happens to the mount after the rider departs. "You've got assets. Use them yourself. Like I said, I'm not your bitch."

There is a pause. "Normally we would. And we'd deal with you later." A longer pause. "First we could not see within the Omega Ministries. Now the area of darkness is growing. Colorado Springs is closed to us. Denver is dimming. Our hands are numb and cannot grip." Control's tone is chilly. "Are you Born Again, Mister McTavish? Are you willing to bend your neck to the yoke of Raymond Schiller's master?"

"Are you telling me you've lost your grip?"

"That depends on the meaning of the word 'lost.'" For a moment Control sounds uncertain. "We are experiencing difficulty conducting operations in north-central Colorado. There is an unnatural storm system to the north that formed overnight, a weather bomb. Flights are diverted, road checkpoints are established. The FBI office in Denver reports that all is quiet on the western front, but pools of darkness expand and the gripping hand is paralyzed."

The pressure on Johnny's ward relaxes a little, and he takes a deep breath. "You think Schiller is to blame? What's he doing? Begun one of the great summonings?"

"Find out, Mister McTavish. Write us a letter, a full and frank report, or tell your friend O'Donnell here. Either way: inform us, let us know what you discover. Be of use to us and we will have no reason to take exception to your presence in our backyard. You have three days. Use them wisely."

Of an instant the oppressive sense of dread vanishes. Johnny lashes out, pulling the compact taser just short of Patrick's sallow face. It's not his favorite weapon, but it's safer—probably. For an uncertain moment he wonders if he's making a deadly error. But the faint glow in Pat's eyes has gone; he slumps forward against his seat belt, then begins to shake and twitch uncontrollably.

Johnny safes the taser hastily, then flips it around, using it as a wedge to separate Patrick's teeth: the fit only lasts a few seconds, but by the time it's over Johnny has crossed a line in his own head. Sometimes people do good things for bad reasons, and sometimes people do bad things for good reasons. He isn't sure which this is yet, but he's hoping for the former.

PERSEPHONE GLANCES SIDELONG AT HER MOUSY GUIDE: *bellwether*, she thinks. The scene is crystal clear. The guards holding the struggling sacrificial victim down wear black wind-cheaters emblazoned with the oracular runes *FBI*. They've got sidearms. There are another twenty congregants—everyone from the course, and a few besides—and the church pastors. Heads are turning. Behind her, a windowless tunnel. Fire doors. Her heart skips a beat as she takes a short step backwards. "Sorry, honey," she says to Roseanne or Lisa or whoever her guide is, and punches her over one kidney: the woman stumbles into the underground chapel as the struggling victim rams his forehead into his guard's nose in a classic Glasgow kiss. The other FBI man sidesteps his follow-through kick sharply and is already pulling a pistol as Persephone skips back two steps and slams her elbow into the glass cover of the fire alarm.

The doors slam shut as the siren winds up to a screech. The emergency lights come on, illuminating the route of her sprint.

She makes it up to the first floor in a breathless run and barely breaks stride as she hits the crash bar on the fire exit. The door opens, and she finds herself on one side of the church, on a concrete path winding between deep-frozen snow piles around the side of another windowless building. She trots to the end of the path, then cuts back to a fast walk, composing herself, trying to look unobtrusive. *Don't draw attention.* Icy cold, she's working on her evacuation route. *At least sixty seconds before they fan out and start looking for me.* The prisoners . . . she winces. But they're the least of her problems. She's blown her cover. What was going on in that chapel was worse than anything even Johnny had feared. *Better warn him as soon as possible, before I use the safe house and wheels.* Just in case.

The church complex sits at one side of a street. Opposite it squats a two-story building, low and wide, with glass windows through which she can see brightly colored posters on the walls. There are desks and chairs: perhaps it's a primary school or kindergarten. It's Saturday, though. Persephone trots across the street, round the unfenced side of the school, and up the wooded slope behind it. There's snow on the ground which will show her tracks—very bad. She can hear alarms now, and a quick glance shows her the other fire doors opening, people spilling out. She turns to ignore them and slides her shoes off—the two-inch heels are no good off the beaten track—then breaks back into a run.

Elapsed time: two minutes. She's past the school, coming up behind another building. It's three stories high with a complex spaghetti-work of gas pipes and ducts behind it, just like a hospital or clinic. A big diesel generator and an enormous tank of fuel sit in readiness behind a chain-link fence, but the rear approach is clear and there are windows at ground level. A couple of them are open. She darts towards them, keeping low and using available ground cover—of which there is much, for the trees come almost all the way up to the building.

Observe, orient, decide, act: words to live or die by. Right now, Persephone is disoriented—on the run, cut off. It's time to go on the offensive, work out where she is and what's going on, then get the hell out of this trap.

Unlike Mr. Howard from Capital Laundry Services, she's seen the things in the silver salver before and knows *exactly* what they are, and by extension, the unplumbed depths of the cesspool in which she has so abruptly found herself treading water. And her day has just gone from normal to nightmare in sixty seconds.

PICTURE THIS: IT'S EARLY AFTERNOON IN A BLANDLY CORPO-rate hotel room in downtown Denver. There are two corpses lying on the floor in the middle of the room. An upturned bathroom waste bin sits on the floor nearby, its former steed's handgun holding it down. It rattles from time to time as the complaints department within expresses its opinion of the accommodation. I am sitting in the desk chair, drained by my exertions—both physical and mental—and taking a few minutes to assess my options.

Here's my situation: the bad guys know where I am. This is obviously undesirable. So this is my plan (which is mine, what I invented all by myself): I am going to run away, very fast. *Simples!*

There are minor complications, of course. First, I'm going to have to notify Lockhart, Hazard, and McTavish. Especially the latter two. Both of whom hung out a big *Do Not Disturb* sign last time I called them.

Second, there are the two corpses. Housekeeping are going to be very unhappy, and I don't think tipping high will cut any ice. I feel a bit sick whenever I think about what I did to them. They were, once upon a time, thinking, feeling human beings; by the time they came knocking on my door there wasn't much left inside them—understatement: they were little more than zombies that hadn't begun to smell—but that doesn't make me feel any better. I want to know for sure who sent them, and why.

(And when I find them I want to give the bastard who wrecked their minds a piece of *my* mind.)

I generally try not to jump to conclusions, but I'm willing to wave my little pinkie in the air and swear that they're not from the Black Chamber. The Black Chamber isn't big on Christianity. In fact, they treat it as a character flaw among their employees. Given that I'm over here to ride herd on an investigation into the Golden Promise Ministries, being doorstepped by a pair of armed Christian missionaries is all but definitive. So, I'm working on the assumption that Schiller sent them and that there's more to GPM than meets the eye.

Thirdly and finally, there's the thing in the bin—the complaints department. I don't know exactly what it is, but a quick look in Dead Guy #1's mouth—quick because I don't enjoy throwing up—shows that it's empty: nothing inside but a nub of scar tissue at the back of his mouth. And unless I'm suffering from auditory hallucinations, he *did* ask me to open the door. So the logical deduction is that the thing in the bucket is some kind of hideous parasite that does double-duty among the Jeezemoids; talk about speaking in tongues.

I need to know what they're capable of. So I'm going to have to contain it, bind it, and see what, if any, control one of these parasites can exert on a victim.

(Yes, I've seen *Invasion of the Body Snatchers*. I never imagined I'd find myself having to deal with an outbreak, but there's a first time for everything.)

First things first: call Lockhart. I reach for the hotel phone and punch in my special calling-card number.

"Hello, Garrison Fitzhugh estate agents. We're sorry, but the office is closed right now. Opening hours are 9 till 5, Monday to Friday. Please leave a message after the beep . . ."

Of course it's closed; it's 8 p.m. on a Saturday evening back home. I clear my throat. "This is Bob Howard. I'm in Denver and I want to talk to someone about a problem with my property. I can't contact the tenants and I just had a call from Environmental Health, who seemed to be upset about an infestation of giant wood lice"—there's no codeword for "alien brain parasite" so I make one up on the fly—"so anyway, I'm not sure how long I can fend them off. Please call back." I hang up. Hopefully that little zinger will rattle Lockhart's cage.

I'm busy doodling an intricate design on the inside of last night's pizza box lid with a conductive marker pen when the phone rings.

"Bob." It's Lockhart. "Sitrep, now."

"This is a hotel phone line."

"Are you in public?"

"No—"

"Sitrep. *Now.*" Going by his tone of voice he is just slightly stressed.

I tell him about the MIBs and the slater from hell that's scritching at the inside of the trash can. Phone codecs are designed to filter out the gaps between spoken words, but I can hear Lockhart's blood pressure rising all the way from London. When I finish, he's silent for a few moments. Then he lets me have it: "Your mission is over. I want you to book the next available flight out of the United States and fly home immediately. Between now and departure, go to ground."

"What about—"

"Bring the parasite if you can, but be ready to destroy it if anyone tries to interfere."

"I meant Hazard and McTavish—"

"Mr. Howard." He's clearly making an effort to sound calm, which is scary under the circumstances: "Let us be quite clear, your part of this operation is *over*. You've been compromised and there has been an abduction attempt. You're on a reconnaissance mission, not a search-and-destroy; that's sufficient justification for us to start making direct enquiries into the, ah, *situation* that certain outsiders were poking their noses into. It's also sufficient justification for you to run like hell and not look back, don't you think? It will be much easier for us to make those enquiries if you are on hand to file an eyewitness report, instead of filling a shallow grave somewhere in Colorado."

"Are you telling me to ditch BASHFUL INCENDIARY?"

A moment's hesitation: "Not exactly, Robert. But you told me they went to ground, and it seems to me that they are eminently capable of looking after themselves. I understand your natural loyalty, and it does you credit. If you can notify them that the operation is terminated, without risk to yourself, then you may do so. But it is impossible to over-emphasize the risk management aspect: we want you back here in one piece, and that is more important than anything else you can do in the field." Lockhart pauses again, as if someone is feeding him instructions. "I want twice-daily verbal reports and I want to see you in person within twenty-four hours. Is that understood?"

I stare at the phone as if it's grown bat wings and fangs. "I understand," I say. *I understand that you're telling me to leave the two contractors you made me responsible for to die in a train wreck*, is what I manage to keep back. *You cold bastard, you.*

"Good. Call me with an update tomorrow." The line goes dead.

I stare at the phone and stifle the urge to scream obscenities. It passes quickly enough, anyway: unprofessional, unproductive, and might attract unwanted attention. Nevertheless, my opinion of Lockhart has just taken a nosedive. Loyalty is—*has* to be—a two-way street in my line of work. This isn't a painful but basically survivable workplace situation like a lay-off or downsizing: Persephone and Johnny are out there right now, being stalked by walking corpses with parasites for tongues and heads full of revelation. If I don't do my damnedest to see them to safety, what does that say about me? Sure, Johnny is an over-muscled asshole with a disturbingly easy-going attitude to killing, and Persephone is just plain disturbing (a bizarre chimera, half sexy Eastwick witch and half KGB hit-woman) . . . but I feel responsible.

So I take a deep breath and go back to urgently doodling on the pizza box.

Summonings and containment grid, field-expedient, 101: if the thing you're trying to contain is pallid, has too many legs, and is about the size of a human tongue, a pizza box will do just *fine*. More to the point, I really want it to be locked down properly before I try using the tattoos to call Persephone or Johnny—it's a trophic eater, which means if it isn't securely contained when I call it'll be all over my frontal lobes like grease on a hamburger before I can say "oh shit."

I'm thinking on the fly, here. (Although now that I'm in middle management I think I'm supposed to call it "refactoring the strategic value proposition in real time with agile implementation," or, if I'm being honest, "making it up as I go along.") Revised plan: box up the complaints department, pack my bags, and go straight to the airport. All that's left is to call Persephone and Johnny, then pull the eject handle, get the hell out of Dodge City before it's too late, go home, and hide under the bed for a week of gibbering reaction time.

I finish doodling on the inside of the box, and collect a handy cable from my travel electronics kit. It's got a couple of pointy contacts; I stab these through various points on the diagram, and plug the other end into my JesusPhone. OFCUT does the rest, and I gingerly transfer the live summoning grid to the carpet in front of the bin.

The complaints department sets up a horrendous racket as I slide the grid under it. Then it stops, abruptly. I'm half-expecting a blue flash and a vile smell, but no such luck: looks like I've successfully contained it. I raise the bin gingerly, ready to slam it down if the many-legged monstrosity makes a bid for freedom. The thing is tightly curled in the middle of the grid, which is shimmering faintly—for all the world as if it's held in place by magic cling-film. Great; all I have to do now is refrain from dropping it.

I disconnect my phone, close the pizza box, and stuff it in the bottom of my go-bag. Then I massage my forehead and steel myself, anticipating pain. I pinch my arm over the relevant tattoo and go knock on her frontal lobes.

Busy.

She's aware of me and she's got the blinds turned down—I'm picking up nothing about her environment, just an icy half-amused, half-angry awareness that pursuit could show up at any moment.

I know, I send. ***I've been ordered to bug out. Do not pass Go, do not collect $200, get the first plane out, and run like hell.***

She doesn't seem to be surprised. My heart sinks.

I think you and Johnny should get out right now, I add.

Why do you think that?

Bad guys sent a wet team for me. They're possessed, some kind of parasite.

I know. She sends me a glimpse of my pizza-box horror, trapped writhing between silver tongs in some kind of ritual. My stomach flip-flops. ***I'm on the run; they were going to plant one of those things on me. I blew my cover. It's possible it was blown before I started, though: they may have tagged me right from the start, in London. Then saw me and Johnny and made the connection from him to you.***

I got a heads-up that the local police and security agencies are compromised and presumed hostile, I tell her. ***I warned Johnny about it.***

Understood. Keep your distance. I'll call Johnny in due course to plan our exit. I've got to go now.

And just like that she cuts me off.

I quickly shave and dress in my all-purpose suit—I may have to bluff my way past some desk pilots in the very near future and it doesn't hurt to look like a civil servant—and stuff one of the pistols in a pocket. Then I shovel the rest of my crap into the case and head for the lobby, leaving the *Do Not Disturb* sign hanging on the door handle.

Next stop: the airport.

10.

THINGS TO DO IN DENVER
WHEN YOU'RE DOOMED

AWKWARD SMALL TALK OVER STALE COFFEE: IT'S NOT HOW Johnny imagined catching up with his former associate, but Patrick is badly shaken and somewhat withdrawn. Johnny is short on time and urgently needs to draw him out, so coffee in an almost deserted Starbucks with a sullen, overweight barista pushing a mop around the floor is the order of the day.

"How long have you been in Denver?" he asks.

"Four years." Patrick's hand shakes as he tips a paper twist of sugar into his espresso. "More or less."

Not long after he left the Network, then. "And on their retainer?"

"About the same." Patrick falls silent for a moment as he concentrates on stirring his coffee with the ritual focus of a heroin addict cooking up the next hit. Not spilling a drop demands infinite patience. "They're bastards. But they look after you as long as you're useful."

"What do they want you to report on?"

"What you'd expect." Patrick half-shudders, half-shrugs. "We're up the highway from Colorado Springs. The holy rollers are big in Colorado. Mostly they're harmless, 'long as you're not a young woman in search of an abortion."

"And sometimes?"

Patrick grimaces. "If there's talk of miracles, wine out of water, speaking in tongues—they ask me to check out a service. It's a bad job, I can tell you, but usually it's boring. When it isn't"—he pauses long enough to pick up his cup with shaking hand—"I'm not there."

"Ever checked out an outfit called the Golden Promise Ministries? Out of Colorado Springs, run by a guy called Schiller?"

Patrick shakes his head. "Doesn't ring any bells."

Johnny keeps his thoughts to himself. Instead, he pulls out his wallet and, after a quick scan, counts out bills. "Here's five hundred. The number on this card is a burner: call me if you see anything that might interest your, uh, employers. Call me when you've got a repair bill for the car and I'll pay the garage for you."

Patrick stares at the pile of fifties. He reaches out and shakily pushes them back across the table. "Not playing that game, Johnny. I'll thank you for fixing my car, but you don't know what they're like. What they do to double agents."

It's Johnny's turn to stare. Then, after a few seconds, he shoves the money back towards Patrick. "Then it's my penance for spoiling your evening, mate. Call me when you've got the bill for the car."

Patrick stares at him, perplexed. "You can't fix everything that's broke with money, Sarge."

"I know. But money helps." Johnny knows exactly what's going through Patrick's mind: *What's happened to my old sarge, then?* He stands. He doesn't want to have to stay and explain. "At least I tried."

He walks out the door, moderately certain that this is the last time he'll ever see Patrick. It's cold, and a solitary snowflake spirals down in front of his face. He goes to his truck, climbs in, and starts the engine. *Maybe I should tell the Duchess,* he ponders. But there's no telling where he'll catch her; best get it sorted himself. He drives away slowly, with a head full of darkness and questions.

It is, perhaps, inevitable that his encounter with Patrick distracts him and leaves him in a disturbed state of mind: old ghosts swirl around just beyond the corners of his vision as he drives back towards the third safe house, less attentive than usual. But as he parks opposite, a pricking in the skin of his chest brings him sharply back to a state of alertness. *Something,* his sixth sense is telling him, *is wrong.*

It's too late to drive on, but—as usual—he hasn't parked directly outside the front door. Johnny stares at the safe house. The warning is worryingly nonspecific: the vague itching and sense of dread tells him nothing useful.

He slides out of the cab, keeping the truck between himself and the safe house windows. He leaves the door ajar as he rapidly scans the sidewalk, then breaks into a jog. The itch fades as he leaves the shadow of the pickup, just another local out for an evening run: it's amazing what people will miss if they're not watching carefully, and he didn't pick this neighborhood to site a safe house on the basis of its vibrant street life. Once out of the direct line of sight from the safe house he crosses the street, re-scans to make sure there are no bystanders, then doubles back. His nostrils flare as he ducks and glides around the side of the house.

There is a kitchen door that opens onto the backyard, and it has a well-oiled lock. The key turns silently. Johnny steals inside like a thief in the night, right hand drawn back and knife in hand. It's of a single piece, the blade oddly flat, the handle an extruded extension: a thing of power, lethal as a cobra. A gift from the Duchess, years ago. The kitchen is dark and still and just as he left it, the tripwire—actually an empty tumbler set on the floor just inside the door—still present; but his skin is prickling again. If there was an enemy already in the house it would be far more intense. *What if they aren't here yet?* Johnny stands up, then passes through the ground floor rooms silently and rapidly, ending just inside the front door. The pizza joint flyer he'd balanced against the front door when he left is still upright. *No, not here yet. Which means—*

There is a bright discordant jangle of shattering glass from the front window on the lounge, to the left of the vestibule he's standing in. Johnny turns, lowering his—*knife to a gunfight,* he absently realizes— as a familiar rattling hiss kicks in. *Gas grenade.*

He smiles, lips peeling back from teeth in a frightening grimace.

Johnny's got his fight.

*   *   *

PERSEPHONE USED TO HAVE NIGHTMARES, WHEN SHE WAS A
girl. Dreams that would drag her shuddering awake, drenched in a
clammy sweat, with her own shriek of terror echoing in her ears.

They always started the same way: with her waking in a hospital
ward, moonlit through unshuttered windows, surrounded by the living
dead.

They were living because they breathed in their sleep, lying cold and
motionless on beds with rusting steel frames, sheets drawn up to their
chins to cover the wounds and evulsions inflicted upon their bodies by
the metal of war. But they were dead, too, because they would never
wake. She could force herself out of bed inside these lucid dreams and
poke and pry at the sleepers, scream her lungs out into their cold blue
ears, to no avail.

There were always twenty beds on the ward, nineteen of them occupied by sleepers. Male and female, young and old, white-skinned and
sallow in the moonlight. She could run to the end of the ward—or fly,
at will—and there was a corridor, and on the other side of the corridor
another ward, another twenty beds. Up and down the corridor the
wards stretched towards a morbid vanishing point in the gloom. She'd
ventured into the corridor, once or twice, but the first few wards she
checked were all the same. And besides, she wasn't alone. She never actually *saw* the Watcher but she knew it was there; a lurking immanence
observing her increasingly frantic explorations, avoiding contact for
the time being as, suffused with a growing sense of panicky terror, she
cast about for relief from the infinite loneliness of the graveyard.

Curiously, it never occurred to her to gaze out through the windows
at the night world her dream had crash-landed in the midst of.

Years later, in her early teens, she'd shyly confessed these dreams
to her adoptive father. It was a tentative gesture of intimacy, as she
began to deconstruct the emotional barriers that she had erected during her childhood in the camps and on the long road out of Srebrenica.
Alberto had taken it seriously, not pooh-poohing it as teenage angst;
rather, he sat her down and delivered the first of a series of lectures on

the interpretation of dreams, with the aid of a copy of the *Liber di Mortuus Somnium.* "Precognitive dreams are not representations of a fixed future," he explained. "Rather, they're echoes of events which hold particular resonance, sufficient to overcome the barrier between now and then. They might not come true, and they are in any event symbolic, not literal predictions. But you should *always* take them seriously." Then he spent an afternoon with her, showing her how to make a dream catcher from cobwebs and feathers, and then how to program it as a screensaver on her Amiga; and she'd taught herself to sleep soundly without waking the rest of the household.

She never learned to like hospitals, though.

Now the night world has crashed through the window and landed in the ward of the dead in the mid-afternoon light, and it's Persephone's turn to be the watcher floating through the corridors, observing and monitoring with a cold knot of horror.

The open window is one of three at the end of a hospital ward bay. There are four beds on the bay: two are occupied. It's very quiet, but for the heartbeat beeping of monitors tracking pulse and ventilation rate. One of the inmates is sleeping, but the other woman follows Persephone's progress with frightened eyes.

Persephone tugs her skirt down, hitches her handbag strap up on her shoulder, reaches for a convenient lie, and offers a smile that doesn't reach the corners of her eyes. "Don't worry, I'm just taking a look around. Journalist."

She walks towards the door at the end of the bay, then pauses as two slivers of fact slice through her mind. There's a *door*. On a ward side-bay. You don't put doors between a patient and the nursing station if there's any risk of acute incidents. Doors are for privacy. And the woman's eyes are still watching Persephone, but her head—

She turns and walks back to the woman. Who lies utterly still on the bed, breathing but unmoving except for her eyes.

"Can you speak?" she asks quietly.

The woman—girl, almost: late teens, early twenties—blinks at her with horrified eyes, then begins to silently weep. Her lips move, as if in prayer. But her body lies still as if stunned, bedridden. Paralyzed. Persephone notices the sealed port of a nasogastric feeding tube nestling by one nostril. No wonder she can't talk: this is a long-term spinal injuries unit.

Persephone pulls her cameraphone out of her shoulder bag and captures the layout of the bay on a slow video scan. She spots the file by the head of the bed, medical notes. She has a queasy feeling. Something here is very wrong.

"You don't mind?" she asks, taking the file. The woman's eyes close. There's a name on the cover: *Marianne Murphy (23) Saved*. Persephone's brows furrow as she pages through the notes, reading and photographing the evidence. Yes, nasogastric feeding. Yes, physiotherapy. But, oddly, no medication. Nothing about vertebrae or spinal damage. Then Persephone comes to the ultrasound scan printouts. Images of a fetus, results of amniocentesis. Her skin crawls. She points her cameraphone at the woman. "Blink if you understand me?"

Marianne blinks. And now, Persephone realizes, the young woman has a name to her. "One blink for no, two for yes." *Blink, blink.* "Are you held here against your will?"

Blink, blink.

"You're pregnant, aren't you? Did they make you pregnant?"

Blink, blink.

"You're paralyzed. Was there an accident?"

Blink.

"Was it the ministry? They did this to you?"

Blink, blink.

The nightmare is solidifying around her. Persephone glances at the sleeper in the other bed, sees a nasogastric tube and a cervical collar to lock the woman's head in place. She can see what's happening here, although she's reluctant to acknowledge it: in the combined spinal injuries and maternity ward the women are prisoners in their own flesh, arrow factories for the full quivers of the theocratic movement. "'In sorrow thou shalt bring forth children,' is that what he said?"

Blink, blink.

Persephone swallows. Very gently, she reaches out and touches Marianne's forehead. "Can't stay. Got . . . got a story to tell. I'll put an end to this. I promise."

Blink, blink.

The crèches and kindergartens of a quiverfull movement, pious mothers raising bountiful families of young believers for the greater glory—ten and twenty children, far more children than most women can bear—need additional ammunition. So they look further afield, to the wombs of young unbelievers taken by the roadside, homeless runaways, addicts, prostitutes. Doubtless they've got a little list, of those who won't be missed. Bait the line, spread the net; carry them down to a quiet hell filled with hospital beds, where they'll be paralyzed and used like wasp-stung caterpillars to nurture their kidnapper's spawn. She can hear Schiller's apologetics echo in her mind's ear: *Nature is bountiful, nature gives us great examples of God's meticulous design for life, including certain parasitic insects—*

Persephone removes her finger, suppressing a shudder, suppressing thought, forcing her body into obedient calmness. She'd like to scream with rage, smash things, forget the job and rescue these women right now: it's a fatal temptation. But it would be a mistake. In fact, if she leaves behind any sign that she's been in this bay she will be signing their death warrants: Schiller will not suffer such witnesses to live and testify against him in Federal court. So she will be heartless and patient—for now.

There is a clipboard by the other woman's bed. She takes it and holds it to her chest. No spare stethoscopes or white coats, unfortunately; the clipboard will have to do. It's a Saturday, so the place should be running on weekend staff. Fifteen minutes have passed since she broke from Schiller's bid to brainwash his new recruits. The alarm will be out. Escape is going to be difficult: it's becoming clear that there is a lot more to this operation than just a rogue church.

She closes her eyes for a moment, composing herself and wiping the expression of feral loathing from her face. Then she opens the door and starts to search for an escape route.

The hospital, as it turns out, is running on a weekend shift pattern:

the wards are almost deserted except for the hunched, unmoving forms of the inmates. There are no televisions, she notes, but a number of bedside lecterns feature bibles that are open at particularly educational passages, displayed before the captured eyes of the bedridden. One of the bibles sits beside an empty bed; acting on impulse she takes it, tucks it beneath the elbow of the arm with which she carries the clipboard.

As she nears the end of the ground floor ward she approaches a nursing station. Two nurses—both women, in green scrubs—are discussing something. Persephone's breath catches, and she makes a peculiar gesture with the fingers of her left hand. Sounds flatten and footsteps fade away as she approaches the desk. Neither of them seem to notice her. It is Persephone's privilege and her burden, to shorten her life's extent in return for the grant of certain powers prearranged; it's not unlike smoking.

"—bed in bay six," one of them is saying. "And there's a prep kit in ward two up back—Ilene will be able to show you."

"When's this new arrival due?" asks the other.

"Not sure, he said there's been some problem—patient tried to run. Doesn't want to comply."

"Oh dear."

There's something wrong with their voices, Persephone notices, with the heightened perception that comes with her occult bargain. She should have noticed it before, the slightly mangled syllables of the believers. *It's the hosts*, she realizes with a frisson of revulsion.

"Well, you go and get the prep kit. I'll make sure the bed's ready when they capture her."

The taller nurse nods, then walks right past Persephone—unseen—in the direction of the lobby.

Persephone spins a blind spot in the remaining nurse's mind and hides within, holding her rage in check. She barely allows herself to breathe until they are alone in the room. Then she lets the shadows slip from her shoulders. "Hello," she says, smiling. "I don't suppose you'd let me borrow your car?"

The nurse stares, mouth opening to shout as Persephone brings the bible around sharply, spine-first, against the side of the woman's head, then drops it and grapples. It's not much of a fight. The nurse has no idea about self-defense, and Persephone has her face-down in a choke hold within seconds, closing her carotid arteries until she stops struggling. Persephone finds it takes a serious effort of will to relax her grip. She wants someone to pay for what's happening here so badly she can taste it.

There is an office off to one side of the reception area, into which Persephone drags her victim. As she begins to shake and snore, coming round, Persephone leans over her and, again, invokes one of her stored macros. An hour of life against a couple of days of deep unconsciousness and subsequent memory problems: a fair bargain, under the circumstances.

A couple of minutes later a woman in hospital scrubs steps out, carrying a shoulder bag. Nobody pays her any attention as she walks out to the two-story car park on the other side of the road from the maternity hospital. (Cameras and robot imaging systems might notice, but Schiller's people distrust what they see through a glass, darkly: and human eyes have difficulty noticing Persephone when she is willing to pay the price of moving unseen.) Neither does anybody pay any attention to the nurse who can't remember where she parked, walking up and down the rows of vehicles clicking her key-fob remote until finally a Toyota pickup clunks and flashes its lights in welcome.

Persephone climbs in, dumps her handbag on the passenger seat, and starts the engine. She doesn't bother with a seat belt, but on impulse checks the glove box. There's a box of ammunition and an odd-looking revolver within: a Chiappa Rhino snub-nose. Expensive and exotic for a nurse, but gunliness is clearly next to godliness for these folks. With a humorless grin she tucks her spoils into her handbag beside the bible.

Then, without any fuss or amateur dramatics, she drives away from her mission, the church compound, and the ward full of nightmares.

DENVER IS A MIDDLING-OLD CITY BY AMERICAN STANDARDS. Founded in the mid-nineteenth century, it's almost as old as the post office at the corner of my street. Most of it is trackless suburban sprawl, residential streets with no pavements for pedestrians alternating with uninhabited retail and industrial zones consisting of air-conditioned and mostly windowless boxes. It is, in short, uninhabitable without a car—except for a small chunk of downtown and the central business district. So my first job is to procure a set of wheels.

There's a Hertz rental agency in the basement of a hotel a couple of blocks away, according to my JesusPhone, so I walk over, shouldering my bag. "What have you got, right now?" I ask the woman at the desk.

"Huhlemmesee . . ." I can't tell if it's an accent or a speech impediment. She rattles away on a keyboard, pounding at a mainframe user interface that probably predates the dinosaurs. Then she frowns. "We're outa compacts and SUVs. Will a coop do?"

A *what*? I blink, then shrug. "How much?"

"The basic package is three-forty a day . . ." I shudder quietly, hand over the magic card, and hastily make some notes on my phone. I'm being robbed blind, of course. The basic package doesn't include insurance, fuel or satnav; by the time it's loaded up for a week (with an option on early drop-off at the airport) I'm looking at the thick end of a return business-class fare to Christchurch via Ulan Bator. "Sign here." I just hope Lockhart's going to approve this.

The car itself proves to be a coupé (rhymes with its typical owner's toupeé): a land-barge with a detachable plastic roof like an aging sales manager's hairpiece. It bears the same relationship to a sports car that a round of golf bears to a half marathon. I sling my bag—complete with sleeping horror—in the boot, plug my phone into the cigarette lighter, and fire up the anti-tracing app from OFCUT. It won't stop a chopper or a coordinated four-car tail team from following me, but it'll work against casual remote viewing. Then I hit the road.

After wrestling my way out of the car park (hopefully without leaving too many paint scrapes on the concrete pillars), I drive for miles beneath sullen clouds that weep a thin drizzle of sleet. The skyscrapers slowly give way to big box stores, drive-ins, streets of cookie-cutter houses, then finally scrub separating anonymous industrial units. More miles and I come to a highway with signage for the airport. Apparently it used to be a strategic bomber base—a flat pancake of snow-capped concrete stretching for kilometers in every direction.

I stick the car in a short-stay car park and head into the terminal, looking for the British Airways desk. It's the regular cattle market of check-in areas and retail concessions, leavened by more public art and shopping than usual for an American airport; there are a lot of delays flashing on the departure board, probably the better to cause the punters to part with their money, and the concourse is heaving with bewildered-looking travelers. I must have hit rush hour or something. It takes me a while to get oriented and home in on the desk. "Good evening," I start, then lay what I hope is a winning hand on the counter: my return open biz-class booking, a passport with a diplomatic visa, and the Coutts card. "I've been called back to London at short notice. What can you do for me?"

The clerk on the other side of the counter is clearly perturbed. "Would you mind waiting here for a minute, sir? I'd like to fetch my manager." *Oops, not good.* Any one of those cards should be sufficient to trigger a bowing and scraping reflex. I nod, and while her back's turned I pull out my wallet and palm my fourth and final card, just in case. The skin on the back of my neck is itching: every time an airport cop walks past I have to forcibly suppress the urge to stare.

A few seconds later she's back, with an older BA staff member in tow—this one wearing the kind of uniform suit that says "management." "Excuse me, sir," she says, assertive with a side order of London accent that's barely been here long enough to go native, "I'm told you need to rebook a ticket?"

I smile at her without showing my teeth. "Not exactly." *Open passport, display visa.* "Head Office want me home on the next available flight. I was *hoping* to rebook my ticket"—*tap finger on full-fat business class booking confirmation*—"or, failing that, perhaps you could arrange something? Via corporate?" *Wave platinum card.* Her eyes are tracking my fingers but her expression is saying something else.

"I'm *really* sorry, sir," she says, looking as if she means it, "I'd love to sort you out, and normally it wouldn't be a problem, but all departures are grounded as of an hour ago."

"What?" I can't help myself.

"It's the incoming weather system. There's a huge storm coming down from Canada and it's threatening to drop twenty or thirty inches of snow on us overnight; as if that isn't enough, there's a tornado warning out. It's a weather bomb. They're still landing inbound flights, but nothing's going out before tomorrow at the earliest, and between you and me I reckon the airport will be closed until early afternoon, if not all day, if that ice storm is as bad as they're saying."

I show my teeth, but keep my warrant card back. "Are you *sure*? Is it possible to charter a bizjet? Just to one of the main hubs, I mean, not all the way to Heathrow."

She's shaking her head. "I'm sorry, sir, but *nothing's* moving. They're even grounding the traffic news helicopters. It'll be the rescue and air ambulance services next. Never seen anything like it. If you want, I can—let's see, I can bump you to first class standby on the next available flight, and if you leave your cell number with me I can—"

I shake my head. "Don't worry," I say. "I'll drive out." And I gather up my papers and leave before she can get started on arguing me out of the idea because I'm afraid she might be right: driving through an apocalyptic ice storm in a convertible isn't the smartest thing I've ever done.

However, I do not get a chance to maroon myself in the Rockies in the middle of a blizzard.

It's not for want of trying, but as I drive out of the airport the snow is beginning to fall. I turn on the windscreen wipers and headlights and turn east, out along the interstate. Traffic is surprisingly light in both directions. Then, after about five miles the traffic begins to thicken up and I see flashing lights ahead. A couple of highway patrol cars are drawn up across the road, light bars strobing, and the cops are out with illuminated batons, waving cars over to one side for an inspection—

No, it's an off-ramp. I slow, going where I'm directed. They don't wave me over, but keep pointing around the curve of the cloverleaf. *More* cops. *Another* diversion. I realize what's going on just before I hit the next cloverleaf. There's nobody behind me, so I slow and wind down my window.

The cop with the light waves at me, then points on in the direction of the on-ramp back onto the highway in the direction of Denver.

"What's happening?" I call. (Just another guy in a suit driving a mid-range coupé: not a target.)

"Road's closed," he yells. "Git moving."

I have no desire to stop and argue with the Colorado highway patrol, so I just nod and keep rolling. The air outside my bubble of rental luxury is frigid; I roll up the window and accelerate back up to highway speed, thinking furiously.

Once upon a time an intelligence officer said, *Once is happenstance, twice is coincidence, three times is enemy action.* I'm not an idiot: I can see the pattern here. First I was doorstepped by the opposition, then I was ordered to scram; meanwhile all flights out of Denver are grounded by an anomalous ice storm, and the cops are closing the roads out of town. Is Schiller really that powerful? The evidence suggests he might be: Lockhart says he has the FBI and local cops in his pocket, and I'm having bad dreams about the Sleeper. Maybe that last one is a coincidence, but if I were a betting man I'd put money on the other stuff being pieces of a really unpleasant jigsaw. I've seen anomalous bad weather before, triggered by a greater invocation—

Oh. Oh *shit*. I do so very badly hope I'm wrong about this.

IT'S LATE AFTERNOON; THE SHADOWS ARE DRAWING IN.

Persephone drives away from the back roads of Pike National Forest without looking in the rearview mirror. Her knuckles are white on the steering wheel. She doesn't un-tense them until she hits US85 and sees the long chain-link fence and open spaces of the Air Force Academy unwinding to her left. She's badly rattled: angry and shaken. It's an unpleasant sensation, familiar from her half-forgotten childhood, and one she has carefully structured her life to suppress. *I fucked up,* she realizes coldly. Schiller's people are on the ball, and if she hadn't cut and run she'd be in that chapel even now, gulping down the choking wine like blood as the host holds unholy communion with her brain. It's anybody's guess whether Johnny is still free; she's torn between the urge to contact him immediately and warn him, and the fear that she'll catch him in the middle of a ruck and spoil his aim. Either way it'll have to wait until she's far enough from her pursuers to stop for a few minutes.

She forces her emotions back under control as she drives, performing the comforting rituals of scan and evasion with eyes wide open for any hint of pursuit. The sky is gray, almost yellowing, promising bad weather. As the miles unroll behind her, her pulse slows to normal and her grip relaxes slightly. She chews over the day's events, trying to make sense of them. The church compound and the clinic in the hills, the ghastly combined spinal injuries and maternity ward, the rite of holy communion with unholy parasites, born again in control of their victims' nervous systems. They're all parts of a vile jigsaw puzzle, but she has a distinct sense that she's missing something. "What are they trying to achieve?" she asks aloud. "What does Ray think he's *doing*?"

Normally she'd be asking these questions of Johnny. She punches the hub of the steering wheel lightly.

"What did he say . . ." *Why aren't we saving them?*

Schiller clearly believes his own spiel. And he's a man with a mission—literally as much as figuratively. "Let's assume he's serious," she murmurs to herself. "He believes his God is coming back to ring down the curtain on the day of judgment imminently. He knows *he's* saved, but most people are going straight to hell. And let's also suppose that he isn't just a sociopath milking a money machine. He's making all that money because he's got something to spend it on. He's going to want to"—her eyes widen—"save *everybody*, by any means necessary." She glances sideways by long force of habit, taking in the passenger seat, empty but for an open handbag holding a book and a gun.

Traffic is thickening ahead; for a while she focusses on the brake lights. The exit for Fort Carson comes into view—nearly there. During a slow patch she pulls out the book, lays it in her lap, and steals glances at it as she pushes her way into the right-hand lane, eyes scanning for exit 141. The clouds are darkening, and occasional snowflakes are hitting her windscreen. The book is a bible, of course. Leather cover, gilt trim, heavily thumbed, with numerous bookmarks poking out like angry porcupine spines near the back cover. "Revelation. Figures." The exit sign slides into view and she takes the exit ramp as fast as she can, then turns north to lose herself in the dusty tree-lined suburbs of Colorado Springs.

There is a quiet residential street, fronted by trees that separate tidily maintained houses at hundred-meter intervals. A relatively small church with a stone-clad steeple anchors one end of the stretch. Persephone drives past it a short distance, then parks. Swallowing bitterness at the back of her throat, she lifts her left leg and rips the blister plaster from the back of her ankle to reveal a temporary tattoo.

Come in, Johnny.

There's an acrid choking stink at the back of her throat, garlic mixed with stale vomit. Persephone gags, feeling muscles spasming, legs pumping. ***Not now, Duchess. Got my hands full.***

"Shit." She drops the link into his head, eyes streaming with the burning itch of an allergic reaction. *Tear gas?* She thumps the steering wheel, angry at her inability to help him. Johnny is up to his eyeballs, the man from the Laundry is bugging out—not without good reason, she admits—and the Golden Promise Ministries is something far worse than they had any reason to suspect back in London. Neither a money machine nor a mere front for occult cultists: it's shaping up to be an enormous clusterfuck. If she had any common sense she'd follow Mr. Howard's advice, collect Johnny, and get out of town.

But she can't shed that childhood nightmare. Can't forget the young woman's eyes tracking her from the bed, trapped in a prison of her own flesh.

Sticking plaster: nail file: a transient pain. To her (immediately suppressed) surprise she's seeing through Howard's eyes. Clearly he isn't terribly experienced at this mode of communication. He's driving, through falling snow on an interstate. She has a sense of confusion and building worry, even anxiety. A road sign looms out of the murky twilight: DENVER. He's driving back towards Denver?—that doesn't make any sense—

Hello again.

He's noticed her. Noticed her and let her think he hadn't. *Watch yourself,* Persephone reminds herself.

Got problems. Johnny's in trouble.

That's not the only problem. Howard's anxiety is infectious. ***The airport's closed by this damn storm, and the highway patrol have blocked Interstate 76. They're diverting all traffic back into town. I'm going to try Interstate 70 to Kansas City, but I've got a bad feeling about this.***

What storm?

There's a really scary weather system coming down from the north. It blew up overnight without any warning. They're talking about most of a meter of snow in the next twenty-four hours or so. Can you spell Fimbulwinter?

Can't be. You're completely cut off?

I won't know until I've tried the other routes, but I think so. What's your situation?

I'm parked up in Colorado Springs. It's not snowing here yet. Johnny's in trouble and I think at least one of our safe houses has been burned.

She bites her tongue, about to raise a delicate topic, but Howard beats her to the punch.

Tell me where you are and I'll come and pick you up. Then we can go find Johnny and get the hell out of here together.

Agreed, she sends, squashing her instant burst of relief.

Then she settles down to wait, and opens the Bible to the first of the bookmarked pages.

11.

THE APOCALYPSE CODEX

⌨

A DOOR IN A DARKENED HALLWAY: TO EITHER SIDE OTHER doors open onto rooms with front-facing windows. A grenade, fizzing acrid fumes from both ends, has just crashed through the window of the day room to the left and is spinning around on the floor like a dying hornet the size of a coke can. Then something heavy slams against the front door, nearly but not quite strong enough to take it off its hinges.

What do you do if you're Johnny McTavish?

You close your eyes.

Johnny braces himself facing the front door, shuts his eyes, and puts his hands together as if in prayer. Between them he cradles a tightly folded sheet of rice paper. Within its folds sits a small RFID chip, pasted to the middle of a design inscribed upon it in conductive ink.

He feels a familiar presence at the back of his head, just as another crashing impact sends the door flying open. Johnny pulls his palms apart. ***Not now, Duchess, I've got my hands full.*** The silence is broken by the hissing of the gas grenade.

Johnny takes a step backwards, and opens his eyes—still holding his breath.

The door hangs open and the fully expanded paper chain lies on the hall floor. Of the attackers there is no visible sign—the paper chain has done its job. He stoops, picking it up gingerly by both ends, then runs forward through the open entrance, holding his breath as he passes the day room doorway (through which a thin mist is drifting). There's nobody out front, but a crew cab pickup with blacked-out side windows and a boxy cargo container on the load bed is drawn up on the street. Glancing sideways, Johnny darts past the pickup, pausing only to bend and slash at the tires. Then he jogs towards his own wheels, not looking back.

(Johnny expects there to be a second pair of operatives around the back of the safe house, and he's got maybe thirty seconds before they stop waiting for the prey to come to them and storm the house in search of their fellows—but by then Johnny intends to be gone.)

The chain sags heavily on the passenger seat as he climbs in and starts the engine. Revving, he slams the truck into second gear and pulls out without lights. As he leans forward over the wheel there's an unwelcome and familiar metallic rattle from behind him. For a moment he's livid with indignation: *What do the fuckers think they're doing, shooting in a residential neighborhood?* Then he clocks it as a hopeful sign—they wouldn't be hitting his tailgate if they were firing on the move—and rams the truck into third. There are no more bullet impacts; he brakes hard, takes a left without signaling, checks his mirrors, and finally turns on his lights when a passing car flashes its high beams at him. It wouldn't do to get stopped by the traffic cops, not with what's sitting on the passenger seat . . .

The paper chain rattles, like the echo of an occult manacle that immobilizes a pair of angry ghosts. But these two aren't ghosts yet, and it's already starting to ripple and distort; there isn't a lot of power in the ward, and sooner or later it's going to degrade, at which point the two game beaters trapped inside it are going to get out. When that happens, Johnny intends to be ready for them. It wouldn't do to find out the hard way that they've got more tear gas grenades where that first one came from.

The downtown Denver safe house has been burned, which means—

if the opposition are halfway competent—that the other two are also compromised. On the other hand, it's a weekday evening, there is a light snowfall, and suburbia beckons. Johnny drives, looking for a certain kind of street, one with too many *For Sale / To Let* signs, too few lit windows and parked cars, unkempt lawns, foreclosed mortgages: the stench of neglect and decay. It's not easy, to be sure, because real estate agents like to hide such signs (they pay landscapers to mow the lawns of empty houses) but he has a nose for the wild places and, presently, he finds a side road where half the street lights are dead and the potholes are unfilled. Slowing, he inspects the houses to either side as he drives. He's after a specific type of vacant property—one with boarded-up windows and a backyard to park in, unobserved by neighbors.

"Just like that caper in Barcelona, Duchess," he mutters to himself as he pulls over, checks for passers-by, then does a three-point turn and drives into the yard of the house he's selected. "Had a bad feeling about that one, too."

The snow in front of it is unswept, pristine; the windows boarded over. He rummages in the back of the cab for a laminated card proclaiming *Big John's Real Estate Services*, lays it on the dash—often the simplest covers are the best—and heads for the front door.

The lock is easy. Once inside, Johnny pulls out a compact LED lantern and closes the door behind him. The house is dark and chilly as a pub toilet after closing time: the electricity is shut off and there's a smell of mildew in the air. It's just right for what he's here to do. So many of the significant events of his career take place in rooms like these, cold and abandoned. He goes through into the combined kitchen-dining room. There's junk strewn all over, and dust. A row of open cupboard doors gape at him like broken teeth in a screaming mouth as he kicks shattered crockery and rotting junk mail aside to reveal the wooden floor. He sets the LED lantern down on a countertop. Working fast with a can of spray paint he scribes the circle, joins the lines, and sketches the necessary sigils. He dumps the paper chain in the middle of the new grid and it jitters, the echo of a ram slamming into a door; working in haste he kneels outside the incomplete grid and links it up to a wire-wrap circuit board and a battery.

The folded chain of rice paper men jerks and jumps for a moment, casting long shadows from the lamp. Then it snaps. Johnny steps to one side so that his shadow is not cast across the circle, and draws both his knives. The heavies in the circle will probably have handguns, and Johnny isn't carrying. On the other hand, the heavies in the circle were dumb enough to go in through the front door. From where they're standing, an instant ago they were storming into a dim hallway; suddenly they're in near darkness in *the wrong place* with a glowing violet circle around them that they somehow can't bring themselves to cross—

"Cover! Left!—"

They're wearing Mall Ninja body armor and black helmets with gas masks and they've got flashlights and lots of spurious accessories bolted to the barrels of their carbines: it's all very Tactical Ted, in Johnny's mildly contemptuous opinion. One of them stumbles sharply in a shower of sparks as he comes up against the edge of the grid.

"You!" He's seen Johnny. The gun barrel comes up. "On the— *Jesus*—"

More blue sparks. The goon takes a dance-step backwards, nearly goes over. His companion is less talkative; there's a hammering roar and a series of flashbulb-bright sparks go off at the boundary of the grid as the bullets strike it and go wherever it is that steel-jacketed bullets go when they run into an energized containment field. He seems to be trying to shoot out the lantern on the breakfast bar.

Johnny is coldly angry. He opens his mouth to speak as the first goon stumbles into the field again, then jitters twitchily backward in a shower of purple flashes. Johnny can barely hear his own voice through the ringing in his ears. "Drop your guns!" he bellows. "Drop 'em now or I'll rip your lungs out and shit down your windpipes!"

The drill sergeant's voice of command usually works on anything short of a meth head's full-blown psychosis, but it's less than effective when punctuated by gunfire in a confined space. The talkative one appears to be frozen, but the second goon, the one with the hate on for light sources, whips round and raises his gun. There's a loud *snick*.

"Drop it, son," Johnny snarls, drawing his right hand back. For an answer, the goon fumbles with the magazine release. That's more than enough for Johnny. He releases the knife and it accelerates towards the grid. There's a crimson flash as the design inscribed on its blade flares white-hot for an instant before it lodges hungrily in the man's throat, and Johnny feels a brief stab of melancholy horror as he takes two quick strides forward across the shorted-out grid and punches the other goon in the face. The man goes down as if poleaxed; Johnny spins knife-first towards the trigger-happy one, but he's already down in a growing puddle of arterial blood. The knife-shaped thing sticking out of his throat is drinking greedily; one glance tells Johnny that the cop's beyond help. There's always a cost for using such occult weapons, and Johnny will pay it later, of that he is sure; but for now he's simply relieved to still be alive.

First he sees to the one he punched out. Johnny rolls him away from the blood, grunting with effort, and turns him into the recovery position. The man's still breathing, albeit noisily—Johnny fumbles a pair of handcuffs from the goon's belt and secures him, then bends to unfasten his helmet and gas mask, keeping one ear alert for police sirens in the distance. Then he searches him.

The one who's still breathing is in his forties, unfit, a salt-and-pepper mustache adorning a flaccid upper lip. The bad news is, he's wearing a law man's badge: Officer Benson of the Pinecrest Police Department. Worse: so is the dead gunman. *Not rent-a-cops*, real *cops*, Johnny decides. Pinecrest: home of the Golden Promise Ministries. *No, not like Barcelona: this is* worse.

Benson is breathing, but won't be answering any questions for a few minutes. Johnny turns to the trigger-happy goon's body, stoops, and takes hold of the knife-thing in his throat. A brief electric jolt runs up his arm: the feeder is intent, gorging, and does not wish to return to its warded scabbard. Johnny grimaces and tugs. There's very little blood as the knife-thing comes free. A thin sheen of red droplets that cling to the blade disappears under his gaze, as if sucked into the metal. He prepares to sheath it, but stops. The dead goon's mouth is moving, opening—

"Well, well, *well*." Johnny pokes at the emerging host with the tip of the blade: it flinches away, avoiding contact. "Fancy meeting a girl like you in a dive like this!" He pulls his knife back, unwilling to use it on such an unclean thing; hunting around for a suitable object he finds the fallen goon's carbine and hammers the host flat with its butt.

Roughly three minutes have elapsed since he completed the grid and unlocked the two captive goons. Police response times to reports of gunshots out here won't be speedy, but they'll be along by and by. Johnny checks on Officer Benson—unconscious, breathing stertorous—then exits the house. He knows a ward that will cause eyes to glaze and slide aside from the building: it needs to be applied to the gateposts out front before anyone comes by to check.

Then he and Officer Benson are going to have a little chat.

IT'S GETTING DARK AND I NEARLY MISS THE BATTERED PICKUP as I drive along the side street, half wondering if she's sent me on a wild goose chase. But something about it catches my attention, and as I slow down I think I recognize the woman in the driver's seat, her hair tied back in a bun, head bowed over a book.

I don't stop. Instead, I drive around the block, checking my mirrors for company and the side streets for other occupied vehicles. Finally, when I'm certain we're alone, I park behind her.

The cab door opens. It's Persephone, wearing nursing scrubs, a battered-looking handbag slung over one shoulder. She pauses beside the coupé and does something fiddly with a ward before she opens the door and slides into the passenger seat. "Drive," she says. "They're a half hour behind me, but that should delay them." I glance at her. Her eyes have aged about a thousand years since the last time we met. I start the engine and pull out carefully, then hunt for an avenue that'll take us south and east, back towards the highway.

After a couple of minutes, Persephone inhales deeply, then sighs as if she's expelling her final breath.

I glance sideways. The handbag is on the floor and there's a book in her lap, open. "Where do you want to go?" I ask.

"Johnny's in Denver." She turns to study me, her face expressionless.

"Head back up the interstate." A pause. "I'd like to collect him. We need to talk."

I turn my eyes back to the road. I don't want to see her expression. "You know I've been ordered home. Do not pass Go, do not collect $200, don't stop to pick up hitchhikers."

"Yes."

"The operation is a bust: we've been blown, and the only thing left to do is to withdraw. All three of us." I can feel her eyes on me as I take a right turn. "Mind you, Lockhart thinks it's a qualified success. He thinks we've got enough evidence to justify him starting an official investigation into Schiller's activities."

Persephone is silent for a while. Then: "He'll be too late."

"Too late for what?"

She doesn't reply immediately, so I let the silence lengthen as I drive. I don't like people trying to pull mystery-man (or -woman) head-games on me. "Pull over," she finally says as we're passing a drive-through Dunkin' Donuts. I turn into the car park and kill the engine.

"What is Lockhart going to be too late for?" I ask.

"Armageddon." She taps the cover of the Bible with a crimson nail.

"Arma-*what*?"

"It's all in here." She opens it, close to the back. "Testament of Enoch, Second Book of Dreams, the return of Azâzêl at the End of Days, the triumph of the elect."

"Testament of . . ." It doesn't ring any bells from RE lessons back when I was in school. "What kind of bible is that?"

"I had to leave Schiller's little indoctrination session in a hurry. It wasn't a teach-in, Mr. Howard; he was making converts. He has helpers—"

"Silver carapace, too many legs?" She tenses as I stick my tongue out at her, then the penny drops. She wiggles her tongue back at me, unsmiling: it's pinkish and she can roll it. "I caught one," I tell her. "It's in my bag. In a grid."

She raises an eyebrow. "Really."

"I was thinking of taking it home to see what the boffins in crypto-zoology can make of it." I pause expectantly. "What about that bible?"

"I took it from the nurse I stole the truck from. Believe me, the clinic she worked in—it would give you nightmares. It's her bible and she is one of them, a true believer, not an involuntary convert." She leafs through it, looking for something. "The first two sections are from the King James Version, I believe. Vanilla Protestant: Old Testament, New Testament. Then there are the Apocrypha, in a separate section. That's not too unusual, even if it contains some rather dubious extras. But then there's *this*."

She points to a page near the back, open recto, a fancy border surrounding a title: *The Final Codex*. Then she turns the page. *The Apocalypse of St Enoch the Divine*.

"Uh—"

She stabs at the page with a finger: "'This is the Revelation of Enoch, Seventh from Adam, which God gave unto him through his son Jesus Christ, to show unto his true servants the things which must be made to pass in the latter days—'"

"Hang on." I rub my forehead. "Enoch is pre-Christian, right? I mean, *really* pre-Christian."

She looks at me slightly pityingly. "Adam's get were peculiarly long-lived, according to the mythos. So the contradiction you're fishing for isn't there."

"Bugger." I focus on the page. "'*Must* be made to pass in the latter days'?"

"Yes." She reads aloud: "'And that the elect of the true creed shall listen and heed, for blessed is he that hears the words of this prophecy and law and sets his hand to building the kingdom of God on Earth. And grace be unto you, and peace, from him which is, and which was, and which is to come. And when the time is as prophesied and the son of God rises from his deathbed in the pyramid of the Black Pharaoh, all men shall bow before him, but first among them shall be the elect of the true creed, who shall be taken up bodily into the seven heavens of the pillars of law . . .'" She stops. "Want me to go on?"

"Please tell me this is a hoax?" Like the fakes titled *Necronomicon* that come out every couple of years and force the poor bloody sods in Records to run around like headless chickens making sure that nobody's got their hands on something they shouldn't (and don't get me started on the full-dress fire drill the first time somebody brought a made-in-China plush Cthulhu doll to the office) . . .

"No." She closes the book. "It's no hoax. But it's best not to overstate things. This is evidence that Schiller's congregation march to a different drumbeat from the other Christian churches. Like all such, they believe in the literal truth of their holy book."

"So they're Pentecostalists with special sauce?"

She nods. "The question is, what do these extra apocrypha mean? What beliefs do they add to the mix?"

"The communion hosts . . ." I stare at the Bible. "That passage. The Apocalypse of St Enoch. Isn't it a bit heavy on the *thou shalt do this and that*?"

"Yes. I didn't have time to read further; I have other worries. But where the Revelation of St John is descriptive, this book is *pre*scriptive. A road map for opening the way and speeding the return of Jesus Christ."

I close my eyes. *That dream.* The skin in the small of my back crawls. "The Sleeper in the Pyramid." The giant step pyramid on a waterless plateau, baked beneath the ruddy glow of a dying star, surrounded by its picket fence of necromantic sacrifices—

"Of course, the trouble with following occult texts blindly is that there is no guarantee that the thing the ritual summons is what it says on the label."

"But they're Christians. If you want to get them to raise something from the dungeon dimensions, *of course* you tell them it's Jesus Christ. I mean, who else would they enthusiastically dive into necromantic demonology on behalf of?"

"I believe the KGB have a term for people like that. They call them 'useful idiots.'" Her expression hardens. "I want to know who is behind them. Or what. Johnny had a theory. I think I discounted it too soon."

"I'd be interested to hear it."

She looks at me oddly. "Why are you still here? You said Lockhart ordered you home."

"He did." I peer at the doorway of the Dunkin' Donuts. "But I don't leave people behind. It's a personal habit." I try to explain: "Lockhart should have known that. He's got my transcript. He could have asked Angleton—my regular boss."

(It's not quite that simple, but some years ago I was leaned on to leave someone behind—and refused. Which worked out for the best, insofar as when a subsequent job went wrong she returned the favor, and we've been happily married for some years now; and if that's not positive endorsement for the idea of not leaving anyone behind, I don't know what is.)

"Hmm. This is your first time working for Mr. Lockhart, isn't it? Mr. Howard, Bob, you are working for *External Assets*. I think Mr. Lockhart regards everyone as disposable—including, ultimately, himself."

"You've worked with him before?"

She shrugs and changes the subject: "I suggest we pick up Johnny and try to drive out. But if the airport is closed and more than one high-way is blocked, that could be very difficult, don't you think? We might be trapped here."

I sigh. "I've been trying not to think of that." I start the engine. "Next stop, Denver."

RAYMOND SCHILLER SLUMPS IN THE BIG EXECUTIVE CHAIR behind his desk. The skin below his eyes form dark pouches in his face, wrinkled and tired. Joe Brooks studies him, concerned. Ray is power-ful, but Joe's seen him perform miracles before, understands the toll that God's work exacts from his latter-day prophet. *Please, Lord, let him be all right this time,* he prays. The last thing the mission needs is for its shepherd to take to his sick bed for a week just now.

"Father." Roseanne—now decently veiled and gowned—sounds as concerned as Joe feels. "Can I get you anything? Coffee and a Danish for your blood sugar? I can call one of Doctor Jensen's residents if it's your sciatica again—"

"Coffee and pastries all round." Ray dismisses his handmaid with a tired wave. He yawns, then focusses on Joe: "I reckon we're going to be here a long while, son."

"Yessir." Joe pauses. "You were right about the Hazard woman. I fed her fingerprints to our local FBI office. And her associate, the Mc-Tavish guy. They got back to me half an hour ago." He wrings his hands together in his lap, fighting the urge to hold his face in them. "It's not looking good."

"Don't blame me!" Pastor Holt is indignant: "How was I meant to know she's some sort of witch—"

Schiller closes his eyes again. "Brothers. No use crying after spilled milk." He raises a hand. "The Holy Spirit showed me what was in her mind. A black and evil faithless one, loyal to the Whore of Srebrenica—Babylon. An apostate and practicing witch. I should have warned you to hold her under guard until the communion service." He opens his eyes and looks at Alex. "What do the FBI say?"

Alex swallows. "The name is genuine. British citizen, naturalized a few years ago. But there's stuff that doesn't add up. She's tagged as a person of interest by a, a bureau in DC that I've never heard of. That's a bad sign; when I asked agents Brooks and O'Neil they'd never heard of it either, so I called Sam Erikson in Denver and he just about shat a brick. Apparently nobody's supposed to know that this, uh, *Operational Phenomenology Agency* even exists. Sam says they call it the Black Chamber, and what goes in never comes back out, and he can't protect us if we draw their attention. And this Hazard woman is of interest to them. She shouldn't be underestimated."

The door opens: Roseanne slips in, followed by handmaiden Julie pushing a trolley loaded with refreshments.

"Julie." Schiller smiles at her; she bobs a nervous curtsey. "I believe you escorted Ms. Hazard between the lecture theatre and her abrupt departure from the communion service?"

"Yes, Father." She licks her lips, nervous and wide-eyed as a doe caught in headlights. Her voice is soft and hoarse. "She said she needed the restroom, so I led her there. I saw her go inside, but Pastor Dawes was paging me to find a clean surplice for communion so I had to go sort that out. When I got back she was still there and it was time for the service, so I led her straight there—" Her words come faster, until she's nearly gabbling.

"Be at peace, my daughter." Ray smiles at her again and Alex tenses. The stink of blame hangs in the air, a cloud of doom floating from head to head: it has just left Julie's vicinity and is now bumping around, looking for a victim to attach itself to like an imp from hell. His expression hardens. "Alex. The cameras."

Alex swallows again: his tongue is dry. This is the delicate bit. "I had Bill and Tony run the tapes. Julie had barely left when the Hazard woman came out of the toilet. She headed for one of the reception rooms, and did something to a PC. Then she went straight back to the toilet, and that's where Julie found her. Near as I can work it out, she then went on . . ." He outlines the Hazard woman's exit via the hospital ward and the car park while handmaid Julie pours Schiller a mug of coffee and passes him a pastry.

"Hmm. And just what exactly did our black sheep get up to on the computer?" Schiller is staring at Alex again, his gaze as black and sharp as an Aztec savage's obsidian dagger.

"I don't know, sir. She rebooted it right after, and didn't leave anything attached. But in view of what happened next, I'm assuming the computers were her target all along, so I've taken the liberty of shutting down the entire admin network and calling in our best computer forensics dudes. They'll be here this evening to take everything apart. They'll be looking for keyloggers, rootkits, spyware—that's my best guess. And when we find it, we'll use it to feed our visitors what we want them to hear."

"I'm glad you've got it all covered. Can you keep it locked down until after Sunday's special service? It would be especially unfortunate if the Black Chamber were to become involved before the Harrowing."

"We'll work on it." Alex licks his dry lips. "Mark and his team have a contingency plan. It comes with an increasing risk of exposure if we run it for too long, but today's Saturday. If we activate the script tonight we can keep the whole city tight until Sunday evening, and maybe even Monday afternoon before the Feds start questioning the story they're getting from their local offices. That should buy time for the main event at the New Life campus . . ."

"Do what you will; I wash my hands of it," Schiller says dismissively. "What of the Hazard woman and her associates?"

"There are two angles to that. Firstly, we're trying to establish what she knows." *Too much for comfort, that's for sure,* Alex thinks. *She had to take a short cut through the Lost Lambs ward* . . . "And we're looking for where she went. We've got a warrant out for her on charges of aggravated assault and grand theft auto, thanks to the nurse she beat up—also firearms theft, because Nurse Stanhope had a pistol in her glove compartment. That's going to get the attention of the State Patrol and every local PD in the region, and Sam Erikson is trying to get her on the TSA no-fly list."

Holt harrumphs. "Can you do any more? Charge her with murder or something?"

Alex shakes his head. "Why bother? These are *real* felonies, they're watertight enough to stand up in court. As long as the judge and jury and attorneys are all churched, nothing will leak; it's always better not to lie, isn't it? Besides, after tomorrow's service and the Harrowing there won't be much she can do. We'll reel her in soon enough. What I'm more worried about are her associates, the McTavish man and her controller—"

"Controller?" Schiller straightens in his chair. He's taken a bite out of his pastry and some color is returning to his cheeks. "The British spy in Denver, right?"

"I haven't heard from Gordon and Lyons. They were supposed to bring him in four hours ago and they haven't reported back. They're not answering their cellphones."

"Really?" Schiller's expression is unreadable. "Gordon and Lyons. Hmm. I would have considered them to be reliable . . ." He takes a sip of coffee. "Be patient." He glances at Alex sharply. "And what of the other man? McTavish?"

Alex swallows. "That's the bad news. Stew went to take care of McTavish himself, with a posse: Benson, O'Brien, and Sergeant Yates. Stew's called in. They tracked McTavish to a safe house. O'Brien and

Benson took the front and—just *vanished*. McTavish exited in a hurry and got away from the deputy. Shots were exchanged. O'Brien and Benson are missing, there were no bodies—"

Schiller puts down his coffee mug and leans forward, his expression intent. "First, the presence in the arena in London—a fellow elect. I could *feel* him out there, watching me. Then this sudden interest from this British agency, and now the Operational Phenomenology people in DC. And an attempt to infiltrate the Omega Course." He clears his throat. "Do you have a picture of this McTavish?"

"Sir . . ." Alex fumbles with his file for a few seconds. "This is the best I—"

He trails off. Schiller stares at the grainy picture, his expression unreadable. "That's him. The elder in the audience. Back row. I could *feel* him. I was right to bring forward Operation Multitude and order the wards of sanctuary emplaced, it would seem. We are under attack. Hmm. Unless, of course, he is drawn to the Mother Church he deserted . . ."

"Sir?"

Schiller puts his palms together before his face in a gesture of prayer. "Almighty Jesus, I beseech you, share your divine wisdom with me . . ." He closes his eyes, breathes slowly, then presently lowers his hands and looks at Alex. "Stewart underestimated McTavish. O'Brien is dead. Benson is unconscious. They are both some distance away, perhaps in Denver. I will tell you where they are when Benson regains awareness.

"Meanwhile, Hazard and her employer are definitely in Denver, in a motel. I know this much by the blessing of Lord Jesus Christ. I can't narrow it down further without the witch feeling God's hot breath on the back of her neck, but our Lord will lead them into our nets by and by." He blinks heavily. "Bring McTavish to me for a visit, Alex. The others you may kill if it's possible to do so without scaring off McTavish, but he the Lord has a use for." Alex is already standing to leave as he hears Schiller continue: "Everyone go, except sisters Roseanne and Julie. We must pray together now . . ."

* * *

LATER, AGONIZED AND PURIFIED, SCHILLER RETREATS TO HIS
private chapel to seek guidance through solitary prayer.

The chapel is a small basement room, accessible via a bare, concrete stairwell branching from the corridor connecting his public office and his private apartments. Dominated by dark oak paneling, crumbling with age—bought from a seventeenth-century church in faraway Scotland that was being renovated—and featuring bare flagstones by way of a floor, the room is dominated by an altar and a featureless, man-sized stainless steel cross bolted to the wall behind the altar.

There is a bible on the altar—a huge, leather-bound affair, its cover studded with clasps and padlocks—and a stone chalice.

It is before these items that Raymond Schiller kneels, eyes closed and hands clasped in fervent prayer. He prays with his whole body, quivering and brimming with faith.

"Lord, hear thy loyal servant." The words leak out through clenched teeth, more of a subvocalized whimper of desire than a verbal declaration: "For though I am but a weak vessel of flesh, damned to eternal torment for my sins, my sole desire is to serve the temple of righteousness and to raise the ancient of days. Lord, hear thy loyal servant. For though it says, 'and in those days the destitute shall go forth and carry off their children, and they shall abandon them, so that their children shall perish through them: yea, they shall abandon their children that are still sucklings, and not return to them,' I have brought mothers to the motherless and children to the barren, to be fruitful and multiply in service to thy will.

"Lord, hear thy loyal servant . . ."

Abruptly, Raymond's chapel isn't so small anymore.

The floor is still flagged with slabs of limestone as broad as a man's arm is long, and the altar waits before him. But the walls have receded into the distance and faded to the color of time-bleached bone, and the ceiling overhead is open to the starry night. Alien constellations sparkle pitilessly against a backdrop of whorls and wisps of blue and green gas, the decaying tissues of a stellar corpse hidden from view by the horizon. Closer, a dusting of silvery specks flicker and flare as they drift across the vault of the sky—the skeletal remains of vast orbital factories, although Schiller is unaware of this.

If Schiller were to rise and walk to the walls, he would find a doorway in the center of each one. And if he were to venture beyond one of the portals, he would find himself leaving a temple atop a step pyramid towering above a desert plateau that stretches towards the distant, parched mountains in every direction that the eye can see.

And he would be able to see the moons, orbiting low and fast, which are blocked from his gaze by the walls.

Report.

The words thrust themselves into his mind like knife-sharp icicles rising from the thing that feeds between his legs, as a vast, chilly awareness slams up his spine and usurps his brain's speech center to give voice to its demands. A bystander would hear nothing, but to Schiller, the still, small voice of his god is louder than thunder.

"I am a damned soul and a miserable sinner . . ."

We will be your judge. But not in this time and place. *Report!*

The force of the demand drives Schiller to his hands, abasing himself before the sarcophagus-shaped altar (which has grown longer and broader, and is now of pale gray stone, embossed with intricate and disturbing knotwork elements that confuse the eye of the watcher).

"Lord! The mission to the leadership of the British government has been an unconditional success! The introduction we seek will be forthcoming within days, and with an endorsement from the Prime Minister, the chair of News Corporation will have no alternative but to see us. Once Mr. Murdoch is one of ours, we will have full access to the largest satellite and news broadcasting organization on Earth to bring our ministry to—"

There is a disturbance in Sheol. Are you responsible?

"Lord? I don't understand . . ."

Four of the hosts I placed at your disposal are missing. Three have been destroyed but another is offline. Report.

Schiller racks his memory, then realizes what his Lord is asking. "Ah, we have a small problem. A cell of spies dispatched by an autonomous arm of the British state has attempted to infiltrate us. We repelled their attack but three of our people were killed in the process. We are now searching for the apostates—"

Three hosts are destroyed but one is offline. What befell the offline host?

Schiller is baffled and terrified. A wind blows through his mind, a desiccating ice storm from an arctic valley where it hasn't rained for a million years, drying up his will and freezing his brain in mid-thought. Then it subsides, as quickly as it blew up: his Lord has satisfied himself that Schiller has no answer to give and is still, at heart, entirely a creature of faith.

Two active hosts were with your minions when they went to apprehend the British spymaster. One of them is dead. The other is beyond my awareness. Searching . . . ah. The expression of surprise is a sharp intake of breath on Schiller's part; his Lord has no lungs with which to draw air, and has in any case long since exhausted the universe's capacity for surprises. ***It is in the hands of an enemy. Our worshipers have met this British agent before. Do not attempt to convert him; bring him alive before Us. He will be of great service in the end times ahead.***

Schiller's body shudders, muscles twitching spasmodically as the most distant echo of his Lord's unhuman emotions bleeds through his amygdala, triggering a fit. Seconds pass; Schiller lies still for further minutes, recovering, before the inner voice addresses him again.

What of the Task? Report.

"As soon as I was informed of the attention we were attracting, I ordered Operation Multitude brought forward. It's very early, but I felt I couldn't take the risk of waiting any longer. So we are bringing forward the ministry to the people of Colorado Springs, and have invoked the miracle of Fimbulwinter, as instructed. The airports are closing, the Great Ward is in place, and we have arranged for highway patrol checkpoints on all the roads we can reach. Tomorrow we will perform the Rite of Awakening and the Harrowing of the unbelievers for the first time before a congregation of seven thousand. If it works as expected, we'll ramp up from there—Colorado Springs today, the whole of the continental United States by this time next month. It will take longer and entail more risks than the original plan, but we can start tomorrow—"

A hundred million souls must be Saved, Raymond, in order to free my mortal husk from this tomb.

"Yes, my Lord. Thy will be done."

Then shall I bring about Heaven on Earth. And all shall be Saved who will accept my host into their heart.

"Thank you, Lord!" Schiller prays fervently.

Bringing you here and protecting you from the forces of darkness that assail me saps my strength in this enfeebled state. Go now, and bring to me the pure of heart that I may take strength from the power of their faith. Go now, and detain the British spy Howard and his employees against my immanent return. Go now, and prepare the Rite of Awakening. Glory to God in the highest!

"Glory to"—Raymond rocks forward on his feet and finds himself once again in a small oak-paneled basement room—"God in the highest!"

IN THE BASEMENT OF THE NEW ANNEX, DOWN A DUSTY STAIR-case with fire doors at the top and along a corridor painted institutional beige and lit by ancient tungsten bulbs (some of which have failed), there is a green metal door. There is no room number or name plate on the door: just a keyhole, an ancient brass handle, and—above the lintel—a security warning lamp, currently switched off. Were it not for the lamp it might be a janitor's closet or a power distribution board. And despite the lamp, the delicate, almost invisible runes of power traced across the surface of the door ensure that most of the people who pass along the corridor mistake it for such.

Lockhart approaches the door with some trepidation. He pauses on the threshold, and an observer would conclude that he is nerving himself before he knocks, briskly.

The door opens.

"Come in," says the room's occupant.

"Thank you." Lockhart steps inside the office and sits down in the visitor's swivel chair opposite the strange metal desk with the hulking hood like a microfilm reader. As he does so Angleton locks the door with a strange silver key which he returns to a matchbox-sized wooden case, sliding it into the breast pocket of his suit jacket.

"What's he done this time?" Angleton asks as he stalks back towards his chair behind the projection turret of the Memex.

Lockhart exhales explosively. "I'm not sure," he admits. "Possibly nothing, yet."

"Hmm." Angleton glances at the elderly analog clock above the doorway. "It's nearly twenty-one hundred hours. Not like you to be burning the midnight oil over nothing, is it? Can I ask why?"

"I'm afraid not." Lockhart's mustache twitches, caught somewhere between a smile and a sneer. "But I was hoping you might be able to help me with a question of character."

"Character." Angleton doesn't seem at all put out by Lockhart's refusal; he leans back in his chair, steepling his fingers. "There's a word I don't hear often enough these days. Especially coming from you."

"Of course not." Lockhart is dismissive. "It's a subjective value judgment and those don't sit comfortably with ticky-boxes and objective performance metrics. It only comes into play when one is off the reservation."

"And is Bob—" Angleton catches himself. "Of course he is. Ask away, ask anything you want. I can't promise an accurate answer in the absence of exact details of the situation, but I'll do my best."

An observer, familiar with the internal pecking order of the Laundry, might at this point be justifiably taken aback. Here is Gerald Lockhart, SSO8(L), a middling senior officer in the backwater that is External Assets—a department most people (who are aware of it) think spends its time keeping track of loaned laptops—grilling DSS Angleton, a Detached Special Secretary (or, as scuttlebutt would have it, a Deeply Scary Sorcerer), one of the famous old monsters of the Operations Directorate: a man so wrapped in secrecy that his shadow doesn't have a high enough security clearance to stick to his heels. But a typical observer wouldn't understand the nature of External Assets. Or, indeed, be aware of Gerald Lockhart's real job.

"Hypothetically, then. Can you think of any circumstances under which you'd expect our man to break cover in the field and disobey an explicit order? That's *expect* him to disobey, not merely signal reluctance before complying, or make use of loopholes."

Angleton's eyebrows shoot up. "Are you vetting him?"

Lockhart shakes his head. "*I'm* not vetting him. It's just a general enquiry I've been told to answer." His tone of voice is flat.

"Oh." Angleton stares at him. "Oh *dear*."

Lockhart shakes his head again. "What are Howard's weak points?"

"Hmm." Angleton stares at the ceiling for a few seconds. "The boy's still hamstrung by a residual sense of fair play, if that's what you're asking about. He believes in the rule of law, and in taking responsibility for his actions. He's personally loyal to his friends and co-workers. His personal life is boringly normal—he's besotted with his wife, doesn't use drugs, has no blackmail handles. In fact I don't think he's got any *noteworthy* character failings—these are all good characteristics in a junior officer. He's not a sociopath if that's what . . . oh." Angleton sits up and leans towards Lockhart. "You didn't give him a clearly illegal order, did you? Put him in a compromising situation or tell him to abandon a colleague or someone he's personally loyal to—" Lockhart says nothing. "Oh dear."

"What is he likely to do? In the circumstances you, ah, speculated about."

Angleton grimaces humorlessly. "He has a history of, shall we say, being on the receiving end of abusive management practices. It has taught him to take a skeptical approach to obviously flawed directives. He'd use his initiative and try to square the circle—do whatever he was told to, while mitigating the consequences. He'd bend before breaking, in other words. He's loyal to the Crown, but he's not suicidal or stupid. However, conflicts of loyalty could be a very sticky wicket."

"Ah." Lockhart pause briefly. "You mentioned loyalty. Personal, organizational, or general?"

"I'm not sure I follow your distinction."

"You said he's unlikely to obey an order to abandon colleagues. What about civilian third parties? Informers and sources? Contractors and stringers? Family members or strangers? Where does he draw the line, in other words?"

Angleton fixes Lockhart with a beady stare. "Bob is too loyal for his own good. The lad's got a troublesome conscience."

"I . . . see." Lockhart nods slowly. "That's what I thought. Excellent." He stands. "Thank you for your assistance. I'll see myself out."

"Just one moment." Lockhart pauses halfway to the door. "Mr. Lockhart. The boy understands plausible deniability. And so do I. But I hope you're not confusing deniability with disposability. That would be a mistake."

"Who for? Howard?"

"No, for you." Angleton doesn't smile. "I will be *very* annoyed if you damage my trainee."

"Dr. Angleton." Lockhart doesn't turn; his voice is a monotone. "I have no intention of burning Mr. Howard. If nothing else, he would be extremely difficult to replace right now. But I have been instructed to establish whether he has the moral courage to do the right thing when he believes he's been cut loose, or whether he'll run screaming for his mother."

"Why would he believe—" Angleton pauses. "Are you expecting the OPA to take an interest?"

Lockhart, by way of reply, opens the door and slips out. He doesn't pause to borrow the key. Angleton stares after him for a moment before silently mouthing an obscenity in a half-forgotten language. Then, his face set in a frown, he turns to his Memex's keyboard and begins to tap out instructions.

12.

WITH A BIBLE AND A GUN

THERE'S A MOTEL 6 JUST OFF I-25, SOUTH OF DENVER. THE rental satnav directs me to it, and there are no highway patrol roadblocks; we reach it around eight o'clock. I head for the front desk. "Hi. I'd like to rent a couple of rooms for tonight? Singles."

"Sure thing." The middle-aged clerk barely looks up from her laptop screen. "Can I see your ID, please?"

I glance around to ensure we're alone, then slide my warrant card under her nose.

"Wait, that's not a—" There's an almost audible *clunk* as the card gets its claws in behind her eyeballs and her jaw sags.

"Our papers are in order," I explain to her. "Two single rooms please, for Mrs. Smith and Mr. Jones."

"That will be—" Her eyeballs slowly unkink.

"Cash." I shove a pre-counted stack of greenbacks at her. "The banknotes are correct." She's still drooling over the warrant card. I wait for her to wake up enough to make the money disappear then pull the card back.

"Let's see." She fiddles with her terminal and the room card reader. "You're in 403 and 404. Have a nice day."

I hand Persephone the Forbidden Room card and keep Room Not Found for myself. She looks at me oddly. I shake my head and walk towards the door—block 4 is across the car park. "Yes?" I ask once we're outside.

"Your card. If they've got OCCINT assets in the field, that's going to be a red flag to anyone nearby."

"True. But they're trying to keep a low profile." I look both ways before crossing: "I reckon they'll go through the regular police first, and I trust you did a good job of muddying the trail with that ward— you stole that pickup truck, yes?"

"They were going to install an alien mind parasite on me—what would *you* do?"

"Probably the same." I swipe the key card. "Let's go inside."

The Motel 6 rooms are basic but adequate, with office desks and broadband as well as TVs and en-suite showers. I've just had time to dump my stuff and do basic set-up. I'm installing a ward on the desk beside the pizza box when there's a knock on my door. It's Persephone.

"Come in." She stands on the threshold, clutching her handbag and shifting from foot to foot, edgy as a vampire with toothache. She sidles past me and stalks around restlessly as I close and ward the door. She pays particular attention to the window, and in particular the cobwebby diagrams I've sketched across the glass with a conductive pen: distraction patterns designed to slide observers' attention elsewhere. "I'm still working on the room."

"Oh, right." She stares at the pizza box. "Is that what I think it is?"

"Yup." I haven't got it wired up to the handy little USB breakout box yet, but it's adequately trapped for the time being. I gesture at her bag. "Is that what *I* think it is?"

"If what you expect is a bible and a gun, it probably is." She plants the bag on the double bed.

"Let's get this room secured before we discuss anything else," I suggest, discreetly palming my JesusPhone. (Thaumic resonance: there's an app for that.) "In case Schiller's people have got a Listener out for you."

"Okay." She reaches into the neck of her blouse and pulls out a discreet chain with a stainless steel cross attached. Before I can stop her she gives the arms a twist, then stabs the ball of her thumb with the tiny knife blade that pops out of the stem like a demented switchblade. "I always carry a concealed athame. It's not ideal, but it works . . . Ouch." I point my phone's camera at her and fire up the thaumometer and, sure enough, the cross is now pulsing violently. She mutters something in glassy syllables that slide around the edges of my mind, then retracts the blade and drops the concealed ritual knife back down between her breasts. "Deafness be upon us, and inner ears stoppered with wax. Will that do?"

I *hate* this ritual magic stuff; it just doesn't come naturally to me, even if I set everything up carefully beforehand—I need a debugger and a proper development environment before I can whip up so much as a *hello, world* invocation. (Hopefully followed rapidly by a *good-bye, world* from whatever I just summoned: that stuff is dangerous.) But she's very good at it. I suppose different people have different aptitudes, but the non-repeatability irritates me—it's anathema to observational science. I force myself to nod. "What else did you find there?"

"Aside from the Bible? That's not enough for you?" She shrugs again, then turns it into a low-grade shudder. "Gods, you don't want to know . . . They're believers, Mr. Howard. Pentecostalist dispensationalists—they are saved, but they are surrounded by the unsaved, and they think their master is returning imminently, and anyone who isn't saved by the time of his arrival is doomed. So they intend to save everyone whether or not they want to be saved, one brain parasite at a time." The shudder is more emphatic this time round. "They're also quiverfull—they raise as many children as they can as ammunition for the cause, because they're not completely sure whether *imminent* means their god is coming in fifteen minutes or fifteen years. There's a clinic in town, with a combined maternity unit and spinal injuries ward for the runaways they've rounded up."

"A *what*?"

"You heard me." She looks away, avoiding my eyes. She's the kind of woman who walls away that which makes her angry, presenting an outward appearance of calm; behind it I'm certain she's furious. "The ends justify the means: we are all to be saved, and it will take a large army to do the saving. As their women can raise larger families than they can give birth to, they use host mothers to make up the numbers. 'In sorrow thou shalt bring forth children'—they take that as an instruction."

"Oh ick." I swallow. "But why don't they just use the hosts to—" Then I realize why: they want loyal brainwashed storm troopers who'll fight for the cause in situations where a parasitic faith module would be a liability. (If you try to smuggle one of those giant wood lice into Dansey House or the New Annex, you won't get very far.) "So they're raising a little army of brainwashed believers, and they have the mind-control hosts to keep down the rest of us. And they've got this clinic"— *if it's real,* I feel like screaming, because the picture she's painting is so vile—"and, uh, what else are we looking at? What are their goals?"

"I don't know for sure." She sounds calm. "I planted a worm on their office network but then I had to break out, so I've got to assume the exploit is compromised. The Omega Course session went off the beaten track yesterday, and this morning they were forcibly installing parasites on the attendees. I think they've decided to bring their plans forward in a hurry. We're going to have to go back in person if you want to know any more."

Urp. Time to change the subject in a hurry. "About Johnny. Do you want to contact him, or would you rather I used the tattoo? Get him to—"

She looks at me. It's a bit like being a nice juicy grasshopper in front of a very sexy mantis. She's wired on something, and I wonder for a moment if she's sourced some nose candy, then I realize: this is what she lives for. Field work: that's why Lockhart was able to get her out here. Persephone is addicted to danger.

"Johnny is coming." Her lips crinkle into something resembling a smile. "He has a passenger to deal with first."

"A pass—" I stop.

They say our eyes are windows on the soul, but Persephone's eyes are more like murky brown pools, utterly impenetrable. Only the muscles around them tense enough to betray her, faint crow's feet of worry radiating from their corners. "I called him as soon as I closed the door." She's not apologizing, merely explaining. "He is meeting old friends.

The Black Chamber are having problems operating in Colorado right now. And the Golden Promise Ministries have their own police force who appear to be experiencing no such difficulties. They tried to take him at one of our safe houses. He is joining us as soon as he deals with an, ah, loose end. Maybe later tonight, maybe early tomorrow."

I swallow. "What kind of loose end?"

"Mr. Howard, Johnny and I are external assets. The whole point of working with us is that you can later swear that you didn't know what we were doing, that we did whatever-it-is on our own initiative." She pauses. "Are you sure you want me to answer that question?"

I stare at her. She's a beautiful piece of work, porcelain skin and not a hair out of place after a day of escape-and-evasion: as beautiful and deadly as a black widow. "I can't countenance murder," I say, with a sense that if I'm watching myself from a great distance—perhaps the witness box at the Black Assizes. "Do you understand?"

"Is it murder if it's another of *those*? Like the thing you took *that* from?" She points at the pizza box.

"If—" I stop and force myself to take a deep breath. "If they're possessed, that changes things. But. Minimum use of force necessary to achieve designated goals. Can we agree on that?"

She looks at me oddly. "Of course we can. Who did you think I am—Murder Incorporated?"

"One can never be too sure," I mutter. "Sorry, sorry, I had to ask." (Because I have dealt with people in the past whose main criticism of Murder, Inc., would be their messy inefficiency.) "Where were we?"

She sits down on the bed, cross-legged. "Motives. I don't know for sure, but I've made some inferences, and then there's this damned book." She glances at the Bible.

"What do you think Schiller's trying to achieve?"

"Besides the usual?" Her laughter is an abrupt bark of released tension. "Well, he's clearly set on converting the entire planet. Isn't that enough for you?"

"I need to know what he's trying to achieve in the short term. Through the Prime Minister." My arms are crossed and I'm leaning against the wall and not making eye contact: defensive body posture redux. "That's my core mission, as I see it. It's why we're here. We *can* admit that the mission's a wash and bug out, but if so, that's not going to help the, the victims." The women in the maternity unit. The pithed, god-struck men in black with their tongues half-eaten. "Come on. What do you know?"

"I don't." She looks frustrated. "Perhaps Johnny will have something . . ."

"And if not?"

"We can go back in if you dare." She cocks her head to one side. "There are ways. Let's say . . . Johnny runs into the Pinecrest police. You have a host, and so does he. We kill it and shell it, then you and he stick your tongues in them and pretend to be police, and I'm your captive. I have a glamour to provide cover against shallow inspection, and—"

"If you think I'm putting that thing in my mouth, alive or dead—"

"That's a shame." She stares at me with those huge, darkly unreadable eyes. "It's a low risk approach. If we make them come after us we hand them the initiative."

I take a deep breath. "Any other options?"

"Oh yes." She nods at the field-expedient pentacle and its inmate sitting on the desk. "That was just the direct approach. There are indirect ones. We could try to hook up that thing and snoop on whatever or whoever powers it, to learn where it comes from. Feed it misinformation, tell it where to go to find us."

I think for a moment. "I've got another idea. Is there any significant risk of them finding us here, if we stay overnight? Other than following Johnny?"

"I don't think so. You warded this room well, I sanitized the path to your car . . ." She thinks for a moment. "What preparations do you need that will take so long?"

"I've got to phone a man about a book," I say. "I need an hour to do some admin work. Then how about we go get some dinner? It's going to be a long day tomorrow."

She raises an eyebrow. "Lend me the car keys in the meantime?"

I chuck the keys her way. "Use them wisely."

* * *

AFTER PERSEPHONE LEAVES I SIT DOWN AND THUMB THROUGH the back end of the Bible, trying to get a feel for the page count. I decide I can discount the first couple of chunks; a quick google confirms that the Old Testament, New Testament, and Apocrypha look like standard factory spec. They might have been tweaked and tuned under the hood, but I don't have time to do more than check the table of contents. The Books of Enoch, however, aren't part of the standard trim level package, or even the deluxe leather upholstery option with sports kit: they're the biblical equivalent of the blue LEDs under the side skirts and the extra-loud chromed exhaust pipe. And when I get close to the end we're off the Halfords shelves and into nitrous oxide injection territory, complete with a leak into the cabin airflow. Using my Jesus-Phone I find a listing of the Books of Enoch on the interwebbytubes, but it sure as hell doesn't include chapters with titles like "The Book of Starry Wisdom," "The Second Testament of St Enoch," and—most intriguingly of all—"The Apocalypse Codex."

The bumper bonus extra features aren't particularly long, they only run to about eighty pages. But they're typeset differently, in a different layout, and the footnotes and glosses don't match up with anything in the front three-quarters of the book. So I place the Bible on the desk, shine the work lamp on it, and pull out the JesusPhone. Then I start photographing and flipping pages. Autofocus and five megapixels mean that just about any pocket camera these days is the equivalent of a flatbed document scanner, and a quarter of an hour later I'm stitching a bunch of image files together and converting them into a PDF. I run it through an OCR package and quickly check that it doesn't mention certain unmentionable keywords (it doesn't: it's not *that* kind of occult text), then I take a deep breath, and do something deeply illegal and, much more importantly, quite possibly unforgivable.

I stick the PDF of the page images on a public file sharing site, then I phone Pete and Sandy at home.

Ring-ring. Ring-ring. Ring. "Wha, who—*Bob?* It's one in the morning! What's up?" Sandy sounds confused and as befuddled as I'd be if you woke me in the wee hours with a phone call. I scrunch up my eyes and wish that I believed in a god I could pray to for forgiveness.

"Sandy, is Pete awake?"

"Yes, but is it an emergency?"

"Sort of. Can I talk to him, please?"

"Hang on." There's a muffled noise, as of a phone being passed from one hand to another.

"Bob?" It's Pete. He doesn't sound very awake.

"Pete? Can we talk privately? I've got a problem."

"What sort of—of course. Hold on." There follows a period of muffled thudding as, presumably, Pete disentangles himself from his bedding and leaves Sandy to go back to sleep. "There, I'm on my own. I assume this couldn't wait for morning?"

"It's sort of urgent." I pause. "What I'm going to say mustn't go any further."

"Cross my heart and hope to die: you know what I do for a living, right? Pastoral care a speciality, spiritual care, too, although I guess that's not what you're looking for . . ."

There is an eerie pins and needles prickling at the back of my tongue. I am going to have to watch what I say *very* carefully: my immortal soul is very much in danger, and I'm not speaking metaphorically. The consequences of betraying my oath of office are immediate, personal, and quite hideous.

"You've probably guessed that, uh, I'm not allowed to talk about my job. But that it's a bit different from what I'm required to lead people to believe."

The hair on the back of my neck is all but standing on end, but the ward doesn't clamp down on me—yet. To some extent it's driven by my own conscience, by my own knowledge of wrongdoing. And as I'm not actually planning on betraying any secrets, I still have a clean conscience. *But.* I'm wearing saltwater-soaked shoes and walking alongside the third rail.

"I've recently come into possession of an interesting document, and I badly need a sanity check. Unfortunately, the only person I know with the right background to give it to me is you."

(Which is entirely true: while the Laundry can probably cough up a doctor of theology with a security clearance and a background in Essene apocalyptic eschatology, it might take them a couple of weeks. Whereas Pete wrote the dissertation and I've got him on speed dial.)

"A document." He sounds doubtful. "And you want a sanity check." *And you got me out of bed at one in the morning.*

"It's a, a non-standard biblical text. Not your regular apocrypha. I'm having to do due diligence on people who are, uh, believers. I'd normally write them off as your regular American evangelical types, but they aren't reading from your standard King James version. And it's kind of urgent: I'm meeting with them in the morning."

"You're *meeting* with—" I can almost hear the audible *clunk* from the mechanism between his ears as his brain jolts into gear. *But you work in computer support in a civil service department,* he's thinking. And almost certainly putting two plus two together and getting five, which is just fine by my oath of office, if not my conscience . . . "Okay, I think."

"I've got a PDF of a scan of the variant bits of their Bible," I say. "Mostly it's the King James version plus a bunch of standard apocrypha, but this stuff is entirely different. I'm going to email you a link to it as soon as I get off the phone. It runs to about eighty pages. If you can take a peek and email me back, what I need to know is: If you start out from a bog-standard Pentecostalist position and add these extra books, what does it do to their doctrine and outlook? What do they believe and what are they going to want to do?"

"That's horribly vague! I—" He swallows. "You really want an opinion from *me*?"

"Pete." I pause, feeling like a complete shit. "You're the guy with the PhD in whacked-out millenarian sects from the first century, right? Work could probably put me in touch with someone else, but they'd take weeks. And I've got to do—business—with these people tomorrow."

"What time tomorrow?"

"I'm in America. Mountain Time Zone. Tomorrow morning—call it three p.m., your time."

Pete whistles quietly. "You're in luck; I was planning on spending the morning working on a sermon."

"I'll email you that link," I promise. "Text me when you've got it, then go back to bed?"

"Sure. God bless."

"And you," I say automatically. Then he hangs up, and I get the shakes. I haven't blown my oath of office—I'm still upright and breathing, not smoldering and crispy around the edges—but I've just bent it creatively. I haven't told Pete about the Laundry, but at a minimum I've suggested to him that I'm not just a boring IT guy, that my job takes me to strange places and involves dealing with very odd people. *If the Operational Oversight*—no, scratch that. External Assets doesn't normally answer to them. But if Gerald Lockhart decides I've exceeded my authority . . . well, he probably *will*, but it is easier to ask forgiveness than to request permission, especially if the gambit works. It's possible I'll be up before the Auditors again. And in the absolute worst case, the Laundry can probably find a use for a Vicar with a PhD in Unmentionable Mythology. They aren't going to be motivated to dump on Pete. I hope. Not with Pete and Sandy expecting a kid. Not because I've gone and fucked up and dragged my work home with me to smear around my social circle.

I feel soiled. I hope I'm not wrong about the significance of that Apocalypse Codex. It would suck to be hauled up before the Black Assizes. It would suck even harder to have gotten my friends into trouble because of a false positive. Mo would never forgive me; worse, neither would I.

I'M BUSY TRACING A SECOND CONTAINMENT GRID ON THE pizza box lid containing Crusty McNightmare when my mobile rings. It's Persephone. "Yes?" I say.

"I'm in the car park. Dinner's on you."

I glance at the gray, many-legged thing snoozing on the oily corrugated cardboard. It's quiescent, but I know better than to poke it—I don't want to risk breaking the ward. The primary pentacle serves much the same function as a Faraday cage: as long as it's locked down this way, whoever owns it can't connect to it and see through its sensory organs. But if it's locked down like that, I can't use it to feed misinformation to said owner. Hence the second, outer ward I'm working on.

Once it's in place I can set up a bridge between the inner and outer containments to let it phone home while I snoop on its communication and introduce material of my own: a man-in-the-middle (or, more accurately, a thing-in-the-middle) attack. But it's a delicate job, I haven't actually tested this particular configuration in the lab, and there's no way I'm getting it down before dessert. So I double-check the outer diagram for flaws in the logic, ensure that it's fully powered up—rechargeable batteries and a frequency generator disguised as a pocket digital multimeter take care of that—and grab my coat. On the way out the door I grab my shoulder bag, complete with phone, camera, and passport; you can never be too prepared.

By the time I get to the car park night is falling, and with it a light dusting of snow. There's a convertible drawn up near the entrance, headlights on and roof up. I walk around the passenger side and Persephone pops the door. "Get in," she says. I obey and I barely have time to get my seat belt fastened before she's moving, fishtailing into the road with a harsh scrabble of grit and ice under the wheels.

"What have you been up to?"

"I got you a laptop." She gestures at the back seat. "And I bought ammunition at Walmart. Then I went for a drive, up north. I tried I-76. Ran into a diversion and checkpoint out past E-470. So I drove around the beltway until I hit I-70. Same deal. The north- and eastbound interstates all detour back into the city. The airport is shut," she adds. "I double-checked in case you have no-fly cooties. They gave me some crap about a frontal system coming down from Canada that's due to dump a meter of snow on us overnight. It's all lies: I checked the NOAA aviation weather reports and NOTAMs. There's a front coming, but it's not carrying snow. So I tried a couple of general aviation fields, even a helicopter taxi service, but they're all grounded."

"But—" I stop dead.

"I drove out to Meadow Lake Airport," she adds. "I went in two offices. The front desk staff were all infected."

I tense. "How did you handle it?"

"There was nothing *to* handle. I didn't go in and say, *Hi, I'm the Big Bad your pastor told you about and I want to hire an escape plane.* One air taxi firm have an enquiry from a dentist's wife called Lonnie Williams on file, and a helicopter company have a phone number for a lawyer's secretary who is setting up a day trip to the Grand Canyon for an office party. Unless Schiller mobilizes the entire population of Colorado to hunt us door-to-door with torches and pitchforks, I left them no leads."

"They'll be looking for—" I stop. She's not driving the stolen pickup, and somehow while I haven't been looking she's changed her clothing and hairstyle from off-shift nursing scrubs to suburban American soccer mom. In jeans and a skiing jacket, ponytail and sunglasses, she's just about unrecognizable as the rich socialite Schiller's people will remember. Still glamorous, though. "You've got paperwork for that cover?"

She nods. "I probably have more experience of escape and evasion than you do." She checks the mirrors and slows, turns towards a downtown thickening of concrete and flags. "I thought perhaps we might try a small brasserie I've heard good things about. Their Kobe steaks are said to be excellent."

Kobe beef? The soccer mom is trying to upgrade to premier league WAG territory. My wallet cringes: despite Lockhart's scandalously liberal approach to expenses I'm probably going to be called upon to justify this in writing, then cough up for it out of my own pay packet. (Unless I can convince the small-A auditor that Kobe is a kind of cheeseburger . . .) "If you insist."

"I insist." Is that an impish gleam behind her shades? "We are not flying out tomorrow, Mr. Howard. Better get a full meal while the meal is to be had."

"What about trains? Driving?"

"Amtrak runs one train daily to Salt Lake City or Omaha, it takes a day either way, and they insist on checking ID. Driving—it's possible, but we'd have to cut cross-country and run past those road blocks. I do not advise it: we would be too obvious, even if we didn't get stuck in a snowdrift and die of hypothermia. If they are infiltrating the general aviation companies, what about the highway patrol?"

I shiver, and not from cold. "You think Schiller's locked down half the state?"

We slow, and Persephone pulls in at the roadside. "Yes. The real question is how soon he'll be in a position to extend it to the entire continental United States."

As she kills the engine I try to force my brain to shift gears. It's painful. "Back up. You think he's organized a total lock-down, blocking escape by air and probably by road, because of *us*? And he's going to *what*?"

"It's not just us, and I have a very bad feeling." She opens her door and climbs out. I join her on the pavement. "We know he has ambitions." She heads for the parking meter. "We know he has a powerful sponsor, and a supply of these parasites, and a messianic desire to bring his salvation to *everyone*. The Omega Course I attended—it wasn't the first, or even the tenth. He's been saving the souls of the rich and powerful for many years, working his way up. He must know that the higher he goes, the greater the risk of exposure. So if he is trying to suborn governments at the highest level, he must be nearly ready to move. And now something has just come up that convinced him to bring his plans forward. Possibly us, I fear."

My stomach rumbles, but I'm not sure I'm hungry. It feels as if Persephone is dredging these fears out of the depths of my own imagination. "He won't be doing this on a whim. Whatever he's planning is close enough to completion that he can't back off and try again later. At the same time, he thinks he can hold the lid down for long enough to—how long can you lock down a city without anyone noticing, anyway? A few hours? A couple of days?"

Persephone shoves quarters into the meter. "If he can conjure up a weather anomaly that matches the weather warning, he might manage a week-long clampdown. And nobody would question what had happened afterwards—especially if we disappear in the middle of it." Light snowflakes swirl in her misting breath. "Winter is not over yet; there can be savage cold snaps."

"Where's he going to get the bandwidth to create an entropy sink that big?" Then my eyes widen involuntarily because I'm having an unwelcome flashback to something that happened more than a decade ago in Amsterdam.

YOU'VE SEEN THE SETTING IN A THOUSAND GANGSTER MOV-ies: the unfurnished room in an abandoned house, empty but for the wooden chair in the middle of the floor, centered in a pool of light beneath an electric lantern hanging from the low, paper-peeling ceiling. A man sits on the chair, his arms cuffed behind the back and his ankles tied to the legs.

In the movies he'd be a good guy, a cop or an investigator perhaps. And the figure in the shadows, the interrogator preparing to ask him questions, would be a killer and a thug. In that respect, this scene is a movie cliché.

The interrogator walks up behind the slumped figure in the chair and grabs a handful of hair. He pulls the prisoner's head back, and with his free hand he smears a ball of cotton wool and baby oil across the prisoner's forehead.

"You can wake up now."

The prisoner snorts incoherently, coughs, drools, and twitches as awareness returns in fits and starts. It's a messy process, never as neat and clean-cut as cinematography portrays. But the prisoner is waking from sleep unnaturally enforced by the ward the interrogator has just erased from his forehead. There's no concussion or intracranial bleeding to complicate things here.

"Would you like a glass of water?"

The victim coughs again and tries to look round at the speaker. Chooses the other direction. Begins to nod, then stops, suspicious.

The interrogator produces a bottle of water and a paper cup. Still standing behind the victim's chair, he half-fills the cup. He holds it in front of the man's mouth and tilts, slowly, taking pains to stay out of his prisoner's field of vision.

After a moment, the prisoner sucks greedily, gulping down the contents of the cup. There is no Mickey Finn moment, no dramatic double take: it's just water. The interrogator re-fills the cup and lets his subject empty it once more before he walks away and deposits it at the other side of the room.

"Do you know who I am?" he asks conversationally.

"Yuh"—*cough*—"you're in too deep." Arm muscles tense, come up against handcuffs. "Let me go now and lessee if'n we can sort this out so you get a day in court, huh? Because if you don't—"

There is a scraping of metal on concrete. The interrogator drags up a chair behind the prisoner and sits, just outside the geometric design sketched on the bare boards around the other's chair. The prisoner, uncertain, trails off.

"Do go on, son." The interrogator sounds amused rather than afraid.

"*Hss.*" There's an odd undertone to the sibilant.

"You can stop pretending." The interrogator leans forward. "Because I know what you are, *minion.*"

The prisoner's voice shifts: "You should join us. Life eternal awaits the brethren of the chosen, perdition and damnation the apostate. For I am the light and the way, sayeth the Lord—"

The interrogator listens to the godbabble for a couple of minutes. It has a nice stirring ring to it, sonorous phrases honed by centuries of preachers: the shock and awe programmed into generations of believers by their priests. But it falls on willfully deaf ears, for though the interrogator grew up thoroughly churched he has long since shed the naive belief in the trinity and the gospels and the crucifixion and the resurrection and the Church triumphant. He knows the truth, knows the creed of the One True Religion, the nature of its worshipers and what passes for its deities.

Right now what interests the interrogator is the state of his prisoner's mind. Because it's certainly not what it ought to be under these circumstances—knocked unconscious and brought round in a situation designed to intimidate, a situation familiar from a thousand entertainments and notorious for ending badly—indeed, the prisoner's attitude is positively abnormal. A normal reaction might run the gamut from panic, fear, and offers of cooperation, through self-pity and ingratiation to anger, even defiant threats. A well-prepared subject might be grimly committed to silence. But a small-town cop accustomed to the casual exercise of force-backed authority will not be well-prepared for capture and debriefing; he'll bluster or break. So: first evangelism, then . . . what?

After a while, the prisoner begins to repeat his offers. The interrogator waits a minute to be sure, then moves on to the next stage: he tosses a small object onto the floor before his prisoner. It's about the size of a severed human tongue, a silvery banded carapace or husk of chitin, somewhat flattened by repeated encounters with a rifle butt. It sparks and sizzles briefly as it touches the ward. "You can stop now," he says in a steady tone that gives no hint of his own state of mind. "Just put me through to head office."

The prisoner falls silent. Then the light flickers.

"*Faithlessss* . . ." There is little humanity in the prisoner's voice, but an odd sharp clicking as of dozens of chitinous legs tapping against the teeth in a dead man's jawbone, a buzzing as of the wings of a thousand flying insects.

"Do you remember me?" Johnny's tone is light, almost mocking. "*Father?*"

I'M HAVING A GUILT DREAM——SOMETHING ABOUT RESCUING A dead man from a burning hotel and hoping he won't eat my face as I climb backwards down a ladder, then finding that he's got no tongue and I've suffocated him by accident—when my phone rings. I roll over, nearly strangling myself in the sheets as I grab for it. It's showing an international call, no caller-ID. "Hello?" I see the illuminated digits of the bedside radio: it's a quarter past five.

"Bob?" It's Pete. "Bob, is that you?"

"Ye—yeah." I sit up and wince, swing my legs over the side of the bed. It's dark. "Returning the favor."

"I looked at the manuscript you sent me." Pete sounds odd. It's hard to tell over a mobile phone, but I could swear he's upset about something.

"Great." I summon up some false cheeriness as I shuffle towards the curtained window. "What did you make of it?"

"You said you're doing business with people who, who have bibles containing this material?" *Yes*, Pete *is* worried. "I'd advise against that, Bob. I mean, assuming your business has anything to do with their beliefs, obviously; if you're just buying office supplies from them that's probably safe, but . . ." he trails off.

I yawn hugely, and peel back a corner of the curtain with one pinkie. Outside it's dark and cold, but flakes of snow are falling just beyond the glass. Very large snowflakes. I let the curtain fall. "How non-mainstream are they?" I ask. "If you had to describe them to a colleague, what would you call them?"

"I'd"—Pete clears his throat—"I'd call them dangerously loopy heretics who are well down the slippery slope to hell, Bob. A hell of their own creation, even if you don't believe in the literal sulfur-and-brimstone variety presided over by a big red guy with horns and cloven hooves. Which these people very likely do, but they think they're on the side of the angels, which makes them doubly bad. They're outside the Nicene Creed and they're not actually Christians, although they think they are—like the Mormons. But while the Book of Mormon is just a nineteenth-century fabrication there's stuff in here that's, uh, disturbing. Very disturbing, Bob. The marginalia—are they yours?"

"Marginalia?" I ask before I can stop myself, then bite my tongue.

"*Not* yours?" Pete sounds relieved.

"*Not* mine. Er, I don't think I'm supposed to have been allowed to have access to the book. If you don't mind keeping that under your hat . . . ?"

"Naughty, naughty! Well, that's a relief because it means you haven't turned batshit crazy on us since dinner last Tuesday. Mo will be relieved. In fact—"

"Pete." I yawn again, but my head's clearing. "What do they *believe*?"

"What? Oh. Hang on, let me check my notes." I wince, but there's no helping it: Pete runs on paper, so there will be an evidence trail of this unofficial consultation. *Damn.* "Let's see. We have a bunch of foundational mythology about the Nephilim, an alternate creation myth to Genesis—that's not so new. We then have a line of prophets descended from Adam by way of Lilith, not Eve, who are able to talk to these supernatural beings, angels or demons. And a couple of confused allegorical stories, sort of like the Book of Job only not as upbeat and cheery. But then there's the new stuff. An entirely new apocalypse that devotes some verses to denouncing St John the Divine as a charlatan—that, right there, tells you we're in uncharted territory. Between you and me, that conclusion is mainstream among serious biblical scholars—but it's not something you generally run across among the literalists. And then the authors construct a bizarre eschatology around the image of a dead-but-sleeping god, whose followers on Earth will receive their reward in heaven if they conduct a series of purification rituals and—it says *bind*—enough converts to resurrect him? That's literal heresy, Bob, insofar as it goes entirely against the two pillars of Christian doctrine, which are that the path to salvation is through voluntarily accepting Jesus as your personal savior, and that he'll return when he's good and ready. It's *not right*." There is a rising note of disquiet in his voice. "There are other hints that something is wrong: lots of elaborate gibberish about the ritual of summoning that requires the participation of two pure-blood descendants of the sons of Lilith. Lots of references to the sacrifice of Abraham, pronouncements of anathema upon the followers of false churches, imprecatory prayers and declarations that anyone who isn't within the circle of salvation is going to regret it, that kind of thing. Who *are* these people, Bob? What are you doing with them?"

I stare at the thing in the pizza box on my desk. "I can't tell you that."

"They're dangerous," he insists. "Bob? If they invite you to one of their church services? You really don't want to go—"

"I got that already."

"No! You're an outsider, Bob. There's this stuff about binding converts. It sounds like some sort of coercion to me, and whoever owned this Bible was very keen on underlining passages relating to it. And stuff about making the unclean vine bear clean fruit whether it will or no. There's a strong stench of the unholy about this book, Bob. Bob? Are you listening?"

I close my eyes. "Pete. You know damn well I'm an atheist." He does, and he forgives me for it because he's Pete. Even though it's a lie; I'm not an atheist these days (even though I wish I was). "I'm not going to visit these folks' church, either." (That *is* a lie.) "But I have to prepare a report on, on their reliability. Deadline's later today. You've been a real help. Is there any chance you can send me your notes?"

"They're on paper . . ."

"Use your phone; photograph each page and send it to me as an MMS. I'll pay you back. It's really urgent." A plausible white lie jumps into my mouth and is out before I can swallow it: "I've got to put the word out before they land a contract to set up half a dozen faith schools."

"Oh dear! No, that wouldn't do at all. But I've only got six pages. It's handwritten, they're not very legible . . ."

"Just send them. Please?"

"All right." He pauses. "God bless, and take care." Then he ends the call.

I open my eyes again, and take a deep breath. I *really* hope I haven't got one of our last remaining innocent friends into deep trouble.

Then I peel back the curtain and let my eyes adjust. It's snowing heavily now, and a thick rind of spongy white covers the car park, turning the vehicles into hunchbacked white boulders. The snowflakes are big, and they fall fast. At a guess there's upward of five centimeters down there already. I shiver, check the time, and go back to bed for an hour or two.

But I can't get to sleep again.

I don't like snow.

Years ago now, when I was young and foolish and ignorant, I got a ringside view of what happens when it snows for forty years. Or rather, of what happens when a team of mad necromancers use a certain very unpleasant ritual to summon up what they mistakenly called an *ice giant*, a monster out of Norse mythology who they hoped would freeze the Red Army in its tracks and secure victory for the Thousand Year Reich.

Well, in the short term their plan worked. Predators from dying universes trump T-34 tanks and B-29 bombers. But their triumph was short-lived: consuming energy from the structure of spacetime, the monster grew and grew and . . . well, when we went through the gate in Amsterdam to shut it down, there wasn't a lot left. A layer of dirty carbon dioxide snow beneath unblinking, reddening stars. A view down a hillside towards a blue-tinged lake of liquid oxygen, a crust of solid nitrogen slowly growing across it. A gibbous moon carved with Hitler's saturnine portrait rising behind the battlements of a dead SS castle . . .

Like I said, I don't like snow—especially the supernatural kind.

13.

FIMBULWINTER

PERSEPHONE HAZARD LIES FULLY CLAD ON TOP OF A MOTEL bed, with her eyes open, staring at the ceiling.

She does not appear to be breathing, but she is not dead. In fact, she is very much awake.

In her mind's eye she is standing on an infinite gray plain, flat and dusty, that sweeps away towards a horizon beneath the utterly black sky above. She is wearing ritual vestments, a gown made to a pattern designed by Jeanne Robert Foster to the specifications of her magus; her hair is bound up with silver wire, and she holds a blunt-tipped knife with two notched ivory blades bound together by a band.

All this is immaterial, existing only within her imagination—but for a practitioner of ritual magic, as opposed to a technician of computational demonology, the set dressing of the Cartesian theater is a matter of great importance. Ritual magic is unpredictable, and the civil service hates it because it relies on the unaccountable exercise of power by the dismally eccentric, if not un–house trained; nor does it work as reliably as numerology or cabbalism, let alone their infinitely more potent and reliable descendants, algorithmic imprecation and computational demonology. Its practitioners also tend to die young and horribly, of Krantzberg syndrome or something worse. But to a trained adept it delivers the power to make a reality from the field of dreams and visions.

The plain she stands on—again, imaginary—is the raw material with which she works. It is also a meeting place, for minds and other things.

Persephone kneels and begins to inscribe symbols on the featureless landscape with the tip of her ritual object. Where it touches the ground it leaves a glowing trail like a line of red LEDs in the dust. She writes rapidly, in a formal dialect of Old Enochian. The featureless plain provides syntax completion and automatic indentation: as she scribes, some of the words change shape and hue subtly. (There are many (many (nested)) parentheses: ritual magic, realtime spell-casting, hasn't been the same since John McCarthy.)

Finally she completes her—spell? theorem?—and watches as a violet border forms around it, shrinking until the words are wrapped in a fist-sized knot of metaphor. It begins to rise, pulling free of the landscape, forming a glowing sphere. "Go," she tells it. It slowly drifts away from her face, until after a meter it stops abruptly and rebounds sideways.

Below it, the featureless ground begins to glow, forming first the yellow outline of a wall, and then an open doorway.

Thaumotaxis: the attraction of magical power. Persephone has constructed a tool that will map the energy gradients around her and sketch yellow contours across the infinite plain, building up a map. If Fimbulwinter is indeed on the way, or if Schiller is preparing a rite of power, the solar glare of the ground will show her which directions to avoid. The map, growing in her mind's eye, will take some hours to mature. But there's nothing like knowing the ground you're fighting over better than your enemy . . .

She can't return to the real world while the spider is spinning the first iteration of its map-web. It's going to take quite some time. She rises to her feet and stretches; then, reluctantly, she raises one leg and pinches the blister plaster on the back of her heel between two sharp fingernails.

Johnny. Sitrep.

He's lying on his back in a dark space that stinks of mildew and neglect: an underfloor space, or a tomb, perhaps. It's bitterly cold but he's swaddled up in a bivvy bag, like a moth in a cocoon.

Duchess? Where are you?

I'm in the Other Place, working on a map. My body is secure and I'm with Howard. Sitrep.

They jumped me as I checked on safe house three. We've been tracked—

I know. Howard took down two of them.

She feels Johnny's flicker of surprise.

Eh? Well, they sent a brick to tackle me. I showed 'em a clean pair of heels and pocketed two. Found a suitable venue and unpacked them and they lit up on me, so I nailed one with Soulsucker and KO'd the less crazy motherfucker. Then laughing boy and me had a nice long chat.

His mood is grim.

I told you I had a bad feeling about this?

Persephone waits. Finally he continues.

The cops from Pinecrest, they're all possessed. *All of them.* And the hosts are, they're . . . they're like that time in Barcelona, Duchess, that hive we ran across. So I did the full smackdown take-me-to-your-leader thing and what do you know, he did. Full-on channeling. The usual all-your-souls-are-belong-to-me bullshit, at which time I terminated the interview, but. But. Their boss is close enough to dial in for a chat, know what I mean? Schiller's almost certainly an elder of the old church, he recognized me that time in London, and he's actually trying to set up one of the great summonings. It's the only explanation that fits, and it does not fill me with joy and happiness. Oh, and before I forget, Patrick says to say 'hi.' He's stringing for the Nazgûl who are having *a spot of bother with Denver.* I don't know about you, but I reckon the shitter is about to blow up under us; I would *strongly* recommend wiping arse and leaving the bathroom with extreme prejudice.

Patrick?

What's Patrick doing here?

He's stringing for the Black Chamber, like I said. They've got their claws in deep—not his fault, by the way. We had a little misunderstanding over him tailing me but it's all sorted now. He says the Nazgûl would be very grateful for any information we could give them about what the fuck is happening in Colorado because their own people can't visit and the local affiliate offices are all compromised. Am I getting this across, Duchess? Because if not, I am really *not very fucking happy* about being here. This level of shit is above even your admittedly stratospheric pay grade, in my opinion—

Persephone has heard enough.

Agreed, and we're leaving tomorrow. How mobile are you? What did you do with the cops?

I've got wheels. As for laughing boy, after his boss used him as a telephone there wasn't a lot left. Nobody's going to find them for a while.

Good. I want you to come round here at first light. She visualizes the motel's location. ***You, Howard, and I are going to try to drive out. But it looks like Schiller's put a cordon around us. If we can't get out, I intend to go for the throat. I want to nail these bastards, Johnny.***

Whoa, you're taking it personal, Duchess?

You bet I am. But I'm going to be professional about it. See you first thing tomorrow morning.

SIGNING OFF, SHE OPENS HER EYES TO SEE WHAT KIND OF web her thaumotropic spider has woven.

Beyond the threshold of her room—a yellow outline surrounding a rectangle of slate-gray emptiness—loop vast whorls and spires of sun-yellow energy. Denver itself is a valley, low and dark, but around it rise ramparts of power. A narrow cutting leads towards Colorado Springs, another valley cupped between high walls of compulsion, but near the edge of the city there rises one leg of a towering arch of light. A torrent of power roaring into the sky, coming out of nowhere and leaping out across the plain towards an answering pillar ten miles to the north. It's so strong it's right off the scale, a multiple reactor meltdown in the middle of the background field of ambient radiation.

Persephone stares at the arch of power for a subjective minute. Then she swears, clicks her heels together, and vanishes from the Other Place.

I'D SET MY PHONE TO WAKE ME UP AT 7 A.M., BUT I'M AWAKE and dressed and waiting for it three minutes before it sounds.

I go into the motel bathroom and splash water on my face, then shave. There are dark bags under my eyes and, not to put too fine a point on it, I look like something the cat tried to bury. I haven't had enough sleep, and what sleep I managed to snatch came with an unpleasant freight of dreams: plateau, temple, sleeper, you know the drill.

There is a shitty filter coffee machine and I use it with malice in mind, dunking two whole bags of Starbucks' oiliest caffeinated charcoal in the cone. As it hisses and burbles I try to check my email on my phone.

Nothing.

Now, there are few existential crises as unnerving for a geek like me (the original feral kind—not your commercialized cash cow as-reimagined-by-Urban-Outfitters-and-Hollywood fashion geek, who is basically a hipster with a neckbeard and worse fashion sense) as being off the net. It takes me a couple of minutes of prodding and poking to determine that the motel's wifi network is up but has no way of sending packets to the wider internet, and AT&T's two-wet-shoelaces-and-a-tin-can excuse for wireless broadband has also shat its routing tables and is drooling in a corner. There are a couple of laptops hooked up to the hotel wifi network—I can see their owners' porn stashes from the shiny new Dell—so it's not my equipment. Frowning, I check for Google. Nope, and if *their* private backhaul isn't talking to the local ISPs we're in major blackout territory. Following a hunch I punch up the maps app and see if I can get a GPS signal. Nothing, nada.

The coffee pot is making drowning-squirrel noises as I do something

I *never* do in hotel rooms, which is to pick up the TV remote for a purpose other than hammering the "off" button. The in-house check-out channel comes up on the screen, but once I start to channel hop I rapidly confirm an unpleasant suspicion. There are too many dead spots. I can see a local news channel, a couple of community spots where amateur dramatics types are playing with their camcorders in a studio that looks like an abandoned warehouse, and of course the local porn buffet. What I *don't* see is anything national: no CNN, no MSNBC, no Hitler Channel or Mythbusters. Not even *Top Gear* reruns on BBC America. The local cableco is clearly having a spot of bother. Mind you, I *do* find the God Botherer Channel, where they're advertising a love-in at some place called the New Life Church in Colorado Springs. Live coverage from two o'clock.

I stare at the screen for a minute, jaw hanging slack. *Ha. Ha. Very funny. Not.* They're even giving directions for how to get there, for any locals crazy enough to drive in this weather, and a special dispensation from Lord Jeebus to say that his faithful won't have to worry about doing four-wheel drifts into oncoming snowplows. Raymond Schiller, Impresario and Evangelist. On stage in the New Life Church this afternoon at three. Bring all the family! A first-class production is guaranteed for all.

With a sense of gathering alarm I rummage through my wallet and pull out the Coutts card. I dial the phone number on it and a robot with a nasal whine tells me it has been unable to connect my call and I should try again later.

"Shit," I say aloud, just as there's a double-knock on the room door.

I'm not usually prone to flashbacks but a split second later I'm flat against the wall with a stolen revolver clenched uncomfortably in my left hand, heart rattling the bars of my tonsils and screaming to be let out. It takes a second for me to realize that cops wouldn't knock—they'd break the door down—and it doesn't *feel* like MIBs.

Feel? I wonder what's up with me. Another funny turn?

There's another knock, quiet and rapid. I slide over, glance through the peephole, and open the door.

"Wotcher, cock," says Johnny, oozing into the room like a diffident landslide. Persephone is waiting behind him, looking up and down the corridor. She's positively tap-dancing with impatience. "Nice piece," Johnny comments.

"Come in," I say, making sure the gun's pointing at the floor. Persephone backs inside, then turns and has the door locked and bolted in one fluid motion. "We're blacked out. No internet, no TV, no GPS, no phone."

"I love it when a plan comes together." Johnny pauses for a double beat. "What, it's not deliberate?"

"We had dialtone at five a.m.," I tell them. "This is new."

"Well." Persephone looks around. "There are roadblocks on the interstates, the airports and general aviation fields are shut down, and now the phone system doesn't work. It sounds like—"

"Enemy action," completes Johnny. He glances at me. "You want to get out, or go in?"

"My orders say to get out, so I'm going to leave the other on the table as Plan B," I say. Persephone is looking at me, with an expression I usually see on Mo's face when I've said something particularly stupid. "What?"

"It's going to be harder to drive out than you think. There is an open gate near Colorado Springs, and someone—I think Schiller—is using it to power a ward around half the state." Now I get it. She's tired *and* wired, simultaneously. Then I do a double take. *Power a what?*

"Seems to me we can try and bug out," Johnny observes. "Might not make it, fair do's. Or we can drop it in my mate Paddy's lap and hope the Nazgûl can do something with it."

"Paddy?" I ask.

"An old mate I ran into. He's making a living as an informer for you know who. 'Course he won't inform on *us* unless I ask him to." He smiles frighteningly. "Or we can go down to see our old friend Ray Schiller and explain the facts of life to him. Pick a card, any card."

I turn to the table and pick up the coffee jug. *Decisions, decisions.* There are only two cups. "Johnny, go get us a couple of mugs from Persephone's room."

He bristles. "Hey, you don't—"

"Johnny, do what the nice man says," Persephone's tone is even. "Take my key."

I am still pouring the second coffee as the door closes. "How far do you trust him?" I ask, turning round to offer her a mug.

"With my life," she says, unhesitating. "Only—" She stops. "You noticed it, too. What?"

I take a sip of coffee and grimace. "He's pushing options at us. And something feels *wrong*."

"He had a religious upbringing: he was brought up to be an elder in the very odd church that Schiller comes from. He ran away to join the army to escape. And now it turns out"—she sniffs at her mug: her nose wrinkles—"he is probably having unpleasant flashbacks."

"Could they have turned him?"

"Out of the question." She shrugs dismissively. "Johnny's loyalty is not in question." Her eyes narrow as she looks at me. "If you think we do this only for money—"

"So you want to go in," I say, as the door opens, "find out what he's using to power the gate and close it. Right?"

There's a heavy *chunk* as Johnny puts a mug down on the desk top. "You've got a map, Duchess, and Mr. Howard here has got a compass." He's looking at the pizza box on the desk, where the complaints department has been quiescent for some time. It rattles quietly, as if it senses doom approaching.

"Johnny," I say briskly, trying to conceal my unease, "you implied your friend Patrick is an OPA stringer, right?"

"Yep."

"So why aren't the OPA crawling all over this town right now?"

"Because," Johnny says patiently, "they can't. Schiller's keeping them out. Paddy lives here; he's their only eyes and ears right now."

"Right." I think for a moment. "Then we need to contact him because he's probably our only way of getting a message out right now. Schiller's big mega-church is in Colorado Springs, and he's starting whatever it is at three this afternoon. At least that's what the ads on cable TV say. I think he's moving to some kind of endgame, and opening a gate is part of it. So here's what we're going to do. *You* are going to go and find Patrick and go to ground with him." Johnny is looking at me oddly, but I push on: "You and I"—I turn to Persephone—"are going to drive down to Palmer Lake and look around. Bet it's some kind of major ceremony—if they're doing what I think they're doing—"

"They'll need lots of warm meat. Understood." She glances at Johnny, then nods. "They'll be processing the flock at the mega-church. What do you want to do about it, Mr. Howard?"

I take a mouthful of the foul wake-up juice. "I think we should confirm what's going on, then relay to Johnny, who's going to tell Patrick to tell his handler what the epicenter is." Johnny nods slowly but holds his counsel. "Then we're going to go visit the church. It'd be a good idea to confirm the picture before we set the Nazgûl on them. Plus, they may be running the abattoir some distance from the buffet. In which case we may be able to rescue a few folks." I swallow again, my throat abruptly dry. "And then I'm going to take some holiday snaps."

I HATE KILLING.

Most people seem to have this escapist James Bond vision of secret agents offing bad guys left, right, and center, then wisecracking about it. Or they think we're some kind of Jack Bauer psychopath torturing the truth about the ticking bomb out of everyone in sight. In truth, killing is a very unusual part of the job and it leaves me feeling sick and depressed for months afterwards—and that's when *someone else* is doing it.

I can count on my thumbs the number of people I have intentionally killed in my decade-plus of service. I've put down a lot of once-living humans whose bodies still moved but whose nervous systems were in service to alien nightmares, but that's not the same. The zombies, like the two who tried to grab me back in the hotel, are not so terrible—you learn to live with the inevitability of it eventually—but the very idea of killing a thinking, laughing, loving human being makes me sick in my stomach and fills me with horror. And that's when it's a bad guy who's got a knife at my throat or who is pointing a gun at me, and I can justify it to myself as self-defense. (Killing innocent bystanders is something I have nightmares about. Once, for a traumatic week, I thought I'd done so; it nearly broke me.)

Anyway, that's why they send me on these missions. As my ex-boss Andy put it, "Would you rather we gave the job to someone who *enjoyed* it?"

It's bad enough when I have to do smelly stuff that lands someone else in the shit. TL;DR version is, I hate killing, and I try to find any possible shadow of an excuse to avoid doing it. (And so does my wife.)

. . . Which is why it feels very peculiar, not to mention distressing, to be in this position.

Schiller's ministry is clearly messing with very dangerous powers. That Bible alone would have been enough to justify shutting him down with extreme prejudice, and as for the rest—the brain parasites, the baby farm Persephone stumbled across, not to mention the Fimbulwinter weather and the Sleeper in the Pyramid—all of those are enough to justify bringing the hammer down *hard*.

I don't like the term "collateral damage"; it trivializes agony and dismemberment, mourning and grief. (*You* try telling the bereaved survivors that you had to kill their family and friends to protect their freedom. See how you like what they say to you.) But if any situation justifies the use of extreme force, this comes close. If Schiller's misguided attempt to wake the Gatekeeper (Is Schiller *really* so naive he believes that abomination is Jesus Christ?) succeeds, everyone in the world will pay the price. These things are not demons or gods: they're ancient intelligences from other corners of the cosmos that are normally inaccessible and inhospitable to our kind. When they get into our world they are as inclined to mercy towards us as cats are towards mice. We make splendid toys for their amusement, until we break.

If Schiller is really trying to conduct a great summoning with the Apocalypse Codex as a reference manual, someone has to shut the gate down before he levers it wide enough to summon his master—a process which probably involves mass human sacrifice, because these nitwits are generally too theory-impaired to realize that if they want to make a nuclear explosion there are more efficient ways to do it than banging two lumps of highly enriched uranium together by hand. And unless the Seventh Cavalry—that would be the Nazgûl—make it over the hill in time, that duty devolves on *me*. Because I'm apprenticed to the Eater of Souls (and how's that for a job description? Junior Assistant Under-Secretary For Eating Of Souls, Fourth Grade) and they made me sign for Pinky's pocket consumer implementation of SCORPION STARE, the original basilisk gun in a box—so I guess from the outside I look like some kind of super-powerful government assassin.

While all the time I'm brokenly repeating inside, like an old-time cracked record, *fuck me, I've drawn the hangman's straw. Again.*

TRY LOOKING AT IT FROM SOMEONE ELSE'S POINT OF VIEW:

Persephone drives slowly into the teeth of the twilight, peering suspiciously at the road from behind wipers that sweep across the windscreen with a rhythmic thud, shoveling the driving snow into the chilly night.

The liaison officer from External Assets slumps next to her in the passenger seat. His face is turned away. He could almost be sleeping, but occasionally he raises a hand to scratch alongside his nose or delivers some other sign of sentience. The other hand rests, palm down, on the small cardboard pizza box in his lap.

The weather is unnerving. Huge snowflakes, fingernail-sized, drift from a sky that dawn has barely brightened to the color of dull slate, warmed by a brassy tint that bespeaks more snow to come. There's little wind and the flakes drop steadily, dulling the sound of traffic from outside the coupé and reducing visibility to a couple of hundred meters.

The municipality snowplows are out and the roads are gritted. Even so, the fresh snow is filling in tire tracks in front of her eyes. Denver gets snow and people hereabouts know how to drive in the stuff, but the sidewalks and trees are already blanketed thickly, and it's getting heavier.

There's a ramp onto the interstate, clogged with sluggish traffic shuffling south. It moves in fits and starts. She glances sideways at

Howard again. A civil service chinless wonder, Johnny thought. Well, the chinless wonder in question broke out through a snatch squad and evaded capture as neatly as any field op in the Network. And the chinless wonder seems to harbor ideas about leading from the front, not dropping the people he thinks he's responsible for in the sticky stuff. And he's inclined to go for the throat when confronted with a fight/flight choice. All in all, he's shaping up extremely positively as far as Persephone's personnel review is concerned. But . . . *holiday snaps*? He's joking, he's mad, or he's holding something back. And she knows which she'd put her money on.

Persephone checks her rearview again, then squints into the falling curtain of snow. A big rig looms up out of the haze on her right, stationary on the hard shoulder. Snow is already mounding up across its hood as she rolls past it in a wave of slush, maintaining a steady forty. A lunatic in an SUV is coming up too damned fast on the left, but at least he won't be yacking on his cellphone on the way to work. "Mr. Howard. Is your phone getting a signal yet?"

Howard's hand moves to his coat pocket. "Nope." He stares at the iPhone for a while before sliding it away again. "Thaumometer's still hot ahead of us, though."

Persephone compares his announcement to her mental map, lurid gold and yellow highlights gleaming like Midas's curse, and finds that the spike of power that marks the portal is right where he said. "Check."

She scans her rearview again. "About the target. Once Patrick notifies the Black Chamber, what do you think we should do?"

Her passenger cogitates for a few seconds. "That depends. If the Nazgûl tell us they'll handle it—then, I think, at that point we should leave as fast as we can. Assuming we're able to, of course. At that point, it's their baby."

"And if they don't? Or if we can't contact them?"

Howard sighs. "Let's cross that bridge when we get—"

There are red-and-blue lights flashing up ahead. Another big rig has slid off the side of the road, and the highway patrol are directing traffic over to the left to pass it. She notices the way Howard tenses. "Do you have a plan, or were you going to improvise?" she asks.

"It depends on whether Schiller's church event is where he's opening the gate, or merely where he's feeding it from," he admits.

"They're separate." She purses her lips. Can't he see that? Doesn't he have the inner eye to observe the magic lighting up the horizon all around? Clearly not—and she doesn't think he's the type to go through life with eyes wide shut.

"Then it also depends on whether the Nazgûl are on the case. I figure I can shut down one or the other but not necessarily both, assuming they're in separate places. If the Nazgûl can shut down the gate I can stop the sacrifices, or vice versa. Or—"

"You are not asking me to take one of them. Why is that?"

She keeps her eyes on the road ahead, but her fingers tighten on the wheel. Howard might notice and think she's tense because of the snow, but he'd be wrong. Clearly Lockhart didn't brief him fully: it's almost as if he thinks *he's* in charge here.

Howard is silent for a few seconds. Then: "I don't think it's fair to ask civilian contractors to do something that could get them killed in the line of duty."

Civilian Contractors? Lockhart definitely left him in the dark, then, or maybe that part of her dossier was above Howard's clearance level. But Persephone finds another aspect of Howard's reply more interesting than his misconceptions about her and Johnny. "What has *fairness* got to do with it?"

Howard looks at her. She keeps her eyes on the road, but can half-feel his curiosity burning into the side of her face. "We hired you for a hands-off reconnaissance mission, not a suicide op. As of the moment Lockhart told me the operation was scrubbed, you were off the hook. You're not part of the Laundry. You don't *want* to be part of the organization. So you've done your bit; game's over, you can go home and collect your pay packet with a clear conscience and a job well . . . okay, a job that *would* have been well done if the snark wasn't a boojum after all." He clears his throat. "I, on the other hand, swore a binding oath to defend the realm against certain threats, of which this is clearly one. Schiller made it my business when he stuck his nose into our tent back in London. Now, my job doesn't stop until it's over. If I was a complete bastard like some of my managers, I'd be looking for a way to blackmail you into giving your all for Blighty. But I tend to believe that the difference between *us* and *them* is that we don't compromise our principles for temporary convenience. So once we've confirmed the target and gotten the word out, I want you to—"

Persephone can't contain her laughter anymore: she starts to giggle. "Oh dear. Is *that* what you think?"

"Uh?"

"You listen to me. I am not going to leave this job half-done, and I am certain Johnny will say exactly the same when you ask him. You are not the only person here with a reason to put Schiller out of business."

Howard hunkers down in his chair. "Oh," he says quietly. "Well . . . thanks. But I don't like to make assumptions."

"Well that's too bad, because you're running on false ones."

They drive on in silence for another ten minutes before Persephone feels calm enough to try to explain.

"The Laundry, Mr. Howard. It's not noted for enabling high achievers, is it?"

"What?" He looks puzzled. "What, you mean—"

"It is a government agency. And government agencies are run as bureaucracies. There is a role for bureaucracy; it's very useful for certain tasks. In particular, it facilitates standardization and interchangeability. Bureaucracies excel at performing tasks that must be done consistently whether the people assigned to them are brilliant performers or bumbling fools. You can't always count on having Albert Einstein in the patent office, so you design its procedures to work even if you hire Mr. Bean by mistake." She pauses to maneuver around a nose-to-tail queue of trucks that are making bad time on an uphill stretch, slowing as she sees red-and-blue lights on the shoulder ahead. "Wizards and visionaries are all very good but you cannot count on them for legwork and form-filling. Which is why there is tail-chasing and make-work and so many committee meetings and reports to read and checklists to fill out, to keep the low achievers preoccupied.

"Now, I suspect Gerald Lockhart didn't brief you on certain . . .

aspects of his department. Like its relationship with what is sometimes jokingly called Mahogany Row. And it's not my place to brief you for him, but you appear to be working on the assumption that the tail wags the dog, not vice versa. So let me put it to you that there's more to the occult intelligence world than institutional bureaucracy. Sometimes a bureaucracy grinds up against a problem that requires a mad genius instead of an office full of patient researchers. And indeed, the mad genii predate the bureaucracy. The Laundry is like an oyster nursing an irritating grain of sand within layers of bureaucratic mother-of-pearl."

The snow is falling in ever-heavier sheets, obscuring the roadside signage and turning the slopes to either side of the freeway into blank white planes. "Sometimes they try to nurture the talent within the organization. You usually work for Dr. Angleton, don't you? Yes, I suspect you're one of *them*. The specialists who come up through the ranks. And then there are the external assets. Lockhart deals with those. Because sometimes the bureaucracy needs people who can do things that bureaucrats are not allowed to do, people who can work outside the law or who have unique skills. The organization needs to scratch its own back."

She thumps the steering wheel hub hard. Howard jerks upright. "What?"

"I am not outside your *agency*, Mr. Howard, I am outside your *organization chart*. And I'm outside it because I am *more useful* on the outside. Bureaucracies are inefficient by design. Inefficiency is the twin sister of redundancy, of overcapacity, of the ability to plow through a swamp by brute force alone. If I was embedded within the organization I would spend most of my time in committee meetings, writing reports, and arguing with imbeciles. I would be far less efficient under such constraints, and I am not a patient woman."

The idiots in Rome, endlessly bickering over who had killed her parents, had tried her patience sorely. And the patronizing men at the Ministry with their *no job for a little girl*. The British organization, at least, had a more pragmatic approach—one reflecting its antique collegiate origins, all the way back to Sir Francis Walsingham and John Dee; never mind its wartime expansion into a special operations team, willing to take anyone whether or not they had been to the right school or university. Buried somewhere in the lard-belly of committee agendas and office politics is a steel spine, and the arrangement they offered her has proven to be very satisfactory.

"The Laundry is stranger and older than you probably realize," she says quietly. "And the core, the informal group the bureaucrats call Mahogany Row, goes back even further. For hundreds of years they existed, a select band of practitioners of the dark sciences, solitary by nature, funded out of the House of Lords' black budget." Howard's jaw flaps, silently; it's always amusing to watch their reaction when they learn the truth. "Mahogany Row, the bureaucrats call it. They don't know the half of it. The larger organization, built from the guts of SOE, was created purely to support the wizards of the invisible college; these days, the civil servants think they're the real thing. But only because the occupants of those empty offices choose not to disabuse them of such a useful misconception.

"I believe Gerald Lockhart may have misled you about our working relationship, Mr. Howard. Perhaps he implied that Johnny and I are contractors who work for the agency. A little white lie that lends us a bit more flexibility than we'd have if we spent all our hours filling in time sheets and attending meetings. That sort of stuff is Gerald's job—dealing with the bureaucracy so that we don't have to. Us? We go places, break plots, and kill demons."

She closes her eyes briefly to consult her memory map, opens them again as a stupid minivan driver blazes past, spraying turbid slush everywhere. There are more flashing lights. The big USAF base is some miles ahead, off to the right, behind a chain-link fence surrounding the area of a medium-large European state.

"Forty to fifty minutes," she says, pressing down on the accelerator. The yellow glare of the gate lies off to one side and astern, just beyond the horizon, lighting up the starless sky of the Other Place. An echoing glare of light lies dead ahead, straight down the highway. "Then we can shut down Schiller's revival service."

She glances sideways to check his reaction to her words. Howard is staring intently at the pizza box on his lap instead of listening.

"What is it?" she asks.

Howard looks up. "I think they're onto us," he says.

MORNING AT THE NEW LIFE CHURCH.

The New Life Church isn't just a church—it's a campus and office complex, with multiple buildings housing the World Prayer Center and a whole slew of small group ministries focussing on specialized niches.

Its worshipers are, in Raymond Schiller's eschatology, misguided at best and damned at worst; or they were, until he convinced the Board of Overseers to give him a fair hearing at a prayer retreat in the compound near Palmer Lake. The Board of Overseers have now been Saved, and are duly grateful. As a sign of appreciation they have agreed to make the main sanctuary available for Ray's big tent event, in a joyous celebration of the Golden Promise Ministries' bounteous commitment to the people of Colorado Springs. In fact, they're pulling out all the stops to bring their flock to the true cause—they've rearranged the main sanctuary for a largely standing congregation and, with the Sheriff's Department providing volunteer fire marshals and a waiver, they've got a roof to cover 8,000 souls. New Life only has about 9,000 regulars at present and barely a third are likely to show for a non-Sunday special organized by a different local church, but Golden Promise have been love-bombing Colorado Springs and environs with advertisements for the event for the past week; and once they're Saved, the new converts will be most zealous in their attempts to bring friends and family along.

Kick-off is due at 2 p.m., for an event that is planned to run all afternoon. It's a tight schedule. The Golden Promise team are supposed to complete their tear-down by 9 p.m. so that the sanctuary can be returned to order for the Sunday morning service. The reality, as Ray has explained to Pastors Dawes and Holt, is that Sunday is cancelled. *Every* day is Sunday in the world to come, and once the New Life Church is rededicated to a higher purpose it will process new blood around the clock.

It's morning at the New Life, although Ray couldn't be certain if his watch didn't tell him so. "Who ordered this?" He frets at sister Rose-anne: "Our Lord sends his storms to protect the flock of the faithful until it's time to take what is ours of right, but if it stops them coming to Church . . ."

"I'm sure it will be all right, Father?" She clutches his day planner apprehensively. "The Lord will provide snowplows and road salt, I'm sure!"

Ray glances at her sharply, but there's no sign of irony in her hope-ful face. Irony is a sin, but his handmaids are faithful followers, pure and chaste even without a host to guide them. He nods slowly. "I'm certain He will." He turns his head to his security chief. "Alex. Our expected drop-in guests. You're ready for them?"

Alex nods. "We have security in plain clothes checking the doors, and the parking garage barrier is manned. I've issued mug shots and everyone's been briefed on the troublemakers; the control room's manned and watching for them." He cracks his knuckles. "They won't get past us."

Ray closes his eyes. "They are approximately twenty miles north of here, coming south along the Ronald Reagan Expressway. Slowly, be-cause of the weather. The Holy Spirit told me so." He opens his eyes. "Now, what of the other task?"

"It's being taken care of. I sent some missionaries." Alex has a habit of becoming uncharacteristically terse when he is discussing something that he thinks Schiller is best insulated from, lest he end up on a wit-ness stand someday.

Ray nods, thoughtfully. "I'll be in the vestry. Bring them to me as soon as you have them, unless I'm on stage; in that case, hold them until I'm ready." He stands and rests a hand on sister Roseanne's shoul-der for a moment—his sense of balance has been erratic this past day or so. "God be with you."

PATRICK IS IN THE KITCHEN, BREWING UP A POT OF TEA, WHEN he realizes something is very wrong.

Moira is upstairs in the bedroom, tucked up and crashed out on a cocktail of temazepam and Imodium to keep her guts under control. The chemo this time round is visibly eroding her, like a too-fast river wearing down a sandstone bed. It cuts into her earlier with each course. She won't be stirring much before noon, but he needs to get moving and buy food, then call the shop about her car. So he's up and about in a pair of worn bedroom slippers and a dressing gown that's seen better days, sluicing hot water around the teapot and getting ready to spoon loose leaf tea into it. The Irish Breakfast blend brings back memories, not all of them bad.

It's unnaturally dark outside, and the weatherman's got no clue about what's happening: there's something on the news about an extreme weather event and a blackout that's hit the phone company— backhoe through a cable, probably, or a fire in an exchange. But Patrick pays scant attention to the radio. Something is tickling his nerves.

He can't say precisely what it is, but his hackles rise. Then, a moment later, he feels it. It's a tight, warm sensation at the base of his throat, in the other tattoo they applied when he signed the contract. *A warning and a threat.* He glances around, taking stock. The kettle is on the burner, heating up. There's nothing visible in the backyard. *Danger.* He's felt it before, this premonition of disaster. It takes him back to an evening in Belfast: taking a shortcut home from the pub via Barrack Street, just off the lower Falls, when he'd realized he was being stalked. Or another time in Marseilles, setting up a fallback route for the Duchess when the same faces kept showing up in shop window reflections behind him. The fetid breath of disaster panting after him.

There is a reproduction grandmother clock in the front hall, patiently ticking away the seconds. Patrick darts through and opens the cabinet door on its front, pushes aside the lead counterweights and disturbs the pendulum that has counted out the twilight hours and months he's spent here with Moira. Leaning inside the cabinet with its muzzle on the floor and the butt close to hand is a sawn-off pump-action shotgun. Five in the tube and one up the spout. He keeps it for emergencies, along with the discreet camera on the front stoop and the screen inside the door. Right now the camera is showing nothing much, just the usual view of the steps and the mailbox, but something about it isn't quite right—

There is a hammering on the door. "Police! Open up!" There's nothing on screen, but right then the tattoo heats up like a bad patch of sunburn and begins to glow.

Out of time for the subtle stuff, Patrick feels an old and familiar fury: *So they want to fuck with me and mine?* Not that he's got much. This run-down two-story house in the suburbs, and his run-down wife, sallow-skinned and exhausted from the cancer, sleeping upstairs. But he will *not* let them pass, whoever they are. He pulls the shotgun, brings it round to bear on the front door, and fires without hesitation.

Click. Nothing happens.

Crunch. The door bows inward near the lock, but the reinforced frame he installed is holding for now—until they bring a jack to bear.

Patrick swears angrily and works the slide, ejects a cartridge, and pulls again. *Click.*

His tattoo is burning hot now. The kettle begins to wind up to an eerie banshee scream from the kitchen as it comes to a rolling boil.

Another cartridge goes rolling across the floor as Patrick squeezes the trigger again: another misfire. He glances down as he reloads, futile—the red plastic tubes projecting from the cartridge bases are glowing cuprous green in the shadows. They're loaded with banishment rounds, but it looks like someone's brought countermeasures.

Patrick drops the gun and legs it towards the kitchen, hunting wildly for anything suitable—the knife rack by the worktop, the kettle screeching its iron lung out—grabs Moira's favorite carving knife and the aforementioned iron jug, skids back into the hall, and turns at bay as the door opens.

They are not the police.

"Motherfucker!" Patrick screams in fury and throws the contents of the boiling kettle at the first intruder. Conservatively attired in a black suit and tie, white shirt, the missionary takes the steaming gush direct in the face without flinching. His eyes glow the same shade of green as the flawed shotgun cartridges rolling underfoot as he steps forward. Glowing green wormlike shapes writhe within the intruder's eyes. "Get the fuck out!"

Patrick lunges forward, carving knife held low. The missionary is spreading his arms wide. Now his mouth opens, revealing something silvery and twitching. The knife is a faint hope. Patrick leans hard and the point sinks into the missionary's chest, right between the ribs, but no blood comes out. And now Patrick's tattoos are glowing nearly as brightly as the low-power bulb in the hall light fitting. The missionary takes another step forward, and the second one crosses the threshold, cutting off any chance of escape through the front door.

Patrick takes a step back, treads on a loose shotgun cartridge, and falls against the wall beside the clock. Door hanging open, chains and counterweights disemboweled—he reaches in and yanks hard on the pendulum, a kilogram of brass on the end of a meter-long steel shank. (The clock was his old man's; the only thing of his that he's bought to the new world.) Raising the improvised shillelagh he takes a swipe at the missionary's head with the counterweight. *Success.* The thing in front of him raises an arm to block, and stops pushing forward. The knife blade sticking out of his chest is oozing slowly, thick and dark.

"Join us," drones the missionary. "We are the Saved. Join us and bathe in the blood of the lamb and be Saved forever."

"Fuck *off*," Patrick snarls, waving the pendulum at the walking corpse. "Get aff my fuckin' patch, motherfocker!"

"Join us—" The missionary repeats the invitation perfectly, like an answering machine from hell.

"Patrick"—another voice from the top of the stairs, one that detonates an emotional hand grenade that sends grief-tainted shrapnel tearing through his heart—"what's going on?"

Only one thing left. Utter desperation and fear threaten to weaken his knees before he can do it. It's a last resort: *maybe they can—*
Help?

Patrick loses consciousness immediately. Someone else looks out through his eyes, someone more detached, with the aloof cruelty of a small boy contemplating the antics of insects trapped in a jam jar.

"Hello," says Patrick's mouth.

The missionaries hold their ground, but look apprehensive. It's like they know their own kind.

"Why don't you tell me why you're here," says Control. "Did Ray send you?"

"Join us—"

"*Bo*-ring." Patrick's body jabs the pendulum into the nearer missionary's face and lets go of it. And then, with an agility alien to a sixty-year-old in poor condition, he stoops sideways and scoops up the shotgun.

"Patrick? Who are these—"

"Oh shut up." He spins towards the staircase and casually pulls the trigger. The detonation is deafening in the confined space. What's left of Moira's upper torso fountains blood as it topples forward, coming to rest at the foot of the stairs. Her head lands face down on the landing.

Control ejects the spent cartridge, chambers a fresh round, and turns back to face the missionaries, raising the shotgun and bringing the barrel to rest under his borrowed body's chin.

"Who sent you?" Control demands, resting a finger lightly on the trigger.

"Why did you kill her? She was Unsaved." The second missionary is more talkative than his taller companion, whose unfortunate encounter with a carving knife has damaged his lungs.

"Who sent you?" Control repeats. "I'm getting impatient here. Tell me or I'll kill the hostage. Then you won't get to eat him."

"We do not eat them!" protests the second missionary. His voice is thick and hard to make out. His tongue ripples fatly between his lips, silvery with twitching legs: it has grown almost too large for this mouth. Soon it will asphyxiate the carrier, and the host will require another body. "We bring them to the Lord."

"All right." Control lowers the shotgun muzzle far enough for Patrick's mouth to swallow convulsively: certain physiological reflexes continue, even if the usual tenant is elsewhere. "Who *is* your Lord?"

"We serve the Gatekeeper of Heaven, He Who Sleeps and Will Rise Again. Come with us. Accept the love of Jesus Christ into your heart and mouth and rejoice in everlasting light for eternity. You, too, can be Saved. Help us tear down the Wall of Pain and open the gates of the pyramid and dance wild and free forever in the silver heat of His gaze!"

Control sneers. "I don't think so!" Then he pushes down on the trigger, and the top of Patrick's skull disappears in a mist of fatty tissue and bone splinters.

IT IS A SMALL MERCY, IN CONTROL'S OPINION: A REWARD FOR all Patrick has done for the Agency, and a final discharge that painlessly clears all debts. (Which are not inconsiderable, counting the group health insurance.) The situation was already non-survivable by the time Patrick became aware of it. He should have grasped this as soon as he realized the CCTV was being spoofed. Or in any event once the banishment rounds misfired when he engaged the enemy.

But Control is now aware of the true identity of the adversary. And that means there's still some hope of saving Denver.

THE TROUBLE WITH GODHEADS, IN JOHNNY'S EXPERIENCE, IS that they can't quite understand how anyone could *not* believe their shit. It seems as obvious as gravity to them, as normal as water flowing downhill and rain following sunshine; everything works the way it says in the book because the book is the inerrant word of God.

Leaving aside the idolatry implicit in taking a mere *book* as a more authoritative source of truth than divine revelation, there are damaging consequences when such a belief system collides with reality. If the world was created in six days six-thousand-odd years ago, then a whole bunch of evidence relating to geology, biology, paleontology, genetics, and evolution has to be ignored—or, much harder, refuted. Which is easy enough if you *don't hold with school-book larnin'*, but it's difficult to practice general medicine if your religion says bacteria can't evolve antibiotic resistance, and hard to be a geologist if your cosmology is incompatible with continental drift.

And then there's the picking and choosing. Men who lie with men are an abomination in the eyes of the Lord. But then, so is the eating of shellfish, if you go back to the original text. And the wearing of garments made from different types of fiber. And tattooing. And witchcraft—or is it poisoning? Different translations disagree. (And what on earth does the bit about what to do if your house contracts leprosy mean?) The early Church fathers cut through the Gordian knot by declaring the Old Testament obsolete: version 1.0, superseded by the new, improved version 2.0. But they couldn't make it stick, hence the thousand-page prologue you have to wade through before you get to read the Gospel of Matthew. And even there, even in the prologue, even after weeding out the obvious Bible fanfic, there's no rhyme nor reason: some churches can't be arsed with the Book of Judith, while some of them cancelled the Maccabees after season two because of dwindling Nielsen ratings.

So you end up with divergent sects reading from subtly different versions of the same book—which in turn is a third-generation translation of something which might have been the original codification of an oral tradition—and all convinced that their interpretation overrides such minor obstacles as observable reality.

Which *still* wouldn't be a problem except that some of the readers think the books are an instruction manual rather than a set of educational parables, a blueprint instead of a metaphor.

Johnny whistles tunelessly between his teeth as he drives.

He's fed up to his back teeth with Godheads. Godheads in the person of his father and uncles and mother and aunts were why he joined up with the British Army when he was sixteen. Godheads following the blueprint for salvation got him into trouble a couple of years later—and then there was the *Légion étrangère*. Because when you're born eldest son to the moderator of a remarkably exclusive brethren in an exceptionally free kirk where they don't believe in sex because it might lead to dancing (which in turn would imply the existence of *music*), the tendency to see demons everywhere never really leaves you.

It took meeting Persephone all those years ago to show Johnny that he was not, in fact, insane: the visions and nightmares in the corners of his vision were, in fact, really there, and that his ranting elders with their taste for spiritual warfare and their ancestral skeletons in a very watery closet were barking up the wrong tree.

Johnny drives.

There is a pricking in his fingertips and an itching in his left buttock that tells him where to point the pickup. Patrick didn't exactly hand him a business card, but they've broken bread and shared a meal: the symbolism is not wasted. Johnny doesn't have much in the way of natural magical aptitude, though like Persephone he has vastly more than most of the arid theory-driven paper-pushers of the Laundry. What he *does* have is a knack for seeing and sensing the unseen and unfelt. Centuries earlier he'd have been doomed to the madness of the witch-finder, but in these enlightened years he's just a regular guy with a talent for spotting trouble before it spots him. And a couple of psychotic blades.

But he has a bad feeling about Patrick.

His itches and hunches take him off the freeway and onto a leisurely cruise around the back streets of Denver. They're drawing him north, into a subdivision dominated by low houses behind rusting chain-link fences, untidy yards showing the detritus of suburbia—dirty plastic slides and paddling pools, aging cars. Patrick and (What was her name? Morag? Moira?) live cheaply and frugally, in one of these houses. Yes, this street, that house—with the black Suburban with blacked-out windows parked casually asprawl the sidewalk fronting it.

Oh. Too late.

Johnny pulls over and backs up until his tailgate is up against the radiator of the big SUV. Then he climbs out and walks up the garden path to the front porch and the door, drawing the pair of knives as he goes and holding them point-down. The door is ajar and there is an itching in his nose, and the skin on the nape of his neck wants to stand on end. A powerful geas surrounds the house, making eyes drift by and ears misinterpret noises. Johnny, however, is immune to such distractions. He kicks the door open and breathes in the stink of death.

He counts two corpses and two bodies that still breathe. Heads turn to look at him, eyes glowing the green of luminous watch dials in the shadows. He raises his knives and they shrink backwards. Two bodies: one male, pretty much headless, a sawn-off shotgun lying to one side. Another . . . *too late.*

"Awright," he snarls, "so whose smart idea was *this*?"

One of the breathing bodies—clad in a dark suit, with a spreading stain of sticky blood drenching the front of its white shirt around the handle of a carving knife—slobbers incoherently at him. The other is less far gone. In fact, by born-again zombie standards he's positively eloquent: "The sinner summoned up a demon from hell, which shot his wife before turning his weapon on himself. You are Johnny McTavish. We have a message for you."

"You do, do you?" Johnny stares at the speaker. He *looks* human— as human as a missionary in his Sunday best—but his voice sounds sluggish and thick. "Stick yer tongue out, mate."

The missionary stares at him. Writhing shadows in the shape of worms twirl endlessly in the depths of the missionary's eyes. Then it slowly opens its mouth, revealing a laminated silver carapace. Johnny stares at it. After a moment, it extends eye stalks and stares right back.

"I should kill you right now. Like the others."

The missionary retracts what passes for its tongue. "Then you would not find it so easy to reach your destination."

The other missionary's slobbering quiets. It's nearly out of blood; even a cymothoan mind parasite can't get much mileage out of a body that's no longer capable of supporting aerobic respiration.

"What destination?" Johnny keeps his knife aimed at the thing's throat. He can feel the knife quivering, eager to carry out its task. He actually has to hold it back, to prevent it from flying out of his hand. It's difficult to hold back, not least because of the black nucleus of rage burning at the back of his mind over what they have done here to Patrick, who was, if not an old friend, then at least a sometime brother in arms.

The surviving missionary isn't wasting energy animating its facial muscles: the hosts do not have much use for human body language. It is as unconcerned as a corpse. "We are instructed to bring you to the High Priest, if that is your wish."

Johnny can't help himself: he laughs incredulously. "You *what*?"

"Our master ordered us to serve his High Priest. The High Priest desires your presence at the service of dedication of the masses. You should come with us." The dying missionary twitches slightly. "You must come with me."

"You have got to be kidding." *Well, it's* one *way in,* Johnny thinks. And with Patrick gone, he has no way of contacting the Black Chamber: that part of this errand is a failure. If Schiller wants to see him, that's awfully convenient. "You aren't going to convert me and you're not going to plant one of those things on me. If you try, I'll kill you. Understand?"

"Come with me," says the walking corpse. "Please, elder. Your brother commands it."

Johnny hesitates for a moment, but curiosity finally makes up his mind for him. "All right. But you're driving," he says.

14.

APPOINTMENT IN SAMARRA

IT'S 11 A.M. AND THE FIRST TRICHLE OF CHURCHGOERS ARE arriving at the New Life Church for today's extravaganza organized by the Golden Promise Ministries. Pastor Bob Dawes is up front on the stage in the big sanctuary, fronting a team—there's a light Christian rock band to get the audience energized, a couple of fire eaters with some fun parables to get across, and a bunch of other distractions to keep the audience focussed while the show builds up momentum.

They'll have help, of course: among the fresh meat will be sitting about five or six hundred of the Saved, those who have already entered fully into the doctrine of the holy ministry and who will live forever in His Glory when the light bringer returns. They're primed to cheer and clap at the right points; nothing will be allowed to fall flat.

It's been a huge project to bring forward at very short notice. Schiller's people have dropped everything, thrown themselves at the job to bring in food and refreshment stands, mobile catering kits, and a mountain of supplies. When you're getting ten thousand warm bodies through the door you've got to keep them fed and irrigated. Luckily New Life expect thousands to show up for peak draws; they've got the sanitation and toilet arrangements to handle it, and the first aid support. They've had advertising airtime playing every hour for the past couple of days on all five of Colorado Springs' Christian radio stations—begging, borrowing, and blackmailing to buy up airtime at short notice—and less frequently on the talk and music channels and the Christian stations with coverage in Denver; all this on top of the continuous roadside advertising campaign they've been running for the past few months. The message is urgent: "Get off your couch and dance with Jesus!" Ray has personally authorized a million-dollar spend on this project at very short notice, and another million on the support infrastructure.

They've even rearranged the main sanctuary for it, brought in additional seating, and laid down red carpet runners on all the aisles.

It is the most expensive birthday party Alex Lockey has ever been invited to. Only he isn't going to be taking time to enjoy the scene—as security chief he's going to be spending the whole session in the control room. *Ah well. The Lord will provide,* he thinks ironically as he waits for Ray to finish with makeup.

"Not too glossy, hon," Ray tells Judy, his makeup girl. "I need *gravitas*. Most of these people don't know me well yet." His eyes turn to Alex. "The missionaries. Any word?"

"Yes. They've found Elder McTavish. He's en route." He pauses. "There was some trouble with a spy working for the Operational Phenomenology Agency, but he's been dealt with. McTavish led our men to him." *And a good thing too,* he keeps to himself. There's no room for loose cannon stringers in this operation. If head office were to get wind of what's going on here before the Sleeper awakens it could cause any amount of trouble.

"Excellent." Schiller does not smile—not while Judy is working on his forehead with a brush: the artist is not to be disturbed—but his satisfaction is palpable. "McTavish will not yet be fully committed. Don't let him see the others after you take them in."

"I certainly won't, sir," Alex assures him. "If you don't mind . . . ?"

Leaving the presence of his master, Alex walks around the periphery of the sanctuary. The huge church is filling up slowly, and there's chatter among the families as they queue for the best unreserved seats;

ushers from GPM, uniformed in blue smocks, are directing them towards aisles where their arrival will cause minimal disruption. Some of them clutch burgers and burritos with their bibles, hot from the booths outside. The food is free, for as Ray puts it, a full stomach is a great way to get the undecided to sit down and listen to the good news.

Alex's two-way radio buzzes. It's Deputy Stewart in the control room. "We need you up here now, boss," he says. "We've got a situation developing."

"Check. On my way." Alex ups his pace. It wouldn't do to let any unwanted interlopers kick up a fuss on the Lord's new birthday.

Not long now, he thinks. His captive host agrees: *Soon we will be reunited with the Lord.* Alex basks in its warm glow of joyful anticipation. Strange to think that such a—his mind flinches from the next word—*alien*-looking thing could be such a source of love and consolation. But it is, and thanks to his wards his own mind is intact enough to appreciate the irony. And when you've worked for the Nazgûl for as long as Alex has, you learn to look beyond surface appearances.

AT THE EXACT MOMENT THAT LOCKEY IS BEING PAGED BY SE-curity in the New Life Church's control room, it's coming up on 6 p.m. in London. In a dingy office block above a row of shuttered shops, somewhere south of the river, most of the windows are dark, for it is far into overtime territory in a time of spending cuts. But in one particular meeting room—windowless, in the interior of the warren of narrow puce-green corridors and beige-carpet-tiled offices that make up the New Annex—the lights are burning late.

Approach the meeting room by way of the corridor and you will see that the door has no windows, and is identified only by a name plate reading M25. There's a strip of lights above it, like a miniature horizontal traffic signal. Right now the red light is flashing.

There's a battered boardroom table in the middle of the room. Eight chairs—equally battered, castoffs from Human Resources—are scattered around it. Someone has furnished it with a large black velvet tablecloth, chain-stitched with intricate designs in conductive silver thread using a sewing machine that is stored in a secure vault room when not in use. A couple of ruggedized boxes full of electronics sit at one end of the table, attached to the cloth by alligator clips and to a wheeled, voltage-regulated battery pack by fat cables. The door is not merely shut, or locked, but barred: physically and by means of less obvious but more lethal wards. These are not the only precautions against unwanted eavesdropping—only the most obvious ones.

"Tell me," the Senior Auditor leans forward, "precisely how long ago Howard was supposed to report in."

Gerald Lockhart clears his throat as he checks his wristwatch: "I was expecting him to be here by now," he says mildly. "I delivered the scram instruction at eight fifteen p.m. yesterday and authorized him to use any means necessary. He should have had sufficient time to make a connection by now."

The Auditor—sixty-ish, male, distinguished-looking, with gold-rimmed half-moon bifocals—exchanges a significant look with his colleague—female, late forties, with the twin-set-and-pearls look of a House of Lords apparatchik. She delivers the next question pointedly: "What *is* the communication situation at present?"

Lockhart grimaces as if he's just been asked to swallow a live toad. "In a word, poor. Phone calls are not connected. Email is not downloaded. SMS messages are not delivered. To determine whether this was specific to our people, I tried contacting various businesses in Colorado. Denver and Colorado Springs and all points between might as well have dropped off the map. The last information I could independently verify was that there is an anomalous snowstorm sweeping down the Rockies, that all flights in and out of those cities and their environs are grounded, and there's some kind of problem with satellite phones."

The female auditor makes a note on her pad. "Have you enquired through formal channels yet?"

"No." Lockhart stares down his nose, refusing to be intimidated. "As I already noted at the last oversight meeting, local law enforcement is believed to be compromised."

"Have you contacted the Black Chamber, directly or indirectly?"

Lockhart takes a deep breath. "That's what we're here to discuss. The answer is 'no,' by the way. Not without your authorization."

The male Auditor speaks again: "So we have established a baseline for this situation." He looks at Lockhart sharply. "Denver. Tell me about its geography."

"Geography? It's on a plateau." Lockhart shrugs. "West of it, everything goes crinkle-cut. East, it slopes gently down to the Mississippi."

The fourth occupant of the meeting room finally speaks. "A *plateau*." His tone is wintry.

"Thank you, Doctor," the female Auditor is snippy, "unless you have anything to contribute . . . ?"

"Yes, it's a plateau," Lockhart snaps waspishly. "With a couple of cities in the middle, and a *big temple*. The parallels to the layout of a certain other plateau in a location formerly subject to regular photo-recon overflight did not pass me by, James."

Angleton nods. He rests his elbows on the arms of his chair, fingers steepled; beneath the harsh fluorescent light from the ceiling tubes, his face looks sunken, cadaverous. "I see." He turns to stare at the auditors. "You are aware of APOCALYPSE CODEX?"

The male Auditor nods. "That is the document that . . ." He glances at Lockhart.

"Yes," says Lockhart, surly at having his work exposed to hostile eyes and critical minds. "The one that was copied during the black bag job at Schiller's hotel. And that Howard so casually emailed to *an uncleared social contact*—" His icy disapproval is profound.

"The, ah, doctor of divinity," Angleton notes with relish, "whose thesis was a study of variant Essene apocalypse cults." He returns Lockhart's glare with a blandly satisfied expression. "Do we have one of those on payroll? I seem to recall Donald Hiller retired nearly twenty years ago without any decision as to a successor being made. How long would it have taken us to locate and vet a suitable consultant if Howard hadn't cut the Gordian knot?"

"But he shouldn't be—"

"*Mister Lockhart*." Angleton leans forward like an angry rattlesnake: "You picked Howard *because* he can think outside the box and improvise solutions in the field. And you sent him out into the field to support BASHFUL INCENDIARY and JOHNNY PRINCE, without showing him the PRINCE dossier or explaining the relationship between Hazard and McTavish and our organization. You are the one who decided that the best way to evaluate his performance under stress would be to handicap him in that respect. You chose your cake. And now you are complaining about the flavor?"

"Dr. Angleton!" The female Auditor sits up. "*If* you please." She glances at her colleague. "Should we action HR about this external contact?"

"Hmm, I don't think so. Not yet. A vicar." The other Auditor picks up a pen and twirls it between his fingertips. "Too public a figure. Background checks only, for now. We can reel him in if he begins to ask uncomfortable questions."

"So." The female Auditor raises a hand and starts ticking off finger joints: "Mahogany Row suggested BASHFUL INCENDIARY and JOHNNY PRINCE investigate a location that has unfortunate resonances with GOD GAME BLUE, not to mention PRINCE's background. Howard was sent to monitor them and provide top cover while they were underground. He acknowledged a scram instruction but is now overdue, and there appears to be a communications blackout over most of populated Colorado. However, he transmitted documentary evidence that confirms GOD GAME VIOLET. The anomalous meteorological conditions suggest that GOD GAME YELLOW is in effect, either now or imminently. INCENDIARY and PRINCE are also unaccounted for. Is that a reasonable summary?"

Lockhart runs a hand through his thinning hair distractedly. "Yes."

Angleton peers out across a bony cage of interlaced fingers. "The black bag job," he says smoothly. "It was deniable, yes?"

Lockhart bristles. "It was a journalist from the *News of the World*, if you must know. He bribed a cleaner. We used a cut-out in the Met to suggest he investigate Schiller—*Freaky Fundie Preaches Polygamy at Number Ten*, that sort of thing." He shrugged. "Our friends at the Doughnut were good enough to send us his cameraphone contents. Totally, utterly hands-off, you may rest assured."

"Ahem." The Senior Auditor interrupts. "I'd like to get back to the situation in hand, which has evidently spiraled out of control in the last day. Thank you for drawing it to our attention." He glances at his colleague. "Do you think we have time to send this back up the ladder to board level? Will it keep overnight?"

Her expression could chill liquid nitrogen. "No." She glances at her watch. "If there's any risk whatsoever that Schiller is attempting to raise the Sleeper I think we should act immediately on our own cognizance."

Lockhart looks as if he's about to say something, but freezes at a glance from Angleton.

"This isn't a regular external operation anymore," the Senior Auditor tells Lockhart, not ungently. "Nor is there any need for it to remain so. You can let go, if you want. A more collegiate protocol is called for."

"Collegiate?" Lockhart pales. "But Hazard and McTavish *are* at that level."

"He's talking about the reciprocal monitoring provisions of the Benthic Treaty," Angleton points out. "Someone has to tell the Black Chamber. Stands to reason, old man." Angleton looks at the Auditors. "Well?"

"Doctor Angleton." The older Auditor pauses to push his bifocals up the bridge of his nose. "I believe you have dealt with those entities in the past. Would you mind . . . ?"

"What? Right here and now?" Angleton, normally imperturbable, for the first time sounds taken aback.

"Can you suggest a reason not to? As this is a matter of some immediate urgency . . ."

Angleton looks round. "Well, we should ward the documentary evidence first. Anything that's not cleared for sharing under these admittedly irregular circumstances. And we should ward ourselves *thoroughly*. And have suitable backup in place to contain any hard contact. Otherwise, no."

"Then so be it." The Auditor looks at Lockhart. "Gerald. When called upon, you will give an account of the inception of this operation, the direction of the external assets, and the status of Agent Howard as their monitor, and a concise report about what they found. You may mention the motivation for this operation, but should not identify the participants in the black bag job. You may discuss material classified under GOD GAME color codes freely—the Black Chamber will already be fully aware of their content—but may not refer to those codewords directly. Do not discuss McTavish's background unless the Black Chamber show prior cognizance of it. If you wish to vary these constraints you may request it of us, but not in the presence of the other party. Am I understood?"

Lockhart swallows. "Yes, I think so. Am I to negotiate?"

"No." The Auditor peers at him over his spectacle frames. "That's Angleton's job. He knows what we're dealing with." He puts down his pen. "I wish we had time to send out for a longer spoon, though . . ."

"I THINK THEY'RE ONTO US," I SAY.

I have been sitting in the passenger seat for the past hour, as Persephone flogs the rental coupé down the interstate in weather only a homesick penguin could love—it's so cold I'm shivering inside my anorak just from looking out the windows—when I realize what's going on.

"Where?" she asks, instantly focussed.

"Not in sight right now." I pause, and glance down at the pizza box. "But we keep passing cops on the shoulder with light bars going. Every ten minutes or so. If you knew you were tracking someone on this highway, wouldn't that be how you'd do it if you had the resources? Station observers every five to ten miles to radio in a sighting, instead of putting a car on their tail which they might spot."

"That would work." Persephone glances at me. "If they knew we were here."

"Yes, well." I tap the pizza box. She swears loudly and swerves. "It shouldn't be able to talk. I put wards on this box that are strong enough to gag a death metal band. But if it's found some kind of back-channel—"

Persephone isn't listening to me: she's chanting something in a tonal language that makes the hairs on my arms stand up, and her eyes are shut. I'm about to make a grab for the steering wheel—we're beginning to drift out of our lane—when she turns her head to the box, then turns sharply frontwards and opens her eyes again. "*Merde.*"

"Yes?"

"It *is* leaking. Bleed-through in the Other Place."

"The other—" *Oh*. That's one of the things about ritual magicians; they use visual or tactile metaphors instead of nice standard well-defined terminology. The Other Place, the astral plane, the land of dreams—it's not a real place like, say, Walsall. But it's a metaphor for a mathematical abstraction, a manifold containing an n-dimensional space where everything is the product of geometrical transformations, including mass and energy and time. Leakage between dimensions occurs there: it's how we summon demons from the vasty deep, communicate with aliens, and try to extract our tax codes from the Inland Revenue. And if she says it's leaking—"I should have grounded it there, too?"

"That might not have worked." Her fingers are white on the wheel. "It has an astral body: separate the two and it'll probably die. It's connected to something in the distance off and to the right. Like a spiderweb. I think it's in the compound near Palmer Lake. *Which is the next turnoff.*"

Signs blur towards us, warning of a junction: turn right for the Air Force Academy. Without indicating, Persephone crosses lanes and brakes hard, dragging us into a sharp turn before merging with a main road below the grade of the interstate. "Hey!" I say.

"We're going to Palmer Lake," she says firmly, "to pay a visit to the Golden Promise Ministries compound while Schiller's people are attending their revival show. Besides, it's lit up like a lighthouse in the Other Place."

"But the church service—"

"Is fuel for Schiller's invocation, yes, but do you think he'll have set up the major summoning itself in the middle of a mega-church?"

It's like arguing with a madwoman, except she's not mad. "But he might have—"

"No. He hasn't had the free run of the mega-church until very recently. If he had, he wouldn't be using it to attract new victims. They'd already belong to him."

It's hard to argue with her logic because it fits the pattern that's emerging, but I really want her to be wrong. A few months back, Mo came home in meltdown after closing down CLUB ZERO in Amsterdam—a circle of cultist fanatics (from this neck of the woods, now that I think about it) who'd decided to summon up something unpleasant. The venue for the summoning was a deconsecrated Lutheran chapel, but the fuel was the kindergarten on the other side of the road. Linked by a path through the Other Place—exactly the MO Persephone is proposing. I *really* want Persephone to be wrong about this.

"If he's got the summoning grid set up in his own compound, then there'll be a connection via the Other Place to the church," I reason aloud. "This is the shortest route to Schiller. Bypasses his muscle, too." I'm whistling past the graveyard at this point, you understand. "As long as he hasn't already woken the Sleeper."

"The Sleeper." She takes her eyes off the road ahead long enough to spare me a sharp glance. "What exactly do you know about it?"

I look at the pizza box on my lap. The complaints department is quiescent, locked down by occult manacles. "It's not human. Dead but immortal. Sleeps in a temple on a high plateau, surrounded by a lovely necromantic picket fence constructed by a genocidal maniac more than ninety years ago. On a planet that's definitely not in our neck of the woods, if not in our universe." I shiver. "It's sometimes known as the Opener or the Gatekeeper." I know more about it than that, but I'm not sure how much Persephone knows and I don't want to provoke my oath of office again.

"That'll do," she says absent-mindedly as she wrestles the car through a sharp left turn onto a narrower street where the snowfall is outpacing the traffic's ability to turn it into slush. "You're mostly right, although I hope your analysis is wrong. Disturbing the Gatekeeper would be *bad*. Not so much in its own right, but because of what's on the other side of the gate." With that encouraging sentiment she hits the gas again; the wheels spin for a few alarming seconds, then we're back on course.

We haul ass through snow-capped suburbia for a few silent minutes. Side roads with scattered houses roll by every few hundred meters. I stare at the pizza box in my lap, nervous and upset and simultaneously keyed-up. The thing inside is in communion with its master: they'll know we're coming. It's probably a directional beacon, too. But by the same token, I ought to be able to use it to probe what's going on ahead. If I dare to shut down part of the firewall I've built around it and stick my head up against it, of course. *That* option does not appeal.

I've been keeping my mind inside my own head ever since the incident back at the hotel, because to say I don't like my new-found proficiency at soul-sucking is a bit like saying that cats don't like swimming. But there may be no alternative, if I want to try spoofing our location.

I take a deep breath. "Persephone. Your map. Can you show it to me?"

She chuckles grimly. "All you need to do is open your eyes, Mr. Howard."

"But I don't—" I stop. *No more excuses.* The inner eye, the vision thing, that's what let me know there were monsters on the other side of the door, isn't it. That's how I saw the feeders under Brookwood last year.

"You're a necromancer, Mr. Howard, not just another button-pushing computer nerd. That's why they sent you here with me. You have the aptitude for ad hoc invocation and control. I think you would be extremely powerful, if you get over your squeamishness. It makes you as useful as a heart surgeon who faints at the sight of blood."

I stifle the urge to swear at her. Instead, I close my eyes as we tear down the highway towards Palmer Lake and the turnoff for Schiller's compound, and force myself to gaze inwards. There is a sudden shift of perspective as the world changes. And then I *see*—

IN THE MIDDLE OF THE TABLE SITS AN ANTIQUE ROTARY-DIAL telephone. It dates to an age when telephones were made of wood and brass, crowned with the royal crest of George the Fifth's Post Office. A separate speaking horn carved from yellowing bakelite or some other more organic substance hangs by a hook from its side, connected by a length of cloth-wrapped wire.

Four people sit at one side of the table: Angleton, Lockhart, and the two Auditors.

The phone sits in the middle of an elaborate double ward, concentric Möbius loops of eye-bending power wrapped around its base. There is no sign of a power source or telegraph wire connected to it. Nevertheless, the audience watch with abated speech as Angleton carefully lifts the speaking horn and dials a series of digits.

"Hello, I'd like to speak to Overseas Liaison, please." He leans across the table, placing his ear close to the speaker. "Yes. This is Angleton. I am calling on behalf of SOE on official business. I would appreciate an immediate conference call with a representative of your Internal Affairs department. This concerns current events in Colorado Springs and Denver." He waits for almost a minute. "Yes, that is correct. As I said, we would like to discuss this matter with you—oh very well."

He hangs up the speaking horn and sits back, arms crossed.

"Well?" asks Lockhart.

"They'll call us back."

"Really." The female Auditor's lips are a thin line. "This is preposterous—did they give any indication as to how long they would take? We have an operation to run—"

Silently, without any fuss, the walls of the meeting room dissolve. The conference table extends, doubling in length, but the far side is ash-gray and the three figures that sit behind it are indistinct shapes, shrouded in cloaks and cowls of black mist, their faces in shadow.

Angleton, clearly unimpressed, nods at the new arrivals. "Good evening. Can you identify yourselves?"

There is silence for a few seconds. Then the leftmost of the wraithlike figures nods, a slight inclination of the cowl that hints at a skull within. "I am Officer Black. This"—a band of mist that might conceal a hand, or some other, less human limb, gestures to its right—"is

Officer Green. And I have the pleasure of introducing Patrick O'Donnell, formerly of the Hazard Network, subsequently one of our freelance informers, now deceased."

The phantom limb stretches alarmingly past Officer Green and flips back the hood covering the wreckage of O'Donnell's head.

Lockhart swears very quietly—but not so quietly that he escapes notice.

Officer Black emits a dry chuckle. "Remember our service motto? 'Death is no escape.' Now, who are *you*?"

Angleton points at Lockhart: "This is Officer Blue. And you can call these two"—he gestures at the two Auditors, who are watching, rapt— "Officers Red and Yellow." A mirthless smile wrinkles the corners of his eyes but reaches no further. "You have a problem. *We* have a problem. And I think it's the same problem."

Officer Black folds his arms. The drape of the fabric suggests extreme emaciation. "However, your agents within the Continental United States are illegals, under Title 18 of the US Code—'gathering or delivering defense information to aid foreign government,' not to mention Title—"

"Bullshit!" Angleton snaps. "As you well know, the UKUSA Treaty exception takes precedence. What's sauce for the goose will do for the gander." He clears his throat. "And before you continue with your *next* point, we felt it necessary to act immediately. In the absence of evidence that your assets in the warded zone had *not* been turned by the opposition, and because of certain other considerations, we could not go through the bilateral coordinating committee. Your late colleague's presence here"—he nods in the direction of O'Donnell's ghostly wreckage—"suggests that we were right to do so. The situation is deteriorating by the hour, so I suggest we discontinue the bluster and concentrate on ways of preventing a meltdown."

Officer Green's hood twitches, but he—or she, or it—passes no comment. Officer Black, however, appears to be considering Angleton's words carefully. Finally he nods. "Would you care to summarize your understanding of the situation?"

Angleton pointedly looks for the chief Auditor's permissive nod before he speaks. "We are dealing with a particularly dangerous cult: Christian millennialists who are reading from some extra books in their Bible. They set up shop in Colorado Springs and have extended their influence through Denver and Colorado in recent years, but they were under our radar until very recently because of the resemblance to ordinary evangelicals. Our interest was triggered"—he glances sideways for permission to proceed—"by their missionary activity in London, and specifically by what appeared to be an attempt to suborn members of our highest level of government."

Officer Black nods again. "Was your concern justified?"

"Yes, I think so." Angleton laces his fingers together in a bony pile upon the tablecloth. He frowns thunderously. "Our officers secured a copy of the Bible used by the Inner Circle of the Golden Promise Ministries. Its apocrypha provide a recipe for performing a Class Five Major Summoning, and a theological imperative to do so. It's a necromantic ritual, like most such pre-modern operations, and prodigiously wasteful—completely unoptimized. The body count just to open the portal is in the hundreds; to actually bootstrap the target entity to full immanence it's in the double-digit millions. Oh, and there's worse: Pastor Schiller has got his hands on a fertile tongue-eater, and is using its spawn to conscript and direct bellwethers. We ordered our assets to scram, but this morning they confirmed that they're having difficulty evacuating and there are indications that Schiller is proceeding with the second stage of the summoning, the build-out. Hence this call."

The Senior Auditor, who has been watching with an expression of distant amusement, takes Angleton's silence as his cue. He abruptly raises his right index finger and points it at Officer Green. "I command you to speak," he says mildly.

The robed and shadowed figure's response is remarkable: it quivers spasmodically, shrinks in on itself, then expands back to original size, emitting a burp of foul-smelling bluish smoke as it does so. A hacking, emphysemic cough follows, which goes on for a long time. Finally, a thin piping emanates from the depths of its hood: "Fuck you!"

Angleton raises an eyebrow at the Senior Auditor, who shakes his head. "Ancient history." He looks back at Officer Green. "I do not approve of your presence at this table. Explain yourself immediately!" He turns to Officer Black. "Your choice of colleagues does not incline us to trust your bona fides," he adds icily.

Lockhart, who has been watching the exchange from the sidelines, leans back in his seat and fans himself, looking faintly aghast.

"I don't work for you anymore, Michael," Officer Green quavers. "Not this century, you bastard." He stretches out an arm, lays a hook-like claw on the other side of the illusory shared table; it appears horribly burned. Then he raises his other claw and pulls back his cowl, to reveal a thing of horror.

The Senior Auditor looks at him evenly. "To betray your oath of office was your decision, not mine." He looks at his colleague, who is shaking her head, appalled: "I don't think there's any point continuing with—"

"Please wait." Officer Black speaks. "This will be investigated." His tone is much less self-assured. "You are correct in your inferences about the Golden Promise Ministries. More to the point, they have raised a ward against us around a substantial part of central Colorado—from south of Colorado Springs to north of Denver. Your people appear to be able to move freely across it because it was programmed to detect our sigil of office. Which is highly suggestive of an internal rogue element, but that is not your concern; Internal Affairs will investigate in due course. That is not all, however. Yesterday an artificial weather system blanketed the area, and all flights are grounded. They have also suborned the highway patrol, the Denver police department, and the local FBI office."

"What about the military?" asks the female Auditor. She leans forward intently. "Aren't there any units within the area that can intervene?"

"No. The only major installation within the zone is the Air Force Academy."

"Well, can't you use them? Arm the students and—"

"The Academy is under investigation for discrimination against non-evangelicals," Black says dismissively. "The faculty and student body must be presumed hostile."

"So you're locked out of the area," Angleton muses. "I take it O'Donnell here was your last remaining asset in Denver?" O'Donnell's shade nods. Something grayish-pink peeps briefly at the world through the shattered eggshell of his skull. "If our people can deactivate the ward from the inside, how well positioned are you to follow through?"

Officer Green pipes up: "We have assets sleeping in place." He grins, heat-cracked ivory flashing in a carbonized jaw. "You are not the only soul-eater, Doctor."

The female Auditor clears her throat. "We want our people back. Preferably alive."

Officer Black looks at her. "If they survive, we will not prevent them leaving."

"Forgive me for saying this, but your people have a reputation for not playing well with allied—"

But she is talking to a blank wall, for Officer Black has vanished into the Other Place from which he came, taking his horror show companions with him.

"Well, I think that went reasonably well, all things considered!" The Senior Auditor remarks to the suddenly small and dingy room, as he reaches for the water carafe to fill a tumbler with a hand that is only very slightly shaky.

Angleton shakes his head. "Longer spoon next time," he murmurs.

The female Auditor is visibly frustrated. "They're relying on our assets to do their dirty work, and they won't even guarantee safe passage!"

"Then they'd better be up for the job, hadn't they?" Lockhart shows his teeth. "Mahogany Row sent them—except for Doctor Angleton's secretary, of course. Who is not without resources of his own."

"One may hope so." Angleton reaches for the table water. "But I admit I wasn't expecting him to have to deal with a challenge of this magnitude so soon."

* * *

ANOTHER PROBLEM WITH GODHEADS, JOHNNY REFLECTS, IS that they can't quite understand how anyone could *not* believe their shit. (He knows this because he started out as one, although he lost his faith before his balls dropped.) Consequently, they have immense difficulty in grasping, at an intuitive level, that someone who used to be one of them might no longer be completely in tune with their ideology.

Here he is, sitting snug in the leather-lined baseball catcher's mitt of a luxury-trimmed Suburban, surrounded by fake walnut veneer and cup holders and power sockets, staring out at a blizzard through tinted windows. Up front a godshattered man in black with a cymothoan parasite in place of his tongue wrestles with the power steering. (At least it isn't one of the hypercastrating variants, Johnny notes with relief; those things give him the cold shudders.) It is apparent that Schiller's people have caught up on their research: they've worked out who and what Johnny is, which is why they've switched from shoot-on-sight to the velvet-glove treatment, like it was all a bad mistake and they want to kiss and make up. It's that damned summoning recipe from the Book of Apocalypse, of course. If Schiller popped out of nowhere then it follows that he may be short on willing elders to help with the ritual.

But it's also fairly clear that although Schiller's people know what he is, they don't understand where he's coming from. It's like something out of quantum mechanics: you can know where something is, or where it's going, but not both at the same time. *Yeah, that's it,* he thinks as he stares out at the swirling blanket of snow: *Heisenberg's uncertainty principle, as applied to dead gods.*

Fuckwits.

"How long have you been Saved?" he asks the missionary.

There is no immediate reply, and he's about to ask again when the husk speaks: "Three years."

Johnny is impressed. Either Schiller's found some way to slow down the parasite's growth or the man has a very strong mind indeed. (*Had* a very strong mind.) "How did it happen? If you don't mind me asking."

The missionary slowly steers the big SUV around a tight curve, peering out through the windscreen wipers as they batter huge slabs of melting snow away from the glass. It's mid-morning, but the light is gray, fading towards twilight. "Before I was Saved I was in the FBI. I'm a back-office forensic specialist, not an agent. Jack—he's our station chief—invited us all to an after-work service one evening, said it'd change our lives. I was . . . *lost* . . . didn't believe him, kind of resented it. But you don't piss off your chief over nothing, and I had nothing else on, so I went." The vehicle rocks slightly as it aquaplanes through slush. "I was scared for a few seconds, at communion, but they had my back. And then everything was *all right*. Jesus came into my soul and now everything is wonderful."

Just like a heroin addict describing his first fix, thinks Johnny. "What does Jesus tell you about me?"

"You're of the prophet's line," says the missionary. "You are one of the Elect." He falls silent for a while. "Jesus says he needs you, for the seed of the elders of the elect is holy."

Well fuck me, Johnny thinks ironically, with a flashback to his dad's lessons, punctuated with blows from the tawse: *For the priests of the Lord are of the house of Levi, and what are we if not the guardians of the holy seed?* That particular beating had been over suspected masturbation, something dad seemed to have a peculiarly superstitious dread of; it had been one beating of many, mostly undeserved. There had been no denying the terror and glory of the Lord in the McTavish household, or the old man's ability to bring home a trawler with a net full of fish *every* time he put to sea and prayed, or the fits and the babbling, and—when Johnny was thirteen—the coming of age ceremony, the service of dedication at midnight on a spume-blown rocky beach, attended by representatives of the distant branch of the family who could no longer stray far from the ocean or pass for human.

"Does Jesus know *what* I am?" He pushes.

"Jesus says you are of the line of the Masters. The prophet's son. Jesus says God wants you by His side when He returns to earth. The elder says you are to help open the way of the Lord."

Johnny leans back, skin crawling. He's got a lot of planning to do before they make it to the church on time. Normally he'd call up the chinless wonder on his tattoo hotline, but this close to so many supernatural parasites would be a spectacularly bad idea. So he's got a bunch of planning to do, starting with, how to take best advantage of the besotted cymothoan host's crush on his lineage—an unexpected bonus of his occult ancestry, born of a line of men who go down to the sea in boats and commune with the things of the deep. On the other hand, he knows from long experience what Persephone will expect of him, and how *she* is likely to react. All that's in question is how to terminate Schiller's operation and get out of this rat trap alive.

After an hour of tense boredom, driving through a twilit blizzard behind an endless trail of brake lights, Johnny's chauffeur takes a gently graded exit from the interstate and turns onto a wide, straight boulevard. Squat, windowless stores and warehouses punctuate the desolation, snow already humped up before them. Traffic, however, is surprisingly heavy, and most of it is going the same way. Finally it begins to bunch up in a queue of turn signals, all heading for the same side road. It's the gateway to the New Life campus: an airport terminal served by sky pilots. It's large enough to have its own internal road network, and the parking attendants, bundled up in heavy winter coats, are working overtime to direct the churchgoing throng to the different parking zones.

Johnny's driver does not head for the regular parking. After a brief word with one of the attendants he turns down a side road and drives around to the back of a building the size of a cinema multiplex. There's a loading bay, fenced off and guarded by cops, bundled up in cold weather gear and stamping their feet to stay warm. One of them holds up a hand.

"O'Neil, FBI." The missionary holds out an ID badge. "Special guest for the reverend."

"Let me see." The window beside Johnny retracts, admitting a flurry of snow and a scalpel-sharp breeze. The cop glances at him, incurious. "Okay, go to bay two. I'll call ahead." His voice is rough and glottal, his cheeks slightly distended. Johnny gives no outer sign that he recognizes the host inside the officer's mouth.

The missionary nods, then drives towards the designated parking spot. It's inside the fence, behind a motorized gate. The engine stops. "Follow me, sir? I am to bring you to his holiness. We must hurry: the feasting of the body and blood of Christ is about to begin."

15.

BLACK BAG JOB

WE'RE DRIVING THROUGH SNOW DESCENDING IN THICK, BLANketing sheets across the street so that Persephone must follow the tire tracks of other cars and trucks. Overhead, the sky has darkened to the color of unpolished iron, gray-black with a hint of rust when the snowfall lightens enough to see it. We're heading for darkness at noon. The trees are sodden mounds of white, rearing up out of the twilight around us as we drive uphill, along a narrowing trail through the outer fringes of a forest.

Seen with my eyes closed, it's a very different picture. The patterns in the darkness (random firing of nerves in my retinas) glow oddly greenish, following the curves of the landscape. But beyond the hills ahead of us there is a waterfall of light, greenish-blue—a bilious tint I've seen before in the phosphorescent gaze of walking corpses—fountaining into the sky in a vast geyser of unconstrained power. Something has ripped a hole in the fabric of reality, and a chaotic flux of raw information is bleeding in through it. I know it's not an artifact of my eyesight because the glowing patterns don't move when I turn my head. It's unpleasant to watch, so much so that after a minute of staring at it I have to open my eyes again.

"There is a fence and a gate coming up in a quarter of a kilometer," Persephone warns me. "There are probably cameras. If you have any useful ideas . . . ?"

"Pull over," I say. This is where some of the tools I signed out of the armory back home might come in handy.

Persephone stops the car, and I rummage in my go-bag. It takes me a while to find what I'm looking for: a small pouch containing a wizened, stumpy gray claw, and a cigarette lighter. I rummage around some more and come up with a small, battered tin: an electronics geek survival kit stuffed full of wires, diodes, capacitors, and bits'n'pieces. The breadboard is already configured, just waiting for me to connect the miniature Hand of Glory to it via a cable clip and plug in a nine-volt battery, then light the thing. I unroll the grounding strap and plug it into the dashboard cigarette lighter. "All set."

"Neat," Persephone observes warmly. "I didn't know they came that small."

"Ever wondered why there are so many one-legged pigeons around Trafalgar Square?" You don't *really* need a hand from a hanged murderer to make one: like so many pre-modern magics, there's plenty of room for optimization tweaks. I hook up the battery. "Once this lights off we should be good for about three to five minutes of invisibility. But it smokes and stinks of burning rotted pigeon, and if you turn up the aircon too high you'll risk blowing it out."

"When you're ready." She fiddles with the climate control, redirecting the warm air towards our feet and turning up the fan. Then she drives on.

I don't need to be told: I flick the lighter and set fire to the mummified claw. It fizzles and sends up a plume of acrid, smelly smoke, and a green LED lights on the board. "Three minutes."

Persephone doesn't answer. There's a fence alongside the road, three meters high and topped with rolled razor wire—casual visitors clearly not welcome. We follow it around a curve and then there is indeed a gate in the fence, overlooked by a pole with what might be the black plastic dome of a CCTV camera on top. Right now it's buried under a shroud of snow. Luckily for us, the gate is open. Maybe they just couldn't be bothered shutting it, with all the traffic to the church? I hope that's what it is. Otherwise, we're in big trouble.

Persephone turns through the gate, onto a single-track road that is almost entirely covered in snow. There's an unpleasant lurch as the back wheels let go, but she calmly turns into the skid and regains control before we end up in the ditch. Then we're driving up the path to the compound, albeit slowly, following the almost-buried tire tracks.

"Let's hope we don't run into anyone coming the other way," I opine.

"We won't." She sounds very certain. "They're all in the New Life Church or the compound ahead. This is Schiller's big day. *That* tells me." I blink and see what she's nodding at. It's just around the next hillside.

I reach into my bag and rummage around for the camera, pull it out, and hit the power button while pointing it at the floor and keeping my finger well away from the shutter release. It pings a cheery tune as it boots, then the screen darkens for a few unpleasant seconds. I'm about to swear and pop the battery compartment—I think it may have crashed—when Pinky's lethal firmware comes up, showing a live view of my kneecaps with an angry red gunsight superimposed. *Eek!* I turn it off hastily. Okay, so it takes ten seconds to boot from cold to full readiness. That's a lot longer than the ordinary camera firmware takes. I should have driven out of town and found somewhere discreet to practice with it before relying on it in a hostile situation, but it's too late for tears now.

"That's for your *tourist snaps?*" she asks.

I nod. "It's a basilisk gun." Her violent flinch would be gratifying if she didn't nearly lose control of the car. "Don't worry, I turned it off. Until we need it . . ." I thread my wrist through the lanyard. Dammit, why do they make these things right-handed? My upper arm still aches; it's going to be painful if I have to use it in anger.

"Oka-ay . . ." She unkinks slightly. "We are about five minutes from the buildings. There is a high street with three smaller roads crossing it. I think we are looking for the church. You may want to keep *that* for later."

She takes one hand off the wheel for long enough to point to the miniature Hand of Glory. I sniff, and immediately wish I hadn't. "Agreed." I blow on it hard, turning my face away before I inhale. It stops burning, but a hideous smoke trail that stinks of burning fingernails rises from the claws. "Are we—"

We turn a bend, leave the trees behind us, and we're there.

I'm not sure quite what I was expecting. The Branch Davidian compound at Waco, perhaps? But GPM isn't poor, isn't marginal or ascetic, and Ray Schiller is no David Koresh. The layout is more like the residential quarters on a military base: a long, straight boulevard with low buildings set to either side, manicured hedges fronting rows of curtained windows, and a church with a steeple at the far end of the road. It's half-deserted right now, going by the empty car parks covered in snow outside closed doors. Probably most of the folks who work here commute in from Colorado Springs.

I'm glad there's virtually nobody about. The fewer people on hand, the less chance I'll fuck up and kill someone by mistake. Or worse, *not* kill someone, by mistake.

I blink, trying to cop a brief sense of where everything is in here. There's a pale green haze in my lap—the complaints department is leaking like crazy on the other side—and what looks like heaps and drifts of green slime all around us: the uncanny residue of its occult origins adhering to the snowfall. The buildings are limned in violet, until I look towards the church at the end which is shining with a harsh emerald light—and the building next to it is *on fire*, a harsh cuprous glare of raw power that shines through doors and windows, leaching through the concrete. "The building next to the church—"

"I'm on it. That's Schiller's residence, I think."

She drives forward two blocks and parks carelessly, opens the driver's door, and bails out in front of the church. A gust of freezing air slams into me; I swear, turn my camera on, pick up the pizza box and my phone, and follow her into an ankle-deep chilly white blanket.

Persephone high-steps towards the front door of the big house, holding some sort of gadget in her left hand (a ward, perhaps, or a smartphone with some nonstandard firmware). Her right hand is buried in her coat pocket. I rush after her. My mood is dismal: I've been trying to keep a lid on it and mostly succeeding, but since we set off on this journey I've had a continual sense of foreboding, and it's getting worse by the second. We should be getting *out* of this rat trap, not burrowing deeper into the darkness. This is a job for the Black Chamber, along with the Colorado National Guard and maybe the USAF, not a couple of deranged external assets (whatever *they* are) and a junior manager who's so far out of his depth—

Persephone is at the front steps when the door opens and a figure bundled up in cold-weather gear leans out. "Can I help—" It begins to say in a woman's voice, as I raise my camera and try to focus past Persephone, who is standing too damn close for the smart autofocus to get a clean lock on. I can *feel* it in the back of my head, feel the sleepy hunger in its mind as it recognizes the thing in the pizza box I'm holding in my left hand and begins to turn towards me, reaching for its gun—

Persephone's right hand lashes out and the figure drops. She's holding some kind of compact dumbbell; she turns and beckons me forward urgently with it. "Get her inside before she freezes."

"It's one of—"

"I *know*. Keep a tight hold on that pizza box."

The complaints department is twitching and writhing in the cardboard, kicking up a fuss: it knows where it is. I join Persephone in the octagonal lobby of an expensively furnished house. Reception rooms open off to either side, and there's an alarm panel behind the door. The one she dropped used to be a fifty-something woman. Now it's a husk with a silvery carapaced horror for a tongue. I can see it, shining green inside the victim's mouth and throat. I can hear its panicky mindless scrabbling for escape now that its carrier is unconscious. I bend over the body and before Persephone can stop me I do whatever it is I did to the missionaries in the hotel (it feels like *biting*) and the host dies. Trying not to think too hard about what I'm doing I push my fingers between the unconscious woman's lips and tug, tug again until the corpse of the parasite tugs free. (The complaints department kicks up a racket, scritching at the inside of the pizza box lid as if it thinks I'm about to eat it, too. Silly mind parasite!) I wipe my hand vigorously on my coat and catch Persephone staring at me. "What's the problem?"

"We have a"—she coughs quietly—"job to do."

"Oh, right." I look around. "Where—" The answer is obvious. Going by the nacreous glow from below, whatever is waiting for us is downstairs in the basement. Of course, they sent the wrong man; this is the sort of job Agent CANDID handles best, preferably in conjunction with a house clearance team from the Artists' Rifles. (But would I really want to put her in my shoes right now if I could make a wish and swap places with her? Probably not . . .) There's a staircase leading upstairs, and a wooden door in the side of the panel behind it which probably leads down to the cellar. I'm about to go that way when Persephone gets in front of me and starts mumbling and waving her hands around animatedly, as if holding a conversation with a deaf Italian-speaking alien.

There's a pop and a flash from the door handle. "Clear," she says quietly, glancing over her shoulder at me. I peer at the door. Yes, there was some kind of ward there; Persephone shorted it out with her sema-phore ritual.

I raise my pizza box. "Okay, you," I say. "Lead me to your taker."

The complaints department scritches and shuffles round, nudging urgently towards the cellar door. Persephone holds it open and I duck through. There's a light switch just inside the door and I thought-lessly flick it, do a double take, and shudder. I lucked out this time—no booby traps—but I am *so* unprepared for a black bag job that it's not funny.

A WORD ON THE SUBJECT OF BLACK BAG JOBS:

Don't.

I'm not a cop and it's not my job to enforce the law, any more than it is the job of any other citizen to do so. (Yes, I know about Peel's Principles: nevertheless, there's a good reason we mostly leave the job to professionals.) I am, however, a civil servant, which means I work for the government, who *make* the laws. Consequently, lawbreaking is something I'm supposed to avoid unless there's an overriding justification in the national interest, and it's not up to me to define what that means.

The situation is murkier when I'm working overseas in other jurisdictions, but I'm normally supposed to obey *both* sets of laws, HMG's and the host nation's. Unless compelled by overriding justification in the national etcetera, of course, or subjected to cruel and unusual circumstances where they contradict each other.

Anyway. Black bag jobs—burglary, bugging, and breaking in—are by definition forbidden, most of the time. Especially since the Spycatcher business. They may be authorized in the interests of national security, but that happens at a level well above my pay grade, all the way upstairs. When I get sent to run a little errand, it has generally been pre-cleared by a committee, or it's covered by standing orders relating to what we euphemistically call "special circumstances." In which case there *will* be an enquiry after the event and the Auditors *will* be there to ask pointed questions and wield the clue-bat if I've exceeded my authority.

This is one of those *jobs.*

I've been ordered home, the mission terminated. Unfortunately the external assets I'm here to shadow have decided that the mission is *not* over, and in any case my withdrawal route is blocked. So I am unofficially tagging along to keep an eye on them and make sure they don't do anything . . . no, scratch that. It's the *official* truth, the *pravda*, but it's not the real deal. What is going on is that Lockhart wants Persephone and Johnny to be here, raising hell, but he doesn't want to be held responsible for the consequences: it might create a stink when the Black Chamber find out about it. At least, I *think* that's the subtext.

Me, I'm here because I can't get out, and while I'm locked in the asylum I might as well take notes on the inmates. That, and obey standing orders if I run into any of the aforementioned special circumstances. As seems regrettably likely right now.

So, you see, Persephone has to do the door-breaking. If *I* break down doors without orders, I might just be breaking the law. She is

too, but she isn't accountable for her actions as long as the other side
don't catch her; I'm not a cop, remember?

Listen, *I* didn't make these rules—I just have to work within them.

Nobody said this job was going to be easy . . .

THE MISSIONARY LEADS JOHNNY FROM THE PARKING SPOT TO
a side door, through the teeth of an icy gale. The door opens onto a
narrow, windowless corridor curving around the side of the sanctuary.
Johnny hears many voices raised in song, their joyous words muffled
by the echoing acoustics of the bare concrete walls.

They come to a door that opens into the sanctuary.

"Please come this way," says the missionary, head cocked to one
side as if listening to words inaudible to others. "Our father will see
you in the vestry."

"Uh-huh." The music is louder near the door, backed by instruments: an organ or synthesizer and electric guitars. It's like a rock
concert singalong, but Johnny can't make out any of the words. "Lead
on," he says, palming his throwing knives. They feel as if they're writhing between his fingers, reluctant to be here.

"Do not be afraid," the missionary adds, "nothing here will hurt
you." Then it opens the door.

Visualize a church.

Make it a *really big* church, the size of a large cinema, with a funnel
of gently sloping terraces set with rows of theater-style seating that
converge to focus on a stage decked with altar, pulpit, and rock band.
In the walls all around, stained-glass windows backed by halogen lights
shine the glory of the Lord; overhead floodlights and stage spots illu-
minate the brilliantly gowned choir and the musicians on stage.

The soundproofing on the door is excellent, because inside the sanctuary the voice of the crowd is nearly deafening as they stand, chanting
along with a holy rolling rock anthem. Johnny's ward squeezes against
his breastbone, beaten back by the passionate strength of the congregation. There are thousands of them—most of the seats would be occupied if the occupants weren't on their feet, singing their hearts out. But

there's something odd about it, because they're not stomping: they're mostly swaying in place, hands clasped before them in attitudes of prayer, and though they sing—

Johnny squints. He can't see to the front of the stage, but follows the missionary along one of the aisles leading round the outside of the congregation. Something is *wrong*. The skin on the back of his neck crawls. There's a glamour here, a monumentally powerful one, stupefying and cloying. He's seeing and hearing what he's meant to see and hear, thousands of churchgoers singing and clapping along to a wholesome Christian rock band between prayers led by the pastor at the front, a joyous act of collective worship.

But every five or ten seats in the rows there's one who doesn't feel *right*. There is something about them that Johnny recognizes: the taint of the old school, the stolid soulless stance of the missionary in front of him. The crowd is seeded with the possessed, positioned behind and scattered among the congregation like fence posts surrounding a flock of sheep. The shepherd has sent his own to bring the flock home. There's a faint smell, too, aromatic burning incense overlaying something slightly fishy, like burning electrical insulation. A powerful glamour lies over the whole congregation like a stifling blanket, leaking into eyes and ears and warping perceptions. His knives are uneasy for good reason: created to cut, oblivious to mercy and mistruth, they are themselves shrouded in this gummy, foggy cloud of mind-sticky deception. And the music, the singing, the chant is deafening—

The chant. Johnny focusses on it, trying to make out the distinctive words that the congregation are repeating. They slide away from his ears, half-masked by the glamour: *Latin?* No, this isn't a Catholic mass. *Think, sonny!* he tells himself, tightening his grip on the soul-stealer knives as he follows the missionary around the next block of seats. *I've heard this before.*

At the O2 Arena in Docklands. On the stage. Glossolalia, speaking in tongues. Specifically: Old Enochian.

"*Hell and damnation,*" Johnny mutters to himself in near-shock, as the glamour falls away from his eyes and ears and he sees what is going on around him with unclouded senses. It exceeds his worst imaginings.

For he is indeed in church, but the shift in perception shows him what lies beneath the glamour.

The pastor still stands behind the altar, but his chant is a continuous incantation in the formal language of magic, and he, too, is one of the missionaries, driven and controlled by the host of an alien Lord. It is a chant of control, binding and compelling, coercing and demanding obedience and submission in the name of the Sleeper.

The rock band and the choir are still there, but they're not playing and singing of their own volition: they're puppets dancing to an alien tune. The sound swells from somewhere deep beneath or behind them, using their voices and their instruments as a vehicle to penetrate the wall between the worlds. Johnny is still far enough back that he has to squint—but there is blood on the guitarists' fingertips, and the choir members eyes are rolled back in their heads as they sway, unconscious in the grip of something that only looks like rapture when seen through glamour-fogged eyes.

The plain steel cross behind the altar is gone, replaced by an iron hoop three meters in diameter, standing on edge. He knows without having to examine it that the rim will be inlaid with glyph-like circuit patterns, connected to external signal generators; different shades of darkness shimmer within the gate's heart. He feels the ghostly fingers of the wind from the abyss pulling on his mind, urging him forward towards it.

The missionaries aren't there to herd the congregation forward, they're in the crowd to hold them *back*, lest they rush the gate and trample each other in the crush.

"Oh, Duchess," Johnny mutters, "I hope you know what you're getting into." Then he tightens his grip on his knives and follows his unwitting guide, down towards the side door at the front of the aisle that leads backstage, where Schiller is waiting to receive his long-lost cousin.

PERSEPHONE STEPS IN FRONT OF ME, CLOSE ENOUGH THAT I can feel her breath on my face. "The Hand of Glory," she whispers; "now would be a good time to restart it."

I fumble in my pocket lining, which has become twisted around a disgusting jumble of bits of scorched pigeon toes, a cigarette lighter, and other peculiar odds and ends. The camera dangles and spins from the lanyard around my wrist as I try to rearrange things—luckily it's in standby mode—until I manage to extract the pigeon's foot. I'm about to light it when Persephone helpfully fastens an elasticated grounding strap to my wrist, and takes hold of the other end. "Thanks." The click of the lighter and the sudden flicker of the butane flame seem deafening in the twilight at the top of the stairs. Then the claw is burning again, sputtering a foul trail of smoke, and everything around us acquires the very slight pallor that tells me it's working. "Okay, lead on."

She doesn't speak, but takes a couple of steps forward, towing me along at the end of the grounding strap like a leashed panther.

There's a fat bundle of cables and some narrow insulated pipes slung from a shelf suspended from the ceiling above our heads as we descend the stairs to what proves to be a narrow corridor with doors to either side: a basement that's been partitioned off into rooms. The complaints department is scritching excitedly at the inside of the warded pizza box and I can feel its eagerness to be reunited with . . . what? Something down here, that's for sure. I have a surreal sense of déjà vu, as if I'm trapped in a live-action game of Dungeons and Dragons or something. It'd be funny if my skin wasn't crawling.

Persephone pauses at the bottom of the stairs and glances at me. I gesture with the box, pointing where its occupant is scritching loudest, towards the door at the end of the corridor. One of the other doors is propped open, and the smell tells me all I need to know: it's a sluice room and basement toilet, currently unoccupied. We tiptoe past it and Persephone stops again outside the end door. "You're sure?" she whispers, and I nod.

I'm half-expecting her to kick down the door, but instead she reaches out, pauses just short of the door handle for a few seconds, then turns it and takes a quick step forward. Somehow that little snub-nosed revolver has appeared in her hand—I never saw it move—but there's nobody in the darkened storeroom to point it at. There is, however, a presence.

The complaints department is going apeshit with delight as I follow Persephone across the threshold and smell burning insulation, a rotting sea-smell like the slops rinsed from a fishmonger's slab on a hot summer afternoon. I hear a loud scritching hissing clattering, like an infinity of giant wood lice. Persephone backs up in a hurry and turns to hit the light switch by the door and nearly clouts me in the gut with her gun. The light is oddly red, and I look past her to see a giant glass-walled tank occupying the middle of the room, its panels smeared on the inside with a thin coat of algae behind which—

"*Hsss!*"

The complaints department is eager to be reunited with its siblings, who seethe and burble in the breeding tank around the sessile, slowly pulsating body of a monstrously large isopod. The mother of hosts sits at the bottom of the tank atop a mound of small, gelatinous eggs, resembling nothing so much as a giant wood louse. There's a dual-purpose summoning and containment grid inlaid on the floor around the tank, of course; even so, I can hear its song of joy, an eternal hymn to the glory that is the father-thing that feeds it. And now it's seen us, because the compact Hand of Glory is nearly burned to a stub and in any case *the bloody thing doesn't have eyes*, and it focusses the full strength of its moronic worship on me.

It wants me to kiss it. Which is okay, because it loves me like I've never been loved before: it feels utter adoration and delight at my presence.

The Hand of Glory is burning my fingertips so I drop it; it fizzles out and I shrug off the grounding strap. Persephone is between me and the tank. That's annoying. I try to sidle around her but she keeps getting in front of me. "Mr. Howard. Bob," she's saying, as if my name means something. "Stop that. *Bob*—"

Something rattles in my hands: in the pizza box. It's unimportant, so I drop it and try to shoulder-barge past her to get to the tank. It loves me, I can tell. It wants me to kiss it so it can be with me forever and save me for our ecstatic union in the Lord's embrace.

"For fuck's sake," says Persephone. She *won't* get out of my way. She's got her feet braced and is leaning against me, trying to hold me back. I get a glimpse of her eyes, dark and wild and scared, and then suddenly she wraps an arm around the back of my head, pulls me closer, and sticks her tongue in my mouth. It's like a parasite's tentacular mouth-parts, questing, looking for a blood vessel to latch onto: I choke with disgust and recoil, nearly biting her before I realize what's happening.

The thing in the tank is spinning a high level glamour—class four, at least. My mouth feels slimy and revolting; Persephone wipes her lips on the back of her wrist as I double over and gag, drooling copious saliva on the floor. Ritual magic runs on sympathy and contagion, and she just hit me with a simple channeling of what she sees when she looks at the thing in the tank to break through the glamour. *It nearly had me . . .* clearly my standard-issue defensive ward isn't up to blocking that kind of assault.

"Better now?" she asks.

I nod, wordlessly, then spit again. "Got to kill it—" She raises the revolver and takes aim. "No, wait." If she shoots, it'll bring everyone within a couple of hundred meters at a run. "Better idea." I stagger backwards, then turn into the sluice room and hit the light switch. There's the usual stuff you'd expect to find: mop and bucket, taps, hose, janitor supplies. I grab a gallon bottle of Liquid-Plumr and squint at the ingredients. Sodium hydroxide, sodium hypochlorite, detergent: *That'll do.* I step back into the tank room, and pass the bottle to Persephone. "Here."

"Wait for me at the top of the stairs. And take your host." I bend and pick up the pizza box, which is rattling away furiously. Maybe the complaints department realizes it's about to become an orphan. I'm halfway up the corridor when all hell cuts loose in my head and the host in the box starts to vibrate and spasm, like a wasp that's been hit by a concentrated blast of insecticide. There's a pungent stink of chlorine inside my head and it feels as if someone is ramming nails in my eyes and ears and tongue. I nearly fall over, but grab the handrail and stumble upwards in the grip of the worst headache ever until I bump into the inside of the door at the top of the stairs. The pain begins to subside, and I take a couple of deep breaths. Persephone's still down there. Is she going to be all right? I turn round and experimentally open my eyes, but the migraine distortions swirling around make it hard to see. "Hey," I call quietly.

"Hey." I startle. She's right in front of my face, nose-to-nose with me. "We made it. Are you okay?"

"I—yeah." I nod. "Just a sec." I pull out my phone, call up OFCUT, and poke it at my ward. The damn thing says it's fine, which is seriously worrying because Jesus nearly had me for a fish supper back there. The mother-of-hosts totally bypassed my defenses. On the other hand, my ward didn't stop me feeling the missionaries back in the hotel. Come to think of it the ward I was using back in Germany and St Martin during the business with Ramona didn't block our entanglement, either. Maybe it just plain doesn't work on soul-eaters? I shut my eyes again. I can feel Persephone in front of me—feel the outlines of her mind, if that makes sense. I try and spread my awareness, but apart from a very faint presence outside the door (the attendant Persephone decked?) I don't feel anyone. I open my eyes. "The good news is, I think we're alone. The bad news is, there's nothing down here but *that*."

A quick nod. "The gate must be somewhere else, then."

I was afraid she'd say that. "Can you tell where?"

She gives a funny little choking laugh. "*You*—no, don't. Don't look in the Other Place. We're almost inside it's mouth."

"Oh." I open the door. "Then we'll just have to do this the old-fashioned way."

The complaints department has shut up since Persephone drenched its mother in caustic soda, but I'm willing to make a wild-assed guess that Schiller won't have hidden an occult portal anywhere where random visitors might stumble through it. We've checked the basement, and the ground floor reception rooms don't look promising, so that leaves upstairs: his private apartments or his office. I shove the pizza box inside my shoulder bag and pull out the gun I took from its human steed. "Upstairs first."

We go upstairs. There's a corridor running laterally across the house and we rapidly establish that one end is residential—guest rooms, bathrooms, and the like. Which means the other end, behind a fire door, is where Schiller attends to business. He has a nice-looking office with decent quality oak paneling, bookcases full of impressive-looking leather-bound volumes, and a public desk flanked by American flags. It's backed by a huge wall-mounted cross. Never trust a religion whose symbol of faith is a particularly gruesome form of execution, say I: but at least this is the abstract kind, lacking the figure of Yeshua ben Yusuf writhing in his death agony. "There's also a private office." Persephone points to a door to one side of the desk. "Do you see any wards?"

I peer at the door. Then I haul out my phone and take a look at it with OFCUT. Augmented reality for the win: my nascent necromantic spidey-sense doesn't see anything, but there's a spiderweb of *really* nasty schematics tingling and twitching all across the door's surface. A fine thread leads from it towards the giant cross. I've got a nasty feeling that if you touch the door without an invitation you're going to get to ride on Jesus's tree, and not in a happy way. It's probably Schiller's idea of a cute joke. "I wouldn't mess with that if I were—"

Bang.

I wince and clutch my head as she lowers the pistol with which she has just blown a hole in the central binding node of the trap-ward. It shorts out in a storm of fat violet sparks and a brain-wrenching twist at right angles to reality. She kicks the door hard, right above the lock. It crashes open and she goes straight into a crouch, covering the room within, which does indeed appear to be a private office. Of course, it's unoccupied. The desk is smaller than the one up front, but there's a much nicer chair behind it, and there are more bookcases and a much more eclectic collection of bindings visible on their contents. I raise my camera, wake it from sleep, point it at the floor, and mess with the settings. *Knowing Brains it'll be here somewhere . . . ah, gotcha.* Basilisk guns able to set fire to wide swathes of carbon-based life forms are all very well, but in my line of work a camera also comes in handy, and this one's a lot better than the one in my phone. I was pretty sure Brains wouldn't have disabled the photographic firmware entirely, just augmented it. I raise the camera and start taking shots, partially obscured by Persephone's panicky head as it snaps round and does a double take.

"Evidence," I say. I should have remembered to do this in the cellar but I was too rattled. I turn to the nearest bookcase and begin scanning. The titles don't mean much to me, but it's a fair bet that someone in the library section will find a picture of Schiller's background reading informative and useful.

"Yes, well." She circles the desk cautiously, leans towards the oil painting on the wall behind it. It's a medium-scale picture of New Republican Jesus descending towards the Manhattan skyline on what looks like a fire-breathing war horse, wielding a spear while a squadron of B-52s circle behind him, outlined against thunderclouds. I guess it's a mission statement for the Christ Militant or something. "Hmm. There doesn't seem to be a safe here."

"You were expecting one?"

"Schiller is not an original thinker; that's not his strength. He probably has a private chapel. Very private, but it is unlikely to be hidden well. So—"

I lean towards the bookcase I've been photographing. It appears to be free-standing, but it's built very solidly into the wall opposite the window, running floor to ceiling, and there's clear carpet in front of it. The carpet strikes me as being rather thin for a plush private office. "Huh." I begin looking at the spines of books. I switch the camera off, then pull out my phone. Again, I scan the books using OFCUT. Most of them glow faintly—contamination from Schiller's hands, at a guess—but it doesn't take me long to find what I'm looking for. "Would a secret door be of interest?"

"A *what?*" She blinks at me. "Oh, of course! Open it, please."

"Want to double-check first?"

"Okay." She steps forward, sees the book I'm pointing to. "*The worm turns.* Very droll. It's safe." It's right next to one side of the bookcase, at door handle height. She pulls it and there's a click and the bookcase begins to pivot—slowly, because it scrubs against the carpet and it's laden with about half a ton of tree pulp.

Persephone follows her pistol into the small inner sanctum hidden behind the bookcase, and I trail behind her—and so it is that I'm close enough that when she says "shit" very quietly it's too late for me to back out.

* * *

JOHNNY FOLLOWS HIS GUIDE PAST THE SHAMBLING. SWAYING crowd, past the queue that snakes across the front of the stage to the altar and round to a side door at the other edge of the platform, down three steps to a red carpet leading through an awning into darkness, then up six more steps and around a corner to a room off the side of the sanctuary.

"Glory!" chant the crowd, but not in English or Latin or any language most humans understand. "He is coming! Glory to God in the highest! The Sleeper awakens! Glory!"

Johnny nerves himself for the coming confrontation.

The door closes behind him, deadening the sound of the damned next door. The vestry is roughly twenty feet on a side, low-ceilinged and windowless. There are lockers lined up against one wall, a table pushed up against the other, and a cold iron circle three meters in diameter propped up against the wall opposite the door. It's plugged into a ruggedized equipment case and a spluttering plastic-clad Honda generator that doesn't quite drown out the sound of the wind soughing into the starless sky behind the open gate.

"Eldest McTavish." Schiller sits on an ornately carved wooden throne before the gate. He wears a charcoal-black three-piece suit under his surplice. His face is gaunt with exhaustion. One of the four missionaries who wait with him hovers solicitously, ready to support him if he falters. His smile is pained. "There are many things I'd like to ask you, if we had more time together."

Johnny forces a smile, aware that it's as unconvincing as a three-dollar bill. "I'm sure there are." He keeps his face pointed at Schiller, but is scanning the room, registering the positions of the missionaries. They're bodyguards, of course, all tooled up, suit jackets cut loose to conceal their holsters. There are a couple of handmaids in long dresses, their hair veiled, waiting beside something that looks like a giant silver soup tureen on a catering trolley. But soup tureens don't usually contain live crustaceans that chitter disturbing thoughts that flood the room with the sickly sweet flavor of a gangrenous god's love. "What exactly are you trying to achieve?"

Schiller straightens his back. A momentary grimace betrays his pain. "The same thing the order's been trying to achieve for centuries, eldest. The difference is, I'm going to succeed."

"You want to bring him back." Johnny crosses his arms. "The Sleeper." Johnny keeps one eye on the open gate behind Schiller. The breeze sighs faintly as it drifts through the portal, into the twilit chamber stone beyond.

"The sleeping Christ, yes. The one whose mortal vessel we call Jesus."

Johnny nods; he grew up with this deviant theology, although he doesn't hold with it himself—the doctrine that Jesus was a supernatural vessel for the Gatekeeper is inner doctrine, but he considers the idea that the Sermon on the Mount was delivered by a sock puppet for the Sleeper in the Pyramid to be somewhere between implausible and hilarious. "You know me through my father, I take it?"

Schiller nods. "You are the eldest son: it's in your blood. Baptized and confirmed in a sister church dedicated to bringing this wandering in the wilderness to an end, obedient to the True Creed. I saw you in the back row in London, shining like a beacon; once your friend Ms. Hazard drew our attention, the genealogy department identified you within hours. You were sent here for a reason. It's your destiny."

"Maybe." *Dead right I was sent here for a reason.* Johnny runs the numbers: two knives, four bodyguards, not looking good—and that's before counting the handmaids and the boss himself, who may look like he's half-dead but that's only because he's pouring his entire will into holding open the gate while his pastors funnel willing souls through it to wake the sleeping god. Threaten his holy mission and he's quite capable of sacrificing himself to bring it all together. No, this isn't like that job in Barcelona, or even that hairy caper in Pripyat: it's worse. So: *Keep him talking.* "What do you think I was sent here to do?"

Schiller chuckles drily. "They thought they could send you here to kill me, didn't they? You and your mistress."

"She's not my mistress," Johnny says automatically before he realizes he's been played. "An' you don't believe that shite about me being here to kill you, else—" He raises a hand and makes a cutting gesture across his throat, letting the blade steal into view just in case the muscle are getting twitchy: message to goons, *It could be you.* "So deal or quit, guv. You've got an offer in mind: make it." *Draw him out. Intelligence is vital.*

"You are aware that it takes two to open the gate fully? As it says in the Third Book of Revelations, fifth chapter: 'for the two elders of the blood of Lilith shall be as doorposts in the House of the LORD, and they shall be as stout beams of cedar: And they shall hold the lintel above them that the father of dreams shall walk under it.' We have— had, until you showed up—a shortage of elders." Schiller coughs. "I am the last of my line. So you can name your price, eldest McTavish. Once our father awakens and returns to bring about the kingdom of heaven on earth, you'll have a throne at his side, and a fiery shield and sword, and any temporal reward you want. Do you want your little witch? Do you secretly dream of owning her, body and soul? You can have her, for merciful is the Lord, and *you*, as one of his prophets, have the power to pardon her for her sins. Would you like a billion dollars? A trillion? Immortality? The throne of England? It's all yours, if you agree to your destiny. What do you say?"

The bodyguards are clearly keyed-up; soul-sucking knives or no, there's no way that one against four is going to end well. Johnny nods, smiling. "Sounds like a great offer," he says, taking a step forward—the bodyguards begin to move and so does one of the gowned handmaids, her sleeve pulling back as she raises the machine pistol concealed in it. "And I'm inclined to take it." The guards pause. "Only one thing"— he's in motion, bounding forward past Schiller—*"first you'll have to catch me!"*

A couple of bullets crack through the air above his head as Johnny dives through the open portal. And then the chase is on.

BUTTERFLIES IN MY STOMACH; IT'S DARK AND THERE'S A

breeze from behind—

A breeze.

There are two types of breeze: man-made, and natural. Sources of the man-made kind include things like desk fans, jet engines, and driving with the window open, none of which apply right now. The latter kind occur where there's a difference in air pressure. Air is blowing from behind me, and it wasn't doing that until we opened the secret door. Which, now I think about it, is a *revolving* secret door. Revolving doors made high-rise buildings with elevators possible by allowing pressure equilibration without blowing the windows out whenever a passenger hit the button for the umpteenth floor; but if there's a sky-scraper in front of me I'll eat my hat. Rather, there is a large volume of low pressure air into which a natural wind is blowing. And in my line of work—

"Keep moving," Persephone says very quietly.

I wish I'd brought a door-wedge with me. Or a flashlight. *This'd be a fine time to be eaten by a grue* . . . I take another couple of steps forward and there's floor under my shoes instead of carpet. *Huh,* I think, just as Persephone throws the light switch.

"We found it," I say, feeling sick.

We're in what's left of Schiller's private sanctum, facing an open gate. It probably used to be a small windowless room, much longer than it was wide, before he had the secret door and the altar installed. But now the light of the bare overhead bulb shows us that one of the walls is almost entirely missing. There's a circular summoning grid installed on edge in front of it, and the damn thing is running. It's the sump the breeze is blowing into, and I feel like throwing up when I see it because I recognize the landscape on the far side: I've only been dreaming about it for nine months or so.

"This is it," says Persephone.

"Looks like it." I walk over to the altar. It's a plain slab of stone positioned in front of the gate. There's an ornate silver cup on it, and an ivory wand capped in gold—ritual objects, at a guess—and a smaller grid that, thankfully, is plugged into a boring old-fashioned lap-top. (Have I said how much I *hate* ritual magic? It makes my head hurt.) "This is the other end of Schiller's operation. Quiet, isn't it? He's pumping lots of energy into it from the other side, from the church downtown, so where's it all going? And what's this other grid for?"

"It's going here—no." She's quick on the uptake. "Okay. The small grid looks like"—she closes her eyes briefly—"yes, it's the source of the ward that's locking out the Black Chamber." Without further ado, she yanks the cable connecting it to the laptop. There is a brief spark and a smell of burning plastic, then she points at the wall. "He opened this gate first. It leads to the site of the ritual. Then he opened another gate in the church to power the ritual. The ritual takes place *over there*"— she points through the gate—"and that which is summoned then comes *here*, to grow free from unwanted attention while it is still young and weak. Yes?"

I try to untangle her syntax: "That sounds about right."

"The women in the hospital," she says conversationally, "haven't been disposed of because they're its prepared food."

"*It*. The Sleeper?"

"Yes. And I'm ending this *now*." And she takes a step towards the gate, crossing its threshold before I can shout at her to wait.

So of course I follow her.

WHEN I WAS A KID MY DAD ONCE TOOK ME UP TO THE YORK-shire Dales, to go walking and see the limestone pavements around Malham. They're eerie landscapes, carved by glaciers and corroded by water over thousands of years—on a bright, dry summer afternoon it feels as if the bones of the Earth are poking through the parched skin of a mummified planet.

This place looks well and truly dead at first sight. I take three steps after Persephone and nearly go arse over tit, for with each pace I land too late, too far away. Lower gravity than Earth, but not too low—this planet still has a breathable atmosphere, which suggests something is still putting oxygen into it. Above me the sky is dark, save for a broad sash of bluish glowing dust that crosses the upturned bowl of the heavens—and a sun, angry and red-eyed and much too small. It's day-time and the milky way (or what passes for the ecliptic of the local galaxy) is visible and the ground underfoot is dry, uneven grit and stone slabs. Mountains rise in the distance, beyond a fencelike series of isolated lumpy posts.

I look away hastily and see Persephone turning, to face the thing behind me.

The gate is a circle of darkness hanging in the air, its bottom edge just brushing the ground. About fifty meters behind it start a flight of steps so wide they seem to reach halfway to the horizon. I look up. Steps, and more steps. And up, and up, vanishing towards a false perspective, a horizon capped by a monstrous pillared building, somewhat like the Parthenon.

"Oh fuck me," I mumble.

The ground under my feet vibrates, as if a heavy truck has just driven past. *Earthquake* is not a natural thought to crawl into an English brain, but it's an understandable one when there's not a truck in sight, nor one within a thousand lightyears for that matter.

"Huh. So this is the Sleeper's plateau?" Persephone observes with bright-eyed interest. "Because it's smaller than I expected—"

There's a scritching in my shoulder bag: the complaints department is enthusiastically pointing the way ahead—right up the side of the pyramid.

"If it's okay by you I'd rather not hang around here: the locals aren't terribly friendly. We have a job to do—close this gate, open the next. Right?"

The next couple of minutes pass me by because I'm in the zone. Persephone, it turns out, is not carrying any high explosives or banishment rounds, so the job falls to me. "Hold this," I say, passing her the camera. "If anything comes at us, take a portrait."

I rummage through my bag, pull out the wire-wrap board and breakout box and my phone, and go to work. The gate is straightforward. Schiller didn't try to booby-trap it; all you have to do to close the thing is toss a coil of wire through it and hit it with a signal at the gate's resonant frequency—

(Memo to self: do not degauss interdimensional portals at close range without ear protection in future.)

"Bob. What do you see?" My work done, I look up: Persephone has been trying to get my attention, waving and pointing across the plain.

I have a premonition, so I look at the fence. Then I look at it again with my eyelids screwed shut. I open my eyes. "We should start climbing. *Now.*"

Persephone heads for the steps. I follow her. She's walking, not running. "What can they do?" she asks as I pass her. "What are their capabilities? You're the expert . . ."

"The fence wasn't put here to keep the Sleeper in, it's not strong enough to do that. It's to keep people who might want to wake the Sleeper *out*." (I can feel them waking up all around us, hanging on their stakes like nests of sleeping hornets. We've got their undivided attention because we're the only moving things for a hundred kilometers around. They're curious about the still-living: I think they see us as a *mistake*.) "And, if someone is stupid enough to open a gate *inside* the fence and stick around for a picnic, they're supposed to deal with that, too. Fuck knows how Schiller managed it . . ." I put one foot in front of the other with careful determination, not so fast I'm going to run out of breath before I reach the top, but not too slowly either. "They're vessels for the feeders in the night. You don't want to be here when they arrive."

Persephone glances behind me. "I agree." She hurries to catch up, bounding gracefully up the steps two at a time on the tips of her toes— for the steps are shallow and the gravity low. "I might be able to hold some of them . . ."

"Me too, for a while." *Step. Step.* (I have a history with the feeders— it's *possible* I can even control them.) *Step.* "But." *Step.* "Don't want to weaken." *Step. Step. Step.* "The defenses." (And my contractors are another matter.) *Step. Step.* There are at least a hundred, possibly two hundred steps to the top of the pyramid, and the air here is as thin as in Denver: I'm already beginning to feel my heart pounding. I feel light-headed too, but not from too little oxygen—there's something about this place that makes me feel as if my skull's too thin and the universe is trying to leak in.

"What. Do you expect. To find up there?" Persephone asks.

"Big temple." *Step. Step.* "Sarcophagus." *Step.* "The Sleeper—" I misstep as the next flagstone under my foot abruptly isn't there, then bashes into my sole hard, then drops away. "Shit!"

"Quake! Drop." Persephone pancakes across three steps and I land hard beside her, taking the impact on one buttock. I gasp and wheeze in the thin air as dust devils rise across the plain and the steps groan and wail beneath us, stone grinding on stone. For a moment I'm terrified that the temple will fall on us: but no, it's stood here for many thousands of years. In fact, the designers will have picked this plateau precisely because it was tectonically stable, so why is it shaking now? *Don't think about that Bob, you wouldn't like the answer.*

The tremors continue for almost a minute. I lie on my back, then as they begin to die away and the groaning and moaning stops I sit up and look down the slope of the pyramid.

One by one, the mummified corpses are helping each other down from the stakes upon which they were impaled. Limping and wobbling and rattling, they shuffle and lurch towards us across the dusty plain, still wearing the scraps of Russian civil war uniforms they wore when they were murdered. Many of them are fully skeletonized, but they're still articulated, and they carry knives and rusty cavalry sabers. They don't have working lungs or larynx with which to hiss *brains*, but you don't need to have seen many Romero flicks to know what they've got in mind.

I catch a flash of light in the corner of my left eye and begin to turn just in time to see Persephone standing, camera before her face, taking aim at the lead zombie before I can tell her not to.

There is a concussive blue-white flare of light from the vicinity of the eater: it's so painfully bright it brings tears and leaves a green-purple haze in my eye. About half a second later the *crump!* of the explosion reaches us.

"Woo-hoo!" Persephone bounces straight up in the air, lands a step higher up behind me. "That was fun!"

"Give me that back."

"Why?"

(It's a Basilisk gun. When you point and shoot one, about a tenth of one percent of all the carbon nuclei in whatever it's locked onto are spontaneously replaced by silicon. There is a slight insufficiency of electrons to go around: the result looks a lot like an explosion, and what it leaves behind is more like concrete than flesh. Red hot concrete full of short half-life gamma emitters.)

"Firstly, you don't want them to start shooting back. Secondly, I may need them."

"Why, can you—" She looks at me and does a double take. "Oh, *that*. Angleton said you—" She swallows whatever she was about to say, hands it over, and we start climbing again. Actually, she may have done us a favor. The other walking corpses are still picking each other up: the blast knocked most of them down. On the other hand they're angry now, and some of them have rusty bolt-action rifles.

We climb again until we reach the top of the steps. I'm gasping for breath and my buttocks and upper thighs feel as if I've been beaten with baseball bats. Ahead of us there's a wall of unmortared giant limestone blocks, windowless and surrounded by a row of pillars the size of ICBMs supporting the roof above. It *is* like the Parthenon in Athens—if the ancient Athenians who built it had been twenty-meter-tall giants. I can see a dark-mouthed opening between two pillars about eighty meters away, and I am at a loss for words to describe my lack of eagerness to go there. On the other hand, our pursuers are wheezing angrily through the gaps in their rib cages and brandishing stabby implements in a most unfriendly manner, as they come surging up the steps below us like a wave of bony hooligans.

I point at the opening wordlessly. Persephone nods, then picks herself up and breaks into a loose-limbed jog.

I stagger drunkenly towards the opening, trying to ignore the grotesque carvings inlaid on the bases of the pillars and the walls of the temple—not so much Achaean as Aztec, but with added writhing tentacles and horned skulls—and follow Persephone up to the threshold. It's a big rectangular doorway about five or six meters high and three meters wide, and the wooden doors that would normally block it have been carefully opened and wedged. *Gee thanks, whoever.* I pause beside Persephone and look inside. It's gloomy, the dim light filtering down from skylights in the ceiling. The roof is free-standing, vaulting high overhead—the classical columns outside are decorative, for there's no forest of roof supports within—and I find myself peering across fifty meters of stone towards a raised dais that supports an altar-shaped sarcophagus. There's a glowing circle in the air beside the sarcophagus and, unlike the one we found in Schiller's office, this one reeks of power, fat and bloated with the life energy of worshipers. There's a faint metallic smell in the air, as of blood, and it makes me feel hungry. I can feel Persephone's mind behind me, wondering at our surroundings; I tap her on the shoulder and she glances at me.

"No time," I say, then take a step forward. The eaters will be reaching the top step soon, and I'd rather not stop to dicker with them. Besides, there are more tremors. They've started again, gentle aftershocks to the earlier screeching and groaning of stones. The ground is vibrating again, as if some huge beast is stirring uneasily in its sleep beneath our feet, and even though the shocks are weaker they're making me nervous.

Then a human figure dives through the open gate towards us, and all hell breaks loose.

16.

THE RESURRECTION AND THE LIFE

"DON'T SHOOT HIM!" SCREAMS SCHILLER AS HE RISES FROM his throne, clawing at its wooden arms in pain as he stands. "Take him alive! 'For I am the way and the life, sayeth the Lord!'"

"Yes, Father," Roseanne says meekly, lowering her FN P90; the barrel of the bullpup submachine gun is smoking slightly where it melted the cuff of her part-synthetic sleeve.

The boys aren't waiting for direction: they pile through the gate in eerie silence, drawing batons and tasers in unison. Their hosts ride them with expert precision, coordinating perfectly to fan their mounts out across the floor of the courtyard on the other side. Schiller shuffles round the throne and takes a hissing breath. "Tell Alex to secure this side, then follow me through," he tells the other handmaid. "Roseanne, help me."

Roseanne goes to his right arm and lifts it across her shoulder. "Father, will you—"

"The prodigal son will serve, willingly or no," Schiller says quietly. "Through the door, Daughter. 'Less'n I'm mistaken Pastors Holt and Dawes are already beginning Holy Communion: I can feel the life flowing back into me as I stand." He takes a step forward, then another, gathering strength as he moves. A few seconds later he lets his arm drop from his handmaid. "Follow me. Alex's men will be here soon. We need to be on the other side to unseal our Lord's tomb."

The cathedral-sized building on the other side of the gate awes Roseanne. She's dreamed of it for years, even before Father Ray took her for a handmaiden; dreaming in awe and ecstasy that she might be the one to quicken the Lord in His sleep. It's far above her place to hold such dreams, she knows, but even so she is determined to be present at the second coming, and she feels an icy spike of rage at the flippant Englishman who so foolishly turned down Father Ray's generous offer. She tightens her grip on her gun's foregrip. For a butterfly-ticklish moment she'd almost thought Father Ray was going to offer *her* to the Englishman as part of his ludicrous list of bribes, not that she does not welcome the idea of fulfilling her duty to be fertile and submit to the husband he will eventually choose for her, but the hot flush she felt for a few seconds in the vestry has left her disconcerted and angry with herself for sinning in her soul.

And so, as she follows the holy father through the portal to the holy sepulcher, her mind is not entirely focussed on the job.

JOHNNY ROLLS AS HE HITS THE FLOOR——TOO SLOWLY. AL- though the bullets cracking above his head like maddened wasps are as fast as normal—and bolts sideways, away from the direct sight-line of the gate.

He knows this place. He heard stories about it on his father's knee as a wean; he knows the layout, for the village kirk reproduced it in miniature. It's in his blood, and he knows just how desperate Schiller must be to complete this ritual now that he's here.

(Set a thief to catch a thief. Johnny will be having some pointed words with the Auditors when he gets home, by and by, if Persephone doesn't get to them first; and then there will be a pointed debate among the invisible collegiate membership of Mahogany Row. But that's of no matter right now. What matters here is preventing Schiller from completing the service of possession that he's trying to carry out—that, and maybe escaping with his skin intact. And the Duchess and that Howard guy Lockhart sent along on this caper as an understudy.)

There's the nave: there, at the front of it is the Altar of the Sleeping Christ, as dad called it—more like the cryonic suspension capsule of an alien nightmare, if you look at it without god-glazed eyes. The ground is shaking slightly beneath his feet. *Are the support systems coming on-line already?* They're elder gods to the superstitious neolithic tribes who had worshiped them, ancient astronauts if you want a more modern metaphor. They're nameless and inhuman horrors, either way. There are benches in the nave, half-melted looking things made out of some kind of crystalline mineral. They're sized for humans but each seating position is punctuated by a gully in just the right position to accommodate a stumpy tail.

Johnny duck-walks behind a pew as the first two bodyguards bound through the gate. He can feel his skin crawling with power in this place, and the throb of blood in his ears is disturbing: there's a curious sense of euphoria, a giddy light-headedness that seems to come on the back of the distant hymns of damnation filtering through the gate from the church sanctuary back in Colorado Springs. *The sacrifices. He's beginning the sacrificial ceremony.* Johnny freezes for a couple of seconds, during which the next two bodyguards arrive and fan out on either side of the gate. The sacrifice of souls joyfully given by their owners is the most potent part of the ritual, necessary to power the invocation that will awaken the Sleeper. All it takes are donations of circulatory fluid from two members of the blood, descended from the ranks of the Sleeper's chosen priesthood—there is some archaic genetic manipulation at work here, and other, more arcane processes—and the rite of awakening may be performed. *Fuck, he's beginning. He needs me here. Willing, or . . . ?*

With a pang of embarrassment, Johnny McTavish realizes that he might have made a really bad error of judgment. Not merely bad: the *worst*. In which case there's really only one thing he can do.

Johnny stands and shouts, "Over here, motherfuckers!"

Heads whip round.

Then knives fly.

* * *

"HAND OF GLORY," SNAPS PERSEPHONE, HOLDING OUT AN open palm just as I hear a couple of gunshots.

I drop to the floor behind a row of church pews perfectly suited to the hindquarters of deep ones. "I've got it in here somewhere . . ." I rummage in my shoulder bag, end up upending the complaints department on the floor, then drop a spare tee shirt on top of it. Something buzzes aggressively—like a rattlesnake—and I jump back before I realize the ward's broken and the giant isopod is free. *Well, fuck it.* I find the second and last mummified pigeon's foot and pass it to Persephone, who's kneeling behind another pew with her pistol held at the ready, then go hunting for the lighter. Which I pass across in due time.

"Make a distraction," she says, "I'm going to sort this out." Then she flicks the lighter, turns transparent, and disappears.

I sigh and power up my camera. Just then I feel an echo of hunger tugging at my attention from somewhere just outside the door. ***Not now,*** I send irritably: ***I'm busy.***

Unfortunately these are not *my* feeders in the night; I get a distinct sense of peevish resentment, and then the hunger pressing in on the edges of my mind redoubles. A moment later there is a great clattering of bones as the front of the picket of the damned reaches the entrance and shuffles across the threshold, luminous green worms writhing and twisting in their sunken eye sockets.

There's a great shout from the other side of the nave, and then a gurgling scream and another gunshot. The first three walking corpses shuffle towards me. Two of them raise tarnished swords; the third clutches an ancient and rust-speckled rifle with a bayonet the length of my arm. They don't look friendly.

I raise the camera and frame them in the viewfinder. One last chance before I blow them back to Molvanîa or wherever they came from, before they got swept up in the Russian civil war and ended up in one of the Bloody White Baron's death trains: ***I am the Eater of Souls! You are mine to command. Halt!***

It's a bit of an exaggeration (if not an outright lie: I am not the Eater of Souls, I'm just his administrative assistant), but for a miracle the half-skeletonized soldiers stop dead just inside the threshold. I sense bafflement and incomprehension.

Report!

The rifle barrel rises, and rises until it points at the ceiling in scabrous salute. ***The watch . . . reporting, Master.***

Another three zombies arrive on the threshold, rocking and shuddering to a halt. There are more behind them, the walking undead ruins of a bloody civil war, staked out to die without hope of perpetual rest beneath the racing moons of an alien world: the sentries on the edge of forever. ***It is him,*** I sense one of them saying, ***it is the Lieutenant come to lead us home.***

(By "home" I do not think he is talking about anything this side of the grave.)

Enemies have come to wake the Sleeper, I tell them. ***They must die. There are two allies, an invisible witch and a man with two knives that eat souls. They must live.***

Must they? comes a question from the ranks. There's always one.

I'll pretend I didn't hear that. Follow me! And with knocking knees, I force myself to stand up and walk out from behind the row of pews and shout, "Hey motherfuckers! Over here!" ***Charge!***

I hope Persephone appreciates my distraction . . .

Before me, the Altar of the Sleeping Christ is a plain sarcophagus carved from a single slab of black granite, inlaid with metallic flecks that form disturbing patterns if you stare at the surface for too long. It's four meters long, far too big for a human unless it contains a pharaonic nest of concentric coffins, not that anyone with any sense is going to go looking inside. Reddish sunbeams track slowly across the dusty flagstones of the temple and drip bleeding from the backs of the empty pews.

At one side of the room, a fight is in progress. Two of the black-suited bodyguards are down, twitching in their death agonies as Johnny's knives suck the souls from their bodies. The other two aren't shooting, but they hold batons as if they know how to use them and they're circling around Johnny McTavish, who—knifeless, now—is at a marked disadvantage.

A woman in a blue gown leads an older man dressed in priest's vestments towards the sarcophagus. He casts an angry glare at McTavish, but seems satisfied by the man's mere presence. It's not far to the altar, and they're arriving just as I shout and start to run towards them. The woman looks up in surprise, then raises her arms as if in prayer in my direction. Only she's not praying.

There's a noise like a sewing machine the size of an airliner punching holes in sheet steel. I throw myself at the floor, but she's not aiming at me—she's aiming *behind* me, at the source of the lurching shadows that careen across the pews. And for all that they're undead the bodies ridden by the eaters aren't bulletproof—break enough bones and they'll be reduced to crawling towards their victims like something out of a Monty Python film, even if the shooter isn't firing banishment rounds. I, on the other hand, am not bulletproof at all, so I hide behind the furniture and make myself one with the floor.

The camera. When I made my throw-self-at-planet move it was attached to my wrist by a lanyard. Now, not so much: I am attached to a lanyard but no camera. I look around but I don't see it—it probably slid under a few pews. Well, sucks to be me. I've got a pistol; it'll have to do.

It takes me a few seconds to get the damned thing disentangled from my jacket, and then I run into a second problem. I'm used to punching holes in paper targets with a standard issue Glock 17, as used by police tactical response teams, MI5, and just about everyone in the UK who is legally allowed to carry a handgun these days. But this thing isn't a Glock. There are odd-looking *buttons* on the side and the grip feels all wrong. It probably has a safety catch. Pausing to RTFM, in a dimly lit temple while my pulse is running at warp speed and a deranged valkyrie with a space-age weapons system chews holes in the landscape, isn't an option: so I mentally consign my soul to wherever it is that dead agents' souls go, flick the switch or button or whatever that's nearest the trigger guard into the other position, and squeeze the trigger in the general direction of the altar—firing under the pews.

Bang goes the pistol, and I nearly bite right through my lower lip as I button up to keep from screaming aloud and giving away my position. My upper right arm is in searing agony where Jonquil and her posh friends made holes in it last year. "*Shit*," I say very quietly. I haven't been working out on the range since the business in Wandsworth, and it's clearly a non-starter. But . . .

Take this pistol. I put it on the floor and give it a good shove, and it goes skittering back behind me. ***Kill the woman with the machine gun.***

Rattle-click-crunch: a feeder is crawling towards me. I can *feel* waves of festering resentment and rage gnawing away at what's left of his mind. For a miracle, he reaches for the gun instead of the warm, pulsing, living leg so close to his jaws. *Leg of master.* He'd bite me if he could—but he's bound to serve the will of those whose taint I've carried ever since the Brotherhood of the Black Pharaoh fucked up bigtime in Brookwood last year.

Wait! I announce, feeling the feeder preparing to lurch to its feet. ***First, find a small silvery box, looks like *so****—I visualize it mentally—***on the floor somewhere. Bring it to me! Then await my order to fire.***

A fresh burst of automatic fire sprays overhead as the nun with the very big gun lays down suppressive fire. There's a crunch, and a wail that dissipates like pollen on the desert wind as one of the feeders falls apart. Then something bangs into my hip. I reach back for it with my left arm, swearing quietly. It's the camera. I push the power button and wait for it to wake up. I hope it's not broken.

About ten seconds have passed: an eternity in a fight.

Schiller is now leaning on the altar, holding a cable attached to a Pelikan case that he'd obviously brought through earlier and stashed behind it. He's exhausted but determined. His handmaiden stands guard beside him, a white-hot blaze of righteous anger, and she's taking regular aimed shots at the walking corpses who are still stumbling in through the entrance, for all the world like a horde of green-haired munchkins in an early computer game. They're not doing well; this isn't what the feeders were intended for. Maybe half a dozen of the brighter ones are still moving, but they're mostly the ones with enough of a residual sense of self-preservation to use the furniture for cover. (If I didn't know better I'd say the others were trying to get themselves killed, seeking release from their deathless agony . . .)

Johnny is—oh dear. Johnny is down. So is another of the body-guards, but another four arrived through the gate from the New Life Church while I was trying to become one with the lithosphere. I can feel his anger and frustration and pain just as I can feel the dry, com-placent yearning of the hosts riding Schiller's goon squad. They've come for Jesus's summoning, and—

Where's Persephone?

I blink, bemused, as I open myself up to the world and listen. I can't taste her mind anywhere around us. It's as if she's legged it back through the gate.

Oh.

Well, *that* royally buggers everything up, doesn't it?

A quick situational audit tells me that I'm up against: Schiller (no mean sorcerer in his own right), Our Lady of the Lewis gun, no less than *six* security guards with pistols (two of whom are sitting on Johnny McTavish—for some reason they're reluctant to damage him), and the goon squad's boss, Schiller's head of security.

In the white hats we have: Johnny (out of action), Persephone (out of area, running so fast she's trailing a sonic boom if she's got any sense), six assorted Russian Civil War-era zombies (only one of whom has a remotely modern weapon), and Yours Truly.

It's not looking good. Especially because—now that I try—I can *feel* the hosts in Schiller's bodyguards. Alas, they're too far away to eat. I could try and get closer, but I suspect it would end in tears.

I glance at the camera. It's up and running, but the case is very scuffed. More worryingly, the battery icon in the top right corner of the display—which is cracked—is flashing red. Either it's about to run out of juice, or being chucked around the floor has damaged the battery contacts. I look up again. The guards are dragging Johnny to the altar like a very reluctant bride, and the madwoman with the machine gun is staring in my direction, eyes narrowed.

For a stomach-churning instant I think she's seen me, but then I realize I'm between her and the door that the pile of semi-dismembered feeders came through a minute ago. *I'm pinned down,* I realize. If I pop up to aim the basilisk gun, it'll take anything from a tenth of a second to a couple of seconds to lock on to a target; meanwhile, I'm in front of the sights of an automatic weapon. Plus, they've got Johnny. And I am not sanguine about killing people I know—especially if they're human and they're on my side.

Fan out, I tell my remaining feeders. ***Move forward quietly. They intend to raise the Sleeper. We are going to stop them.***

Then I begin to work my way forward beneath the pews, worming along on my belly like the snake in Schiller's Garden of Eden.

"DEARLY BELOVED." SCHILLER CHUCKLES WETLY: "NO, WRONG service. We are gathered here as it is prophesied, to bring about the second coming of the Christ Militant, who with fire and the sword will sweep all before the triumphant armies of his elect, that the unbelievers be cast forever into the fiery lake and the reign of God on Earth be brought about. It is to our eternal regret that we could not complete the planned conversion of the unbelievers, but the atheist servants of the British Government were upon us, greedily spying on our secrets; and so we must bring down the curtain on this aeon of sin and perversion as soon as possible. Shed no tears for them, for their damnation is of their own doing."

He coughs, then clears his throat noisily and spits to one side of the altar. Then he turns to face the dark-suited guards who hold Johnny before him, in front of the sarcophagus.

"Elder McTavish, the rite of awakening may require the presence of two elders of our bloodline—but only one of them needs to be willing." Schiller frowns theatrically: "It will go better for you if you are Saved first and take Jesus Christ as your personal savior. What do you say?"

Johnny tenses; the guards hold him down, kneeling before the altar. They've handcuffed his wrists behind his back and one of them is in the process of fastening shackles to his ankles. He looks at Schiller with weary contempt. "The thing what's buried under that stone ain't *Jesus*, me old cock. You've been 'ad."

"Really?" Schiller smiles, evidently amused. "I think not, and you're going to burn in hell for eternity unless you change your mind in the next thirty seconds. But don't take my word for it; Christ will return and prove me right. Enough idle chatter. Sister, pass me the chalice and the needle."

There is a large silver goblet on the equipment case by the altar. Roseanne scans the temple again, looking for signs of motion among the pews or in the pile of dismembered body parts by the far entrance: she sees no threat, so she reaches out with her left hand to take the vessel—but her eyes never stop their endless scan of the space before her. It takes her a couple of seconds to find the packet of sterile needles on the top of the Pelikan case by touch alone, but she manages it in the end. Schiller takes a needle and abruptly rams it into the ball of his thumb, squeezing it over the chalice.

"Bring him here, the son of Adam's other wife," Schiller calls.

"Fuck you—" Johnny's sudden struggle is not unexpected, and a rabbit punch to one kidney gives the guards time to bend him over the altar, face-down.

"In the name of the Father, and the Son, and the Holy Spirit," Schiller intones, "I bequeath this soul unto the tender mercy of our Lord Jesus Christ who sleeps dead but undying beneath this stone." There is a knife in his hand as he leans forward to cut.

The situation, I decide, *is non-survivable.*

Go, I tell my minions, and pop up from behind my pew like a kamikaze photography buff.

Shots crack out.

Roseanne, the blonde handmaiden with the gun, fires simultaneously with the skeletal horror I donated my pistol to. She's fast and practiced, and a crackling trail of bullets smashes the feeder's rib cage to splinters, then wrecks the arm that holds the pistol.

The feeder's shot misses.

For a horrified split second I stare down the muzzle of her gun as she points it at me with an expression of frustration rather than hatred on her face: *Why won't these pop-up nuisances just give up and die?* she's wondering. I watch for an eternity, waiting for the fucking camera to display a green gunsight around her, while her gun clicks, once, and a box pops out of one side. She begins to rotate her arm, turning her gun side-down to eject the empty magazine, and just then there's another gunshot and a red stain splashes the back of her headdress.

"Behold, the Lord will rise again, washed in the blood of the lamb! And the apostate gets his just reward!" Schiller shouts at me, as blood from Johnny's throat gouts across the sarcophagus, splashing into the chalice. Fury and pride twists his face. "You're too late!"

Take out the guards, a familiar voice whispers inside my skull.

What the fuck? I spin round and raise the camera, taking aim on the four armed missionaries who are between me and the gate. The red battery icon flashes—

"He's not yours to kill!" Persephone's voice rings out.

Then there's another crash of gunfire as I simultaneously see four green targeting boxes appear on the camera's display and click the shutter button—

I've never looked directly into a basilisk gun's target before. It's a major design fail; I shall have stern words with Pinky when I get out of here.

Go to the gate, Howard, go now.

I shake my head, unable to see past the green blotches and purple outlines of the four guards, frozen in the crackling flares of magnesium-bright light that have etched them into my retinas. There are more shots. I realize that staying upright isn't a good idea, so I sit down hard, feeling dizzy.

Schiller's down. I'll rescue Johnny. Persephone's in take-no-prisoners mode, going by the icily professional feel of her thought.

Johnny's dead—I saw Schiller cut his throat—

—It won't be the first time I've had to raise him. Go!

Everything is very confusing when you're half blind and in the middle of a firefight, but I could swear the bench is shaking beneath me.

What about you? Don't you need a hand?

A blast wave ripples through me, like a giant door slamming in the near distance. I hear more shots.

I'll be fine. And I can sense the belief in her mind, a solid rock of self-confidence sufficient to hole a battleship. ***You're out of your depth. Go, now!***

I don't have to be told a fourth time. I stumble towards the gate, fumbling my way past the pews of long-dead alien worshippers, the blazing human candles of the burning bodyguards, my compass the bright and mindless hymns of the faithful.

Somehow I find my way to the other side, and an empty vestry in the middle of a temple full of lost souls. And that is where the Nazgûl find me amidst the other mortal wreckage, burned and half-blinded by the light, clutching a broken camera full of secrets.

Epilogue

AFTERMATH

THE DUSTUP IN THE SLEEPER'S MAUSOLEUM HAPPENED LAST
month, but I've only been home for a couple of days. Mo was just
about mad with worry when I rang the doorbell at seven o'clock,
bleary-eyed and sweaty, straight off the red-eye from DC to Heathrow.
Economy class, of course; it may be painful, but I'm not stupid—after
the mission ends, it's back to business as usual.

I slept for about six hours, ate, slept for about eighteen hours, and
spent the next day in a zombie-like haze. Today's the first day I've been
sufficiently compos mentis to go back to the office. Lockhart, I gather,
is chewing the carpet. (*Good.*)

You can blame the Black Chamber for the delay. Officious as any
other component of the labyrinthine American secret state, they had to
first satisfy themselves that I was not, in fact, an enemy agent. The carte
blanche helped—or at least convinced them to make some phone calls
first, rather than shooting me out of hand—but was not sufficient on
its own to dig me out of the crater I had landed in. However, some
pointed nagging from somewhere up the ladder at Dansey House—up
the ladder from *Angleton*, I should add—eventually shook me loose.

Not that they were keeping me in twenty-four-hour lockdown in the brig at Quantico; I had my own private five-star hospital room to occupy while recovering from superficial burns and concussion, to say nothing of suspected neurological insults that required multiple appointments with an MRI machine to rule out Krantzberg syndrome.

Persephone and Johnny—if they survived—I don't know about. They disappeared and the Nazgûl won't tell me anything, and I wasn't asking questions that might give away anything they're not supposed to know I know. However, I've got some fragments, and I can speculate:

I can infer that Persephone did *not* do a runner, but in fact used the Hand of Glory to conceal her side-trip to Schiller's vestry in the New Life Church, where she did her best to wreck the link between his pastor's sacrifice of souls and the power source in the Temple of the Sleeper. Then she came back to rescue Johnny—and me.

Did she succeed? I don't know. Like I said, she and Johnny disappeared while I was lying on my back in the vestry seeing stars.

I'm pretty certain that Persephone saw to it that Schiller didn't make it out of the temple alive after he tried to sacrifice Johnny. She's nothing if not possessive.

I'm pretty sure Schiller cut Johnny's throat—I saw the blood. And the blood of two elders of the priesthood of the Sleeper were spilled upon the altar while it was hooked up to a grid powered by the prayers of thousands of god-raped worshippers. But the Sleeper—or Jesus, depending on which eschatology you choose to run with—did not clamber out of his sarcophagus and start rampaging across middle America. Maybe they got something wrong? Mind you, the tremors under the plateau suggest someone turning over in their sleep. The fimbulwinter that gripped central Colorado prior to Schiller's summoning is very worrying, but the thaw afterwards suggests the information bleed between the walls of the worlds was staunched in time. Or at least prevented from turning into a flood.

Which finally brings me back to the present, and the inevitable fallout from the operation. Which, I gather, will involve a lot of committee meetings that I won't trouble you with.

CLASSIFIED APPENDIX

GOD GAME RAINBOW
- -

WARNING: Copies of The Apocalypse Codex report containing this version of the appendix are classified GOD GAME RAINBOW.

(Copies omitting this version of the appendix are classified GOD GAME with one additional single color code from: RED, GREEN, BLUE, VIOLET, PURPLE, SILVER.)

If you are not cleared for ALL of the codewords listed above you MUST IMMEDIATELY commit this report to secure document storage (level 3 or higher).

You MUST IMMEDIATELY report any uncleared access to this document to the designated Section Security Enforcement Officer for investigation, even if you have not read the classified appendix and you believe you were issued the document in error.

YOU MUST UNDER NO ACCOUNT READ BEYOND THIS PAGE.

THE SITUATION MAY BE NON-SURVIVABLE.

Persephone raises her head slowly and peers out from behind cover.

She and Howard are crouched at one end of a roughly rectangular space about the size of an aircraft hanger. There are doors in the middle of each wall, and rows of strangely shaped pews—cast or grown rather than built—marching the length of the floor. A raised dais or stage at one end supports a huge stone sarcophagus, and an active summoning grid at the opposite side of the temple from the door they entered by hangs in midair before the far entrance, lit from beyond by the harsh glare of electric lights.

"Hand of Glory," she says, holding out her left hand as a familiar figure dives through the gate back to the real world, followed by the harsh crackle of gunfire.

"I've got it in here somewhere . . ." Howard mumbles apologetically behind her as she searches for a target. The shots cease; instead, four more figures rush through the gate, chasing Johnny. They're clearly armed. There are more figures, indistinctly seen against the back-lighting of the gate.

The situation is as bad as anything Persephone's ever seen: she,

Howard, and Johnny against at least four gunmen who control the egress they need to escape through—and Johnny wouldn't be running away if he thought he stood a chance. It may, in fact, be non-survivable.

Howard finally produces the small, gnarled lump, then fumbles for a lighter as Persephone waits impatiently. Seconds stretch out interminably. Three more figures come through the gate. Meanwhile, behind her, she is acutely aware of the feeders driving the dead husks of their victims forward and up the stairs. If Howard can control them there might be some hope of salvaging the situation . . . otherwise, not.

Howard clumsily fumbles a cigarette lighter in her direction.

"Make a distraction," she says, careful to keep the incipient tremor out of her voice—whether driven by fear or anger, adrenalin surges are infectious and can be devastating. "I'm going to sort this out." She puts down her pistol temporarily, flicks the lighter, and ignites the pigeon's foot. Then she pockets the lighter, picks up her pistol in her free hand, and stands up.

Mind still, calm, in the moment: *They can't see you.* And indeed, the fighting figures are oblivious to her. There's always the moment of cold terror suppressed purely by force of will when you rely on another's prepared occult toolkit to shield you: all it takes is a quality control error and you're naked in the gunsights. But no, the Hand of Glory is burning steadily.

Persephone opens her inner eye and looks round, taking stock.

Everything is light.

Beside her, Howard is a green silhouette; she hears him mumbling in the privacy of his own head, hears the hungry-tasting answers from the shamblers beyond the door, themselves limned in light, but barely visible as shadows against the vast, solar glare coming from beneath the floor of the tomb. The portal through which Schiller's people are coming is a blinding violet hole in space, and a luminous umbilical cord links it to the sarcophagus, which is itself an extrusion protruding from the frozen explosion of power beneath the floor. The river of light pulses slowly, like the heartbeat of a sleeping whale. Persephone can't quite shake the feeling that if she could see the Sleeper's body—embedded in the depths of the nova-glare beneath her feet—it, too, would be pulsing.

A shout explodes from the far side of the pews and echoes shatter from the walls. Then there's a scream in a different register, gurgling, abruptly cut off. Knife to the throat, if she's anyone to judge: Johnny giving a good account of himself, she thinks, as she quietly hurries towards the portal. Another pistol shot hammers out and she whips round towards the shooter, but it's not aimed at her. Schiller's men in black have hemmed Johnny in between the sarcophagus and the far wall. He's taken one of them down and is using his remaining knife to hold off three—that's not going to end well, although they seem curiously reluctant to shoot him. But Schiller's got more missionaries, and they're guarding the gate, and they've seen the feeders in the night. That's what the new shooting is about.

Come on, Howard, give me my distraction!

Persephone's dilemma is this: she can deal with the gate, or she can deal with Johnny's assailants. If she takes the latter, she'll even the odds—but give herself away. And while the gate is open, Schiller can bring reinforcements through as well as continue to feed the sleeping horror.

It's not much of a dilemma.

Schiller and a handmaid step through the gate while she's still four or five meters away. *This* presents her with a dilemma—shoot Schiller and hope it'll derail his summoning? But as she raises her pistol and sights, the handmaid turns, the sleeve of her gown falling away from the curved black foregrip of a P90: and then there's a shout from behind.

"Hey motherfuckers! Over here!"

Persephone drops to the floor as the handmaid whips round towards her, bearing on Howard—whose distraction has surfaced at *precisely* the wrong moment—and braces the bullpup gun with both hands. It looks weirdly as if she's raising her hands in prayer until the deafening roar of bullets erupts. Lips pulled back from her teeth in a rictus, Persephone crawls forward between the pews as the woman unloads. She's close enough that a shower of hot brass cartridge cases rattle and spill across the floor around her, dangerously close to her back until she rolls sideways and stands—still clutching the burning

Hand of Glory—and walks around Schiller and his guard, cat-light on her feet, then steps through the gateway back to the New Life Church. *Don't worry about Johnny. Don't think about Howard. They're behind you. Think about what's in front.*

What's in front turns out to be a squad of men in black clogging up the floorspace of a windowless locker room as they crowd in towards the gate. Persephone dodges sideways to avoid the elbow of an arm that's cradling an AR-15 in a tactical sling, falls back against the wall beside the gate. Beyond the doorway to the vestry an eerie chant pounds away in time with the slow beat of the green light. Schiller's reinforcements swarm through the gate at the double; only seconds later, the room is empty but for one man, who stands beside the equipment case that's plugged into the grid to energize it.

Persephone takes a step towards him and raises the butt of her pistol, judging precisely where to strike.

He looks round and meets her gaze. "Ms. Hazard: Hello. I've been expecting you."

Persephone freezes in place and glances sidelong at the Hand of Glory.

"Don't worry, it's still burning." The man smiles, not showing his teeth. He has other defenses—her inner sight shows her the tattoo pulsing at the base of his throat. It's a familiar sigil. As she recognizes it, a cold metal finger fumbles up against the back of her head. "Drop the gun, please." She complies. "Jack there may not be able to see you, but he can touch you and hear you."

"To whom do I have the pleasure of speaking?" she asks, trying to maintain a shred of dignity as she lowers the compact revolver.

"I'm Alex Lockey. Yes, kick it over there. I handle Mr. Schiller's security."

"You do, do you?" She pauses. "And why is Raymond Schiller's security a matter of interest to the Operational Phenomenology Agency?"

Alex's smile vanishes. "You don't get to ask the questions here." His backup, standing behind her, plants a hand on her shoulder, restraining, even as he rests the muzzle of his pistol against the base of her skull. "I could tell you, but then I'd have to have you killed, and that would be a terrible waste."

"Let me guess?" At the minute flicker in his eyes she continues. "The Black Chamber has always relied on non-human assets, hasn't it? To a much greater extent than any of the European agencies. But now the great conjunction is beginning, and you've got a huge landmass to defend. You've also got a population who are geographically dispersed, many of whom subscribe to frankly implausible religious beliefs that will badly impair their ability to recognize the truth about what is happening. So you've got to find a solution to the religious lunatic problem—to people who will mistake the Black Chamber for Satan and his happy helpers—and to defending the United States. It's only natural to look for the biggest stick. And that thing"—her gaze tracks towards the gate—"is the biggest stick that comes to hand. Am I right?"

Lockey stares at her, poker-faced. Which almost certainly means *yes*. Persephone presses on, playing for time and a momentary lapse of attention: "So this is a false flag operation. Schiller isn't leading it, even if he thinks it's all his idea; he's just a useful dupe. If he succeeds, you stand to gain control of a truly monstrous weapon (and thin the herd of god-struck liabilities in the process); if he fails, the Black Chamber could deny all knowledge and responsibility, ask for help in hammering down the lid again if necessary. Trouble is, you still need a second elder of the blood in order to complete the awakening ceremony, don't you? And the supply of elders from that particular wee free kirk is more or less a monopoly of the British government. So you trailed Schiller through London to get the Laundry's attention, relying on Johnny's background to ensure that we were sent to investigate—"

"Enough." Lockey doesn't look amused. "Eighty percent, Ms. Hazard. Such a shame—"

He begins to step sideways, out of line with the pistol at the back of her head. It's the cue Persephone has been waiting for. She reaches backwards and jabs the burning Hand of Glory into her guard's eye in one fluid motion, turns sideways as he shrieks. The pistol shot—twenty centimeters from her right ear—is a hot hammer blow against the side of her face. She continues her turn and brings her other hand up, grabs the slide of the automatic, then twists, using it as a lever to break the shooter's grip. Jack stumbles, still shrieking, hands reflexively going to his face. The automatic discharges into the ceiling as she yanks it away, then shoves him backwards.

Off-balance and clutching his face, the hapless Jack—another of Schiller's black-suited missionaries—stumbles towards the open gate. But he doesn't stumble through it. He falls across it sideways, legs intersecting with the glowing edge of the portal at ankle level, shoulders and head hitting the side.

There is blood; lots of blood.

Persephone spins to bear on Lockey.

Lockey is diving for the revolver, which lies inconveniently close to the door to the church. Persephone is holding Jack's pistol by the slide in one hand, the Hand of Glory in her other. *Only one thing for it.* She opens her mouth and shouts a word that will cost a year of her life, at least.

Time slows to a crawl around her. The air thickens to the consistency of jelly; light dims, sounds dull. Movement is sluggish, like swimming. Lockey hangs in the air, falling slowly as she lets go of the pistol she took from the hapless Jack, moves her hand to catch it by the butt as it drifts gently floorwards. Her other hand is abruptly heavy, gripped by pins and needles. She struggles to turn and aim one-handed through a period that feels like minutes but is probably a fraction of a second, then to squeeze the stiffened trigger mechanism.

The gun heaves against her hand, sparks and smoke billowing from it; she can see the bullet as it drills a hole through the turgid air towards Lockey's head. His hand is centimeters away from the revolver as the cartridge case slowly wobbles free of the breech of her stolen pistol, drifting through the red glimmering twilight.

Time snaps back to normal and Lockey jerks, then is still.

Persephone takes a deep, whooping breath and shudders like a leaf from head to foot. Her left hand is numb and tingling; her right feels as if she's taken a kick to the wrist; and her stomach feels light and sick with the memory of what she has uncovered. But she can't stop now:

if this isn't a rogue operation within the Black Chamber, dissent among the Nazgûl with a gaslight scenario to confuse and bamboozle the intruders, reinforcements will be along very soon indeed.

She walks over to the equipment rack, identifies the cable feed under the gaffer tape from the altar in the church, and pulls the plug. There's a fat spark and a quiet bang from inside the switch box. For good measure, she puts the pistol to the socket and shoots the terminals at close range. It's risky, but less risky than chancing Schiller's people to make a field expedient repair. Then she turns to face the portal to the Sleeper's tomb, and swallows—because despite appearances, she is not fearless.

A MONTH LATER:

It's a bright late-spring morning in London. I let myself into the New Annex via the unmarked door beside a closed high street chain store. I head upstairs towards my office—still hanging off the side of IT Facilities, after all these years—pausing to grab a mug of coffee and say "hi" to Rita on the front desk on my way in. I'm not putting things off, honest, it's just that I expect the unexpected to happen today, and I'm bad at dealing with unknown unknowns while low on caffeine.

It's a small office and I don't have an outside window, but I *do* have a nice Aeron chair these days (downsizing elsewhere in the civil service has left us with a surplus of lightly used executive furniture) to go with the five-year-old Dell desktop with the padlocked-shut case and ancient light-bleeding seventeen-inch monitor that is apparently considered suitable for IT staff at my grade. I plonk myself down behind it and am just beginning to get my head around the scale of the sewage farm that is a month's worth of missed committee meeting minutes when the door opens.

I glance up, surprised, and my guts turn to ice. My visitor is a tall, late-middle-aged man in a suit, and I've seen him three times before in my entire career. I don't know what he's called, he's just the Senior Auditor, and if he takes an interest in you it is usually because something has gone *very* badly wrong.

"Uh, hello," I say.

He looks at me over the rims of his half-moon spectacles and essays an avuncular smile that reminds me of my childhood dentist just before he reaches for the drill. "Good morning, Mr. Howard. Do you have a minute?"

"Uh," I flail for words, then gesture at the solitary visitor's chair. "Sure." Too late, I realize that there's a heap of unclassified literature clogging it up, the better to conceal the suspicious stains and the two rips from which protrude chunks of grubby yellow furniture foam. (I was meaning to replace it at the same time I snagged the Aeron, but got side-tracked . . .) I stand up hastily and grab for the paperwork, which retaliates by making a bid for freedom and sliding in a messy avalanche to the floor.

"Ah, security by obscurity." The Senior Auditor perches on the edge of the chair and waves me back to my seat. "I gather you arrived home the day before yesterday. How are you feeling, Bob?"

The first name takes me by surprise, so much so that I start to stutter: "Oh, um, I'm f-fine, o-over the jet lag—" He's watching me with sympathetic eyes, deep brown with pupils so huge and dark I feel as if I'm falling into them, down into a sea of stars—

"Ruby. Seminole. Kriegspiel. Hatchet." The nonsense words ricochet from side to side of my skull like bullets; my tongue feels like leather and I can't look away. "I'm sorry about this, Mr. Howard, so I'll make it quick. Execute Sitrep One."

From a very great distance I hear my own voice, in a cadence not my own, say, "Subjective integrity is maintained. Subjective continuity of experience is maintained. Subject observes no tampering."

"Exit supervision," says the Senior Auditor, and I flap my jaws soundlessly for a few seconds, taking deep breaths. He breaks eye contact. "I'm sorry to have to subject you to that, Mr. Howard, but I'm afraid it's the lesser evil—the alternative would be a month or two under observation in Camp Sunshine, and we need you operational too badly to spare you for that long."

"What"—I swallow—"kind of tripwire was that?"

"You've seen *The Manchurian Candidate*." The Senior Auditor raises an eyebrow. I nod: I'm bluffing, but I can look it up on Wikipedia later. "The Black Chamber have been known to forcibly install back doors in the minds of foreign operatives who fall into their hands, turning them into sleeper agents. After your experience in Santa Cruz eleven years ago . . . we felt it best to take precautions. It's a standard precaution for all field agents who are tagged for fast-track development."

"And I'm not—" I pause. "No, if I was, you wouldn't tell me. You'd use me as a conduit?" I'm grasping for straws.

He shakes his head, somewhat sadly: "No, Mr. Howard, I'm afraid we'd have to decommission you. If we couldn't excise the damaged tissue, that is, but that kind of neurosurgery has a poor prognosis."

I am taking deep whooping breaths. *"Aaagh—"*

"I'm very happy to say that you're fine," he adds hastily. "Would you like a minute to—"

I wave wordlessly.

"You're probably wondering why I'm here," he adds awkwardly. (I manage a nod.) "I am here to clear up some loose ends from GOD GAME RAINBOW. First, before we continue—I'm required to ask you this: Is there anything you would like to disclose to me in confidence?"

"Uh. Um . . . such as . . ." I manage to ask, but it feels like my brain's still freezing from whatever he just did, combined with the realization that if my traitorous nervous system had given a different answer I could be *dead.*

"Oh, anything you'd like to confess." He emits a self-deprecating chuckle. "Excessive expense claims, bribes, embezzlement, you're working for the KGB as a double agent, that sort of thing. In confidence, with no disciplinary outcome indicated if you make a clean breast of it to the Audit Commission at this point." He looks at me hopefully, like a kindly uncle expecting me to confess the origin of the scratches on the door of his new Jaguar.

"Um, er"—*stop that*—"well, Gerald Lockhart gave me a rather exotic credit card and instructions to use it in a manner that's not consistent with our usual expenses policy. Does that count?"

"Perhaps. What did you use it for that might be inappropriate?"

"Well." I rack my brain. "He told me to fly business class and stay in a higher class of hotel than I'd have used on a regular travel account. When given the scram instruction I rented the first car I could get, for a week, unlimited mileage in case the airport wasn't available. Oh, and I ordered out for some items when in the hotel—including a pizza." He frowns minutely. "But I needed the pizza box to make a field-expedient containment grid for one of Schiller's hosts, which I used to locate the breeding pool." His frown clears. "I tried to keep receipts, but the Black Chamber confiscated them." Along with the contents of my wallet, my passport, the pizza box, my IronKey, and everything else I was carrying.

"Well, I think we can find a way to retroactively approve the pizza and the car hire," the Senior Auditor says gravely. "And I shouldn't expect the hotel and air fares will be a problem if you were ordered to use them. Is there *anything else*?"

Anything—why is he asking—realization blinks on like a five-hundred-watt light bulb. "Oh, yes, yes there is." I explain about Pete and the apocrypha and my misgivings about the whole business, and he nods every thirty seconds throughout the whole sorry story. Finally I wind down. "That's what you were after, right?"

He's silent for a few seconds, then finally nods again. "Yes, Mr. Howard, it was. Thank you for telling me. I'll take the matter under advisement. We may have to call you in for a formal debriefing, but in view of the circumstances I don't think you have much to worry about." He stops. "You have reason to believe otherwise?"

I nod, glumly. "My wife will be furious when she finds out."

"Hmm." He cocks his head to one side, watching me. "Don't you suppose she would be even more upset if you got yourself killed and failed to stop Schiller waking the Sleeper?"

"Uh—maybe." There are some domestic disagreements you can't win: it's in the rules, or something. "If I was allowed to talk to her about it—Lockhart overrode our usual waiver."

"Well, if you have any trouble, talk to me and I'll see if it's possible to override *that*. Meanwhile, CANDID will come round eventually," says the Senior Auditor. "She has a level head on her shoulders." He clears his throat. I barely have time to flinch, just as my younger self did whenever he heard the dental drill spinning up; he's a deft touch, is our Senior Auditor. "Now, as to why I'm *really* here, I'd like you to accompany me upstairs to a personnel hearing in one of the executive offices."

TWENTY-EIGHT DAYS EARLIER:

"Hurts like a motherfucker, Duchess," Johnny opines, touching the dressing taped around his throat. He wears an open-necked dress shirt, the better to conceal its alarming proportions from casual witnesses.

"I'm not surprised." Persephone doesn't move her head or shift her hands from the steering wheel, but he can see her gray eyes flicker to examine him in the rearview mirror. "Try not to do that, Johnny. It takes longer to heal if you stress it."

"I thought I was dead for keeps this time." He shudders. "And Schiller was going to resurrect me." He leans back in the leather-and-walnut embrace of Schiller's Lincoln limousine and focusses on the back of her head. Her hair is tied in a chignon beneath a chauffeur's cap that matches her black suit as she drives steadily towards the rising sun. There are more strands of gray in it than there were just a week ago. Nevertheless, she drives like a machine: over the night just past they've covered nearly seven hundred miles.

"Sorting you out when you get yourself killed is *my* job," she says, exposing a flash of jealousy. "You didn't think I'd leave you to him, did you?"

Johnny shrugs, then winces in pain. "Looked a bit hairy for a few minutes there, Duchess. This retirement caper isn't as peaceful as I expected." She doesn't reply. Miles pass, then he tries again: "Seems to me if it wasn't for Howard we'd both be in the shitter. It's a total clusterfuck."

"What makes you say that?"

"Lockey and his backers suckered us. They suckered everyone too damn well. Assuming the fish ain't rotting from the head down, he locked the Black Chamber out before they even realized they had an incursion. If he hadn't tried to overreach hisself by fishing in our backyard . . ." Johnny's thousand-yard stare is focussed far beyond the vanishing point of the highway ahead. "An' then the old poacher-gamekeeper match-up turned sour on us."

"You're assuming he didn't do that deliberately. Play us for idiots right down the line." Persephone is silent for almost five minutes. Her expression is distant. "He got Mahogany Row's attention, and they sent us. Do you suppose it was deliberate? That he'd worked out that we'd have the right kind of asset and trailed himself through London just to ensure that someone like you would show up on his doorstep?"

Johnny's eyes widen in surprise. "I really hope *not* . . . !"

"Oh yes." Her face in the mirror is pale. "At least, Lockey didn't deny it. The bloodline is rare outside of the western isles. And the organization's done a good job over the past few decades of ensuring that the believers don't stray, and the stray don't believe. But Lockey only needed two of you—Schiller and someone else—to make it work. I'm thinking we were set up."

Johnny digests this for a minute. Then: "Schiller's dead."

"I would say so, yes. At least, he was on the wrong side of the gate when I unplugged the generator that was powering the control node. Along with whatever he managed to awaken."

"The Sleeper? It's *awake*?"

"Probably. Maybe. I was very much afraid that it was finally stirring from its sleep when I went back through the gate, and it certainly seemed restless." Her knuckles whiten on the steering wheel. "It'll be weak, though. To wake it is the easy part—feeding it until it's strong enough to act is the hard bit. That's what the mass sacrifice was about. It may be awake but right now it's trapped in the temple, barely conscious, with nothing to feed on but Raymond Schiller. And if the Nazgûl thought they could control it, they're going to learn otherwise really soon."

"So, what now?"

"What, next, you mean?"

"Don't act the ingenue with me, boss, it won't wash."

"We go home." Her voice is tired. "We conduct the post-mortem. Then we dig in for the phony war."

"Ah." His eyebrows rise with enlightenment. "You think it's going that way?"

"I am certain of it." He sees her frown in the mirror. "At least we got out of there alive. What did you think of Mr. Howard's performance?"

" 'E came through better than I expected, keeping up with you, Duchess. Is 'e still alive?"

"Probably. I passed him on the way out. Unconscious." She pauses. "He's got potential. If only he can get over his squeamish side he'll be a very useful asset. And I think we can work on that."

"So you've made up your mind, have you? Despite the aforementioned clusterfuck?"

"Yes. We've got to take talent where we can find it, and it's not Howard's fault the mission was a qualified failure." She taps the fingers of her right hand on the wheel boss. For a moment there's a flash of bitterness in her eyes. "You win some, you lose some. And when you lose, you have to pull yourself together and go back for more. Otherwise, the other side wins by default."

"A HEARING?" I MANAGE NOT TO SQUEAK. "DO I, UH, WOULD I be advised to ask for an advocate? Or legal advice?"

"It's not that kind of hearing." The Senior Auditor actually looks *cheerful*. "You're not in the frame for GOD GAME BLACK running off the rails. In fact, you've come out of it smelling of roses. Or, at least, not covered in sewage. For one thing, you survived. For another thing, so did the executives you were sent to support."

"But what about—"

"Come on." He stands up. "You've already worked most of it out for yourself, but we still have some procedures to go through, forms to file, that sort of thing."

"Forms for *what*?"

"Forms for Human Resources to document your permanent transfer to External Assets as an executive assistant. BASHFUL INCENDIARY's report on your performance was quite positive, and you seem to have come through Gerald Lockhart's stress test with acceptable results. The one thing everyone who has ever supervised you agrees on is that you'd be wasted in middle management. So you're not going there. Instead, you're being diverted onto the other career ladder, the one most people in the organization don't know about.

"Welcome to Mahogany Row, Mr. Howard. And may whichever god you choose to believe in have mercy on your soul."